LOVE'S REUNION

Gently he lifted her chin. Then his mouth was seeking hers, finding it, covering it, possessing it, at first tenderly, then more eagerly, coaxing alive in Jessica a fire she'd forgotten existed. As many times as she'd remembered the embraces she and Christopher had shared, this moment of feeling his lips on hers was a new experience—a wonderful one . . . warm . . . overwhelming.

"I have waited for so long," he murmured, "to feel this way again."

He led her to the couch, drew her down beside him, kissed her again deeply. "I will never be able to get enough of you . . ."

Other Avon Books by
Jo Ann Simon

HOLD FAST TO LOVE
LOVE ONCE IN PASSING

Love Once Again

JoAnn Simon

AVON
PUBLISHERS OF BARD, CAMELOT, DISCUS AND FLARE BOOKS

LOVE ONCE AGAIN is an original publication of Avon
Books. This work has never before appeared in book form.

AVON BOOKS
A division of
The Hearst Corporation
959 Eighth Avenue
New York, New York 10019

Copyright © 1983 by Jo Ann Simon
Published by arrangement with the author
Library of Congress Catalog Card Number: 83-90053
ISBN: 0-380-83345-x

First Avon Printing, June, 1983

AVON TRADEMARK REG. U. S. PAT. OFF. AND IN
OTHER COUNTRIES, MARCA REGISTRADA, HECHO EN
U. S. A.

Printed in the U. S. A.

WFH 10 9 8 7 6 5 4 3 2 1

To Maine,
My new and much-loved home.

*With acknowledgment and
special thanks to
Julie Garriott,
copyeditor beyond compare.*

1

The air was bitterly cold, piercing to the bone. The numbing chill forced its way into her consciousness, prompting Jessica Dunlap to open her eyes and stare about her.

She stood in a small room with rustic pine furnishings, roughly plastered walls, a low ceiling, and a wide board floor, unpainted and worn in places. None of it was recognizable.

All was very still; only her breathing and the muted whimperings of the month-old child in her arms disturbed the silence.

Yet what Jessica was seeing couldn't be real! A moment before, she'd been standing in the warm bedroom of her twentieth century Connecticut home. It was Christmas morning and the sun had been streaming brightly through the window as she held her son in one arm and approached her husband, who sat expectantly on the edge of the bed. His smile had been brilliant, his arms outstretched in welcome as she'd stepped forward.

But she remembered how, suddenly, that smile had been wiped from his lips . . . how his image had seemed to begin fading, drifting in and out of focus before her. She blinked her eyes, thinking something was wrong with her vision. Then she'd heard his pleading voice as though from a distance, calling to her, begging her to come quickly, to take his hand. His eyes . . . those beautiful, vivid-blue eyes, fading before her own horror-struck gaze . . . were filled with alarm and urgency.

She'd rushed forward, reached desperately for his hand. She'd barely been able to see him any longer. "Oh, God," she'd prayed. "Let me find him!" Then she'd felt him . . . felt his warm, strong fingers closing tightly around her own . . . . and then he was gone.

Now this cold, strange room; she and her son alone; no sign of the tall, dark-haired figure with his vibrant blue eyes, his warm smile, his comforting arms.

All color had drained from her face. It couldn't be true! After all they had shared together, she couldn't have lost him!

It had begun so unexpectedly a year and a half before, on May 5, 1978, that otherwise unexceptional day when Christopher Dunlap, elegant, privileged English nobleman, had entered her life. She remembered so well now driving over the winding country roads that afternoon, from her office toward home, the Connecticut landscape green and glorious with budding spring. Suddenly, startled by unnameable sensation, she'd glanced to the supposedly empty passenger seat beside her to find him seated there, dressed in the long-tailed jacket and tight breeches characteristic of the early nineteenth century. At first she'd stared in disbelief—she must have been seeing things! But there'd been nothing imaginary about him. He'd been real; he'd been there as much in the flesh as she. Yet how and why had he come to be in the car beside her? She'd felt fear, then outrage, at his ridiculous behavior. How she'd smirked at his presumptuous attitude and speech, laughed at the affectation of his dress and at the absurdity of his apparent belief that he was living in a world one hundred and sixty years in her past. Yet how quickly her scoffs had turned to bewilderment and astonishment as he'd displayed proofs of his identity: gold coins, a small fortune's worth and none bearing a date later than 1811, although they looked almost newly minted; a packet of letters he said were written to him and by him, the earl of Westerham, all dated 1812 and seeming too authentic to be denied.

His stupefaction was equal to her own, yet he was the first to be convinced of the truth—extraordinary as it was—that he was a man swept out of the world of 1812 England into twentieth century America, carried forward in time by a phenomenon neither could explain.

Thus had begun their life together . . . a fairy tale, the meeting of two people whose paths would never have crossed had not fate thrown them together to share an unimagined relationship. As they'd faced each day, never knowing what force had brought them together or whether they would be separated with the same suddenness, Christopher had learned to adjust, to accept with some equanimity the wonders of modern technology: television, electricity, indoor plumbing, automobiles, airplanes. In the months that followed, he'd begun making a place for himself in his strange new world, surmounting the obstacles that faced him, gradually discovering that his life in the twentieth century was becoming more important to him than the life he'd left behind.

He had fallen in love with Jessica, and she with him. They had come to share the intense love of two people who wanted to spend the rest of their lives together without the specter of separation hanging ominously over them. They had to try to discover the truth of Christopher's destiny—whether or not he would remain in the twentieth century, or be swept back in time to his own world. They'd traveled to England, to the ancestral estate he'd left one hundred and sixty years before, hoping to find in the family archives some evidence, some proof of whether or not he had returned. It had taken many days—nerve-racking ones for Christopher especially.

But the facts he'd finally discovered in an old diary had filled them with joy. Christopher Robert Julian George Dunlap, ninth earl of Westerham, born 26 June 1780 in Cavenly, Kent, England, at the age of thirty-two a renowned and sought-after member of London society, a man rising in prominence in the House of Lords, had, on 5 May 1812, disappeared without trace from the world he'd known.

A search for him had been conducted, but nothing had been uncovered, and in due course his title and estates had ceded to his cousin and heir, who'd lived to a ripe old age as the tenth earl. The former earl apparently never had returned to reclaim what once had been his, and his disappearance was still considered a mystery.

They'd felt so secure then, so happy in their conviction that they weren't going to be separated by time, that Christopher was to remain in the twentieth century; that they could live their lives as normal people, loving without fear. They'd returned to Connecticut and embarked on their future with vigor and high expectations, purchasing a home in the country, starting the horse breeding farm that was Christopher's dream. Their son, Christopher Jr.—Kit—had been born a month before, and they were justly proud of their healthy, handsome child.

Jessica had carried him into their bedroom early that Christmas morning. Christopher's expression had been jubilant as he'd sat on the edge of the bed, arms spread wide. "Let me wish my fine son a Merry Christmas, too," he'd called.

Tears welled in Jessica's eyes, a blinding, stinging heat, as she thought of what had come next . . . what had occurred in those last moments. Where were she and the child? Where was Christopher? *Why* weren't they all together? Was he near by? Or—and a feeling of dread swept through her—had she lost him forever?

She tried to analyze her surroundings. Through the windowpanes harsh daylight flooded the room in which she was standing; slanting rays of sunlight cast white-gold trails over the simple furnishings. Behind her was a narrow bedstead, at its head a washstand bearing pitcher and bowl. To her left was a fireplace, in the recesses of which hung a soot-blackened kettle on a swing arm. In front of her was a plank table and two ladder-back chairs.

Beyond the windows was a winter landscape, a few inches of snow blanketing the frozen earth. In the distance stood a large white house several stories tall. The house, the lay of the land, were strangely familiar to Jessica. Dormer windows poked out from the gambrel roof, and various additions to the house branched off to the back and sides. A wide drive running along the side of the house led to two large barns and a small cottage edged by a stone wall that climbed the low, rolling hill to the rear. Near the barn a rough wagon was parked, and beside it were several other pieces of horse-drawn farm equipment. Wispy white trails of smoke were floating from the three large chimneys of the house.

The scene might have been from a Currier and Ives print, so perfectly did it embody the atmosphere of a nineteenth century New England farm. Was that *precisely* what it was?

She thought again of that last instant in the bedroom —of her husband's hand gripping hers. Was that the link? In making that physical contact, had she and the child moved with him into another plane? Had they, too, become travelers in time? Yet if that was the case, why weren't the three of them together? Had they made that physical contact only to be carried in different directions?

The baby began to fuss, screwing up his tiny face, clenching his small fists. Jessica gently rocked him, adjusted the folds of her robe and his blanket. Wherever she was, whatever had occurred, she had to carry on, however frightening the thought was.

As the baby quieted, she rubbed a finger across his smooth cheek and thought of the day she and his father had named him. There'd never been any question that he'd be Christopher Dunlap, Jr., but in arriving at a diminutive to avoid two Christophers in the house, they'd disagreed.

"Chris sounds more American," Jessica argued.

"And you know how I despise that abbreviation directed toward me," he retorted. "You have some deep dislike of the name Kit? It is what I would have been called had I been named for my father."

"I don't have anything against Kit, but *I* think of him as Chris."

"And *I* as *Kit*—from the moment the doctor told me we had a son and held him in the air for us to see."

She'd looked up at him sidelong, and saw he wasn't about to change his mind. "Okay . . . but I want first choice in naming our next child."

"Do you?" His brows lifted. She could see the laughter in the eyes that had been so serious a moment before.

"What's fair is fair."

"Agreed, my love. What interests me is that you are already thinking about our next."

"Eventually, Christopher," she'd grinned. "Eventually."

Now she wondered if "eventually" would ever come. Her sigh was deep and painful. She couldn't think of that now . . . not now.

Again becoming aware of the cold, of the need to protect her son and herself, she stepped quickly toward the bed, noting the thick down quilt spread over its narrow width. Wrapping the warm folds around her child, she laid him in the center of the bed, where he'd be safe for the moment. The insulation of the quilt wasn't nearly enough. On the fireplace hearth was a basket of kindling and a few neatly stacked logs. If she could get a fire lit, it would solve the immediate problem of the cold.

She could find no matches, but on the hearth was an object she guessed might be a flint. It took her some frustrating moments of fiddling before she was able to raise a spark and ignite the dried leaves she'd scattered under the kindling. When she was sure the fire would continue burning of its own volition, Jessica returned to her son. He was sucking hungrily on his closed fist. In a moment she would have to feed him, but first she needed some warmer covering for herself. Her thin nightgown and robe were no protection against the cold air.

Hoping there might be something in the cupboards along the wall, some spare blankets if nothing else, she reached for the latch of the first of the two doors. Beyond was a storage room, its walls lined with wooden shelves holding various items, from mason jars to rags. The second door opened into a smaller closet, where various articles of clothing hung from wooden pegs. She was grateful for her luck. There were a worn, woman's cloak and several long, faded, drab-colored, full-skirted dresses, all old-fashioned, a century or more out of date. A pair of high-topped, laced lady's shoes rested on the floor next to a small trunk, its hide coverings and leather straps cracked and dried with age. She lifted the lid of the trunk and found half a dozen folded articles at its bottom—an old shawl with a torn fringe, several pairs of darned wool stockings, a limp linen camisole and a petticoat of the same material, clean but yellowed with use and age.

She took from the closet the heaviest of the dresses, a deep-gray wool with long sleeves and a high, plain neckline. The bodice was fitted and buttoned down the front to just under the bust, where the high-waisted skirt was gathered to fall in straight lines to the ankles in the style of the early nineteenth century. Jessica removed her robe and dropped the dress over her silk nightgown, retaining the latter for added warmth, and drew her long dark hair from under the collar to fall in a gleaming mass down her back, then fastened the buttons of the bodice. Although the dress had been made for a shorter, heavier set woman and was somewhat baggy on Jessica's slim form, it was warm.

Returning to the opened trunk, she reached greedily for the wool stockings she'd seen there and, leaning against the doorjamb, pulled them over her numb toes. She looked back to the trunk and drew out the tattered shawl, which she wrapped around her shoulders, at the same time discarding her own lightweight, uselessly decorative robe into the trunk. Jessica closed the old humped lid and picked up the leather shoes on the floor near by, taking them to the bed to try them on. The shoes were snug, but they were better protection for her feet than the flimsy satin slippers she'd been wearing. If she laced them loosely, she could get by.

Standing, she tested them, then went immediately to her son. He was fussing, hungry for the feeding he should have had an hour earlier. Jessica could feel a fullness and soreness in her breasts, brought on by the delay, and knew a moment's guilt for having neglected the baby. Taking Kit in her arms, she pulled one of the ladder-backed chairs before the fire, which was still flaming heartily. At least his tiny hands felt warm now as they pressed against her. She studied her son's face, so small, so perfect in its innocence: the minute nose, the fading red pressure marks of birth that now only slightly tinged his forehead, his lightly etched brows and lips—so like his father's—his chin, already showing the barest hint of the Dunlap cleft, the cap of dark hair curling with infant fineness over his round head.

She loved him so, it was like a warm tide surging through her; a tide that reminded her of her feelings for his father. Already, despite the shock of the abrupt change that left her feeling dazed, the thought of Christopher brought a yearning, an aching emptiness that she knew would never be assuaged until she had found him and they were together again.

The worst of the chill had left the air. The quilt protected Kit, but as Jessica touched him tentatively, she found his bottom wet. *What* was she going to do for diapers? . . . She thought of the old petticoat in the trunk. It wasn't the sturdiest of articles, but if she could tear it into strips, it would work. With a gentle hand, Jessica burped the air bubbles from Kit's system, then rose and placed him carefully on the bed before she went to the trunk and pulled out the old petticoat. The material ripped easily in her hands, and in almost no time she had a square of cloth of approximately the right size. She folded it, then removed her son's wet diaper and replaced it with the dry linen.

The baby, comfortable again with a full stomach, was already beginning to doze off. Jessica covered him carefully, gently dropped a kiss on his rosy cheek, and went to lay another log on the fire.

She was bending over the hearth, settling the log in place with the fire tongs, when a knock sounded on the door. Startled, she nearly dropped the tongs. Had she been hearing things? The knock sounded again, more firmly, this time accompanied by a woman's voice. "Hello! Is anyone there?"

Hesitantly, with a deep fear, Jessica moved forward. She had no choice but to answer the door—yet what was she to say to the unknown woman on the other side? How could she explain her presence?

"One moment," she called, forcing into the tone of her voice a steadiness she didn't feel.

The wooden latch stuck for a moment under her trembling fingers, then gave way suddenly as the door swung inward, letting a cold rush of air into the room.

A middle-aged woman stood on the stoop. Her mittened hands held closed a voluminous hooded cloak, which she let slide open as she stepped briskly into the room. Beneath her cloak the woman was wearing a deep-green wool dress of the same high-waisted style as Jessica's, but with lace trim about the neck and sleeves. Kindly-looking brown eyes gazed at Jessica as the woman drew the hood back from her gray-streaked brown hair, which was pinned in a bun at the back of her neck.

"I am Amelia Beard." Her voice, though pleasant, was cautiously reserved as she scrutinized the dark-haired young woman before her. "Mistress of this farm. And you must be the new maid sent up from New York. I saw the smoke coming from the cottage chimney and came to investigate. The agency didn't give me your name, only vouched for you."

"Jessica Dunlap." She took the small hand that was extended to her. Her voice quavered as she absorbed the woman's words, barely daring to believe in the authenticity just given her.

"But we expected you a week past," the woman exclaimed. "What delayed you?" For all her mild aspect, Amelia Beard was also clearly a perceptive woman.

And at the moment she was a very puzzled one, as well. This young woman before her was not at all what she'd expected. Too attractive. Was there something to be learned here, under the surface of things? Miss Dunlap's appearance didn't fit that of serving maid.

"We had begun to think you had changed your mind," she said. "I can understand how difficult it must be for a young woman accustomed to city life to uproot herself and come to the Connecticut countryside, but I assure you we have most of the comforts of the city, with the schooners sailing frequently in and out of Eastport harbor. Of course, with this war of Mr. Madison's it has been difficult. Let us hope 1814 will bring an end to it." She paused, wagged her head. "But what delayed you? You came by stage?"

Jessica could only nod mutely to the last question as she

rapidly digested the information just given her and tried
desperately to maintain her composure in the face of her
astonishment. Two facts stood out. She was in or near
Eastport, Connecticut, the town of her birth, where she'd
lived for most of her twenty-nine years of life, where she'd
met Christopher, where she'd conceived their child. But
this wasn't the Eastport of *her* living twentieth century
memory. This *was*, just as it appeared to be, the Eastport of
the early nineteenth century!

"True," Amelia Beard continued, unaware of Jessica's
turmoil, "they would not chance sending you up the Sound
in a packet. The British have stayed to the east of us—but
who knows how long that will remain the case? But why
did you not come directly to the house?" She peered
quickly around the room. "And where is your luggage?
Have you unpacked?"

Jessica's mind was working rapidly, manufacturing a
story that followed along with what Amelia Beard was
telling her. Lying was an unfortunate necessity.

"I'm afraid I've lost my luggage. When we stopped along
the way, it was discovered that the baggage straps on our
conveyance had broken and several articles were missing,
my luggage included. Someone was sent back to check
along the route, but he discovered nothing and . . . and
presumed the straps had broken while we were fording a
stream. The fallen baggage must have been washed
away."

Amelia Beard shook her head. "Well, not a new tale.
The performance of the stages can be most disgraceful.
You did not walk to the farm from the stage stop, I hope?"

"A traveler coming this way was kind enough to give me
a ride, but because of the early hour, I didn't want to disturb you. The cottage was open. It was cold, and I lit the
fire. I hope you don't mind."

"Mind? My dear, had I known you were arriving today
—on Christmas of all days—I would have had the cottage
in readiness for you. And you with no luggage!" Her lips
pursed. "I am certain we can find something for you in the
house. The maid's uniform will give you a change of clothing, at least. And I have two grown daughters of about

your size. One or two of their older gowns should suit for the time being."

All the while Amelia Beard had been speaking, she'd continued appraising Jessica. Now she tilted her head slightly to one side. "You are a very comely young woman—not the usual sort to be seeking such a position. Those with looks such as yours are usually long since wed, snatched up immediately—" She stopped abruptly, her eyes catching sight of the band on Jessica's finger, and widening. "But you *are* married!"

"I . . . yes . . ."

"I had no idea! The agents said they were sending a single woman."

"I didn't tell—" Jessica was cut short by the sudden wail from the side of the room. Her face paled as Amelia Beard swung around, eyes riveting themselves to the small, blanketed mound on the bed.

"What is this? Sounds like a child . . . a babe?"

"It is." Jessica sought vainly for words of explanation as Mrs. Beard walked toward the bed.

"An infant! Yours?"

"Yes, mine."

"You never told us! The agents certainly did not. There was no stipulation in our agreement for a mother and a newborn babe. It will interfere with your work."

"Please let me explain."

But Amelia Beard was already lifting Kit from the quilts, soothing and cradling him with experienced hands. "Hush, hush. Yes, quiet now. My, but it has been a long time since I held a child of your size in my arms." She looked piercingly to Jessica. "Girl, boy?"

"Boy."

"His name?"

"Christopher. We call him Kit."

"And his father?"

Jessica hesitated, then rushed into the story she'd been formulating in the last few minutes. Her sentences were clipped, her voice breathless in her nervousness and her revulsion at having to weave such a lie. "My husband's a seaman." Remembering how Christopher had loved sailing and the sea, the profession was the first to pop into Jessica's mind. It also provided a handy excuse for his present absence. "He signed on with an American cargo vessel that sailed over six months ago. He knew that, with the war, it wasn't a wise move, but he needed the work. I stayed at our lodgings in New York, waiting for him. Then the child was born. My husband should have returned long since. The money he had left was running out. I had to find some work to support the baby and myself."

"Did you inquire at the shipping offices? Could they give you no information about your husband's vessel?"

"I am embarrassed to say I didn't know at which shipping office to inquire, and I don't know the name of his vessel. It was only to be a short trip."

Amelia Beard's expression was thoughtful, and Jessica waited with clenching stomach; this cottage was all she had. It afforded no luxuries, but at least it offered warmth, protection. If she and Kit were cast out, what might befall them? Where would they go? What would she do?

"Why weren't you honest?" Amelia said finally. "Why did the agents give me a lie?"

"I needed a job so badly, I didn't dare tell them. I accepted the position hoping that when I arrived, you would understand. I didn't know what else to do; I had to find work, and this position was by far the best offered. I could find nothing available in the city, and I didn't have the resources to wait. I am terribly sorry for the deceit."

Mrs. Beard's brow was furrowed. She liked the girl; her immediate impression was, on balance, a positive one. Yet . . . to show up on her doorstep with a baby, a missing husband—one could only wonder if her story was true. "It is not what I expected," she spoke firmly. "There are some from whom I would never believe such a tale, but you have the look of an honest woman about you, and you are wearing a ring—no brass trinket that, either." Her eyes again rested on the white-gold band, adorned with sapphires, on Jessica's finger.

"It was my husband's mother's . . . a family heirloom," Jessica explained. Here at last was a bit of truth.

"He comes from a prominent background then? A colonial?"

"English. He came here looking for a better life."

Amelia nodded. "Came upon hard times—no need to explain. Two generations ago my family, too, came from England seeking a new start. But these are bad times to be in your husband's profession—the blockade, the British impressing our sailors—enough to make one's blood boil! Didn't we fight fairly enough for our freedom? I lost two uncles in that war. Mr. Beard, too, lost some of his family. General Tryon burnt most of this town to the ground. I heard stories of those days from Mr. Beard's father . . . how the family helped those from town who lost everything to the redcoats' torch."

She wagged her head, then another thought crossed her mind. "Your husband will know where to reach you?"

"I left word at our lodgings in New York." As she spoke, Jessica prayed that Mrs. Beard would not ask where those lodgings where.

Fortunately Amelia Beard didn't ask, and Jessica realized from the look in the woman's eyes that she had accepted the story. Jessica's relief was . . . almost palpable, yet she knew this was only the first of many obstacles she would find in her path.

Already there was the obvious question of the maid she was being mistaken for. Where was the other woman? Since a week had passed since she was due to arrive, Jessica could only hope that the woman had changed her mind just as Mrs. Beard had begun to suspect.

Amelia Beard's tone of voice found a more sympathetic note. "I can understand why you were not honest with the agents. Positions for women in your situation are few and far between. Not that I like . . . evasiveness, but you have come to us now, and we will make the best of it. I think you will work out."

"Thank you—thank you so much. You are very kind."

"It is just that I've been blessed—sometimes it is a curse—with being able to see through to people better than most would care to be understood." She smiled. "You are not English yourself, are you?"

"American."

"I thought so. You met your husband here, then?"

"Yes."

"No family of your own?"

"They are all gone." That, too, was the truth. She had no family to reach out to now.

"Sad. . . . And you seem a well-educated lass—certainly more so than the regular house servant. Life can deal cruel blows. We have all suffered a few. Now—let us find a place for the babe in the kitchen. Kit, you called him?"

Jessica nodded.

"I have an old cradle we can put by the kitchen fire. Cook Fletcher will tend to him while you work—no doubt she will spoil him—and Rachel, the kitchen maid, can give a hand. We can spare you time from your duties to feed him. Not much over a month old is he?"

"Just a month."

"He'll need his mother. Never could see putting a child this age in the hands of another. It would be best if you stayed with us in the house for the present. We have a spare room near the servants' quarters."

"Oh, Mrs. Beard, that's not necessary. It's so very good of you, but Kit and I will be comfortable here."

"Not as comfortable as in the house." Amelia Beard had made up her mind and was not to be swayed. Whether the story of a missing husband was true or false, the young woman was not of the common stock. She showed refinement, intelligence, a good background. And she was obviously suffering. Amelia felt an almost motherly urge to give her some protection. "The babe's too young. You will stay in a room upstairs that's large enough to be used as a nursery."

"I don't want to intrude on your family."

"You will not intrude, you will be very welcome. I have always loved little ones. Well, fetch your wrap, and we will go up to the house. A good breakfast is what you need, and Cook will have it ready."

As Amelia Beard moved toward the door, still holding Kit, Jessica went to the closet to collect the old cloak she'd seen hanging there. She pulled it around her shoulders, and Amelia wagged her head.

"You have naught but that old thing to protect yourself? A wonder you have not already caught your death. Well, come along. It is but a short walk, and you will be warm soon enough."

The snow crunched under her boots as Jessica hurried after Amelia Beard, down the narrow path from the cottage, across the drive and up a short walk to the back of the main house. They entered from a small roofed porch, on one side of which cords of firewood were neatly stacked, into the kitchen of the farmhouse. Jessica felt a comforting blast of warmth, mingled with tantalizing cooking smells, as Mrs. Beard opened the door and hurriedly preceded Jessica into the room.

"Well, Molly," Amelia called to the plump and rosy-cheeked woman who stood at the table kneading dough. "A surprise for us all—our new maid has arrived. She was staying in that drafty cottage for fear of waking us on this Christmas morn! Can you imagine! A good thing I went to investigate that smoke from the chimney. Come in, Jessica, come in. Warm yourself, and Molly will give you a bite to eat."

Closing the door behind her, Jessica stepped forward across the brick floor. A tremendous fireplace filled most of the back wall of the large, low-ceilinged room. A wide range of utensils hung from the beams, and spacious cupboards were set against the walls. The cook was working at a long harvest table that stood in the middle of the room opposite the hearth. A white gathered cap covered some of her graying blond hair, and she wore a gray homespun gown, the front of which was almost entirely covered by a starched white apron. She looked up curiously.

"Jessica," Amelia Beard continued briskly, "this is Molly Fletcher, our cook. I know you will find her happy to help you until you are familiar with your duties. Molly, this is Jessica Dunlap."

Molly smiled warmly as she wiped her floury hands on her apron and stepped across to meet Jessica. "Welcome, dear, and a Happy Christmas. 'Tis a good house to work in.

You'll be happy here." Her voice held traces of an English country accent, and its pleasant intonation immediately put Jessica at ease.

"I am glad to meet you, Molly."

"Aye, the same—but you look a bit weary."

"As she is bound to be," Amelia said, "after her journey and with no food in her stomach. I promised her one of your good breakfasts. Have a seat, Jessica." Amelia waved her hand in the direction of the table, which Jessica took after removing her cloak and draping it over the back of a neighboring chair.

"I have some hot porridge right here on the fire," Molly smiled, "and warm bread. A glass of milk, too. In better times I would offer a bit of tea, but it is hard to come by these days."

"The British blockade," Amelia Beard explained to Jessica. "Although I imagine you were faced with the same scarcities in New York."

Molly went to the cupboard for a wooden bowl, filled it with steaming porridge from the pot on the hearth, and, setting it and a spoon on the table before Jessica, then fetched a cutting board with a loaf of fresh bread, a crock of butter, and jar of jam.

Mrs. Beard still had Kit bundled in her arms, so well protected by his blanket that even his tiny face was hidden. It was as Molly passed with a mug of milk for Jessica that she noticed the child and stopped dead in her tracks.

Amelia laughed at the expression on the cook's face. "Another surprise for you, Molly. Jessica has brought along her babe." Amelia was already slipping the folds of the quilt away from Kit, who fidgeted at the loss of the cozy warmth.

"Well, I'll be," Molly exclaimed. *"Tis* a babe! And such a lovely one!"

"Yes, a fine lad," said Amelia proudly, sounding as though Kit were her own grandson. "I was a bit taken aback when I learned about the child, but I believe we will all get along very well. Where is Rachel? I want her to run up to the attic and find the old cradle. We can set it here by the fire, and Jessica can tend to him between her chores

. . . though I am sure the babe will not be lacking attention."

"Rachel's in the dining room setting the table for breakfast. I'll go and fetch her." Molly bustled away through the swinging door at the far end of the room, and Amelia Beard took a seat in one of the kitchen chairs, perfectly content to continue holding Kit while Jessica finished her meal. The porridge, flavored with cinnamon, immediately warmed her, and the milk she sipped was far richer and creamier than she'd tasted before.

In a moment Molly came back into the kitchen with a slender, dark-haired girl dressed, similarly to the cook, in a gray gown, a long, starched apron, and a white cap on her head.

"Ah, Rachel," Amelia Beard greeted her. "Merry Christmas."

"Merry Christmas to you, ma'am."

"I had not intended to give you extra duties on Christmas, but I need you to fetch something from the attic. Under the eaves you will find an old wooden cradle. Bring it here to the kitchen. Then also gather some linens and a blanket or quilt."

"The cradle?" The girl was obviously puzzled by such an odd request.

"Yes." Amelia smiled almost conspiratorially. "We have a need for it . . . as you can see." She turned so that Rachel had a clear view of Kit.

"A baby!"

"Indeed so, and his mother is seated right here at the table. Rachel, I would like you to meet our new housemaid, Jessica Dunlap."

The girl swung around, surprise written on her features.

"Jessica, this is Rachel Coombs, kitchen maid," Amelia continued.

Jessica smiled to the girl, but Rachel merely nodded and turned back to Mrs. Beard.

"Well, hurry along, Rachel. We want to get him settled."

Rachel bobbed quickly and scurried away.

"Once we get the child comfortable, Jessica, I will take

you through the house, but let me explain a bit about your duties while we have a moment. You will be responsible for the cleaning of all the rooms in the house, although there are several guest rooms that will not need more than a weekly dusting, and a good cleaning twice a year. You will not be expected to serve at table—that is Rachel's job—except on her day off or to help her out during a large party. You will have one day off a week, and on Sundays you are welcome to come with us to church service. It's a bit of a trek, so in the worst winter months we attend only when the weather is clear. Cook takes care of the marketing. Once a week Jeb Latham, our farmhand, takes her into town in the wagon, but I am sure you will have no objection to giving Cook a hand with the heavier shopping should she need assistance. It will be a good opportunity, too, for you to get out to Eastport and see the area. This northern section of Eastport is known as Silvercreek. Before the Revolution, it was a small town on its own. There is still a small market, and a meetinghouse, and of course the mills, all up and down the river. You will find it a pleasant place to live."

"I am sure I will," Jessica said evenly, but her mind had caught on Silvercreek. Amelia Beard had just confirmed that Jessica was in the very neighborhood where she'd lived with Christopher in the twentieth century. Now she understood why the Beards' house had looked familiar. She could picture it as it had appeared in the nineteen seventies. Minor exterior changes had been made by then. The cow pastures around the house had grown back to woodland, but the barn remained, and, in a modernized form, the cottages. She guessed there would be other buildings in the area that would be familiar to her, too. Perhaps she could even visit the site of her twentieth century home, she realized suddenly with a start. The house wouldn't be standing, since it had not been constructed until the eighteen thirties, but Jessica could walk over the grounds where she and Christopher had found such happiness together. Again she felt a knot of anguish in her stomach. Oh, Christopher, she cried inwardly, as she sat, outwardly composed, at Amelia Beard's kitchen table. Where are you, my love? Please, please be somewhere near by!

Rachel bumped into the room then with the bulky cradle, jarring Jessica's thoughts back to her present surroundings.

"That's going to need some dusting," Molly observed. "I'll just brush this flour off my hands . . ."

The cook had already grabbed a rag and was approaching the cradle, but Jessica intercepted her. "Let me do that. You still have your bread to finish."

The cradle was a sturdy and beautifully crafted piece, obviously made with love, and the activity helped to keep Jessica's whirling thoughts and fears at a safer distance. By the time Rachel returned bearing linens and blankets, the cradle was spotless.

When Jessica had finished fitting the blankets and sheets into Kit's new bed, Amelia Beard rose with the child in her arms. "Well, that looks nice and cozy, young man. You should be very comfortable for the time. Shall I settle you in? . . . There. . . . Ah, no, you do not enjoy being left in there by yourself, do you?" She smiled down at Kit, who had begun to whimper.

Jessica tucked the quilt securely around her son and took one of his chubby little fists. "Shhh, sweetheart. You can't expect someone to hold you all the time." Gently she rocked the cradle. "Yes, that's a good boy. How tired you must be after all the confusion. Close your eyes." After only a few minutes Kit drifted off in the contented sleep so peculiar to infants.

"He should be all right now," Jessica whispered.

"Yes," Amelia agreed in the same hushed voice. "He's peaceful now." She rose, and spoke softly to Cook. "I'll take Jessica on a tour of the house now. Keep an eye on the child."

Cook nodded.

Before leaving the room, Jessica gave one last, tender look at her son.

"Never you worry," Molly smiled. "The babe will be in good hands."

"Thank you."

Quickly Jessica followed after Amelia Beard's retreating figure, through the kitchen doorway into a narrow hall that was noticeably cooler than the kitchen.

"Back there," Amelia motioned leftward, "are the servants' stairs and the cellar entrance. But since I want to show you the main rooms, we will use the front staircase." She turned to the right and followed the narrow corridor into a spacious front hall, to the rear of which rose a graceful white-bannistered staircase, then went straight to the double doors to the right of the hall and swung them open.

"The dining room is in here. As you can see, it is convenient to the kitchen. No need to begin your duties until the morning, but then be sure first thing to take out the cold ashes and light a new fire, dust, and sweep. Rachel will take care of the table. We will need a morning fire, too, in the front parlor across the hall."

As Mrs. Beard spoke, Jessica observed the large, square room. The gleaming dining table and chairs were of elegant construction, perhaps Chippendale, as were the side pieces arranged along the walls. Yellow satin draperies adorned the four tall, paned windows. A pewter chandelier hung from the ceiling over the table, and a fire was blazing in the fireplace opposite the door. Pine branches were spread upon the mantel in keeping with the holiday season. The table was set for three, and serving dishes sat, ready for use, on the sideboard.

"I see my husband and daughter are not down yet, but then I am an early riser and generally up well before them. You will have a chance to meet them shortly." Amelia turned and, with Jessica at her heels, stepped out into the hall. She closed the doors behind them and motioned across the hall toward a matching set of doors. "Over here is the front parlor, which we use daily."

It was a room of warm colors, slightly larger than the dining room. A tall, white fireplace faced the door. The wood floor was partially covered by an oriental carpet of beige, gold, and a touch of red. Arranged before the fireplace were a sofa and two wingback chairs, upholstered in colors to complement the carpet. Deep-rose draperies hung at the windows. Along the walls were various straight

chairs and tables, and a Sheraton secretary, its satiny finish glowing.

Jessica was impressed with the beauty and good taste
the large room displayed in all its aspects. "It's lovely."

"Thank you," Amelia smiled. "Many of these pieces are
family heirlooms. Others Mr. Beard and I acquired over
the years. I take pleasure, and probably a bit too much
pride, dear, in decorating and maintaining the house at its
finest. We will go out this way"—she pointed toward another set of doors, at the back of the room—"into the back
hallway."

They proceeded across the corridor, to the first of two
doorways.

"This is the summer parlor," Amelia explained. "A set
of French doors open into the garden and make it quite
pleasant in the warmer months."

The room was about half the size of the front parlor and
decorated in lighter colors—pale greens, sunny yellows.

"We rarely use this room in winter," she added, "so for
now you will need to do little more than an occasional
dusting and straightening."

The tour continued, bringing them to the next doorway
along the hall: Mr. Beard's study, Amelia advised. It was
furnished in deep reds and browns. A large desk was
placed opposite the fireplace, a floor-to-ceiling bookcase
covered the wall behind, and two leather armchairs sat on
a thick Turkish carpet before the fireplace.

"Mr. Beard spends a great deal of time here on his business matters, and he's very particular about his desk—do
take a care not to disturb any of the papers when you are
cleaning. It may seem disorderly, but I assure you, he
knows precisely where everything is. One more room to
show you downstairs, and then we will go up to the second
floor."

They followed the hall away from the center of the
house, toward a set of doors slightly more ornate than the
others in the house and possibly, Jessica thought, of more
recent design.

"This is the ballroom," Amelia swung the doors wide.
"It will be chilly in here. Obviously, we do not light the fire

unless the room is in use. The ballroom is our little extravagance in the house, added by Mr. Beard's father after the Revolution, since he entertained so extensively for his business."

How marvelous! Jessica thought as her eyes scanned the interior. The whole end of the house was given over to this long, high-ceilinged room. Tall windows to the right and left let in light that bathed the room in brightness, glinted off the two crystal chandeliers suspended from the ceiling, and made golden trails on the parquet floors. The furnishings were few: side chairs along the walls, and a long table pushed to one side. Still, the splendor of the room took Jessica's breath away. "Do you and Mr. Beard entertain often?" Her voice echoed in the huge expanse.

"We have a large party once or twice a year. Now with the war, of course, not as often. The last big affair was our daughter Mary's wedding last spring. Quite a celebration."

"I can imagine."

Amelia smiled softly at the memory. "There were over a hundred guests. The ceremony was performed in the garden with a ball afterward. And such a beautiful bride she was! That is a mother's pride speaking, but it did go off well. She and her husband, Roger, also live in Eastport in a small house he inherited from his grandfather. It is convenient for them, now that he is employed in Mr. Beard's mercantile business."

"And you have another daughter at home?"

"Elizabeth. You will meet her shortly. She is our younger child, just eighteen, and a lively one. Mary is more serious. You may meet her as well today, since she and Roger will be joining us for our Christmas dinner. Well, I had best show you the upstairs and the room you and Kit will be using; then you will have time to rest and settle in before the servants' party. All the help have Christmas afternoon and evening off for their own celebrations in the kitchen. Molly prepares a feast, and other friends come in. You will enjoy it, I am sure."

As she spoke, Amelia led Jessica back to the front hall. As they approached the staircase, Jessica heard voices and looked up to see a distinguished-looking, heavyset gentleman of about fifty descending the stairs, at his side a lovely blond young woman.

"Bertram and Elizabeth! Merry Christmas!" Amelia Beard called gaily.

Elizabeth was the first to reach Mrs. Beard's side, dropping a kiss on her mother's cheek. "The same to you, Mama."

Mr. Beard came forward to give his wife a jovial squeeze. "Merry Christmas, my dear. A lovely day." His lively blue eyes looked over to Jessica, who stood as unobtrusively as possible a few paces behind Mrs. Beard. "And who have we here?"

"Oh, Bertram, you will not believe . . . but this is our new maid arrived just this morning, and quite a troublesome journey she had, losing her luggage in a coach mishap."

"Well, young woman, we had about given up hope of your arriving at all, but welcome."

"Let me introduce you properly." Amelia motioned Jessica forward. "Bertram, this is Jessica Dunlap. Jessica, my husband, Mr. Beard."

Jessica extended her hand. "I'm pleased to meet you, Mr. Beard." An instant later she remembered that in this era it would be more customary for a servant to bow or curtsy to an employer.

Graciously ignoring her faux pas, Bertram Beard accepted her hand and returned the light pressure. "The pleasure is mine, Jessica. Most unfortunate about your journey, but I hope you will be happy with us."

"I am sure I will."

"And, Jessica," Amelia continued, "this is my daughter, Elizabeth. Elizabeth, Jessica Dunlap."

Although Elizabeth was smiling, there was a coolness to her manner, an air of superiority lacking in the elder Beards. Jessica became very aware of the dowdiness of her own appearance—the worn and mended drab gray dress, opposed to the pale-blue satin and lace concoction adorning Elizabeth's trim figure. Still, she instinctively forced her chin up proudly as she smiled, then nodded. "How do you do, Elizabeth."

"So you are the new maid." Elizabeth's gray eyes swept over Jessica, missing nothing—neither the worn gown nor the lovely face. "Somehow I was expecting someone quite different. You are not from Eastport."

"No, from New York."

"Well, I shall have plenty for you to do. Being without a maid for the last month has left my wardrobe in a shambles." And, at the puzzled look in Jessica's eyes: "Mama did tell you that one of your duties would be to assist me, since as yet I have no personal maid."

"No . . ."

"My apologies, Jessica," Amelia said quickly. "I should have mentioned it, but with all the confusion this morning, it slipped my mind. Elizabeth can advise you when she needs your assistance. Your regular household duties will take priority, of course."

Elizabeth smiled, satisfied. Jessica only nodded in acknowledgment.

"Both go have your breakfast now," Amelia said to her husband and daughter. "I will join you when I finish showing Jessica the rest of the house and her room."

Elizabeth looked up. "She is not staying in the cottage?"

"Temporarily I thought I would give her one of the attic rooms. Come along, Jessica."

Amelia headed purposefully up the stairs. Jessica followed quickly, wondering why Amelia Beard hadn't told her husband and daughter the whole story . . . about Kit, about her being a married woman.

As though reading her mind, Amelia answered that question as soon as they were out of earshot of the others.

"I will tell them about the child and your situation when we can talk privately. It's not a subject to bring up in the front hall, with all the explanations required."

"Do you think your husband will object?"

"Bertram? Heavens no. He has a generous heart for others' misfortunes, and he gives me free rein in household matters. He has enough to keep him busy with his mercantile business, the mill and the farm."

They arrived at a landing at the top of the stairs, from which halls led off in two directions. "Only two bedrooms are in use now, obviously, and there are four other guest rooms. The master bedroom is over here." Mrs. Beard turned to the left and led Jessica into a large, sunny room that faced out to the road in front. From this height Jessica had an excellent view of the river across the roadway, and of the pasture and woodland beyond. An old canopy bed was centered at the back wall, with a Queen Anne style dresser between the front windows and a small lady's desk snuggled into a corner near the fireplace.

"The dressing room is in here. I require no help with my dressing, but if you would keep the room tidy and see that a fire is lit every evening before we retire . . . the fire in Elizabeth's room as well. Jeb will bring up the wood, and Rachel sees to the morning hot water. Oh—and while we are here, I have some infants' gowns I saved from my daughters." Amelia bent before the carved blanket chest at the foot of the bed, and opened the lid. She lifted out a few articles before nodding in satisfaction. "Yes, here they are, and in remarkably good condition. Let me see . . ." She held up several small white gowns. "This should do, and this, for the time." Handing the garments to Jessica, she replaced the other articles, closed the lid of the chest, and rose. "That should keep the child warm, and Rachel will show you where to find linens for the babe."

Jessica fingered the fine, hand-sewn gowns, the delicate embroidery around the bib. "Thank you so much. I will take very good care of them."

"Not to worry. They are well made, as I can vouch for myself, and in the next week I will have Mr. Beard bring up some yard goods from the store so you can sew up some new things for the babe, and a new maid's gown for yourself."

As moved as she was by her employer's generosity, Jessica cringed at the thought of creating little gowns like these, or a dress for herself. She could sew passably, but she always used a modern sewing machine and dress patterns. Only with a great deal of practice could she hope to come close to duplicating the fine hand stitching that Mrs. Beard seemed to take for granted.

She had no time to worry about it then, since Amelia Beard was already leading her back to the hall, past the stairwell and toward the first door on the right.

"Elizabeth's room. Here I think you will have a bit more of a chore. Dear though she is, the child is not particularly tidy." Her words were evidenced very clearly, as they stepped into the room, by the crumpled heap of bedcovers on the mattress, the quilt dragging on the floor, the nightgown draped over the back of a chair, the dress discarded on another; and, on the dressing table, by the spilled powder and hairpins, the silver-backed brush and comb dropped in the midst.

Despite the disorder, Jessica could see that it was a lovely room of delicate feminine furnishings in pale blue and rose. It was more cluttered than the Beards' room, but charming, with the same front, river view.

"Oh, my," Amelia clucked. "Well, no time for you to straighten this today. Tomorrow morning will be time enough. I am a neat person myself and have always wondered where I got such a child. Her father often teases her that she should have been born with a personal servant in attendance." Shaking her head again, she directed Jessica back to the hall. "There are two other guest rooms along to the right here, though there is no time to take you through today. We will just stop a moment in Mary's old room before I take you up to yours. There are some old gowns of hers in the wardrobe that I was going to give to the church charity. Perhaps one or two will fit you. You will want something prettier than that," she added, nodding toward Jessica's gray dress, "for the festivities this afternoon."

Opening the door to the bedroom behind the master suite, she stepped briskly across the carpet to the large mahogany wardrobe and began flipping through the dresses hanging within. "Mary is about your height and weight."

Jessica watched as Mrs. Beard slid the gowns along the rod, and sighed at a beautiful royal-blue silk gown with creamy lace panels adorning the bodice and soft folds of the skirt, at another elegant full-sleeved red velvet dress.

But Amelia Beard passed these right by as obviously unsuitable as a maid's attire. She finally settled on a simple, high-waisted, green wool dress with long tight sleeves and a high neck adorned only by a small white collar, and a brown tweed walking dress that was unrelieved by any such accent and not much-more complimentary than the gown Jessica was wearing. But both were serviceable, warm, and very well made.

"These should do." Amelia handed Jessica the gowns, then went to the dresser and returned with a pile of folded white cotton and cambric. "And a nightgown and change of underthings, mended I am afraid, but still a lot of wear in them."

Carrying the undergarments, Amelia went back to the hall. "I will show you your room now. Left here, and up the back stairs. We have one spare room in the attic that we keep for guests when the house is full. There is a small cot there, too, that we can use for the child."

The stairs were narrow and steep, bending up under the eaves and opening into yet another narrow hall.

Amelia gestured toward a door on the left. "Rachel's room is there. Cook's, down on the right. To the other side the servants' workroom and storage areas. Your room is here." She opened the first door on the right. "As you can see, it is cozy, and there is a small fireplace." She strode over to the bed and dropped the undergarments on it. Jessica noticed some hooks on the wall by the door and hung the two dresses there, then surveyed the room. The furnishings were simple, but adequate: a maple four-poster bed and a nightstand, a rough dresser, a washstand with pitcher and bowl, an old rocking chair near the fireplace, braided rugs on the wide-board floors, and a narrow cot pushed into the far corner of the room.

"I thought," Amelia continued, "if we slid this cot up beside the bed with some rolled blankets along the edge to keep him from falling, it would work very well for the babe."

"Yes," Jessica agreed, "and it's close to the fireplace, so he'll be warm."

"Unfortunately we only have one cradle, and it would

seem better to leave that in the kitchen so he will be in a safe spot while you are working. Cook will be there to keep an eye on him."

"She really won't mind?"

"Molly adores children. Never had any of her own and makes up for the lack with the neighborhood youngsters—always one or another of them coming to the kitchen door begging a cookie and cup of milk. Not that I mind—keeps the place lively. Well, you should be all right for the time. I will go down and join my husband and daughter. If you are in need of anything, ask Cook or Rachel. Tomorrow being Saturday, the household will sleep in, so there is no need for you to be up too early at your chores, though do see that the front parlor and dining room are tidied and the fires lit in both rooms. Mary and her husband will stay the night, so we will be five for breakfast. On weekdays we are up by eight, except for Elizabeth who often rises later. I will no doubt see you later, but Merry Christmas, and welcome."

"The same to you, Mrs. Beard—and thank you so much."

The older woman smiled. "If you follow the back stairs all the way down, they will bring you out to the kitchen hall."

"I'll put these things away, then go down."

"Good day then, and do not worry over my husband's re-action to the child . . . I sense it may still be on your mind. He will raise no objections."

With that she hurried away, closing the door behind her. Jessica let out a sigh of despair, her mind spinning with all that had happened in the last few hours. Slowly she walked to the windows and stared out at the snowy scene as she tried to compose her thoughts.

Despite Amelia Beard's warmth, she found this all terribly frightening and felt nervously unprepared for what lay ahead. She had only the smallest clue to the running of the household. Nothing in her own twentieth century had prepared her for the lack of labor-saving devices, the need to light fires, to carry water from a hand pump, to empty chamber pots. There would be no vacuums or commercially available cleaning aids for her now, just brooms and dustpans, soap and water. Not that she doubted her physical ability to handle a maid's chores—she was healthy and strong; but she did wonder if she could carry it off efficiently and not make herself look like a fool. The Beards and their servants would expect her to have experience in all this, to say nothing of a familiarity with the habits and customs of the time.

Shaking her head slowly, she longed for Christopher's guidance. This was his era; he could have told her what to expect, what to do. Not that he'd ever had to work in a servant's capacity, but as a man who'd once had many servants, he could give her enough clues to carry on. She tried to remember now all that he'd told her of his life in England—the day-to-day details, what he'd expected of his servants, the little inconveniences that she'd never had to consider in her twentieth century world. Of course, when they'd talked, neither of them had dreamed that Jessica would one day face such rigors. There'd only been the fear that Christopher would return to his own time.

It was with an effort that she kept the tears from flooding her eyes; from breaking down and giving in to the miserable ache inside. She felt so terribly alone . . . so terribly lost and frightened! Where *was* he? Would they ever find each other again?

She squared her shoulders, took a deep breath. There were things to be thankful for, too, and she forced herself to think of them. She had a place to stay, a source of income; Amelia Beard had accepted her fabricated story, and she was sure that she didn't suspect Jessica to be anything but a contemporary of hers; Jessica's modern speech blended in well enough with the working-class New England accent that no one would ever question it.

Before leaving the room, she paused in front of the small mirror over the washstand and examined her reflection. It was the same face that had stared back at her from her twentieth century bathroom mirror the night before: the high-cheekboned face, the straight nose, the full mouth; dark lashes framing green-flecked hazel eyes. There was nothing in that reflection to tell what had transpired in the last few hours, yet she knew that in one instant, her whole life had changed drastically, and perhaps tragically.

She sighed heavily, then moved determinedly toward the door.

2

The kitchen was a scene of bustling activity as she stepped inside. Both Rachel and Cook were busy, Cook removing fresh baked tins of bread from the brick ovens built into the fireplace, Rachel chopping onions and carrots at the table. These scents, mingled with that of roasting goose, were enough to make Jessica's mouth water.

Cook glanced up to see Jessica. "Ah, you're back. Good as an angel he's been. Not a peep."

"I'm glad to hear that." Jessica smiled. "You're busy enough as it is."

"That I will not argue," Molly chuckled.

"Can I help?"

"Let's see. The bread's done. Why don't you fetch the pie fillings from the pantry and start filling the shells? Pantry's over there beside the back door."

Jessica found the three brown pottery bowls with no trouble and carried them in to the sideboard. It took only a few minutes to fill the shells. By the time she'd finished, Cook was already at the table rolling out the top crusts and covering the pies. She slipped them into the ovens and wiped her hands on her apron. "Well. That's done."

Cook then went to check the goose in the tin roaster set on the hearth directly before the fire. Jessica had seen examples of these open-front, closed-back roasters in restorations of old homes she'd visited, but she'd never seen one in use before. Apparently it was efficient, for she could hear and smell the juices of the skewered roasting goose dripping and sizzling on the hot metal.

"Bird's doing just fine," Molly said, rising. "Got most of

the cooking done this past week, so there's not too much to
be done today. Have a cold baked ham down in the buttery
for our meal, and plenty of tarts and pastries and a plum
pudding. The master and mistress don't care for it but
they're happy enough to let me make one for our Christmas celebration. Wouldn't have been Christmas at my
home without a pudding . . . Ah, here's Rachel with the potatoes." She motioned to the girl to leave the sack by the
table. "Jessica and I will take care of those. You'd best go
in and clear away the breakfast dishes. We still have to set
the table for dinner. What time are Mary and her husband
arriving?"

" 'Bout twelve, I thought I heard the missus say."

"Fires all going?"

"Jeb helped, and brought in extra wood."

"Good. Just a matter of finishing the cooking, serving
dinner and clearing away, and the day will be ours."

Jessica was bending to move the sack of potatoes closer
to one of the chairs at the table when she heard Kit's
whimper. She looked over to see his tiny face frowning.

"Best go to him," Cook said calmly. "Certainly has been
a good child with all the confusion."

As Jessica drew back the covers and lifted her son from
the cradle, he immediately quieted, soothed by her soft
voice. "What a good boy you've been, sweetheart. Yes,
mommy's here." Cuddling him, she kissed his soft brow.
"I'll be back in a few minutes," she said to Molly. "I just
want to run up to my room to feed and change him."

"Up to that drafty attic? You didn't light a fire, did
you?"

"Well, no . . ."

"Then pull up a chair here in the warmth. No one will
intrude. Jeb's busy seeing to the livestock." Molly was already moving a chair around so that it faced toward the
fire.

Jessica could make no protest without seeming foolish,
but she'd never nursed Kit in front of anyone but Christopher before, and was embarrassed. Trying to hide the
blush she felt warming her cheeks, she went to the chair
and loosened her bodice. Cook and Rachel went about their

work paying no attention to her. As discreetly as possible, Jessica put Kit to her breast to nurse, listening to the quiet conversation of the other two as the baby fed. When he was satisfied, she burped him and rebuttoned her dress. But now he was wet.

"Rachel." Jessica rose and approached the young woman. "Mrs. Beard said you would tell me where I could find some linens for the baby, and some blankets too, for the upstairs bed."

"Soon as I finish cutting this bread."

"No, I don't mean for you to go. Just point me in the right direction."

"Up the back stairs, in the hall outside the second floor landing. You'll see cupboard doors to the left. In the first cupboard, bottom shelf, there's some old linen towels. Blankets are in the next cupboard."

"I'll be back in a moment."

"No hurry," Molly called. "We're about finished. Pretty yourself up a bit for the party. Some of the neighbor folk will be coming in."

"So Mrs. Beard told me."

" 'Twill be a time, and the babe can stay here in his cradle."

Jessica found the second floor cupboard without any trouble. As she searched for the linens and blankets, she heard the sound of voices drifting up from the front entrance hall, calls of greetings and Christmas wishes; the Beards' eldest daughter and her husband must have arrived. The realization spurred Jessica to hurry her task. She selected about a dozen of the old linens and three blankets, closed the doors, and slipped up the remaining flight of stairs and into her room. Now, with Kit so wet in her arms, she especially noticed the chill. Placing him on the bed between two pillows, she went to the fireplace and lit the kindling and leaves already set on the grate. The wood was dry, and the fire sprang up quickly. She placed two small logs on the flames, then went to her son, changed Kit and replaced his wet gown with one of the fine hand-sewn ones lent to her by Amelia Beard. Wrapping him in the quilt she placed him on the cot, at the outside edge of which she laid two rolled blankets to form a barrier. Now for herself; but she suddenly realized there was no water for washing. Checking Kit to be sure he was secure, she hurried back down the narrow stairs to the kitchen. In a few minutes she was climbing back up again, a copper water bucket dragging on her arm. It took awhile to navigate the stairs with her burden, and she pitied Rachel, who had to lift these buckets up twice a day, every day. Kit was still quiet when she returned to the bedroom. She carefully filled the washbowl on the stand with warm water. In the only drawer of the stand, she found a hand towel and a small bar of soap. Stripping to the nightgown she'd worn all morning under her dress, she dunked the cloth in the water, lathered it generously, and washed hastily, rinsing and drying before the still chill air brought too many goose bumps to her skin. Taking the end of the rough towel and dipping it in clean water, she rubbed it over her teeth. The effect was far inferior to that of a toothbrush, but her mouth felt a little fresher.

After changing hurriedly into the fresh undergarments Amelia Beard had given her, she looked toward the dresses hanging on the wall pegs. Which to wear? The green dress seemed the obvious choice. Not only was it more becoming, but the color was in keeping with the holiday season. Undoing the buttons, she slipped it over her head. The wool was soft, perhaps with a touch of cashmere in its weave and not the least itchy against her skin. She was delighted to find the dress fit well; a shade too tight in the bodice, but overall it flattered her figure.

There was no brush, but she found a ribbon that could be pulled from the lacings of one of the nightgowns, and used it to tie her long hair up on top of her head. It wasn't a very stationary arrangement, but it would hold for the time. She took one last look in the small mirror. Her face was paler than usual, but overall she made an attractive appearance.

Banking the fire and gathering her son in her arms, she went downstairs.

The long kitchen table had been cleared. Dishes were laid out on the sideboard, and Rachel was hurrying in and out of the kitchen, serving the family their Christmas dinner. From the sound of laughter and conversation drifting in from the dining room, Jessica judged they were enjoying themselves. Rachel nodded to Jessica as they passed in the kitchen doorway, her eyes and her suddenly pursed lips conveying that she had noted Jessica's change of hairdo and gown.

Molly Fletcher wasn't so silent, however. "My, aren't you a picture! But I'd thought you'd lost your luggage."

"Mrs. Beard lent this to me. She had planned to give it to charity."

"Always say charity should begin at home." Molly lowered her voice as Jessica went to the cradle and gently placed Kit within. "And don't you mind the other one—Rachel. I notice she's a bit cool to you, but I think her nose is out of joint. She was hoping to get the housemaid's position herself. 'Twould be a step up in the world for her, but no doubt the mistress thought her too young . . . only seventeen. Now fetch that apron hanging on the peg there, so you don't muss that lovely dress. I'm heating up the water for the dishes, but you can start setting out our table. Plates are in the cupboard there. Just stack them at the end of the table. Not sure how many are coming in. I'll just get the coffee and dessert tray ready to go into the dining room, then go and tidy up myself."

Rachel pushed through the door with a tray of dirty dinner plates and wineglasses, which she slid onto the wooden counter top beside the wash basin.

"Can I help you with that, Rachel?" Jessica offered, hoping to break through the girl's coolness.

Rachel's brows lifted in surprise. "Well, if you don't mind scraping the dishes and settin' them in the tub, that'd be a help."

As Jessica began scraping the leavings into a slop bucket that she learned would later be taken out to the hog, Rachel left the room again with the coffee tray and dessert dishes.

The water was hot, and Cook poured a quantity of it into the wash basin, mixing it with cold water from the hand pump. "I'll be back shortly," she said as she hung her dirty apron in the pantry. "Good of you to help Rachel. Not your responsibility, but I'm sure the girl will appreciate it."

"I don't mind," Jessica answered. "I'd rather be busy."

The activity did help to keep her worries to the back of her mind. She had half the dishes washed and on the drying board by the time Rachel returned from the dining room with the rest of the dirty dishes. The girl seemed amazed at Jessica's progress.

"You didn't have to wash."

"You have enough to do, and I'm sure you want to get ready for the party."

"I did want to change, but I can finish up."

"Then let me dry these, at least, and put them away."

The two worked silently together until the kitchen was tidy again, and Rachel left the room to change her dress. Cook returned, and she and Jessica began putting the food out on the table when the back door banged open and a wiry man entered, a cap covering his gray hair, his arms loaded with firewood. He gave Jessica a startled stare. "Party start already?"

"No. I'm Jessica Dunlap, the new housemaid."

"Pleased to meet ya. Jeb Latham, farmhand. Wanted to bring in this load of firewood. Gonna be needin' it this afternoon. S'posed to chill up."

"They'll be wanting some in the parlor," Molly commented.

"Yep. In the bedrooms, too. Be back shortly. Smells good, Molly."

"My cooking always does," she said, and winked at Jessica as Jeb departed.

Rachel slipped in wearing a far more flattering blue cotton dress with white collar, and moments later they heard voices outside the back door, feet stomping across the porch. The color on Rachel's plain cheeks showed her excitement. Jeb returned to the kitchen with a couple of dusty bottles under his arm. He grinned slyly at Jessica. "Makin's for the punch. Molly got the bowl out? Yep, I see it." He went to the sideboard as Molly greeted the first of the visitors, a man and two middle-aged women.

"Martha, Sarah, Rufus . . . Merry Christmas!"

Molly's greetings were echoed by the others as the three visitors shrugged out of their outer garments, but the noise had wakened Kit, and Jessica hurried over to take him from the cradle. Respectful of the bustle as the new arrivals stepped into the room, Jessica moved with Kit to one of the chairs behind the table, and sat down. Kit was quiet now, content to be held and take in the activity of the room. It was a moment before Molly made introductions.

"I'd like you to meet our new housemaid, Jessica Dunlap, and her babe, Kit. Jessica, this is Martha White and Sarah O'Neil, who work at the Lathrope farm across the river, and Rufus Butts, one of the hands at the Tyler mill."

Jessica smiled to them all. The women made the expected exclamations over Kit, coming closer to get a look at him, fuss over him. Kit responded, putting on a show with a loud gurgle.

"There'll be others dropping in," Molly said gaily, "but go ahead and start in . . . and Jeb's got the punch ready."

"Sure do!" Jeb smiled, ladling the concoction into small glasses. "Pass it around, Molly, and we'll toast the season."

Jessica found the warm, fruity drink very tasty, and guessed that it had been rum in the dusty bottles Jeb had carried in. Plates were passed and filled. Jessica managed with no trouble to hold Kit in one arm and eat with the other. She gave him a sampling of pumpkin pie from the edge of her spoon, and he smacked his lips for more. "Just a little," she said softly. "Too much spice will upset your stomach."

By the time the first of the plates were scraped and stacked in the sink, other guests began arriving; some to join in the eating, others just to share a glass of Christmas punch. It became a very lively gathering, and Jessica, as long as Kit was content, was able to sit back and enjoy and listen. Among the women there was the usual neighborhood gossip. Since Jessica didn't know any of the local names, the talk meant little to her, but it was interesting enough anyway to hear that George Lathrope was courting one of the Lockwood girls in town; that the Berkleys were thinking of selling their farm and moving west to

Ohio; that—hushed whispers here—Cora Greene, the eldest daughter of one of the poorer local families, was said to have gotten herself in the family way. From the men came snatches of conversation about the farm and mill, but predominant was talk of the war. Most of the men opposed it, angry at what the conflict was doing to coastal trade. Milled flour from their farms was a drug on the market, molding in barrels by the docks in Eastport, and sugar, coffee, tea, West Indian rum, and any other commodities not locally produced were scarce and carefully hoarded.

Eventually, as their gossip wore thin, several of the women wandered over to ask Jessica friendly questions about herself. Although Jessica was sure that some would go home to speculate about her story, there were no raised eyebrows as she told of a husband who was out to sea and not returned by the time Jessica had left for Eastport. The local women knew how hard life could be on a young female alone with her child.

After an hour Kit began to fuss, and Jessica took him up to the privacy of her room to feed and change him. When she returned, there was a new addition to the crowd in the kitchen—a man of about her own age, blond and attractive. He stood talking to Molly as Jessica stepped through the door. His eyes quickly swept over her, widening.

Cook, vigilant as before, didn't miss his look. "Ah, Lucas, you've not met our new housemaid, arrived this morning no less from New York. Jessica Dunlap and her son, Kit. Jessica, this is Lucas St. John, who's foreman up at the sawmill."

Lucas gave her a warm smile, a flash of even white teeth; his blue eyes crinkled at the corners.

Jessica extended her free hand. "Good to meet you, Lucas."

"Pleasure's mine. Welcome to Silvercreek."

"Thank you."

"Very pleasant party," he said. "Molly always does a good job of making everyone feel at home."

"According to the look and sound of it, that I do," Molly

chuckled. "And there's Mary and Peter Dodd just coming through the door. I'll leave you two to chat."

"So you arrived only this morning," Lucas continued easily.

"Yes. I was delayed on the trip up."

"Not the time of year to be traveling by coach from New York." He spoke in more cultured tones than many of the others in the room. Jessica wondered at the difference, but without her having to find a tactful way to ask, he explained more about himself.

"I settled here only a few years ago myself. Came down from New Bedford, on my way to New York to make my fortune in one of the counting houses or shipping offices in South Street. Had some cousins here in Silvercreek I thought I would stop and visit. When they offered me the job as foreman of the mill, I would have been a fool to refuse. So here I am, and it's not a bad place to be." He grinned, glanced over to where Kit was lying contentedly in Jessica's arms. "How old is your son?"

"Just a month."

"And your husband?"

Jessica had been expecting the question, and repeated the story she'd told the others.

Lucas frowned. "Not a happy situation, but not hopeless either. I would expect his ship put into a safer port to wait out the war. It has been nearly impossible, even for some of the wiliest privateers, to slip through the blockade into New York."

"I know," Jessica answered softly.

"He will know where to find you?"

"Yes. I left word at our former dwellings."

"It must have been a difficult decision to make . . . coming up to Connecticut."

"At the time I had no choice." And how true *that* was, Jessica thought.

Lucas nodded. "Well, I think you will be happy with the Beards. From all I've heard they are good employers."

"Mrs. Beard has been very kind. I only met Mr. Beard and their daughter briefly."

"Elizabeth?"

Was it only her imagination, or was there a sudden spark of interest in his eyes? "Yes, Elizabeth."

"Quite a young woman." For a moment he stared off into the distance, a slight smile on his lips. "And not lacking for suitors. What did you think of her?"

"She's very lovely, but as I said, I have only been introduced to her . . . though I understand I will be attending her."

"Oh?" His brows lifted quickly. "That should be interesting."

"What do you mean? Is she difficult to work for?" Jessica didn't really need confirmation, having sensed that much herself.

He smiled. "I'm putting ideas into your head. I meant nothing by that comment."

Jessica didn't believe him, but didn't think pressing the point would gain her anything.

"Besides," he added, "I am in no position to advise you on Elizabeth's finer, or lesser, traits." A dancing light jumped into his eyes. "But do put in a good word for me should the opportunity ever arise."

Taking his last remark in the joking vein he intended, Jessica laughed. "I will praise you to the heavens . . . should the opportunity ever arise."

He reached out and patted her arm—a purely spontaneous and friendly gesture. "Well. I have some other visits to make. Best be going. Again, a pleasure meeting you. Living so close, we will see each other again soon. Take care of yourself and the child."

She returned his smile and watched as he moved away through the crowded kitchen saying his good-byes, stopping to chat a minute with Molly and Jeb, then collecting his hat and coat and stepping out the back door. A very nice man, Jessica thought, warmed by their encounter, and one who might be more than just a little bit interested in Elizabeth Beard. A pity. Little though she knew of Elizabeth Beard, she felt that Lucas could have a hard road ahead if his interest lay in that direction.

She shook her head, dismissing the speculative thought, and glanced up to find Rachel staring at her so coldly that Jessica felt chilled. As soon as their eyes met, Rachel looked away and moved into the crowd.

What had brought *that* about? Was Rachel upset at her talking to Lucas? Yet what was there in conversation to prompt such anger?

Jessica remained at the party a while longer, but she was tired, and despite the merriment of the people around her, she was growing melancholy, too. She was reminded too sharply of Christmas a year past and the joy she and Christopher had shared—Christmas Eve with their closest friends in to share their dinner, later all of them singing carols; and after their guests had left, she and Christopher opening their gifts before the fire. She remembered so clearly his delight with the statuette she'd given him of a mare and foal grazing . . . the same statuette that by uncanny coincidence had sat on his desk at Cavenly one hundred and sixty years before. It was that night, too, that he had given her the ring that now graced her left hand, one he'd had made to duplicate his mother's wedding band, the traditional ring of the brides of the earls of Westerham. And when they had gone to bed that night, she recalled their tender lovemaking, the happiness that had filled her as Christopher had held her gently in his arms and let one hand caress her cheek, then brush the hair from her brow as he told her of his joy at being there with her; told her how very much he loved her.

She lowered her head to hide from the others the sudden tears that had flooded her eyes. How could she go on without him? How could she survive in this strange world—survive anywhere—without the man she loved as much as life itself? She listened to the laughing voices around her, thinking how in contradiction that laughter was to her own torn and aching emotions. But there was Kit. She had their son to care for, and for his sake she *must* summon all her strength.

Jessica took several slow, deep breaths to compose herself and waited until the worst of the wetness was gone from her eyes. Then she collected Kit from the cradle and said her good-byes to the guests.

As she hurried out the kitchen door before her composure shattered again, she missed the long, sad look Molly cast her way.

3

He felt disoriented, as though wakened suddenly from a deep sleep. As he sat on the edge of the bed, he shook his head quickly to clear away the cobwebs, then looked at his surroundings again. This was wrong . . . he was sure of it . . . this narrow room of grimed ochre walls, chipped paint, one filmy window from which a few brave rays of sunlight were filtering through. The bare floor felt cold against the soles of his feet. From somewhere behind him came the sound of very loud snoring. He glanced up to the tattered calendar tacked to the wall just above the iron bedstead—the single effort made by some unknown person to enliven the dreary expanse of plaster. A four-masted schooner was sketched on the upper portion of the calendar; below that appeared "James Petrie & Sons, Shipper's Agents." The month exposed was December. Yes, it was December; he remembered now that it was Christmas Day. His eyes moved on to the numerals printed beside the month. 1813. No, that couldn't be correct. Heavens, 1813 was one hundred and sixty years past. . . . Suddenly all that was so hazy came flashing back. Oh God, he thought. No! it couldn't be!

He didn't have to look around to know that Jessica and his son weren't with him. Too clearly he recalled the last moment they were together, desperately reaching for each other's hands, he knowing all the while that it was useless, hopeless; nothing could stop the wheels of fate that had already been put in motion; nothing could stop him from being thrust back to where some cruel fate had decided he belonged—torn from the side of the woman and child he loved as much as life itself.

He closed his eyes in an effort to block out the unpleasant truth. Back in his own world—yet where? London? Certainly not Cavenly. No room in that great house would dare to look so decrepit as this one. Through the dirty window he saw a scattering of three-story brick buildings; beyond them a forest of ship masts standing at their moorings in the blue-gray waters of a narrow harbor. Definitely not London. He knew that city too well, and no spot along the Thames remotely resembled what he was seeing now. Where, then, *was* he? He glanced again to the calendar, to the fine print beneath the advertiser's name. He strained forward to read it: "Burling Slip, New York City."

There was his answer. It made no sense, but then nothing in his adventures of the last year and a half could be deemed logical. His senses were in full clarity now as he rose from the bed, tightening the belt of the robe that appeared to be his only possession.

The snoring in the background had ceased some moments before, but he only now became aware of it and turned to see another narrow bed, its occupant just lifting himself on a forearm to gaze bleary-eyed at Christopher's tall figure.

"Uh. Didn't know I had company," the stranger muttered. "When you blow in? Must have been dead to the world not to hear ya." With a calloused hand he rubbed the top of his disheveled head. "Rum was flowin' a bit too free last night. Head's feelin' it today. Willis Mawson's the name." His eyes squinted against the daylight.

"Christopher Dunlap."

"Dunlap, eh? You come to Hester's often?"

Christopher looked puzzled.

"This here boardin' house," Mawson laughed, then winced at the pain. "You must of tied one on yourself, don't even know where you are."

Christopher nodded slightly, but remained silent to see where the conversation would lead.

"Where you from, or you a local man?"

"Connecticut."

Willis Mawson hoisted himself from the bed, a husky, broad-shouldered man in his mid-thirties, nearly six foot. Again he groaned, as he put a hand to his head. "Devil rum. Oughta swear off the stuff. Will till day after tomorrow, no doubt. Leastwise you can't be in no better shape than me." He reached for his breeches hanging over the iron bedstead, pulled them on and slipped the leather suspenders over his shoulders. "Brisk in here. No wonder—fire's out. Well, don't stand there in that fancy dressin' gown, man. Get some duds on afore you freeze to death."

Christopher swallowed. How could he explain that he had no clothing but what was on his back? He decided on a blunt statement. "I am afraid I find myself in the embarrassing position of having misplaced my luggage."

Mawson stared at him. "Misplaced your luggage? If that don't beat all—" Suddenly the man burst out with a loud guffaw. "But I'll bet my last pay you had it with you when you stepped in here last evenin'."

"I do not recall . . ."

"Well, you didn't walk in here wearin' that thing, man, and I don't see no other clothes lyin' about."

"Very true, but—"

"I've seen it happen before. First night in town. Someone sends you up Five Points way. Next thing you know you got this little lady on your arm, escortin' you to this tavern and that, full of promises, liquorin' you up. When she knows you're too far gone to know up from down, she lures you to one of these boardin' houses, romps a bit on the bed, and when you're out to the world, walks out with everythin' you've got. Ayuh, somebody saw *you* comin'."

Christopher didn't need to confirm or deny what the man said. Mawson had made up his mind, and Christopher was grateful for the avenue of explanation being offered him.

"A regular greenhorn, you were," Mawson continued amiably. "These seeming country misses, so innocent actin' you'd think their bubble hadn't been popped. I was taken in myself that way a few years back. What about your purse? Don't suppose you had enough sense to stick it under the mattress before your romp."

"In my jacket pocket."

"That would be the first to go. Musta had some fine duds or she wouldn't have bothered with the baggage. They resell the good stuff for a nice price. What bothers me's I didn't wake up through none of this. Really musta had a load on. Good piece I hope she was, for all of that."

"I hope so as well."

"Don't remember that either?" Mawson laughed again. "Worst parta them whores, they sometimes slip a powder in your drink." The man grew thoughtful. "So you're out on the high seas without a sail."

"I am afraid so."

"From Connecticut, you say? I catch a bit of limey in your speech—high-class limey."

"I am an American."

"Didn't say you weren't, but with all that's goin' on, one wonders. What part of Connecticut you call home?"

"Near New Haven."

"Know that harbor. New Englander myself. Used to work at the shipyards up in that area till I came down to New York. Afore that I hailed from Maine. Much good the move's doin' me now, with the war lockin' up the harbor and the yards all closed down. Nothin' goin' on but a few ships sneakin' up the Sound and down the Hudson. No need for new vessels when more than half we have are stuck in port."

"Is it that bad in New York?"

"Ayuh. Bad as you can get. Take a peak out that window. What d'ya see? An ocean of masts—not one of 'em able to sail, with that damn blockade. Weren't like that a few years ago. Couldn't unload 'em fast enough; had new ships slidin' into the river once a month." Mawson started walking around the bed toward the pine dresser on the far wall. "You got interests down here? Representing one of the Eastport shippers?"

"No. I came on my own."

"Got work?"

"I shall be needing some."

"What's your line?"

"Anything I can find at the moment."

Mawson had opened the drawers, tossed a pair of rough corduroy work pants in Christopher's direction, then a heavy flannel shirt. "Ain't the newest, but they'll cover you. Here's a pair of longjohns, too. Gets nippy down on the water. See if Hester can't help you out with some boots and an overjacket." Mawson grinned. "She's got a collection of stuff left behind by boarders who left in more of a hurry than they'd have liked."

"I appreciate this."

Mawson shrugged off the thanks.

As Christopher dressed, the other man went to the narrow washstand, the only other piece of furniture in the room besides the dresser and beds, poured some water from the pitcher into the cracked washbowl, and began splashing his face. He then lathered up some soap and spread it over the bristles on his cheeks.

"How long have you been in New York?" Christopher asked the man as he shaved.

" 'Bout four years now. As I said, musta been a fool to come south. Hear they're still buildin' up in Maine . . . then again, can't believe all you hear."

"But the blockade runs the length of the East Coast."

"Ayuh. My guess is the British're lookin' for a little neutrality up there on the Canadian border, and they're softenin' up the locals by keepin' the yards open. Mistaken if they expect any allegiance from that neck of the woods. We Down Easters got minds of our own. What d'you do yourself?"

"A bit of everything."

"Know the sea trades?"

"Somewhat. I did some sailing at one time." Christopher didn't add that the sailing had been on his own yacht, and he had been captain, not crew.

"Take it you're a single man."

"I am." There was no point in telling Mawson the truth that he was married. It could only involve a long and very fictitious explanation.

"So you came to New York seekin' a new fortune?" Mawson had finished shaving and examined the results in the small mirror over the washstand.

"It would appear I have not had much success thus far."

Mawson grinned. "Ain't that the truth! Here—use my razor if you like. Strop's hangin' there off the edge of the washstand. Still, somethin' musta brought you down to New York. You got some education, sounds like."

"I suppose. I thought I would see what opportunities presented themselves before I made a decision. Now, with my resources reduced, I will have to find a new course."

"Mayhap I can help you out. Nothin' comin' in from overseas, but the coastal and Hudson packets are still slippin' in. I'm workin' as stevedore at one of the docks and could use a new laborer. Others waitin' in line for the job, but I could get you in. Wouldn't be fancy work . . . unloadin' cargo and gettin' it off the dock into warehouse, but the pay's six dollars a week which ain't bad for these times."

Christopher didn't need to deliberate. He needed to stay alive, and disoriented though he felt at the moment, he knew this was an offer he couldn't refuse.

"When can I start?"

"Tomorrow soon enough?"

"I am grateful."

"Least I can do for a greenhorn who loses his fortune his first night in New York, though with that education of yours, you'd prob'bly fit right in at one of them import houses. Problem is, none of 'em's hirin', with shippin' at a standstill."

Christopher finished shaving and wiped the remnants of lather from his face with the handtowel. "I can understand."

"You hear a lot of gloom and doom these days down at Tontines, yet every so often a privateer pulls in and things liven up. Cargo goes faster'n it's unloaded."

"Some shipping does get through the blockade, then?"

"Not enough to keep any but the big houses alive. Chancy business, but I know men got rich overnight who had an interest in a privateer."

Christopher was thoughtful. Because the war had had its beginnings in his own native era, he'd studied its history extensively while in the twentieth century, and he

now drew what details he could remember to the forefront
of his mind. Peace would come in another year, almost to
the day, yet news wouldn't reach New York until two
months later. By the spring, the British would flood the
New York market with goods that had been scarce during
the war, causing prices to plummet. Some would see it
through, but others would have a very sorry time indeed.

"You 'bout ready?" Mawson asked. "We'll see what
Hester has out for breakfast. Mayhap some food will stop
this head of mine from poundin'. I'll settle with her for
your first week's board. Don't imagine you settled any-
thin' last evenin'?"

"I do not recall," Christopher said mildly.

Mawson chuckled. "No, I'll bet you don't."

After they'd eaten, Mawson, who was proving to be far
sharper and more well-versed than his uneducated country speech would indicate, took Christopher on a walking
tour of the waterfront. It was a new city to Christopher,
but the sights and sounds surrounding him on the streets
and along the wharves were not alien. This, after all, was
his time, his world—the twentieth century had been the
alien one. The cityscape of two- and three-story brick and
wood framed structures was familiar, as were the packed
dirt and occasionally cobbled lanes, community wells in
the center of intersections, the litter of refuse and animal
droppings piled in the gutters, stray dogs and hogs rum-
maging about; horse-drawn wagons and carriages passing
on narrow alleyways that during the work week would be
clogged with traffic, the street peddlers pushing their bar-
rows even on this Christmas Day—for the poor there was
no time for celebrating.

As they came down Pearl Street to the heart of the commercial district, they passed the offices and warehouse
fronts of textile jobbers and auctioneers. On Peck Slip,
leading down to the East River and the wharves, there
were more warehouses, and agents' and brokers' offices
with lettered signs hanging from the lower story doorways. Docked vessels filled the slip waters between the
rows of buildings, their bowsprits right up over the side-

walk. The tang of salt in the chill wind masked the scents
of tar and the effluvium in the polluted slip waters.

A forest of bare masts formed an ever-present backdrop
as they followed the slip to South Street and the wharves
jutting out into the East River, skirting barrels and bales
and lengths of coiled rope. The area was eerily deserted
but for an occasional down-on-his-luck seaman staggering,
a bottle of rum in hand, between the wharves and buildings.

Christopher shook his head at the scores of sleek wooden
hulls, their proud masts lifting toward the sky, that rested
silently at the docks. He turned to Mawson. "All this shipping is laid idle by the war?"

"All of it. A sin. You can see why there ain't much
chance of you finding work in one of them importin' houses
down the street."

"At this rate, the ships will rot at their moorings."

"The owners did what they could—shoveled salt in the
holds to keep the timbers—but it's a sad sight. Helped
build a couple of these beauties myself—that there brig
Ezekiel Jones, for one." Mawson lifted his hand and
pointed upward. "You see them upended tar barrels the
shipowners stuck over the mastheads? We call 'em Mr.
Madison's nightcaps. Fittin' tribute, don't you think, to
the way this war has put our shippin' to sleep?"

"Fitting indeed."

"You should see the Hudson yards. Every one of the
merchantmen put in there is wearin' one o' these little
bonnets."

As they continued down South Street, Mawson pointed
out the offices of some of the more prosperous firms: flour
and grain merchants, textile importers, china and cutlery
merchants, the offices of T. H. Smith & Sons, tea merchants, whose selling room, Mawson informed him, was a
showplace on the street. Everything was deserted and
locked up tight for the holiday.

They left South Street at Wall Street and headed away
from the river. The street was a far cry from its skyscrap-
ered counterpart of the nineteen seventies. Though even
now the heart of the financial district, the buildings—

impressive Federal and Georgian style bank fronts side by side with the unostentatious offices of marine insurance agents—were of a far less lofty scale. There was a dignity to the area, and one could almost detect the scent of money in the air.

Dusk was falling by the time the two made their way back to upper Pearl Street and had their simple evening meal in the dining room of Hester Reed's Boarding House. Christopher noted thankfully that the downstairs rooms of the house—the parlor and the dining room—were a great improvement over the unrelieved dreariness of the bedroom he and Mawson shared. The house was old, and both rooms were warmed by huge old fireplaces that the chilled roomers kept stocked with firewood scavenged from wherever they could find it. Their fires brought a coziness to the winter evenings, shutting out the cold and casting a mellow glow over the threadbare parlor furnishings and the long, battered table and unmatched chairs in the dining room. Old prints and framed needlework decorated the walls, and rag rugs covered the pine floors from which most of the finish had been worn by the boarders' heavy boots. The effect was a welcoming one, and Mawson and Christopher enjoyed the camaraderie that evening as they sat down at the table with six other men. Their chipped china plates, remnants of a fine old service, were piled high with plain yet good and filling victuals. Three of the other boarders were dockworkers like Mawson, lucky enough to have found and held their jobs. One was a stable hand at a bustling establishment on Water Street that catered to the trade of the merchant princes; another was employed in a dry goods shop up on the Bowery; and the last was a shy young man apprenticed to a silversmith. There were two other beds in the house, vacant and available to those looking for a room for a night or two.

The dinner conversation ranged over many topics, from the situation on the wharves to the latest brawl down at the Ship's Tavern. The dry goods clerk spoke of a wealthy Bowling Green matron coming into his shop that day and, at a price equal to most working men's three months salary, purchasing an English china service that had been run in through the blockade. The silversmith's apprentice agreed that, yes, they were getting commissions, too, some clientele coming in to buy ready-made ware because good English silver wasn't readily available. But in the next breath the dockworkers spoke of work so scarce they wondered if they would be kept on for their next day's pay.

"But it'll catch up with them," the stableman countered. "These merchant so-and-sos, livin' off their bank accounts. Things the way they are, just you wait to see how soon they'll be drained to nothin—just like the rest of us— livin' from one day to the next."

The other men nodded, but the heartening thought of the rich brought down to their own level gave them no real consolation from their own worries.

Christopher listened with great interest throughout the meal, but by the time he was draining the dregs of his second mug of ale, the shock of his suddenly and profoundly changed circumstances and the strain of assimilating so many new experiences and information so quickly, were taking their toll. His mind and heart were unable to accept the overwhelming sadness of having been torn from his wife and son. He felt this New York scene would soon vanish, all a very bad dream, and he would wake to find Jessica in his arms, his family united again in their Connecticut home.

The loss was unacceptable; Christopher denied it as another, denying the death of a loved one, might look up from time to time, half expecting that loved one to enter a room. He cocked an ear, hoping for Jessica's familiar voice; waited for the soft pressure of her hand on his shoulder; could almost catch a whiff of that subtle perfume she always wore, the scent of which followed her from room to room. How he loved her! It was as though her very essence had become part of him.

He jerked his thoughts back to the roomful of strangers, realizing with a stab of pain that he was back in his own time. . . . Yet no more could he put his twentieth century life out of his thoughts than he could forget to breathe. And that life was Jessica. What was she doing at this moment? How was she taking the morning's events? Was she

too feeling a grief too deep even for the release of tears?
Would she and the child be able to carry on without him?
He had no fears for her financial well-being. In the fore-
sight that he might be swept from her side, he had made
financial provisions. But emotionally! Their love had been
so very dear, so very deep . . . and still was. What would
she tell their friends and her family of his disappearance?
That he had just walked out the door and left them? He felt
sick at the thought, but what other explanation could she
give? She couldn't tell the world the truth. And would she
be able to begin a new chapter in her life . . . one that did
not include him? *Did he want her to?* Jessica was young,
beautiful, with a child to raise. It would be unnatural for
her to spend the rest of her life alone. She deserved to have
another man to love her, to share the future with her, to be
at her side through the good and the bad in life. But God!
Another man and Jessica . . . another man calling her his
own, lying in bed beside her! The thought brought a pain
that left him without breath.

Many hours passed before he slipped off into a dream-
filled sleep; hours during which he laid on his back on the
thin mattress, staring at the ceiling, or out the window
where the moonlight cast the city scene into a hazy relief.

Why me? he asked himself over and over. Why was I the
one fate chose to send on this incomprehensible and painful journey?

Willis Mawson proved to be a good friend. Early the following morning, they left for the Schemner facilities—
several large brick warehouses three stories high with
dusty, paned windows, fronting up to the crushed shell
pavement and worn planking of the unloading area beside
the slip waters. By the time they arrived there, Mawson
had briefed Christopher thoroughly on what to expect of
his employer and what would be expected of him, and frequently during the day he materialized at Christopher's
side to offer helpful directions, and advice. It wouldn't do
to have the newcomer's inexperience show to the other laborers, all suspicious of a new man on the docks during
these hard times, when steady work for experienced labor-

ers was almost impossible to find. Christopher did his best
to live up to Mawson's expectations. He pulled his weight
with the other men, moving and positioning barrels, bales,
and crates for the derrick to lift from the hold and the deck
onto the dock. No mechanization was there to aid them. A
mule, harnessed to ropes straining over the derrick pul-
leys, hoisted the cargo into the air. Once on the dock, the
cargo was sorted. Cargo to be warehoused was stacked on
wooden dollies, wheeled up the ramp to the second story of
a brick building facing the slip, and unloaded.

The days were long, with the winter cold numbing a
man's fingers and piercing into his bones. Working hours
began at the crack of dawn and lasted until darkness, with
a break for a noon meal of biscuits, cheese, and a tumbler
of New England distilled rum. The fiery liquid was the sta-
ple drink of these men, who tossed down another tumbler-
ful in late afternoon, any long-term effects of the alcohol
worked off by their muscle-straining labors.

Although his body gradually adjusted, in the first few
days Christopher felt the strain, the weariness of sore
muscles not used so strenuously since the days of his construction site job in the twentieth century. Slowly, he got
used to working with raw hands chapped by the cold, to
never feeling warm despite the layers of clothing on his
body, to suffering feet so sore he felt every one of the cob-
bles he trod in the streets as he and Mawson trudged the
mile back to their lodgings each evening to a hearty meal
of stew or boiled beef and pork washed down with three fingers of rum or a mug of ale. During and after dinner they
talked and compared notes of their days with the other
boarders; but usually, exhausted, Christopher and Mawson were asleep in their beds by nine.

Only on Saturday nights, with a day of rest to anticipate, did they stop off at one of the local taverns. Glad for
a break at the end of a long week, the crowd was often bois-
terous, the talk loud. Fistfights broke out occasionally on
the street in front. Generally they were amicably settled,
the two opponents smacking each other on the back and returning, laughing, to the tavern for another round. The

tavernkeeper, an old seaman himself, took it all in stride, barring his doors only to the chronic troublemakers.

And so the days progressed, long and mind-deadening, into late-January, with no break in the work schedule until a blustery afternoon when the force of the freezing winds off the river made unloading impossible.

Instead of returning to their rooms, Mawson took Christopher down to Tontines Coffee House, the popular meeting place of New York businessmen whose interests were connected with the sea. The inclement weather had drawn many to the congenial rooms of the brick structure on the Old Slip, and a brisk hum of conversation greeted the two dockhands as they stepped through the entrance doors into the hallway. There, dozens of notices were posted: announcements of vessels and cargoes for sale, names of arriving and departing coastal and river packets, news of the war. The notices were few, Mawson advised, in comparison to prosperous days. But at Mawson's words, Christopher couldn't stop a thought from flashing through his mind: if only it were possible to post a message here for Jessica; if only there was the remotest chance that she would see it and they would find each other again. But even as he considered the idea, he knew there was no hope. It seemed heartbreakingly obvious that he had left his wife and son in the twentieth century. He turned his attention to the crowded room before him.

Standing in groups or seated at the clutter of tables was a wide mix of men: importers and shipowners in long-tailed morning jackets and tailored overcoats, top hats in hand; agents and brokers just as nattily attired; captains and first mates in pea jackets and caps, dockworkers in rougher, less uniform attire. Many men stood in a group to one side of the room, their conversation especially animated. Christopher and Mawson moved closer to see what was going on. In a moment Mawson jabbed Christopher's ribs. "Sounds like one of the privateers made it in. Let's learn more of this."

"Took advantage of the rough seas last night to slip right through the blockade," they heard one fellow say.

"The Brits were too busy keeping their tubs afloat to pay any mind." The remark was greeted by a burst of laughter.

Mawson tapped the shoulder of a well-dressed gentleman beside him. "What vessel?"

"*Night Hawk.* One of the Griswold boys' ships. Appropriately named, wouldn't you say?"

Mawson grinned. "Know the vessel. Where'd they put in from? What kind of haul?"

"West Indies. Sugar, rum, coffee. Captured a British merchantman bound for Bermuda on the way up, unburdened her of a nice cargo of English-made goods, then left her to find her own way home." The gentleman chuckled. "Most of her cargo is sold already. Some of the brokers—myself included—were down at the dock at three this morning, soon as a messenger brought word she was in."

"Who's captain?"

"Jonathan Wilkes. That's him up there." He pointed toward a gray-bearded man who was lifting to his lips a shot of brandy poured from a flask that an appreciative listener had pulled from his pocket.

"Heard of 'im," Mawson nodded. "Runs a tight ship. Good man."

"And so buoyed by his success," the gentleman added, "that he is set to head out again as soon as the *Night Hawk* can be reprovisioned and loaded. I have heard the Griswolds want to ship out some of the upstate flour that's been choking up their warehouses."

Christopher had been listening with great interest, and now spoke up. "That might be pressing his luck a bit."

"Or taking fortune by the tail."

"I am not saying I do not admire the man for his courage —this city needs more like him. The sight of all these idle vessels sickens me."

The gentleman eyed him. "As it does anyone whose livelihood is tied up in those ships. What is your interest in the port, sir?"

"Little at the moment. I arrived in New York only a short time ago, and Mawson here was kind enough to find me work up at Schemner's."

"Mawson?" The gentleman asked. "Willis Mawson,

would it be?" And at Mawson's nod, "Yes, I know the name. One of the best ship's carpenters in New York before the war shut down the yards at Corlears. Good to meet you." He extended his hand. "Robert Bayard, broker. Import, export."

Mawson accepted his hand. "Heard of you, too. See you're stayin' alive."

Bayard grinned ruefully. "Barely. Last night's cargo will keep my head above water for the time."

"This here's Christopher Dunlap," Mawson introduced. "Down from Connecticut."

Bayard turned again to Christopher as they shook hands. "Connecticut, eh? Yet I hear a British accent. What brought you to our fair city in these terrible times?"

"I came to Connecticut from England some years ago, and you might say I arrived in this city seeking new ventures, although I ran into a bit of misfortune from which Mawson very kindly extricated me."

"I am sorry to hear that . . . about your misfortune. Not too serious, I hope."

Both Christopher and Mawson chuckled.

"One of them Five Points girls," Mawson explained, "stripped him of his valuables when he couldn't be held accountable."

"I see." Bayard had difficulty concealing his grin. "One of the lessons to be learned in this city—generally in an unforgettable fashion. What was your business in Connecticut, Dunlap?"

"Horse breeding, some investments, although I turned all my assets into cash before leaving for New York," Christopher responded, coming as close to the truth as he dared, "which made the theft of my valuables my first night in the city that much more unpleasantly memorable."

Bayard's expression grew serious. "My sympathies."

"You said you had gotten some of the *Night Hawk* cargo?" Christopher quickly changed the subject. He saw speculation in Bayard's eyes and did not want any further probings into his past.

"A bit, not as much as I would have liked. The bidding, as you can imagine, was steep."

"Not the times to be makin' a quick fortune," Mawson commented.

"Not unless, like the captain here, you have Lady Luck's flag flying from your masthead."

"I imagine," Christopher said thoughtfully, "there are other ways money can be made."

"Yes, if you are referring to the likes of Astor. But his business in furs was established well before the war. He has the funds to buy out and mortgage the failing merchants who have lost their shirts because of the war, but that hardly says a great deal about making it rich without a fortune already behind you."

"No doubt he will make it richer still," Christopher added, "in twenty years, when the property values on this island increase several fold on the titles he bought out for a song."

"What makes you think they'll increase that much?" said Bayard, cocking an eyebrow. "Most of the island above Canal is nothing but farmland. Who would pay exorbitant prices for real estate when there's land to spare for the asking?"

"Someone will. This city will grow, and there is no place to grow but upward."

"Perhaps in many years, but the city is dying at the moment for lack of commerce . . . losing population."

"The war will not last forever."

"No, but the British could prove victorious."

"Doubtful. They have been involved for too many years in a war far closer to their home front, and it has drained them."

"What you say is true, but since the peace in France, they've added a discomforting number of ships to reinforce their blockade."

"I am only speculating."

"Yes," said Bayard. His eyes hadn't left Christopher throughout their conversation. "Well, if I am to make any profit on this cargo I have just purchased, I had best see to its disposition. A pleasure meeting you Mawson, Dunlap.

My card. Do stop by my offices sometime." He shook hands with his new acquaintances. "And I imagine I will see you both here at Tontines again before too long."

"Ayuh," Mawson nodded.

Christopher watched thoughtfully as Bayard disappeared through the crowd toward the door. He'd liked the man and had a feeling that their meeting might one day prove worthwhile to him. He tucked Bayard's name and address away in his mind for future reference.

4

Jessica's first week in the Beard household was a blur of activity and adjustment, and she was left with little energy or time for introspection or self-pity.

She'd gone down to the kitchen that morning after the Christmas party to find Molly already busy preparing breakfast. With Kit fed and settled in the cradle by the fire, Jessica had only a few minutes to eat a quick meal before taking up her new duties. Molly's thoughtful guidance was invaluable as Jessica gathered up dustpan and brooms, ash bucket and dust rags, and set out to light the dining room fire.

She'd felt like a fumbling mass of nerves and ineptitude as she struggled to get a fire roaring and the room warm before the family descended for breakfast. She'd lost valuable time in the task and had to rush with the dusting of the table and sideboard, sweeping the crumbs from the previous day's meal off the carpet, and scraping from the table the worst of the dripped candlestick wax. When the room was finally presentable, she'd moved on to the parlor, where she repeated the cleaning ritual; only there was more to be done in this room—more furniture to be dusted, torn bits of wrapping paper to be picked from the carpet, a tea service to be removed. She'd just about finished the parlor when she'd heard the sound of footsteps and voices issuing from the main staircase. As she briskly swept the carpet, she thought of her vacuum cleaner at home and how she'd taken that luxury for granted.

Lugging the now heavy bucket of ashes, she went on to the study. The men had used this room the day before.

Dirty brandy glasses littered the side table and the desk, cigar ashes lay scattered on the rug. Jessica went first to the fireplace and, kneeling at the hearth, began shoveling. It took three trips, once she'd finished with the cleaning, to bring the tea service, the glasses, the ash bucket, and her cleaning materials back to the kitchen.

"Not a peep out of him," Molly had assured her as Jessica bent over Kit's cradle. "How about a bit of coffee? It's left over from the family's breakfast."

"That would be wonderful," Jessica had sighed. How she'd been longing for a cup of that rich restorative all morning, but with supplies short because of the war, the servants were allotted leftovers.

Afterward, revived, Jessica had headed upstairs to start the bedrooms. The Beards' room required little work except to make up the bed, clean out the fireplace, and lay a new fire to be lit that evening. Amelia Beard certainly was neat. No clothing was left discarded in the dressing room, and dirty linens had been placed in a sack, which Jessica carried from the room with her after she'd emptied and wiped the washbowl and put out fresh towels.

Next was Elizabeth's room, and Jessica dreaded the thought.

It was far worse a sight than it had been the previous morning. Now there were three dresses flung over the chair, a nightgown dropped on the floor. The dressing table top was hidden by the articles strewn over its surface; a book lay open on the rug beside the bed; water had been splashed on the floor from the washstand, and a dirty hand towel lay crumpled by the bowl.

Sighing, she had started with the bed, untangling the sheets and blankets and carefully smoothing the quilt. She'd stuffed the dirty nightgowns in with the other laundry and shaken out and rehung the lovely dresses in the wardrobe, checking first to see if they were soiled. Jessica had mopped the floor, dusted, swept, and cleaned the fireplace. She was just arranging the crystal vials and silver-backed brushes on the dressing table when the door of the room had opened and Elizabeth stepped in. Although her

eyes had swept the room, she made no comment on the
drastic improvement.

"Ah, Jessica, just the one I wanted to see," Elizabeth
had said haughtily. "I have some things that will need
mending if you will take care of it this afternoon." Going
to the wardrobe, she'd carelessly withdrawn a couple of
gowns. "Here, the hem is torn. And on this one the lace.
And these petticoats." She took several from the dresser.
"I forget where they are ripped but I put them aside for
that reason. That should do it for now." She'd tossed the
petticoats on the chair, then went to the dressing table to
extract a folded lace handkerchief from the drawer. "In all
the confusion yesterday I neglected to advise you I will
need you both in the morning and in the evening to help
with my dressing. Rachel has been filling in since the last
maid left, but she has so much to do . . . and then, it is not
the responsibility of the kitchen maid. I will expect you
this evening. We will probably be retiring about eleven."

"Very well." Jessica's tone was mild, though she was
seething at Elizabeth's imperious attitude.

Elizabeth had seemed about to leave the room, but at the
door she turned for one parting comment.

"Mama tells us you are married, with a child."

"Yes."

"And your husband is out to sea." The gray eyes in the
pretty young face were narrowed. "But, then, mama always has had such a soft heart for a sad story. By the way,
in this house I am used to being addressed as *Miss* Elizabeth by the servants. And see that my oil lamps are filled.
They were sputtering last night." With a rustle of silk
skirts, she was out the door.

Jessica had glared after her, her hands clenched into
fists in an effort to contain her anger. The arrogant little
brat! She had the greatest urge to tell Elizabeth precisely
what she thought; precisely *who* she was—not the meek
and mild servant that Elizabeth seemed so anxious to put
in her place, but an intelligent and sophisticated woman
who'd once owned a house in this very neighborhood, who
was a successful businesswoman, who'd been married to a
man whose social stature made the Beards' seem insignifi-

cant. She'd chastised herself for the last thought—she was beginning to sound as petty as Elizabeth—but, oh, the girl made her angry! Yet despite her fury, or perhaps because of it, she realized just how thoroughly her hands were tied, how dependent she was on this employment. She had no choice for the moment but to grit her teeth and bear it. All of it.

Roughly gathering up the garments needing mending, Jessica had carried them up to her room, then returned to the bedroom to finish the cleaning. As she stepped down the hall toward the bedroom behind the master suite, where she presumed the Beards' elder daughter and her husband had slept the previous evening, the door to that bedroom had suddenly opened, and an attractive brown-haired young woman stepped out, stopped abruptly as she saw Jessica in the hall. Her startlement had quickly passed, and in a moment she'd smiled.

"You must be the new maid. Mother mentioned you had arrived. I am Mary Weldon."

"How do you do." Jessica had immediately liked Mary's friendly and unaffected manner, so like her mother's—and so unlike her sister's—and returned the smile. "I was just going in to clean the room, but if you prefer I will come back later."

"Not at all. I only came up to get my shawl." She hesitated for a moment, then spoke again, softly. "Mother has told us of your misfortune. I am truly sorry."

"Thank you."

"She says your son is a darling."

"I tend to think so." Jessica grinned.

"Before we leave tomorrow afternoon, perhaps you would not mind if I stopped into the kitchen to see him."

"Please do."

"I know my mother is aching for the chance to coddle him again, and . . . well, you see, Mr. Weldon and I are expecting our own at the end of summer. We made the announcement to the family last evening."

"Congratulations!"

Mary had flushed. "We are both delighted, as are my parents, but I have never had much opportunity to be near

an infant . . . heavens, not since Elizabeth was born. Of
course, there were the neighbors' offspring, but I never
paid a great deal of attention to them at the time."

"Well, Kit would enjoy all the attention he can get," Jessica had laughed, "that I can promise you. Please do come
by and see him. If I'm not there, he probably will be. Cook
is keeping an eye on him while I work."

"Thank you, I will." Mary had smiled graciously. "And
welcome. I hope you will be happy here."

"I am sure I will."

With another quick smile, Mary had turned and departed down the hall. Jessica went into the bedroom, but
the encounter had left her feeling better.

In the early afternoon she'd toured the cellars with Rachel—the laundry, the buttery, the wine cellar, and the
storage rooms. And all the while she'd worried about Kit—
felt guilt at having left him so long in the care of others.
Then there were linens to be folded and sorted in preparation for changing the beds the next day—and the mending
Elizabeth had left her, which took longer than she'd expected because of inexperience with the fine stitchery required. The work had been interrupted when Mary made
her promised visit to see the baby. It was a pleasant diversion, however, Mary's warm personality putting Jessica
completely at ease as they had chatted of newborns, the
months of waiting, the preparations to be made. Jessica
couldn't help wishing that Mary lived in the house, and
not her overindulged younger sister. It was amazing that
two such opposing personalities could have been raised in
the same family.

Jessica's last task of the day had been the most burden-
some. She'd steeled herself before climbing the stairs to assist Elizabeth with her undressing, promising to bite her
tongue. She'd succeeded with an effort as she'd unbuttoned Elizabeth from her gown, hung it in the wardrobe,
and helped the girl into a lacy nightdress. She said not a
word of thanks to Jessica and criticized her for not being
quick enough.

"I will catch my death if you do not hurry with that
nightgown. No, the pink one, as I told you!"

Jessica had remained silent as she dropped the soft folds over Elizabeth's blond head and held the matching robe as the girl slipped her arms into the sleeves. She'd retrieved the discarded camisole and petticoat from the floor while Elizabeth had seated herself at the dressing table and begun removing the pins from her hair.

"I do believe in one hundred strokes a night, but I am so weary this evening. Would you, Jessica." It wasn't a question.

Jessica had taken the silver brush being handed her and started to brush Elizabeth's long tresses.

"You really should do something with your own hair," the girl had commented as she appraised Jessica's reflection in the mirror. "It is quite untidy."

"Yes, I know, but if you will recall, I lost my belongings, and having no pins, have had to make due with a ribbon."

"Well, take some of these old pins of mine. I was going to throw them out anyway." Elizabeth had reached into one of the dressing table drawers, removed a dozen bent pins and dropped them on the glass table top.

"That's very kind of you," Jessica said, forcing a shade of gratitude into her tone.

"We cannot have the neighbors thinking one of our servants is not neat about her appearance."

"Quite so."

It was after eleven-thirty before Elizabeth had let her go. Jessica was drooping by the time she collected Kit and climbed the stairs to the third floor. Only six hours of sleep, Jessica thought as she settled the baby, undressed, and climbed beneath her own quilt. How long could she keep up a schedule like this? But within seconds of dropping her head on the pillow, she was sound asleep.

Once the holidays were past, Jessica slipped into a routine. There was no question that her work was physically demanding, but she was getting more rest now that the family was on a normal schedule and retiring earlier in the evenings. Bertram Beard was always pleasant on the few occasions she saw him in the house. He was away the better part of the day, either at the mill or at his business in town. In even the coldest weather he had his gelding saddled for the three-mile ride into the center of Eastport.

With her first week's wages—one dollar—Jessica made a trip to the corner market and bought hairpins, a hairbrush and a toothbrush, the latter of which she was surprised to find, and some inexpensive cream for her chapped hands and lips. Little was left from her wages by the time she returned to the Beards', but her purchases had been necessities.

Much to Jessica's relief, Kit was adapting easily to his new environment, receiving more than his share of attention, thanks both to Cook and to Amelia Beard, who was in the habit of dropping into the kitchen while Jessica was at her duties to cuddle and play with the child. Under Mrs. Beard's efficient management, the household ran smoothly. Her orders were always tactfully given, and followed through by the servants without the smallest complaint, but still Amelia complimented Jessica several times on the job she was doing.

"I have absolutely no fault to find," she told Jessica one morning. "Everything is spotless, and Elizabeth seems pleased with the assistance you are giving her."

Jessica was so very tempted to comment that that was a wondrous thing, since Amelia's youngest daughter certainly never had any praise for Jessica when they were face to face, only more and more demands. But Jessica realized that such a remark wouldn't go over well. Amelia was aware of some of her daughter's faults, but was totally blind to the depth of them. Jessica just smiled and said a polite thank-you to Mrs. Beard.

"And I wanted to tell you," Amelia continued, satisfied that everything in the household was going as it should, "that I have had lengths of material sent up from Mr. Beard's store—a nice, sturdy cotton for a new uniform for you and some soft flannel for the child. I have left the bundle on the hall table. You can take them up to the workroom and begin anytime you wish."

What Elizabeth did with her days Jessica wasn't quite sure, although she did see the girl drive and walk out with her mother a few times on short trips to a neighbor's home.

There being so little of a constructive nature to occupy Elizabeth's hours, Jessica could almost sympathize with her; no wonder she complained of boredom. Jessica did notice some rather good watercolors of scenes around the farm—some completed, others half-finished—laid to dry on the desk top in Elizabeth's room.

"Are these yours?" she asked the girl one morning.

"What? Oh, the paintings. Yes. It is something to pass the hours."

"But they're very good. You have a talent."

"Do you think so? Yes, I suppose . . . that is what Mama is always saying. But where shall the painting ever get me? A poor substitute for a bit of social life. Do you realize in a few months I will be nineteen? And not a single suitor! At my age Mary was constantly attending balls and parties, but because of this foolish war, I must sit at home and twiddle my thumbs!" From her tone one would have thought the war had been declared just to spite her. "Not that I wish to make a marriage like my sister—that little box of a house in town without even a maid, scrimping and saving and still oozing contentment now that a baby is on the way. I intend to find a man who will let me live in style, with a home suitable for entertaining. But how I shall ever meet anyone in this dull community, I should like to know! . . . No, Jessica, that is not the gown I wanted. The yellow one. Perhaps at least the color will make me feel like spring."

As Elizabeth fiddled with her golden curls before the mirror, Jessica dutifully returned the gown to the wardrobe and brought out the yellow dress and a creamy ivory shawl that Elizabeth would wear with it.

At least for Jessica there was no question of boredom—tediousness, yes, but with floor and furniture waxing, silver polishing, and window cleaning in addition to her normal chores, she never lacked for something to do.

It was not until late January that she finally got up the courage to visit the site of the home she'd shared with Christopher. She'd thought of it many times, but had been afraid of her own reactions to that place where they had shared such happiness. Jessica had walked through other sections of the neighborhood, always searching for that one handsome face that meant all the world to her, remembering those brilliant blue eyes and the beseeching, torn look in them in those last moments before they were separated. She continued to hold on to a slim thread of hope that she would meet him—though in such a small, close-knit community, if a handsome, dark-haired stranger had appeared, someone would have mentioned it.

Molly offered to watch Kit, so, wrapping her worn cloak securely around her, Jessica set out alone down the drive and onto the lane in front of the house. The day was sunny and warm for late January. The river, iced at the edges, rippled over its rocky bed at the base of the embankment, the rushing water glinting in the sunlight. She knew if she went North up the lane where it cut into the hillside following the course of the river, she would come to the sawmill where Lucas St. John worked. They'd still been sawing planking and boards in that mill when Jessica was a child in the twentieth century, until a tremendous flood had washed out the dam, and the old mill buildings had been left to fall into disrepair and finally collapse in a pile of worn timbers. Nothing marked the site in the nineteen seventies save the remnants of the dam foundations, clinging in places to the rocky riverbed.

Today she turned south toward the crossroads of the small community. A short distance up the frozen, rutted dirt road was one of the many millponds along the river, this one formed by a dam just below. Opposite it, an open pasture, part of the Beard property, stretched away into the distance.

At the crossroads a few hundred yards ahead, the buildings became more clustered. Two wood-framed mill buildings adhered to the river's edge. The first of these, Molly had told her, was a part of Bertram Beard's holdings. Jessica smiled. That same building, enlarged and converted to an inn, was still standing in the twentieth century. On the opposite corner was a clapboard structure. A hand-painted wooden sign swinging from the front of the building identified it as the local market where a variety of items could be purchased, from dry goods to groceries. Situated diagonally across the road was a substantial saltbox farmhouse of seventeenth century construction, and Jessica recognized it immediately. The building looked much the same now as in the nineteen seventies, when it had been restored and refurbished. By then, of course, the barns and outbuildings were long gone, and the farmland surrounding the house had been split into building lots, each with its nondescript dwelling. The latter-day view certainly suffered in comparison to the charming scene now before Jessica's eyes.

Turning down the road to the left of the crossroads, she followed its narrow, rutted width toward the river and the arched stone bridge spanning the water just below the dam. Barely wide enough for one horse-drawn vehicle, it was a rustic version of the bridge across which Jessica had once almost daily driven her car.

How little this scene had changed. It was almost eerie. She surveyed the tall trees, now winter skeletons, standing proud to either side of the sloping, rocky banks; the ice coated pond above the dam; the weathered, wood mill building perched at the edge of the pond with its water wheel turning slowly; white-frothed water falling steadily with a dull roar over the stonework of the dam and into the river below. She remembered so clearly the many times in the twentieth century when she'd come to this very spot to lean on the railings, as she was doing now, on a warm summer's evening or amid the chill snap of winter, listening to the rushing water, gazing up into a black-velvet, star-spattered sky with the old buildings surrounding her; feeling the history of the place, the age, the beauty; imagining former inhabitants and their lives . . . some long-dead resident crossing the bridge, perhaps pausing in this very spot to gaze at the falls. There'd been such a sense of peace, of continuity—it had been so easy to forget the jarring modern world around her; to feel in spirit with a gentler lifestyle.

And now she was in that past she'd imagined, was seeing it with her own eyes. But now there was no peace, only a feeling of terrible loneliness and loss.

Eventually she turned from the view, her mind full of

memories that weren't memories at all but a vision of what was to come. Sighing, Jessica continued across the bridge in the direction of her former home. With her emotions churning, she wondered if it had been wise to come this far. Yet this was something she knew she had to do.

In the future a few houses would shoulder up to this lane where now there was only woodland and field, a large barn and ramshackle shed. But up ahead of her today, straddling the space between river and road, was another mill, quiet now on this Sunday morning and looking very different from the residence it would become. And opposite the mill, on a slight rise of land that blended with the field and the woods beside it, was the spot where her home would one day stand.

She left the road, climbed over a weathered gray stone wall. Mentally she pictured the buildings, the landscape. Here would be the route of the driveway, and there the flower garden; across the drive, the barnlike garage, and here the path to the back entrance of the house. Her mind full of memories, she followed its would-be route.

Stepping through the imaginary doorway, she paced slowly through the rooms, remembering the architectural detail, the furnishings.

First the large kitchen along the back. She could so easily envision the round table before the window, where she'd sat in nervous anxiety the day she discovered she was pregnant; she could remember how she'd run crying into Christopher's arms as, finally, he came through the door, and he'd soothed and comforted away her fears of bearing a child when its father's destiny was so uncertain. The joy in his eyes had been her happiness.

Then there was the paneled dining room, the harvest table where she and Christopher had shared their first dinner together—two strangers, stunned by the unfathomable accident that had brought them together; yet, looking into each other's eyes, they'd sensed the depth of what might grow between them.

Finally the living room with its large old fireplace where, months later on the couch, with their love binding them together, they'd snuggled before a blazing fire.

As she closed her eyes, the memories seemed so real—Christopher sitting beside her, gazing down with eyes of love, reaching out his hands. She could hear his deep voice, his elegant English accent, feel his touch on her shoulder, the softness of his lips on her brow. She could feel him pulling her close into the strong protection of his arms. Only as she leaned forward into the embrace did reality pierce through the images that had taken hold of her mind.

There was no house! There was no Christopher! Just an empty field, the sun slanting down on the dried grass and snow beneath her feet. She mustn't cry! If she let the tears come now, how would she ever stop them? If she was to survive, she couldn't give in to the pain inside and let it be her master. She couldn't give up hope. She would find Christopher again—she *must* find him! She and Kit . . .

She stepped forward, blinded by the wetness in her eyes, forcing her feet back to the road, toward the bridge, up beyond the crossroads, past neat eighteenth century dwellings where chickens scratched in sideyards and an occasional milk cow poked a head over a board fence. The lane was quiet, all activity stilled on this day of rest.

Why had she gone up there, rubbing salt into the soreness of missing him? Why hadn't she realized to what extent the memories of him would overwhelm her?

A farmer's wagon rumbled by, its bed stacked with hay. A man on horseback, dressed in town clothes and a curly brimmed top hat, passed. Jessica glanced up; but his eyes were dark, his features not those of the one she was seeking. He lifted his hat briefly to her; she nodded in acknowledgment and continued walking.

Only when she became aware of the cold seeping through her shoes did she turn back. Weariness had numbed her senses, and Kit would need to be fed.

5

As though paced by a metronome, the hours and days clicked by, one after the other. Jessica survived; Kit thrived and grew. Though there were times when hopelessness seemed about to overtake her, in the busy activity of the farm there was always some impetus to snap her away from despondency. Snows had come, blanketing the world in fairy-tale white. Sleighs and work wagons on wooden runners skimmed over the lanes. Foot travelers trudged with heavy boots through the drifts.

One cold but sunny February afternoon, Lucas St. John came to the farm with a large bundle under one arm. Molly answered the knock on the kitchen door. "Ah, Lucas, good to see you! Come in out of the cold and let me get you a warm drink."

He grinned. "Not an offer to be refused." He stepped quickly past Molly and smiled at Jessica, who sat at the table polishing silver. "How are you?"

"Just fine. This is a nice surprise. I thought you would be busy at the mill."

"Things have been a bit slow the last few days." He placed his burlap-wrapped bundle on the floor, shrugged from his heavy jacket and hung it on the peg by the door, then took a seat at the table. "Actually, I stopped by to see you."

"You did?"

"I have a little something for Kit. With so much time on my hands, I put together a sled for him."

"Lucas, how good of you!"

Lucas colored a bit. "It is nothing fancy, but I thought he might get some pleasure out of it."

"Is this it on the floor?" Jessica put down her polishing rag and wiped her hands on her apron. "Let me see it."

As Molly handed Lucas his hot drink, Jessica knelt and pulled away the burlap covering to expose a three-foot sled made from an old barrel from which the staves on one side had been removed. A sturdy handle and cord were attached to the front.

"I thought you could bundle him and lay him inside, give him a ride across the yard out there."

"Oh, yes! He'll love it, though he's getting so rambunctious I may have to tie him in. Thank you so much, Lucas."

"If Kit enjoys it, that is all the thanks I need. I see he is awake. Shall we try it out?" He looked over to where a wide-eyed Kit in his cradle was watching the adult goings-on. "Can you spare the time from your work, Jessica? If not, I would be happy to take him out."

"Of course she can take a few minutes." Molly interrupted, smiling broadly. "You two run along. I'll be watching from the window."

In no time at all Jessica had Kit bundled; and with her own cape wrapped around her, and Lucas following with the sled, she stepped out the back door into the snow-covered yard.

"Over here on the other side of the drive," Lucas suggested. He placed the sled on the snow as Jessica carefully tucked Kit within. At first the child wasn't happy about leaving his mother's warm arms. But when Lucas gave a tug on the rope and the sled slowly began to slide over the snow, his delight gurgled forth.

"He likes it," Jessica laughed, striding beside Lucas as they set out across the broad sweep of lawn. "I believe you've made a friend for life, Lucas."

"You think so?" Grinning, he picked up his pace to a trot. "For this afternoon, in any case. He does seem to be enjoying it. Shall I pull him a little faster?"

"I don't think he'd mind," she called, returning his grin as she picked up her skirts and hurried after Lucas and the skimming sled. In that moment of play in the icy air, seeing her son's pleasure and good health, Jessica felt an inner glow; she was almost her old self again. A burst of laughter escaped her as Lucas slipped in a snow drift and went sliding down onto his bottom.

"Oh, Lucas, I don't mean to laugh, but if you could see yourself, all covered with snow—" As she rushed up to the fallen man, she laughed again; but the sound was halted by the suddenly serious, intense expression on Lucas's face. He stared up at her, and for a moment neither of them said anything.

When he spoke, his voice was almost husky, deep-toned. "You should laugh more often, Jessica. It becomes you."

"Does . . . does it?"

"Yes. Unquestionably. This is the first time I have seen the sadness leave your eyes."

Jessica dropped her gaze, flustered. "Today has been fun. I haven't had much time just to relax."

"I know, and I have sympathized with you . . . a great deal."

Another moment's silence, then the twinkle was back in Lucas's eyes, a wide grin on his face. "Well, don't just stand there. Be a lady and help this gentleman on his feet again."

"I'm sorry."

"A hand will do. I cannot seem to get my footing."

They'd frolicked for another half hour before Lucas had to get back to the mill. There'd been no more seriousness, only the cheerful bantering of two friends. Perhaps that look in Lucas's eyes, that tone in his voice, had been Jessica's imagination, she thought as she waved Lucas off down the drive, thanking him again. It was Elizabeth who interested him, and although Jessica liked Lucas very much, she knew she was not ready for a more serious involvement. No, it was only in friendship and good-heartedness that he had come. She was sure of that, and the afternoon had been pleasant. She felt so much better for it.

She settled Kit in his cradle for a much-needed nap and went on to finish her chores. As she slipped through the kitchen door into the hallway, she didn't hear Rachel's hushed comments to Molly.

"So, Miss Hoity-Toity's finally gone back to her work. Not like the rest of us who don't have time for an hour or two of play."

"She needed the respite. She's been working hard and is tired."

"I'm sure, but not too tired to flirt around with Lucas St. John."

"Hush, child," Cook said in a firm reprimand. "Lucas came by as a simple friendly gesture and brought a sled for the babe. If you had eyes in your head, you'd see there was nothing else there. Her mind's on another—that husband of hers."

"Ha! Wouldn't be surprised if that story was all a bag of wind."

"Rachel! I won't have you talking like that. The girl's a lady—never seen one so well-mannered in service here."

"Thinks she's better than the rest of us, that's the truth." The girl smiled slyly. "But she's in for an awakening. Miss Elizabeth didn't miss none of that scene out there on the lawn. Lucas is beneath her touch, but she won't have him foolin' around with her lady's maid. Told me as much herself a few minutes ago."

"Neither you or Miss Elizabeth do yourselves any credit with such talk!" Molly's eyes flashed.

"Hmph. Well, the 'lady' Jessica may have pulled the wool over your eyes and the mistress's, too, but see if Elizabeth don't take her down a peg or two."

"And what mischief have you got on your mind, child?"

But Rachel was already gone, and Cook wagged her head sadly. She could see she'd have to keep an eye out for Jessica's welfare. The young woman had enough of a burden on her mind without Rachel's petty troublemaking. And that Miss Elizabeth . . . another crafty one, bending her parents round her little finger.

During those evenings as winter slowly slipped past into the early days of spring, Jessica often sat with Molly before the kitchen fire, Rachel generally preferring her own room and her own company. One early March night, as Molly put up the dough for the next day's bread and Jessica stitched diligently on a new uniform, the two talked easily across the broad kitchen table. Jessica was proud of the four garments she had completed for Kit and was hurrying to finish the new uniform for herself. Only a few more buttons and the hem remained to be done.

An understanding woman, Molly never pried during their chats, but she was perceptive of Jessica's moods.

"You've been blue these last weeks," Molly said one evening. "It's your husband on your mind."

Jessica nodded. She'd adamantly refused to give up hope of finding Christopher, yet it was difficult at times not to give in to growing despair when she could discover not the smallest clue to his whereabouts. Earlier that day she'd traveled for the first time with Molly on a marketing trip to Eastport, still grasping onto the thread of hope that she might find Christopher. But as thoroughly as her eyes had perused the crowds on the street and in the shops, she'd seen no one of Christopher's description. The center of town had been a mass of pedestrians, horsedrawn vehicles of all sorts fighting their way over the mud and icy slush of the main street, the New York to Hartford stage clamoring by—its six-horse team snorting, their hooves echoing on the wooden bridge that spanned the river, pulling to a jangly halt at the post stop at Whitlock's Tavern. Jessica hadn't been free to roam about on her own. She'd stayed in Molly's wake to help the older woman with the shopping, as Jeb left them off in front of the stores then went to find a spot to tie the horse and wagon. They'd gone first to Beard's Mercantile, one of the largest and most prosperous shops in town, its shelves stacked with a variety of merchandise from yard goods to hardware, despite the scarcities caused by the war. Bertram Beard had greeted them jovially, sending one of the clerks to find the items on the list his wife had sent along, then chatting at length with them and taking up so much of their time that they'd had to rush up the muddied brick sidewalk to the grocer's; on further to the butcher's. Jessica had hoped for some time to explore town, but with the afternoon growing short, Molly had hurried her back to the wagon, and they'd headed immediately to the farm.

Molly's voice broke into Jessica's thoughts. "I know you're distressed, with all good reason, but there is much that could stop him from coming, you know. Not many can get through the blockade. Give it time, child, and try not to lose hope."

Jessica nodded, wondering what Molly would say if she knew the truth. Yet Jessica was all too willing to cling to any shred of hope that somehow, someday, they would be together again.

"You're English, aren't you, Molly?"

"Aye. What makes you ask? You're not thinking that puts me on the King's side in this fighting."

Jessica grinned, shook her head. "My husband is English, too.

"Is he now? I'm from Sussex myself. Came over as a girl and met my husband while I was working as kitchen maid in one of the New York inns. Luckier than many I was, getting an honest job and not being lured into the brothels like some of them poor girls. William and me came up to Connecticut soon after when he took a job at one of the shipyards down in Eastport. Some good years we had till that accident in the yard killed him."

"I'm sorry."

"Aye, I am, too, but that was a long time ago now. The shipyard owners were good to me—found me this position with the Beards. Been here ever since. What part of England is your husband from?"

"Kent."

"Not far from my village as the crow flies, Kent being the next bordering county, but I didn't do much traveling about before I set out for America. My family were tenants on a nice little farm, but times were bad. That was back in eighty-nine, when I left."

"Do you ever hear from them?"

"Now and then. It's only my sister and me can read and write a hand. At one time I was hoping to have her come and join me here, but she married." Molly was looking thoughtfully at Jessica. "You're not from the working class yourself, are you?"

"No."

"Thought not. Carry yourself like a lady. Won't go prying into the whys and wherefores of your being here, but you're a strong young woman and you'll do just fine." She paused as she placed the kneaded dough into a crockery bowl. "Miss Elizabeth been behaving herself any better?"

"She has her moments."

"Needs a firm hand, she does. Much as she tries my patience at times, don't think too ill of the girl. Working too hard at growing up and being a lady, and with all the attention she gets, no wonder her head's been turned."

"I know. I try to keep that in mind, and I know she's bored."

"Pity there's no girls her age near about. Well, you ever have a problem, you come to me, and I'll see what I can do."

To welcome in the spring and take everyone's mind from the war that seemed to drag on interminably, the community planned a Sunday social early that April at the meetinghouse on the corner. A very democratic affair, it welcomed all the inhabitants of Silvercreek, from the most prosperous of the gentry to the lowliest servant. Food and drink would be provided, and perhaps a little dancing if one of the local musicians felt inclined to bring along his fiddle.

Despite the melancholy of her mood, Jessica couldn't help but feel a touch of anticipation. To be out with people again, to put aside the forced servitude that sometimes threatened to get the best of her proud spirit, would prove a welcome respite. How wonderful to once again be able to don a flattering dress, to make an effort to look her very best. Not that she'd neglected her appearance, but her position in the house had forced her to disguise her attributes, made her feel dowdy, especially in comparison to the elegance of the young mistress.

Sunday morning she washed and dried her long hair before the fire and brushed it until it gleamed, then fastened it in an arrangement of soft waves atop her head. She chose the green wool dress, by far the most attractive in her limited wardrobe. Its color brought out the green in her eyes—eyes that had so often lately been dulled by weariness and despair. For a moment, as she glanced at her reflection in the mirror, her skin glowing, the color warm and rosy on her cheekbones, she once again felt the strong, vital Jessica that she'd been in the twentieth century.

The entire household set off on foot shortly after noon—the Beards in one party; Cook, Rachel, Jeb, Jessica and Kit in the other. Jeb looked stiff and formal in what he referred to as his Sunday-go-to-meetin' clothes, but he seemed proud of his appearance, such a gentleman that he took Molly's plump arm for the brief stroll. Molly was clearly delighted by his gesture, her rosy cheeks growing rosier, a shy smile on her lips making her seem almost girlish again. At the sight of the two of them, Jessica smiled. How nice that these two good people, both alone in the world, should find pleasure in each other's company. Rachel seemed preoccupied with her own thoughts, but then she rarely encouraged conversation. None of Jessica's overtures of friendship had succeeded in breaking through the girl's icy distrust, and Jessica had finally given up trying. It seemed that the women of the house were equally divided around her—Amelia Beard and Molly Fletcher were warm and supportive; Elizabeth and Rachel seemed eager to do everything in their power to make life a misery for her.

The meeting hall was crowded as they stepped through the door, its utilitarian interior warmed by a fire and the crush of bodies, taking the chill out of the early spring air. Rachel immediately moved off toward a group of young women. But like a mothering hen, Molly kept Jessica under her wing as they moved further into the room, exchanging greetings, Molly introducing her to those Jessica hadn't already met. Jeb had found his own cronies and was soon lifting a punch glass to his lips. The Beards, the Lathropes, and a few other neighbors of their social stature were congregated near the fireplace, where chairs had been set out for the ladies. Jessica had never met the Lathropes, although she'd heard Elizabeth talk of them often, and of their son, George, a dark-haired young man who was courting Willa Lockwood, a wealthy girl from Eastport.

Along one wall a table groaned under its burden of home-cooked delectables—every household had contributed something—and already some of the children were helping themselves, particularly from the dessert end of the table, slyly looking about for their mothers, and when sure no one who cared was watching, popping sweets into their mouths.

Jessica spotted Lucas St. John almost at the start. He seemed to stand out from the other men, and it was obvious many of the laborers looked up to him as a leader. Lucas smiled and lifted his hand in greeting to Molly and Jessica, but it was toward Elizabeth, prettily chatting with George Lathrope by the fire and making the most of her charms, that Lucas was constantly gazing. If Elizabeth was aware of his stare, she certainly gave no indication of it as she tilted her head to hear something George Lathrope was saying. The young Lathrope was obviously flattered by her attention.

Jessica was aware that she, too, was eliciting some interested glances from the men. Still, Miss Elizabeth was daughter to one of the wealthiest and most respected men in Silvercreek; Jessica Dunlap was a mere servant.

The excitement and strange faces didn't seem to bother Kit. He was an angel; alert, fascinated by the hubbub. At five months he was strong for his age, very aware of what was going on around him, more precocious, others had told Jessica, than any babe they'd seen in a long time. Jeb was already building him a small playpen to be set up in the kitchen when he grew too rambunctious for his cradle. But after all, Jessica often thought, given the child's background, was it surprising he was out of the ordinary? He was the issue of two people born over a century and a half apart, his father of noble lineage; and Kit himself had made a journey through time at the tender age of one month.

Molly took Kit as Jessica went to fill a plate at the table, then settle herself in a chair beside Molly to eat and to observe the crowd while Molly offered bits of gossip about some of the neighbor folk. They were momentarily interrupted from their chat when Amelia Beard came over.

"Jessica," she asked with a warm smile, "I don't mean to disturb your meal, but would you mind terribly if I stole your son for a bit? I have told Beatrice Lathrope so much about the child, and I would like to show him to her."

"Of course, I wouldn't mind. As a matter of fact you make me very proud."

"As you have every right to be. Such a fine boy. And never to worry, I will take good care of him."

"That I don't doubt."

Jessica handed Kit up into Amelia's capable arms. The child, so familiar with Mrs. Beard from her visits to the kitchen, gave her a baby smile and was immediately tucked close to Amelia's motherly breast. "I will not keep him as long as I'd like," she said as she stepped back toward the fireplace with the five-month-old in her arms.

"Quite a sensation he has made," Cook commented after Amelia Beard left.

"Do you think so?"

"Aye, no question of it. But he's a lovely child, and the mistress needs somethin' to occupy her thoughts. Always loved children, she did, and with Miss Elizabeth nearly grown and leaving the nest shortly, no doubt, this child is a blessing to her, though Mary will be presenting them both with a grandchild the end of summer. Master Kit will no doubt have his nose put out of joint at that happy event. If I guess him, he'll be taking his first steps by then, so forward he is."

As Amelia joined the group by the fire, one of the local fiddlers took out his instrument and moved to a corner of the room. He tuned the strings, and soon the lively notes of a country dance were ringing through the hall. The crowd separated to leave a space for dancing, and several of the younger couples, all of them servants and farmhands, stepped in to fill the gap and form a set. The dancing was lively, the dancers merry, as though to make up in one swift moment for the deprivations of the last year and a half. Very few of the revelers cared about the politics leading up to the war. Though angered by the British impress-

ment of sailors and interference with U.S. shipping, they
did not share the sentiments of the western and southern
"War Hawks" in Congress who had urged President Madison into the war in the hopes of expanding United States
territory into Canada, and as a means of combating the Indian attacks along western borders that these men felt
were inspired by the British. All the coastal New England-
ers knew was that the war had curtailed shipping along
the east coast and, by cutting off their markets, spelled
economic disaster for them all.

Jessica watched them move through the steps of the unfamiliar dance. Christopher had shown her the elegance of
a ballroom waltz, but there'd never been an occasion for
him to teach her the other popular dances of his era. As she
sat observing, Kit still with Mrs. Beard, she was approached by a likable young man of her own age, Elias
Jones, who worked at Bertram Beard's mill. He asked her
to join him in the next set. That Jessica was married was
common knowledge, and Elias's invitation could not be accepted. She refused as politely as she could, telling him
that she had decided not to dance that evening. He accepted her refusal graciously, smiled, and stepped away.

From where Jessica was seated, it was not difficult to notice the scene being played around Elizabeth. George Lathrope had finally moved away to sit beside his intended,
Willa Lockwood, whose expression had become more and
more irritated the longer he had remained talking to
Elizabeth Beard. But Elizabeth was not left alone for long.
Jessica had noticed Lucas gradually working his way
through the crowd until he appeared at Elizabeth's elbow.
Lucas may not have been garbed in finely tailored jacket
and breeches, as George Lathrope was, but something
about his carriage made an instant impression.

Elizabeth's response to Lucas's greeting was not notably
warm—that much was clear to Jessica even from across
the crowded room. It was obvious Elizabeth considered Lucas far beneath her touch. She was not a girl to settle for a
mill hand, foreman though he was, and she wasn't mature
enough to see beneath to the man's potential. Still, aside
from George, no other young men present came up to

Elizabeth's standards, and a compliment from even a mill hand was better than no compliment at all. The two chatted for a few minutes, Elizabeth moving to end the conversation when Mrs. Lathrope, a stately looking matron, approached her. The girl didn't even attempt to introduce Lucas to the woman, only nodded her head and turned her back on him. Jessica saw the momentary flash of pain and humiliation on his face; then he set his shoulders and walked back to the men gathered around the punch bowl.

It was not long after that he strolled over to where Jessica was standing, Kit once again in her arms.

"I have not had a chance to say hello," he smiled, "or to tell you how lovely you look this afternoon."

"That's kind of you to say."

"I only speak the truth. I see the little fellow is doing well. How are you?"

"Well enough."

He studied her. "The way you say that makes me think you could be better."

"The work is very tiring at times," Jessica said evasively, even though she knew she needn't fear being honest with Lucas.

"And? You've not heard any word of your husband?"

Jessica shook her head.

"As I told you before, that is not a reason to think the worst."

"I know."

Seeing the distress on Jessica's face, Lucas changed the subject. "I will probably be seeing a good deal of everyone at the farm in the next few weeks. Bertram's planning an addition to the barn. I am cutting up the order now and will be making some of the deliveries myself."

"Jeb has mentioned that he needed more stabling for the milk cows. Are you busy at the mill?"

"The work is coming in here and there, but little building is going on. Everyone's afraid, waiting for the outcome of this war. If some of my men had not enlisted with the Connecticut militia a few months back, I would be laying them off."

"The times are bad."

"Which only goes to show the Federalists were right in wanting to stay out, although there is a lot of Republican sentiment in this area."

Jessica had heard enough talk of local politics to know that although the state as a whole was Federalist, the Democratic-Republican Party, proponents of Jeffersonian dogma, had a strong foothold in Eastport and had been one of the few groups in the state to favor the war.

"And what are your leanings?" she asked Lucas.

"Federalist. I never had any great feeling for this conflict—certainly not enough to risk my neck. Of course, if it comes down to the line, I will enlist."

Jessica nodded, sympathizing with Lucas's opinion.

"I was just going to get myself a glass of punch," he commented. "Can I get one for you?"

"If it's no trouble."

"No trouble at all." As Lucas slipped off into the crowd, Jessica had an opportunity to glance around the room. She was pleased to see Molly and Jeb with a group of their contemporaries talking in a corner of the room. Mr. and Mrs. Beard were enjoying a country dance together, its tempo more sedate than some of the earlier numbers. Elizabeth was also up dancing with a gentleman who, his age and bearing suggested, was one of her father's friends and not a contender for the girl's hand. Elizabeth's expression was one of boredom as she moved gracefully through the configurations, and soon her face was hidden from Jessica's view by the other dancers.

When Lucas returned and handed her a glass, he lifted his in a smiling toast. "To peace—in the near future."

Although Jessica knew that the war *would* end, the Americans victorious, in less than a year, she only returned his smile with a simple "Agreed."

"Do not think me impolite for not asking you to dance, but there is obviously another gentleman who has first priority on your attentions." As he spoke he glanced at Kit, who was squirming in his mother's arms.

"Yes, I'm afraid he does have first priority—aside from

which I've already told one young man tonight that I would not be dancing."

"Oh? Can I guess that Elias was that poor young man? I noticed him watching you earlier, trying to build up his courage at the punch bowl."

"I'm flattered, especially that he should be taking notice of an old married woman like me."

"He meant no offense."

"I know. He was offering friendship . . . as you are." A momentary silence fell between them; then Jessica spoke. But for the rum punch loosening her tongue, she might never have broached the subject. "Tell me if it's none of my business, Lucas, but it's Elizabeth who has your eye."

Seeming not the least bit put out, he said calmly, "No doubt that is obvious to all. Much good it does me, as I am sure you have observed. What were you thinking when you asked—of how little chance I have?"

"No, not at all."

"Afraid to give me your real opinion?" And at her silence, "I would rather you be honest with me. I think of you as a friend."

"I am your friend. All I can say is that Elizabeth is young . . . she doesn't know what she wants. I am really in no position to pass judgment."

"What does she *think* she wants?"

"From the little she has said to me, an established man who will give her everything her parents have given—wealth, prestige."

"What I thought myself. She has no use for a man just building his fortunes; nor for one not of her class."

"Not if it means she has to deprive herself. I don't mean to be cruel, and perhaps I am wrong. *I* can see your potential, Lucas, but I don't know if Elizabeth can."

"She has changed in the last year . . . had her head turned. I met her at a community party, much like today's. She hadn't been out much in adult society until then. I think I can be honest in saying we were attracted to each other from the start—there was a real look of interest in her eyes. We danced; she flirted. We parted on very good terms, yet I guess I was a fool to get my hopes up. The next time I saw her, there was a change in her attitude. It was as though she had been reminded of who she was, and who I was. We danced once that evening, but in the months that followed, when I approached her, she became increasingly aloof. I have just been too thickheaded to face the truth."

"Perhaps when she grows up a little . . ." Jessica offered feebly.

Lucas gave a wry smile. "Perhaps. I *am* sorry, Jessica. I had not meant to stand here and cry out my troubles over another woman."

"I started the conversation," she reminded him. "And I don't mind listening."

He placed his glass on a nearby table. "Well, thank you. Whether you intended it or not, you have given me much to think about. We will see each other soon?"

"Yes, I hope so."

It was an hour later before Jessica, Molly, and Jeb left for home. Kit was fretting, Molly tired; and Jeb had had more than his fill of punch. Jessica had already fed, bathed, and settled Kit when the Beards arrived home. Cook prepared them a cold supper, then plopped into a chair, her feet up on a stool. She and Jessica talked quietly, both tired, as they waited for the Beards to retire. Fortunately the family went up early; it was just before ten when Elizabeth called Jessica.

The young woman wasn't in the best of spirits as Jessica entered her bedroom. Frowning, she threw her shawl over a chair. "What a tedious afternoon and evening. I thought Mama and Papa would never leave, and how my head ached!"

She turned to let Jessica unbutton her gown. "Although it would appear at least *you* enjoyed yourself this afternoon."

"It was pleasant." Jessica's voice was noncommittal.

"Only pleasant? No need to be so subtle. Everyone saw you flirting with Lucas St. John."

"He only came over to talk for a moment."

"It certainly appeared to be more than that."

"You are mistaken."

"Do not tell me how to interpret what I saw with my own eyes! Lucas is very handsome, is he not . . . handsome enough to tempt even a married woman?" A small, malicious smile touched her lips.

"I do not know precisely what you may have inferred in seeing us chatting, but Lucas is no more than a friend. And there is surely nothing wrong in our conversing. I saw him speaking with you as well."

Controlling her irritation, Jessica helped Elizabeth from her gown into her nightdress, then hung the gown in the wardrobe as Elizabeth sat down at her dressing table and began to remove the pins from her blond curls.

"That is quite different," the girl said pettishly. "Of course Lucas would come over to me. It is known that he has a tendre for me though we are not social equals. But in your case . . . soon people will begin wondering, if they have not already done so, whether there is some truth in the rumors going about the neighborhood."

"What rumors?"

"Now, you do not need *me* to enlighten you there. Surely you are as aware as I am of what people are saying."

"No, I am not aware. I have little contact outside this house."

"Well, really, Jessica, to show up on our doorstep with an infant . . . a missing husband who has yet to show his face. Is it not obvious that people have begun to wonder if there *is* a husband—or ever was?"

Although Jessica had almost been expecting Elizabeth's insinuation, her face paled in anger. "And I wonder where those rumors might have started. The neighbors I have met have all been exceedingly kind and cordial to me."

"One wonders how long that will continue to be the case when you give so little appearance of the faithful wife. Rachel tells me it is not the first time you have carried on with Lucas. She saw your true colors the first day you were here, at the Christmas party, and with my own eyes I saw you and Lucas carrying on out on the lawn this past winter."

"Neither you nor Rachel has any right or cause to make

such accusations! Nothing I have done warrants them. Since the day I came to this house, you have disliked me; I don't know why. But I will not stand by and let you insult me—particularly when your remarks are so wide of the truth!"

"And what might the truth be?"

"Precisely what I have told you. I love my husband more than any man on this earth, and my greatest desire in this world is to be reunited with him!"

Elizabeth began running a brush through her hair. "Hmmph. Well, I am certainly anxious to meet this paragon . . . a shiphand, is he? I have seen many of that profession down at the Eastport docks, loading Papa's ships." She wrinkled her nose disparagingly. "But perhaps *he* is exceptional."

"He is—very exceptional."

"I will not be needing you further tonight." Elizabeth dropped her brush on the dressing table and swiveled in her chair to face Jessica with narrowed eyes. "Only, might I remind you who is mistress here, and who is maid. I would hate to have to go to Mama and tell her of your disrespectful tongue and tone—"

"You may tell your mother what you wish." Jessica's anger had reached the boiling point. "But I will not sit back and be abused or have my reputation slurred. Obviously I need this work, but there is a limit. If your mother wishes to dismiss me, that is her decision. However, you can be sure I will be quite frank with her about my treatment here, and I don't think she will be very pleased."

Jessica stormed toward the door, not waiting for Elizabeth's reaction.

When she reached the kitchen to collect Kit, she found Molly dozing in her chair. Lifting the still-sleeping child from his cradle, she gently shook Molly's shoulder. "I'm going up now."

"Oh . . . already. Must have dozed off." The woman dropped her feet from the footstool to the floor and yawned. "I'll be going up myself. Long day."

"Yes, a long day," Jessica said. She was in no mood to be sociable now, or even civil. "I will see you in the morning."

"Aye, good night, dear."

"Good night."

In her room Jessica shut the door firmly behind her, deposited Kit on his cot, and began pacing the floor. She felt tied up in knots, angry, humiliated, as she mentally reviewed the scene in Elizabeth's bedroom. The showdown she'd almost been expecting had come, and she'd certainly put her foot in it. Elizabeth wouldn't take Jessica's words sitting down. She was probably already in her mother's bedroom giving a very one-sided picture of what had occurred. Well, if all was lost, then it was lost—Jessica would find some way to take care of herself and Kit . . . how, she had no idea at the moment, especially if she were sent off without reference. If only she had thought more clearly about the future before she'd spoken! But it had been beyond her ability to take any more of Elizabeth's insinuations, the degradation of her position; her pride was too great. Nothing in her past had prepared her for this servant's world. Not submissive by nature, she could not think and feel like the other servants, who accepted their lot and had few ambitions beyond rising in the household echelon.

What would Christopher have done? He'd had to adjust to a step down in stature. But he had never been forced into servitude; he hadn't been asked to numb his mind and his spirit.

At this thought and the memories it brought with it, such a sense of desolation flooded through her that her knees felt weak. Going to the edge of the bed, she sat and buried her face in her hands.

Of what good was it to think of what Christopher would have done? He was gone! She might very well never see him again. Yet he would have depended upon her to take care of their son; he would have told her to look inside herself for the strength to go on, reminding her that they'd discussed this very possibility of separation. She could almost hear his voice whispering encouragement in her ear.

"I need you, Christopher," she cried silently. "I need you now!"

6

With the end of the winter storms and the melting of ice from the harbor, the citizens of New York were sure the time was ripe for an attempted British invasion of their island. The men at the docks and at Tontines spoke in low, worried tones, some considering moving their families off the island into the countryside. Fevered activity at both the Castle Williams and Castle Clinton fortifications on Governors Island and off the Battery insured that all was in readiness in the event of an attack; small scouting vessels moved stealthily along the coastline, keeping a watch on the movement of British ships and sending any news back to the city.

Christopher listened calmly to the speculations and fears of other New Yorkers, knowing the invasion would never occur. It was a period of waiting for him, of persevering, of giving the pain in his heart some time to heal. He was getting to know this growing metropolis very well, from the tip of the Battery up to Canal Street and beyond, once renting a hack and riding as far north as the quiet environs of Greenwich Village and the still-sylvan lands to the east of that community. Some building was going on north of Canal as the population outstripped the original city boundaries, but the majority of it was clustered to either side of the Broad Way, where the mansions of merchant princes had begun rising before the war. Farther to the east and west were scattered wood frame dwellings and spanking new rows of middle class town houses with their three-story brick Federal facades.

Where the Broad Way stretched farther north, following

the Post Road and stage routes toward the Haarlem River, there was nothing for the traveler to see but miles of open countryside, fertile farmland, country estates, posting houses and inns along the stage route—a very beautiful and soothing sight indeed, Christopher had been told, if one wanted to escape the bustle and congestion of the city proper.

A controversy was at the boil over the development of this open land; in New Yorkers' minds the concern took second place only to the war. The Commissioner of New York's Plan, drawn up by John Randal, Jr., showed the whole of the island above 14th Street cut into neat squares, with streets and avenues running monotonously north-south, east-west, without park or commons; with hills to be leveled, streams and ponds filled and culverted. A loud and angry outcry had gone up when, in 1811, the plan was published. Christopher heard protests everywhere, from Robert Bayard and even Mawson, who generally was not one to concern himself with anything unrelated to shipping and the sea.

"It's idiocy!" he'd exclaimed one evening in the Ship's Tavern as he, Christopher, and a few other dockworkers sat together polishing off a few ales. "Never saw a more foolhardy scheme. What man wants to be cooped up in a boxed-out city with nothin' to see beyond his window but a score o' streets and buildin's just like the one he's on!"

"Certainly not you, Mawson," Christopher smiled. "We all know you would fast fade away if out of viewing distance of a harbor."

"Ayuh. But 't'would kill any man's spirit. And how they plan fillin' all them streets? Take half the folks livin' on the East Coast to do it."

Christopher made no response, knowing that indeed one day, in order to accommodate the population, those blocks would be filled with buildings tall enough to dwarf even the imposing steeple of Trinity Church.

"Couldn't agree with you more, Mawson," nodded one of their fellow drinkers. "Never heard tell of a town with all straight streets. Look at London, one of the finest cities of them all—not that I hold any likin' for them Brits, now, but least they got the sense to let a place grow up the way it should, according to the lay of the land and a man's habits. Bah! Plan's a fine waste of tax money, that's what it is!"

Christopher's explorations, however, rarely took him up into the contested area of town. Foot travel confined him to the narrow, meandering streets between the East River docks and the Hudson. His course might bring him down Water Street or Pearl, through the commercial district, perhaps stopping at Samuel Fraunces's tavern for an ale; then down onto State Street, which curved behind Battery Park, the gracious homes along the street facing out toward the park and the blue harbor beyond; north again past Bowling Green, up the Broad Way, the address of some of the most prosperous inns and hotels as well as private residences in the city, then up beyond Trinity Church to the new City Hall with its surrounding park. At other times he would wander west to the banks of the Hudson and, standing on a rise of land, view wharf after wharf of idle merchantmen. The majestic cliffs that were the New Jersey Palisades rose in the distance, trimming the wide, smoothly flowing river.

Only once did he venture to Paradise Square and the Five Points District, on the site of the old Collect Pond, north of the upper end of Pearl Street. Since it was the notorious reputation of this area of brothels, taverns and unsavory characters that had saved him on his first morning in New York, his curiosity was aroused. As he stood at the corner of Cross Street, overlooking the square where five streets converged to give the district its name, he saw a scene of sometimes sad and rundown two-and-a-half-story, gable-windowed buildings, snug against each other, smoke spewing from every chimney. On each corner was a grocery or a liquor store, shouldered up to a tavern or a down-at-the-heels boarding house. The square was alive with pedestrians going in all directions, ducking in and out of the taverns and stores, fighting for a right of way with the abundance of pigs routing freely in the trash-filled gutters of the muddy street. Raucous calls and jeering voices echoed across the square; a peal of female laughter drifted out from one of the taverns. Over his head a window was flung open. Only experience with the life in his own nineteenth century London gave him the presence of mind to step quickly to the side before the contents of a chamber pot sloshed malodorously onto the sidewalk to trickle off into the gutter.

From down the sidewalk a brightly gowned young woman approached, rouged lips and cheeks garish on her otherwise pretty face. As she neared Christopher, she appraised him openly. She paused beside him and looked up with large brown eyes, her smile a clear invitation. Firmly, he shook his head in the negative.

"Can't believe you mean that, sir, else what're you lookin' for in these streets?"

"Not interested."

With a pout and a whispered obscenity, she moved on in search of a more willing prospect, her skirts swishing over the dirty cobblestones.

Christopher didn't remain much longer. The place and its inhabitants reminded him too forcibly of the Seven Dials and East End slums of London—so forcibly that for a moment he felt that he was back in that city again. With a shake of his head, he turned back to the more respectable areas of town.

In the warmer spring and early summer days, Christopher found a haven in Battery Park. Walking over the green lawns under a leafy canopy, he could stand at the promenade at the water's edge to gaze out over the harbor, in the distance the hills of Staten Island, before him the round stone fortification of Castle Williams on Governor's Island. A brisk, salty breeze carried away the more unpleasant city smells as it blew in off the water. He could fill his lungs with the clean air, think back to spring mornings at Cavenly . . . cantering his stallion across the endless fields and pastures of lush green, soaring over hedgerows, walking down a meandering woodland path enjoying the mingled scents of damp earth and new-mown hay, the perfume of field flowers wafting on the breeze. How different things were now—how much had happened since the days when he was the earl of Westerham, lord and master of his own magnificent estates.

He was never alone in the park. There were many pedestrians strolling the paths: workers like himself, or fashionably dressed residents of the town houses along State Street and the Broad Way. The women wore high-waisted dresses, unfurling parasols to protect their complexions from the sun. Their escorts were top-hatted gentlemen in morning coats and breeches of the finest broadcloth; immaculately white cravats were tied elegantly at their necks. Unescorted young women, too, mixed with the crowd, plying their trade, though more discreetly here in the park; and young children scampered across the grass under the watchful eye of parent or nursemaid, their calls and laughter filling the air.

Christopher saw a young child just learning to crawl across the blanket his mother had set out in the sun, and felt the sharp stab of his loss. Kit would be that age now, just learning to navigate on his own; just beginning to explore his world. Was Jessica at that moment sitting on the sunny lawn of their Connecticut home, watching Kit move in just such a way, relishing the glorious spring? Did they miss him as much as he was missing them? He tried to imagine his son as a toddler, as a growing boy, a young man. *His* son. What a wonderful sound those words had. Whatever else he had lost, at least he would always know that he had left behind something of himself; that the love he and Jessica had known, oh, so briefly, had borne fruit . . . a son, a family line that would forever link them together. Would Jessica tell their son of his true heritage? Of the Westerham blood in his veins? That had the child been born in a different age, he'd have been a nobleman, heir to an earldom? Once they'd discussed it, and agreed that when Kit was old enough to understand, he should know the incredible truth of his father's journey through time. Yet now, with Christopher gone, perhaps Jessica would decide the truth was better left unsaid. If she did, how could he blame her? What other choice did she have? He would never know her decision. A feeling of sorrow swept over him.

Yet despite his suffering, physically he couldn't have been in better condition. The labors at the docks had firmed his already hard muscles into perfect tone and now, with the warmer weather, had brought a rich tan to his arms and face. He was sometimes aware that covert glances were cast his way by women on the streets, by ladies passing in sleek carriages; but he was unselfconscious of his own tall, broad-shouldered frame, his handsome features: his gently curling dark hair, the chiseled planes of his face, his strong cleft chin, his penetrating blue eyes. His proud bearing demanded attention despite the rough workingman's clothes upon his back. But the admiring glances had little effect on him. There was only one woman who could rivet his attention, and she was in another world.

So many times on a crowded sidewalk, he'd glance up to see a woman of the same height or coloring; perhaps a pair of dark-lashed greenish eyes, a face of the same cast as Jessica's. His heart would begin pounding; he'd rush forward —only to find a stranger, any perceived resemblance to Jessica fading into nonexistence. And then he'd think himself a fool. After all, what hope did he have of finding her here?

Mawson, who'd developed an interest in a serving girl at one of the more reputable taverns, found Christopher's lack of interest in the opposite sex surpassingly strange. Not once in the months he'd known Dunlap had he known the man to satisfy his needs with a woman.

"Hell, man," he said, exasperated when Christopher once again refused his offer to introduce him to a woman. "What ails you? That mess up in Five Points can't have put you off to the ladies! One bad apple don't ruin the whole bunch."

"I know, Mawson, and it was my own stupidity that evening that did me in."

"Then let me set you up with a nice girl. Abbey's got a friend, pretty as can be. Wouldn't be just no rollin' in the sheets. Abbey's a nice girl—only waitin' tables at the tavern to help out her family. Her father was put out of work when the shipyards closed. Wasn't as lucky as me."

"She seems like a fine young woman."

"That's a fact. And so's her friend. What do you say? This comin' Sunday? Take the girls for a stroll?"

"I appreciate your offer, Mawson. Honestly I do. I am sure the girl is delightful, but I think not."

"You're not lookin' for another one of them tumblers, are you?"

"If I was, I would have no difficulty in finding one."

"Then what the devil's eatin' at you? Ain't natural. One'd begin to think that—" Mawson stopped abruptly.

"*What* would one begin to think?" Christopher's voice was deceptively mild.

"Now calm yourself, man. Didn't mean that to sound the way it did. No one's thinkin' a thing. Leastwise not me."

"I sincerely hope not."

"Just seems to me it'd do you a bit of good to get out with some female flesh once in a while instead of broodin' 'round by yourself."

"Your point is well taken, Mawson, and I can see you will give me no peace until I give you some explanations." The truth was out of the question, of course. Instead Christopher manufactured a story close enough to the truth that he wouldn't inadvertently contradict himself one day.

"There was a woman . . . I do not like to speak of it, but I loved her very much. I still do. I wanted to spend the rest of my life with her. It ended very unfortunately."

"Didn't mean to pry. We've all had our ups and downs with the ladies."

"This was a bit more than that. There is no point in going into the details. Suffice it to say I have not gotten over it yet. I need time to think and be with myself for a while. I suppose you might say my first evening here was an angry reaction."

Mawson was silent, registering the seriousness of Christopher's tone. "So that's the way it was. Often wondered. Always thought you too sharp a fella to get taken in like the veriest greenhorn. Sorry for my earlier remarks."

"Understandable."

"That one of the reasons you pulled out for New York?"

"Yes."

"And why you don't talk much about your past?"

"Do I not?"

"Not noticeable; an' I've got to know you better'n most."
Christopher only nodded.

"Won't bother you again 'bout the women. Just tell me if
ever you're interested."

"I shall, Mawson."

"Call it a night, mate?"

"Ayuh, that we should." Christopher grinned. So perfectly did he mimic the other man's speech that Mawson
looked up startled.

"Not used to hearin' my own talk 'round here lately . . .
not since the war started up, leastwise. You funnin' me,
Dunlap?"

"Not at all, but occasionally I feel so starchy."

"True, you could let a bit out and not miss it."

"I was speculating, too, that the 'ayuh' can only derive
from the old English 'aye,' which makes you more a British speaking person than most of the citizens in this country."

"And here's the bottom of my tankard to you, limey,"
Mawson laughed.

"We will discuss this further another evening. For now,
to Hester's and to bed."

"Ayuh." Mawson winked.

It was midsummer, and news of the war was not good.
The New York papers carried headlines and front-page articles of General Ross and his British troops landing in
Maryland; of his destroying the American resistance at
Bladensburg. The Americans were not adequately prepared, and the British continued their rampage, marching
on to Washington to torch the town, setting fire to the Cap-
itol and White House and any other structures that happened to be in their way.

News of the conflagration in Washington reached New
York August twenty-fifth, riders arriving at the *Gazette* offices, their lathered and exhausted mounts barely standing beneath them. When the headlines broke, the citizens
of New York went into a panic. New York could only be

next. More armaments went up at the Williams and Clinton fortifications. Alarmed citizens readied personal arsenals of rifles and pistols, some so outdated they would prove worthless in an actual confrontation. For days the atmosphere in the city was like a stick of dynamite ready to go off. Yet the panic was brief, for the British stayed to the south. General Ross was killed attempting to take Baltimore, and the British offensive lost its momentum.

There was some good news that summer, too, coming in from the northern front—news reaching New York days after the actual event, the messengers getting to the city on horseback or riverboat. Brown and Scott took Fort Erie, holding the British at the Canadian border, and later the Americans were victorious at the Battle of Champlain.

Knowing the outcome, Chrisopher went through that summer feeling far removed from the anxieties of his fellow New Yorkers. He was yet too immersed in his own dilemma to be actively aroused by what was going on around him.

Only as the leaves began to turn crimson and gold, the blue skies darkening with flocks of wildfowl winging south, did Christopher begin to come alive again slowly. Life forces both within him and without pushed him forward, told him he must continue though everything he had ever wanted was left behind. He could not waste the rest of his life in an orgy of self-pity.

The vein of self-preservation ingrained in those who are meant to be survivors turned his thoughts toward a seed of an idea that had lain dormant in his mind for nine months —an idea of how he might make some money for himself, even in these troubled times. He had no guarantees it would work, but the gamble was one he felt fairly safe in taking. He knew that though the Treaty of Ghent would be signed December twenty-fourth, news of the peace would not reach New York until February. By early spring shipping in and out of New York would be booming again. Suddenly the imported goods that had been so scarce and had brought such high prices during the war would be a glut on the market. The bottom would fall out, and those holding high-priced inventories would be forced to sell at a loss.

His plan was to anticipate the market fall, to contract sales of imported goods to local merchants for spring delivery at price levels well below those other importers would dare to meet. Then he would sit back and wait, and when shipping resumed and the market fell, as he knew it would, he would buy in, fulfill his contracts and still walk away with a profit.

It was not his intention to make a killing; only to make sufficient profit to get himself off the docks and to bankroll himself in some more lucrative enterprise within the shipping trade. He liked the business—it was something he could sink his teeth into—and he had already picked up a great deal of knowledge from listening and talking to merchants and brokers at Tontines. He and Mawson had run into Robert Bayard several times again and Christopher knew Bayard would be a valuable contact if he was to bring his plan to fruition.

Christopher spent the next several weeks with pen and paper, outlining his idea, calculating costs and profit margins. After dinner in the evenings, tired as he was, he'd sit at one of the parlor tables working at his figures.

Mawson was a silent observer, until finally, one night, curiosity got the better of him and he came to look over Christopher's shoulder.

"What you up to now, man? Don't work you hard enough at the docks?"

"Just a little scheme I have, Mawson."

"First you said anything to me 'bout it."

"I will explain all to you in due course. At the moment it is just speculation."

Mawson rubbed his fingers through his thick brown hair and yawned. "Well, I'm up to bed, and I'd advise you the same. Sun'll be up early as ever in the mornin'."

"I will be upstairs shortly. I am almost finished here."

"Ayuh. Hester'll start chargin' you for the extra lamp oil soon."

In mid-November Christopher took a few hours off from Schemners. He needed names and addresses of prospective buyers, and only a man with Robert Bayard's connections could provide those for him.

As he entered that man's office, Bayard greeted him jovially. "Well, this is a surprise, Dunlap. What brings you to my humble place of business on a working day?"

Christopher returned the man's firm handshake. "I have a little proposition I wish to discuss with you, Bayard, and I am also needful of your valued advice."

"You flatter me. Have a seat. Can I offer you tea, or Madeira?"

"Madeira?" Christopher's brows lifted.

Bayard grinned. "I reserved a case for myself from the last privateer haul."

"Such an unwonted luxury cannot be refused."

Bayard poured two glasses and handed one to Christopher. "So tell me what is on your mind. I admit you have sparked my curiosity."

"I am considering a business enterprise." Christopher began cautiously outlining his idea, omitting any reference to his foreknowledge of future events. As he spoke, he saw growing skepticism on Bayard's face but the man listened politely. "Obviously," Christopher continued, "I have no intention of doing anything to compete with you or I would not be here asking your assistance. All I am asking from you is a list of contacts—not your customers, but assuredly you know the names of others presently on the sales logs of your competitors. Names, addresses. I will carry it forth from there. You will in no way be involved, your name never mentioned."

Bayard shook his head. "I do not understand, Dunlap, how you feel you can possibly come out of this alive. There is a war going on. I have enough difficulty procuring imported goods at top dollar. What makes you think you can sell short, let alone below other importers' levels, and find the goods to cover it? You have discovered some secret cache hidden away from the rest of us?" The last was meant to be a joke, but Christopher didn't smile.

"It is a deep seated feeling I have. This war cannot go on much longer. It is at an impasse. The British are tired. They have been fighting steadily on different fronts for the past ten years. This country is suffering economically, seeing the foolhardiness of the stiff-necked pride that got us involved in this altercation. We have already sent a party of negotiators to Europe. I feel the end is in sight."

"We have discussed this before, and I agree as to the direction of events, but the war could drag on for another six months . . . a year. You would be a ruined man."

Christopher nodded. "It is a definite possibility, but the risks are all mine. I would stand responsible for any losses incurred. However, should there be a profit, I would intend to cut you in for a percentage in return for this favor I am asking."

Bayard chuckled. "Profits? You really are optimistic. In your shoes I would be more concerned about getting out alive with the shirt still on my back."

"I choose to look at the bright side."

"What kind of percentage?"

"Shall we say ten percent?"

"Ten percent." Bayard fingered his chin, glanced out the window as he took a sip of Madeira. "As you said, there is no risk to me."

"None at all. Only the opportunity for some unexpected income."

Bayard turned back to Christopher. "In all good conscience, as your friend, Dunlap, I have to tell you that I think you are a fool to even consider the idea. The odds are not in your favor—in fact, they are quite against you. I do not want to be in a position of someday looking back and saying I did not warn you quite strenuously."

"Your advice does not go unheeded, Bayard."

"Yet you exude such confidence, you almost make me believe that what you predict will come to pass and you will come out the winner."

Bayard put down his glass, leaned his arms on the desk. "All right, I will throw in with you. It will take me a day or two to complete a list of possible contacts."

"I did not expect you to have it at your fingertips." Christopher smiled. "I appreciate this, Bayard, and in the meantime I will draw up a written agreement on your ten percent."

"No need for that. As unwise as I think your present course, I believe you are a man of honor. I will take your word as a gentleman that should the unlikely occur, I will get my cut. Shall we shake on it?"

"My pleasure." Christopher took the other man's hand across the desk. "And, again, my thanks. I do not think . . . I sincerely hope . . . you will not regret this day."

7

Six months later Robert Bayard had occasion to look back on that November day and the decision he'd made with considerable pleasure. Incredible though it was, Dunlap's predictions had hit right on the nose. Bayard pondered whether the man had a sixth sense; but he didn't question the means, only delighted in the ends as the notes began fattening his bank account.

Christopher, although he had never doubted he would have some success, was amazed at the extent of his profits. He had been able to write up far more advance sales than he had anticipated. Most of his buyers had thought him a consummate fool to sell at such low levels, but they were more than willing to cash in on his lack of business acumen.

The paperwork had been far more than Christopher could handle alone in the evenings, and he had hired a young man as clerk to write the delivery orders and invoices he had prepared the evening before. He and Mawson remained at Hester's Boarding House through the middle of March, both still putting in full days at Schemners. As the shipyards at Corlear's began opening up again, however, Mawson moved back to his shipbuilding profession, and it wasn't long after that Christopher felt sure enough of his own finances to go off on his own as well. Mawson had long since been let in on Christopher's plans and was extremely helpful, through his contacts on the wharves, in finding Christopher warehouse space. On the ground floor of the leased warehouse facilities, Christopher opened a small office.

The long winter months had given him time to decide precisely what he wanted to do. Beginning with local routes—the coastal Connecticut towns and those along the Hudson—he was going to start his own shipping business, C. D. Enterprises, providing his coastal New England customers with New York-imported merchandise and bringing their local goods back for sale in New York. He'd already leased a small schooner, but his eventual plans went beyond leasing vessels. He wanted his own small fleet and, using Mawson's shipbuilding expertise, had hopes of beginning construction on an oceangoer in the not-too-distant future.

When Christopher approached him, Mawson had reacted with typical Yankee caution.

"Admire what you've done, Dunlap. Wouldn't have thought to take such a gamble myself, but sure you're not bitin' off more'n you can chew?"

"I plan to go carefully. As you know, I will be taking the schooner up the coast in a week or two and personally contacting prospective customers. When I return I should have a better idea of how quickly to proceed."

"Well, you know I'd be glad to help you out when the time comes. What's Bayard think of all of this?"

"He, too, advises caution." Christopher smiled. "I am sure he is waiting to see if I will fall flat on my face in this second round."

By early summer Christopher proved his detractors wrong. His first trip was fruitful, bringing in more prospective business than he'd dreamed. Christopher himself initiated the contacts with prospective buyers, bartered his cargo in trade for other cargo or sold his goods outright, then bought New England-produced goods to be brought to New York and auctioned off there. Though his face was a new one and his reputation unknown, no merchant argued with the hard cash crossing his palm.

Though the trip on the whole was a good one, there'd been bad moments, too—one in particular when his schooner had pulled in Eastport harbor. He'd had no idea just how strongly that familiar scene would affect him until he'd stood on the deck and viewed it with his own eyes. Although the cluster of buildings along the harbor banks bore no resemblance to his memory of the scene, the lay of the land was the same—the small islands grouped around the mouth of the harbor, the salt marshes, the low hills, now mostly farmland, rolling back from the Sound. Memories came flashing back of the times he and Jessica had walked along the pebbled beach he saw in the distance. It was sand then, a popular spot for sun worshipers. He remembered her laughter, the wind blowing the hair back from her face as she'd reached out for his hand, run with him over the hot sand, wrapped her arms around him as they'd collapsed, exhausted, on the breakwater.

"I love you," she'd whispered.

"I love you, too."

"This child of ours," she'd said, pressing her hand to her slightly protuberant belly, "is beginning to make himself felt. I don't think he likes the exercise."

"Nonsense," he'd laughed. "Any child of ours will be an athlete, but perhaps *you* should slow down a bit."

It was June then and not long before that they'd returned from England with the wonderful news that Christopher was not returning to his own time; at least, all evidence pointed in that direction. They had reason for happiness. The obstacles to their loving and planning a life together were gone. Was it possible that that joyous moment had occurred nearly two years before?

He felt an oppression bearing down on his shoulders as the vessel slipped into her mooring and he stepped off onto the busy dock. For the first time since embarking on his new career, he was only going through the motions of conducting business. This place brought back too much pain . . . too many remembrances.

It was only by chance that he concluded a lucrative deal with a local merchant in desperate need of a lot of Christopher's English-made textiles. He shared his noon meal at one of the local inns with a representative of the firm, a pleasant young man named Roger Weldon, who'd been down at the docks when Christopher's schooner had pulled in. He had immediately approached Christopher when he saw the notice of goods being offered. Over lunch the young man not only completed the sale, but contracted for future shipments to Beard's Mercantile of the same quality merchandise, promising an increase if the initial shipments proved satisfactory.

As they left the inn and Christopher turned his footsteps back toward his vessel, he knew he should feel some satisfaction, yet the shadow of his memories left him dazed and disoriented. He was tempted to stay in the town for the night, and the next morning hire a hack and ride north to the area where he and Jessica had lived, to the site of their former home. But what purpose would it have served? She wasn't here—she was somewhere one hundred and sixty years in the future, and no amount of searching would bring her into his arms again. All it would bring him was torment.

Instead, in an effort to run away from the reminders and the emptiness in his heart, he ordered the vessel to set sail immediately for the next port of call.

He returned to New York two weeks later with a full hold of local goods and immediately began procuring the imported goods to fill the orders he'd taken.

Once a week thereafter Christopher's schooner sailed out from the South Street wharves. A month later, when the volume of business proved more than she could handle alone, he leased a second schooner, then a third, and began serious conversation with Mawson over the construction of a larger cargo vessel to ply the sea routes. That was where the money could be made—in the West Indian and European trade. Within the next year, Christopher planned, he would be a member of the group of international shippers.

A freshly painted sign hung outside his office door on Burling Slip, and now three young clerks worked diligently at desks in the back room. Bayard, not ready to consolidate his own business with Dunlap's but seeing that his friend was on the road to success, agreed for a small percentage to keep his eyes open at the docks and auction rooms for merchandise that fit Christopher's needs and could be gotten for a reasonable bid. The two men were not in competition with each other, and the arrangement worked well.

Mawson, seeing that there might soon be good use for Christopher's merchantman, finally gave in to his friend's pressuring. Yes, he'd agreed, he would rather be working to line his own pockets than those of the big shots up at Corlear's. He consented to a quarter of the partnership—all he would accept without making a monetary investment; but the business had grown beyond Christopher's ability to manage it alone, and Mawson more than earned his partnership by overseeing the maintenance of the vessels and the stowing and unloading of cargo when the ships put in. Of course, the drawing of plans for construction of the merchantman was his first priority.

Christopher and Mawson left Hester's for more prestigious quarters on Beaver Street near Bowling Green, leasing a small town house and hiring a daily to do the cooking and cleaning. They'd been able to lease the three-story, seven-room brick house furnished—of prime importance to two bachelors with no domestic belongings—and Christopher converted one of the small downstairs rooms into a study where he and Mawson could work in the evenings.

Their new address was of particular delight to Mawson. His courting of Abbey Miller had become more serious, and he was now only a few blocks south of her family's residence. His evening visits to her residence had become an established rule, a situation Christopher could not let pass without comment.

"So, my man, it would appear I will soon be looking for a new roommate."

"Eh? The two of us ain't makin' enough to keep the place goin'?"

"Far from it. However, I hear the distinct sound of wedding bells in the not-too-distant future."

"Do you now." Mawson grinned. "Plannin' on gettin' hitched?"

"I was talking about you, as well you know."

"I don't believe in rushin' into anything."

"True, a year's courtship is a bit hasty."

"Ayuh. Been on my own for over thirty years. Pays to be a bit cautious."

Christopher laughed outright. "Any more cautious, Mawson, and you will be saying your wedding vows in a white beard."

"Don't know that's a bad idea either." But Mawson winked broadly.

With Mawson's time so fully and happily occupied, Christopher looked to Robert Bayard on those evenings when he felt inclined to have a night on the town. Himself a bachelor, Bayard was more than happy to accommodate him, and the two frequently shared dinner or an evening of drinks at one of the businessmen's establishments in the city.

Christopher's absorption in his growing business was his only outlet, and he had yet to seek out the company of a woman. Still, he was a virile and healthy male, and his abstinence had been an extended one. Though his pain at the loss of Jessica had diminished little, purely physical needs more and more frequently were forcing themselves into his awareness.

On a warm evening in July, Christopher left his offices to meet Bayard in the dining rooms of Younger's Tavern on Pine Street. It was a gentlemen's restaurant and a popular meeting spot for the conclusion of business deals. That night the smoke-filled rooms were crowded, but Bayard, being a regular customer, had been ushered to a table in the far corner of the paneled interior. The two men had a pleasant dinner—cuts of juicy roast beef, new potatoes, and fresh vegetables from one of the up-island farms. Replete, they settled back to talk over a decanter of port. By the time the last of the wine was poured, both were very mellow, yet neither felt inclined to end the evening.

"What do you say," Bayard suggested. "I had planned to conclude this evening at Madam Noir's. Why not join me?"

Christopher smiled. He had heard of Madam Noir's, one of the more fashionable brothels in the city. There a man could enjoy a tumble between the sheets with one of a number of carefully chosen and beautiful young ladies; and should he desire, he might also enjoy musical entertainment, liquid refreshment, or a fine dinner. "Taking advantage of one of my weaker moments, Robert?"

"Not at all. Have a nightcap with me. You will be under no obligation."

Shrugging his assent, Christopher drained his glass. Why not? he decided, but by the time they had walked a few streets north and the night air had begun to clear his head, Christopher had second doubts about his decision. He was about to voice his change of mind and turn back toward his town house when they reached the discreet entrance of the establishment where a uniformed doorman stood to the side of the marble stoop, casting a critical eye over prospective customers. Apparently Bayard and Christopher passed inspection, for he bowed and held the door for them as they stepped inside. Christopher was impressed by the elegant taste exhibited in the furnishings of the front hall; this was not at all what he had expected. A fashionably though modestly dressed woman stepped out from the side of the hall and spoke in soft tones.

"Good evening, gentlemen. May I take your hats? And what might we do for you tonight? A late dinner?"

"No, " Bayard smiled. "The gold room I think, Matilde, for after-dinner drinks."

"Very good. If you will follow me."

She moved off down a short hall to the left, past a large candlelit room from which issued the sounds of low conversation over clinking china and silver; on to a second doorway, where she paused and opened the door to a long, rectangular room where couches and chairs were grouped cozily. The only lighting was from candles in wall sconces and in the chandelier above the center of the room.

"Marie Jeanette will be singing later, gentlemen," their hostess informed them.

"Very good," said Bayard.

"Have a good evening." She moved silently away, and Bayard led Christopher forward.

"By the fireplace here would be comfortable, don't you think, Dunlap?" He seated himself in one of the upholstered chairs, and Christopher took a seat on the couch.

"Quite interesting, Robert. I admit to being pleasantly surprised."

Bayard chuckled. "Wait until the evening progresses."

On the low table before them were full decanters of French brandy and wine, silver boxes of Havana cigars, all things intended for a gentleman's relaxation. "Brandy?" Bayard asked.

Christopher nodded, continuing to survey the room and its few occupants. Seated here and there were several other well-dressed men, at their sides attractive women dressed to the height of fashion, their gowns of the finest cut and fabrics, suggestively flattering. There was quiet conversation, yet the candlelight gave the illusion of privacy. He was still bemusedly observing the other guests when two young women seemed to materialize from nowhere—an exotic brunette and a silvery haired blonde.

The brunette spoke. "So, Robert, you are out on the town again. I am delighted I was free this evening."

"Ah, Diedre," Bayard responded. "How could I long forsake the pleasures of your fair countenance. Come, have a seat. May I introduce a dear friend of mine, Christopher."

The brunette, smiling, motioned to the young woman beside her. "And this is Catherine."

The blonde acknowledged the gentlemen with a soft turning of her lips, her eyes clearly registering pleasure when they rested on Christopher. With a soft swishing of skirts, the women seated themselves, Diedre in the chair nearest Bayard, Catherine on the couch beside Christopher. Bayard poured each of the ladies a glass of wine.

"You have chosen a good evening to join us," Diedre said pleasantly, apparently the more gregarious of the two. "The entertainment will be excellent."

"So Matilde informed us."

Christopher, listening to the conversation going on next to him, was very much aware of the woman seated next to him. Undeniably attractive, she had a lovely figure, clear skin, even features, and lovely deep-blue eyes. She leaned forward to take her glass of wine, and the gesture alluringly exhibited the deep cleavage between her creamy breasts. She looked up into his eyes.

"Tell me, sir, have you been in New York long?"

"Well over a year."

"I wondered. I have never seen you here before."

"No, I have not yet visited this establishment."

"Welcome, then, and I hope you will enjoy yourself."

Christopher's lips twitched. "I will endeavor to do so."

The blonde smiled knowingly. "What is your line of business?"

Their conversation continued easily. The ladies were well versed in politics and the arts, so the talk was intelligent and interesting to both men. In London circles Christopher had been exposed to similarly articulate courtesans, but because he hadn't expected to find their like in New York, he was intrigued and let himself be carried along by the pleasant atmosphere more easily than he might have otherwise. The scent of perfume drifted in the air, filling his nostrils. How long it had been since he'd smelled close at hand that luscious, female scent.

He poured himself another brandy and sipped it slowly, enjoying the languorous mood the alcohol brought on. A small white hand tentatively touched his sleeve. He looked over to his companion's warmly suggestive eyes gazing up at him, silently seeking. Without volition his gaze drifted lower to her decolletage, the pearly mounds rising and falling with each breath she took, forcing him to remember the feel of satiny skin, the delightful pleasures of a woman's curves in his arms. As she slid her body closer against his on the couch, cuddling into the circle of his arm, the enticing warmth of her seemed to burn through the layers of his clothing. He felt himself grow hard with a need he'd too long denied; a need that increased into urgency as she laid her hand on his thigh, then in a moment brushed her fingers along its length.

His arm tightened about her shoulder. He felt her lips at his ear, heard her whisper: "Shall we?"

He nodded, and without even saying good night to Bayard, who in any case was engrossed with the woman at his side, Christopher rose and followed her from the room.

Within minutes they were in an exotic bedroom, its main furnishing, a satin-draped bed, crying out to be used.

The young woman—he didn't even remember her name—
slid into his arms. She lifted her face, her lips full and
moist. Hungrily he met her lips with his own as she
pressed and slowly moved her hips against his now throbbing loins. Her fingers expertly slid beneath his jacket and
pushed it off his broad shoulders; then she loosened his
neckcloth, the buttons of his shirt.

"What a handsome man you are," she sighed, discarding the shirt, her hands returning to caress his bare
flesh, rubbing through the mat of hair on his chest, over
his shoulders and down his muscled back, around again
to his abdomen, her fingers teasing beneath the waist-
band of his breeches, unfastening them . . . slowly caressing lower, all around his throbbing manhood, but
never touching it.

He groaned in an agony of delight, his fingers fumbling
with the buttons of her gown, tearing them in his haste,
pulling the flimsy material off her shoulders, down to her
waist, freeing her swollen breasts. He grabbed impatiently
at the soft flesh, his thumbs rubbing over the nipples until
they stood hard and erect.

"Slowly," she whispered, catching his hands. "Let *me*
take care of *you*. It will bring you more pleasure that way."

Bringing her breasts up against his chest, she eased her
hands around to the small of his back and pressed his
breeches down over his buttocks. He shivered at the sensation of her touch on his flesh, down the back of his thighs.
Coaxing him back to a seat on the edge of the bed, she
knelt before him and quickly pulled off his shoes, then
reached her hands up to draw his breeches the rest of the
way off his legs, slowly, her fingertips skimming his thighs
and calves.

She stood to undo the last fastening of her gown so that
it slithered off her hips and dropped to the floor, leaving
her smoothly curvaceous body glowing like ivory in the
candlelight.

She stepped toward him, and he tried to reach for her;
but she motioned him back and again knelt before him, between his thighs. Her lips and tongue began a deliciously
leisured ascent over his tingling leg muscles, along his

sensitive inner thighs . . . teasing closer and closer to his
manhood . . . her tongue finally flicking with tiny strokes
at his taut and burning member until he was moaning, his
hands clenching the edge of the mattress. And still she
wouldn't let him reach for her, as she lifted her head and
instead nestled the soft silk of her breasts against his
loins; tantalizingly she eased their fullness up and down
along either side of his staff.

Christopher could take no more. With a strength born of
urgency, he reached down and drew her up, pressed her
down against the satin bedcovers. Yet even in the throes of
his passion, unbidden, the image of Jessica flashed before
his eyes. His Jessica . . . his beloved Jessica! Quickly he
covered her waiting form with his aching one; thrust into
the warmth of her, deep and hard, pressing for the contact
he craved, again and again, in growing ecstasy, until he
felt his passion exploding in dizzying waves; until, spent
and drained, he lay inert upon her.

For several moments he didn't move. He was conscious
of her hands soothing the muscles of his back, but only
vaguely. The release of his physical need, so long con-
tained, had left him exhausted. Slowly he rolled to his side.
Dazedly focusing on her smiling lips, he looked down at
the woman to whom he'd just made love, and felt a sicken-
ing lurch in the pit of his stomach. This was a stranger.
The image of Jessica that had burned itself into his mind
had been no more than that—an image . . . a fantasy. He
shook his head and lifted himself on his elbow.

"What is the matter?" the young woman asked, puzzled.
"You look as though you have seen a ghost."

"Perhaps I have," he said, throwing his feet over the
side of the bed. God knows, this wasn't the first time in his
life he'd relieved his needs on a doxy, high-class one
though this woman was. In England, mistresses had been
an accepted part of a well-to-do man's life. But this was the
first woman he'd made love to . . . even been tempted to
make love to . . . since Jessica. For some reason the realization frightened him; made him understand, with a
stab, just how irrevocably he'd lost her. Perhaps what sick-
ened him most was that he'd thoroughly and completely

enjoyed taking this woman as though he were a rutting animal. Not that he had ever felt there was any sin in enjoying sex—it was natural, healthful—but that he should have had to drink himself into oblivion, then vent his passion on the first woman he could get his hands on . . .

He strode around the bed and reached for his breeches.

The young woman sat up, alarmed by his actions. "Did I do something wrong? You're not satisfied?"

He couldn't take his self-loathing out on her; she had done what was required of her . . . more than what was required. "No, you did nothing wrong. It is a personal matter. You were very generous, and I shall be generous, too." He reached for his billfold and extracted some notes, which he placed on the dresser top.

"You don't have to do that. I expected nothing extra. You seem a fine man, and I enjoyed giving you pleasure."

"And I thank you." Christopher hurried on with his dressing, tieing his white neckcloth with far less than its usual neatness. "Please do not blame yourself for my hasty departure." He shrugged into his jacket, adjusting it across his shoulders. "As I said, it is a personal matter."

"Will you come again?" Her voice was almost pleading.

For the first time since he'd left the bed Christopher looked directly into her large, beseeching eyes. "I do not think so." Quickly he turned and, before she had a chance to say more, left the room.

8

Though Christopher never again ventured into the establishment to which Bayard had introduced him, his social life was broadening through his business contacts. As word spread of a handsome, unattached gentleman rising rapidly in the ranks of city businessmen, hostesses were only too anxious to include Christopher on their guest lists. His inborn charm and his polish, to say nothing of looks that set women's hearts to palpitating, soon had half the female population of social New York in thrall.

Although the entertainments were diverting, his main purpose in attending the functions was to cement business ties. Christopher's heart remained entirely his own. Even as he swirled around a dance floor, partnering an attractive young woman in the steps of the newly popular waltz, he remained unmoved, immune to her charms. No woman, even the cleverest, sparked the fire in him that Jessica had aroused without even trying. His disquieting reaction to his sexual encounter at Madam Noir's led him to tread carefully; still, he realized that many other men had suffered losses as great as his and had yet gone on to build new and lasting relationships.

Jessica was surely lost to him. Why did he have no desire to start again—to at least try to find some happiness with another woman? Was it that the old vein of cynicism that had once gripped him in London was again taking hold? Before Jessica, he had believed that true happiness was impossible to find, a state of mind that had no basis in reality. If he ever did form another attachment with a woman, it would be purely a matter of convenience.

Christopher's polite aloofness only incited women's interest all the more. Amused by the flirtatious overtures directed his way, he was careful to let no one young woman take his courteous responses too much to heart. The majority of young, gently bred ingenues were too shy to press themselves on him, and the more sophisticated women he could handle easily, experienced as these women were in the subtleties of social repartee.

Of course, occasionally there was an exception to the rule, as happened one evening at a dinner party at the Lennox home on State Street. Christopher had made the acquaintance of one particular young woman previously at a large party a few days earlier, and because he had found her light on her feet, he had asked her up for two dances during the course of the evening. He'd thought nothing of it at the time; he had paid her no special attention while they were dancing except to ask the usual polite questions. In his estimation she was a child, if more outgoing than the regular ingenue.

As he entered the Lennox drawing room that evening he would have had to be blind not to notice the young woman looking up with excited interest. He shrugged it off, and later, as he circulated the room, paused for a moment before her chair to say good evening.

The young lady dimpled prettily. "A much more delightful one since you have joined our company, sir."

"You flatter me."

She giggled, then lowered her voice to a more intimate tone. "Mama said it was very forward of me to accept two dances with you last we met, but I might be forgiven with such a fine gentleman as yourself."

In a chair behind, Christopher could see the young woman's mother smiling; actually, he was sure, gloating. He had been this route before in London, and groaned inwardly. "It is your charm, ma'am, the gentlemen are seeking, and I am being heartless in denying the others your company."

"No, never," she blushed. "You tease me, sir, and you are far too modest. You are quite the handsomest and most admirable man I have met."

"Do you think so?" Desperately glancing up from her enraptured face, Christopher sought for an avenue of escape; found it across the room. "Ah, there is my good friend, Bayard. I must have a word with him. I know you will excuse me."

"Oh, most certainly. I have heard of the importance of your business interests."

Bowing quickly over her hand, he strode away, but his relief was short-lived when he learned, as the company adjourned to the dining room, that he was to be seated beside the same young woman at dinner.

She chattered unceasingly as they took their seats, undismayed by his coolly noncommittal remarks. By the time they were midway through the first course, Christopher would happily have gagged her with his napkin. He prayed for some interruption to divert her single-minded onslaught into the details of his personal affairs.

"But surely, sir, you must have led an adventurous life," she persisted eagerly, "only so recently in New York and already your fortune made."

He glanced down into her innocent blue eyes. "It is not common knowledge, but if you promise not to breathe a word . . ."

"Oh, no, of course, I would not!" She was fairly dancing with anticipation.

He dropped his voice, his expression dead serious. "I was a pirate . . . captained my own vessel, the *SKULLBONES*. There was not a ship that could outrun her. Ah, what times! The blood we let in the West Indies; the gold and booty we took. Quite enough to set me up *very* handsomely in New York when I arrived." He lifted a forkful of food to his mouth, chewed it nonchalantly. "That was in the past, of course. Now my income is quite honestly earned."

"Oh! My!" the young lady gasped, pressing her hand to her breast. "I—I had no idea."

"No, most do not. And we would not want it to get around. Some of these New Yorkers can be so peculiar and old-fashioned in their morals."

"T-true."

"Morals which I am delighted to see you do not share."

"N-o-o-o."

"Of course, as I said," he frowned, "I would not want to learn that word of this confidence had gotten round." He carelessly picked up the rather sharp knife at the side of his plate.

An incoherent noise escaped her lips.

"Are you quite all right? A sip of water, perhaps? You appear to be choking."

Christopher's dinner partner could only shake her head in the negative, her blue eyes now staring at him as though he'd suddenly sprouted horns. He covered his mouth with his napkin to hide a grin, and throughout the rest of the meal the young woman had not another word to say to him.

On most occasions he did not have to resort to such drastic measures, and he sailed through the social scene unaffected—until he met a woman who was quite out of the ordinary.

Bayard came to him in his office late one afternoon with two beautifully lettered invitations in hand. He threw them on the desk in front of Christopher and wasted no time in getting to what was on his mind.

"From Nathaniel Wilson. Invitations to a reception he is giving at his Broad Way mansion this weekend."

"Wilson?" Christopher shook his head. He'd been working on accounts, and the figures were still in his mind.

"Yes, Wilson, as in N & D Wilson & Company."

Christopher sat back, instantly alert. N & D Wilson were the biggest textile wholesalers in New York and proprietors of several booming dry goods shops in the city. He had been eager for the opportunity to get them as one of his accounts. The goods he brought in from New England would go quickly on their shelves, but Nathaniel Wilson, the man who made all the decisions in the firm, had been unavailable for months. "I thought he was out of town."

"Yes, he was abroad visiting some of the British textile manufacturers. He has just returned to the city. Do you realize what this invitation means, Dunlap?"

Christopher nodded. "How many others are invited?"

"From what I understand, it is a select gathering, the crème de la crème."

"Well, there is no question about attending, is there?"

"None at all."

Christopher picked up one of the engraved cards. "Reception, Dancing and Supper Following," it read. "Formal, I gather," he said, raising a questioning eyebrow to Bayard.

"White stockings and all."

"We had best hire a carriage then. I will pick you up at eight forty-five?"

Bayard grinned.

The two gentlemen, debonair in silk-lined capes, top hats, long-tailed dark evening jackets over pale waistcoats, knee breeches, and immaculate white stockings, were ushered through the grand doorway of the Wilson mansion at precisely 9:05 that Saturday night. They were received in a large marble-floored hallway where their hats and capes were taken, and then led through into a long drawing room to the left. A stately, very English butler announced them as they stepped forward into a room furnished with priceless European antiques and lit by three candle-filled chandeliers.

A portly but robust man of medium height immediately came forward to greet them. He extended his hand.

"Dunlap, Bayard. I am happy to see you could come. Nathaniel Wilson."

"Delighted to meet you, sir." Christopher returned the firm handshake.

"I have heard a great deal about you, young man, since my return."

"I am honored."

"And, of course, Robert Bayard is a name already well known in New York circles."

Bayard bowed his head in acknowledgment.

"You gentlemen would both appear to have been doing well since the war." His bright eyes were merry, yet acute.

Christopher smiled. "We have endeavored to stay in the black."

"I have just returned from abroad myself."

"So I have heard. You had a worthwhile trip?"

"Extremely so. Ah, but now is not the time to discuss business, and I do get carried away. Perhaps we three will have an opportunity to speak together later. For now, come in and join the company." He led them forward. "These gentlemen I believe you know. Phillip Hone, George Griswold. Mrs. Griswold."

The gentlemen shook hands, and Christopher and Robert paid polite compliments to the lady.

"And Jerome Weitz, another up-and-coming entrepreneur in our town."

Christopher had heard of Weitz, a banker and real estate speculator who, like Astor, had lent money to hurting merchants and property owners during the war and, through foreclosures on delinquent mortgages, was now the possessor of considerable real estate holdings on the island. With postwar property values climbing to the skies, the man's future wealth was assured. Christopher nodded to the dark-haired gentleman before him. Weitz looked to be in his late thirties. He was tall and slender, with sharp yet attractive features and brown eyes that fairly snapped with intelligence. "A pleasure to meet you, Mr. Weitz."

"And you, too. Robert and I have had the pleasure before. How goes the brokerage business?"

"In the last year, quite well." Bayard smiled.

"Yes, those of us who survived the war should prosper now. Good to see you again."

Nathaniel led them off. "One other party I would like you gentlemen to meet." He paused near where a group of men and women were chatting by the fireplace, then motioned to a woman at the back of the group. "Rhea, come here for a moment, will you?"

A raven-haired young woman in a ruby satin gown stepped around her companions and took Wilson's arm. Christopher could almost hear Bayard's intake of breath, and he was similarly impressed. Here was one of the most beautiful women he had seen in a long time—a classic beauty, tall of stature, slender of form. Her lips were full and red, her features even—perfect—her face an oval from which her black hair swept back from a high, white forehead into a coronet of thick braids wrapped about the top of her head.

"Gentlemen." Wilson beamed. "I would like you to meet my daughter, Rhea Taylor. Rhea was widowed during the war and is now spending some time with me. Rhea, Robert Bayard, one of our more prosperous New York brokers."

Bayard took her hand and bowed over it. "My sincerest compliments." His dark eyes were alight. "I wonder where I have been wandering in this city that I have not made your acquaintance before now."

She laughed, a tinkling sound that warmed the air. "It is not you, sir, but I who have been wandering—in England with my father, and prior to that I was residing out of town, observing a period of mourning for my late husband."

"My sympathies on your loss . . . but a pleasure to have you with us now. Will you be staying in the city for long?"

"Indefinitely."

"Delightful."

"Yes, I am sure we will be seeing each other in social company again."

Her father interrupted to complete the introductions. "And this, my dear, is Christopher Dunlap, one of our newly established shippers, who, I might add, has been banging on my doors for business."

Rhea hadn't look at Christopher fully; now she did. Her eyes momentarily widened, then her lashes lowered and she smiled.

Christopher felt his chest constrict. Those eyes. Greenish, dark-lashed—Jessica's eyes—even of the same shape, with the slightest uplift at the outer corners.

He took her hand and lifted it to his lips. "Your servant, ma'am. It is indeed a pleasure to make your acquaintance."

"The pleasure this evening is mine as well," she smiled. "You are English?"

"I was born there."

"And retain the beautiful accent. I must tell you how much I enjoyed that country. Where in England were you born?"

"Kent."

Her brow wrinkled. "Did we go into Kent, Father? Oh, yes, I remember now. We visited one of the estates there for a party. Orchardhaven, I believe it was called. Very lovely—one of those magnificent old homes in which we Americans are so lacking."

Again Christopher felt a thrill go through him as memories pushed to the back of his mind for so long came spinning forward. He knew well the estate she mentioned. It lay less than twenty miles from his beloved Cavenly, and was the home of Sir Giles Gresham, one of his old cohorts. God, it seemed years since he had seen him. Giles—mad, wild, good-looking; the two of them tearing about London, racing high-perch phaetons across the countryside on a bet, or sitting at the card tables at White's until the wee hours of the morning. And here was this young woman in New York speaking of a world he'd thought he'd left far behind.

He couldn't question her, and only said: "Yes, I know of Orchardhaven. I am glad you enjoyed England."

Others approached Nathaniel Wilson, to greet their host and be introduced to his daughter.

"Perhaps later this evening," she said quietly to Christopher, "we might chat again at greater length. There will be dancing and a late supper."

Christopher nodded. "It would be my pleasure."

She smiled, but the glance she gave him might have been a touch. Then she turned to her father, who was again calling her name. Christopher and Bayard wandered off. There were many businessmen there of their acquaintance, and it wasn't long before they were deep in conversation.

It wasn't until after the dancing had begun that Christopher saw Rhea again, moving about the ballroom from this group to the next, a charming and gracious hostess. It was difficult to keep his eyes from following her—she was by far the most attractive woman in the room—and he was not the only member of the male sex who watched.

Bayard was up on the dance floor with the daughter of a gentleman whose export account he was cultivating.

Christopher leaned back against the wall, his arms crossed, and observed with great amusement the agonized expressions crossing his friend's face as Bayard tried to keep up the pretense of being enthralled by the company of the rather overweight and very plain girl on his arm. Christopher was just about to throw him a teasing wink when he felt a touch on his arm. He looked down and saw Rhea standing next to him.

"You seem far away, sir. There is someone on the floor who interests you?"

"Yes, indeed there is. My friend, Bayard. I am musing about the lengths to which one goes in the furtherance of business."

She glanced out to the floor, and smiled. "Yes, Clarissa Matthews. I have not seen you up dancing."

"No. I have been content to observe for the moment."

"I understand the next number is to be a waltz."

"Is it?" He turned toward her and was caught again by her green eyes. Almost involuntarily, he asked the question she was awaiting. "Perhaps you would do me the honor?"

"Most delightedly so. I have been waiting for you to ask."

"Have you?"

Her gaze didn't leave his. "Ever since we met so briefly in the drawing room and our conversation was so abruptly ended."

The musicians switched to a new melody, and Christopher gave Rhea Taylor his arm and led her to the floor. Taking her hand in his, he placed his other on her waist, and they began to swirl through the steps.

She leaned back and looked up into his blue eyes. "I must admit, Christopher . . . and you do not mind me calling you by your first name?"

"Not at all."

"I must admit that I was hesitant about having the waltz played this evening. The dance was accepted in London, but standards are not necessarily the same in New York, and before going abroad with my father, I was out of society for so long."

"Your father said your husband was killed during the war."

"Yes. We were in Washington. William was secretary to the senator from Pennsylvania and had a brilliant career ahead of him. Unfortunately, when the British invaded Washington, he thought it his duty to go out and stop them, and joined one of the local companies."

"A tragedy that he should die so young."

"If only he had listened to me and fled that terrible conflagration . . . well, that is in the past now, is it not? And I was young when I married—perhaps too young."

"Your mother?"

"She died when I was a child. Father never remarried."

"Did you grow up in New York?" Gripping her more tightly, the better to steer her out of the way of a less graceful couple who seemed intent on running them down, Christopher noted that she did not seem at all averse to the closer proximity of their bodies. She was smiling up at him.

"Yes, I grew up in the city, and am glad to be back. England provided a much needed change, but this is my home."

"I would agree, this city has much to offer. Particularly of late."

She did not miss the offhand compliment. "I take it you are not married."

"No."

"And how long have you been in the city? I recall Father saying your shipping business was newly established?"

"It is, and I have been most fortunate thus far. I have been living in the city a little over a year."

"And before that?"

"Connecticut."

She was thoughtful. "I understand you are interested in doing business with father?"

He grinned. "Most undoubtedly so. Your father's account is one of the most prized in the city, and I believe I could suit his needs well."

The dance ended. They walked to the side of the floor, and she paused a moment beside him, once again riveting him with her green eyes. "I shall put in a good word for you." Then, in silkier tones, "I enjoyed the dance. Do not leave without coming to say good-bye to me."

"I would not think of it." He smiled, slowly; a smile she returned in kind as she turned and moved gracefully off the floor.

She was waiting for him when, well after midnight, he went to bid good night to his host. He had a very pleasant surprise as Nathaniel Wilson, cheerily shaking his hand, suggested an appointment in his offices later that week, setting a time and date to which Christopher readily agreed. As he turned to find Bayard and collect his hat and cape, Rhea appeared before him. The ruby gown, so stunning with her black hair, looked as fresh as it had hours earlier. She laid a hand on his sleeve.

"Sneaking off without saying a good night to me?" she teased.

"Never would I have denied myself such a pleasure. I was merely trying to locate my friend."

"I saw him a moment ago out in the hallway—but wait, there is no need to rush off. Did you enjoy yourself?"

"Very much so. You give an excellent party, Mrs. Taylor."

"Rhea."

"Rhea," he repeated softly.

"Did you by chance have a word with my father?"

"Indeed. A very pleasant word or two. We have an appointment to meet later in the week."

"Excellent. You see I keep my promises."

"For which I am most grateful."

She smiled, a brightness that was reflected in her green eyes. "Think nothing of it, although I will tell you I never act without good reason."

"And you had good reason?"

"You make a very favorable impression. You fascinate me, and I do not think I have misled Father in judging you to be an excellent businessman."

"No, I do not think you have, either."

"Good. I like a man convinced of his own worth."

Christopher's eyes danced. "You are suggesting I am arrogant?"

"Although we have just met, I do not get that impression," she laughed. "Confident and self-contained, yes . . . and well aware of the effect you have on women."

"You are very observant."

"I try to be, though one cannot know everything by merely observing."

"Quite correct."

"We shall have to talk again in the future so I may see how accurate my assessments are."

"I will look forward to it."

"As will I." And most eagerly, her expression told him. "Until then, Christopher, it has been a pleasure meeting you."

"The pleasure was mine, Rhea. And thank you for a delightful evening."

"You are most welcome." She looked at him directly, fully, then slowly smiled. "Well, I will not keep you any longer, and there are other guests I must bid good night. Much success in your meeting with Father." And she swirled gracefully away, toward other guests.

As he and Bayard drove home, Christopher was thoughtful. Intriguing woman. Beautiful, intelligent; not one of these starry-eyed ladies looking for giddily impassioned love. Yet such a desirable young woman must be looking to form some kind of attachment. Perhaps her father had thrown the reception at least partly to present her to the most eligible men in New York. Was Christopher a candidate? If that was the case, then was he interested in such an attachment? In a purely analytical way, he reasoned Rhea would fit his needs handsomely—she was most attractive, quite charming enough to be the perfect hostess, sophisticated enough not to expect from him that which he could not give; and she was the daughter of one of the most successful businessmen in New York, whose goodwill would be a valuable asset to Christopher.

He realized he was attracted to her. Not in the same way or with the intensity that he'd been attracted to Jessica, but his response to this woman was far more than his usual indifference. Then again, it was early yet, and to jump to conclusions in one evening was foolishness. As he reined the hired team onto a narrow street off the Broad Way, Bayard broke the silence. "What are you mulling over, my friend? The fair Mrs. Taylor . . . or the prospect of concluding business with her father?"

"That, too."

"The lady did seem *quite* interested."

"Do you think?"

"I would give much to be in your shoes."

"As they say, the grass is always greener . . ."

"In this case, infinitely so."

Christopher laughed.

"I have always felt," Bayard mused, "that I would be quite well satisfied to find myself an heiress, or at least a young lady whose father's business interests would enhance my own. A plain girl would do, as long as she was presentable; one cannot afford to be too choosy. But to find the former attributes packaged as exquisitely as in Rhea Taylor . . . ah, it is like riches dropped from heaven."

"Robert, you get carried away."

"I only say that when one is offered such a gift, one must be a fool to pass it by."

"I hear you well, my friend."

They were approaching Bayard's lodgings. Christopher slowed the team and pulled them to a halt beside the stone steps. "Is not a shipment of tea due in off one of the Griswold vessels Monday?"

"So it is." Bayard stepped down from the carriage. "And only you would be minding mundane business matters after such an evening. I would suggest you direct your thoughts to more interesting contemplations—black hair, green eyes, curves in the most delightful places, connections whose bank accounts will no doubt soon approach the million dollar mark—"

"Do get inside, my friend. With you thus playing the clown, I am beginning to think you indulged in a few too many brandies tonight. See you on Monday, Robert." And with a flick of the whip over the horses, Christopher started off at a brisk trot in the direction of his home on Beaver Street.

Although he never went out of his way to do so, Christopher saw Rhea Taylor frequently in the following weeks. They were often invited to the same social gatherings, Rhea never failing to come to his side to converse at length, making it no secret that she found him charming company. Once, as he was walking along Battery Park, she and her father met him in their carriage and stopped to chat and offer him a ride back to his lodgings. He refused, but the significance of the offer did not elude him.

His meeting with Nathaniel Wilson had gone well. Wilson, offering Christopher an opportunity to prove his merit, had placed several orders for New England-manufactured goods and had been otherwise helpful during their discussions, relaying inside information on not commonly known undercurrents in the business community. There'd been a few veiled probings, too, about Christopher's impressions of his daughter, to which Christopher had responded pleasantly but noncommittally.

Still, with Rhea so willing to encourage him and remove any obstacle from his path, he felt himself subtly being drawn closer and closer to the lady. Not that she was forward; she was expert enough to know just how much encouragement to give.

Not until late summer did their relationship take a major turn. They were both attending a reception at the City Hotel, the elegant hostelry on the Broad Way, raved about for its superb service and the excellence of its appointments. He had come alone, as had Rhea, whose father was away on business. Rhea's widowed status gave her the freedom to occasionally go out unescorted.

It had turned out to be a rather stuffy affair. Several businessmen Christopher had hoped to see had not attended, and by eleven he was feeling bored. The presence of Rhea, as stunningly groomed and gowned as ever, her conversation sparkling and adroit, was a much welcome relief. Since she was suffering from the same boredom as

Christopher, shortly after eleven she suggested he escort her home and stop in at the Wilson mansion for a nightcap.

The summer evening was clear and balmy as they walked the short distance up the Broad Way to her father's home. She was in a playful mood and soon dissipated Christopher's boredom with her terse and humorous comments on some of the company they had just parted. Both were chuckling by the time they arrived at the mansion doors. They were admitted by the butler, who must have been sitting in wait for his mistress's arrival.

"Henley," Rhea said as that starchy gentleman took Christopher's hat and gloves. "I believe you met Mr. Dunlap at the reception we had here last month."

The butler bowed. "Yes. Good evening, sir."

"Good evening to you, Henley."

"Mr. Dunlap and I will be in the small drawing room," Rhea continued gaily, taking Christopher's arm. "Would you bring us some refreshments? Brandy for the gentleman and Madeira for myself. And there is no need for you to wait up, I will show Mr. Dunlap out."

"Very good, madam." Henley bowed again, and Rhea led Christopher down a neighboring hallway, pausing at a door that faced the front of the house. "I thought this room would be cozy," she said as Christopher held the door for her to precede him. "We would lose ourselves in the formal drawing room."

It was a warmly decorated room of dark wood and Chippendale furnishings upholstered in yellows and browns. Rhea went to the couch, indicating Christopher take a seat beside her.

In a moment Henley entered and placed a tray of refreshments on the tea table in front of the couch.

"Will there by anything else, madam?"

"No, thank you, Henley, this is fine. Good night."

After the butler had slipped silently from the room, she leaned back against the cushions, slid off her low-heeled satin shoes, and wiggled her toes. "Ah, that feels good. My feet were weary."

Then she curled her legs up beneath her on the couch, and turned so that she was facing Christopher. In a more

petite woman the action might have seemed kittenish; in
Rhea, with her tall, elegant form, the resemblance was
more that of a graceful she-panther.

"You do not mind my informality?" she said lightly.
"After all, it is just the two of us." Casually she ran her
hand down his back. "You should relax as well. What are
you afraid of . . . that I might seduce you?"

"The thought crossed my mind."

"Would that be such an unpleasant fate?"

"Unpleasant is not the word I would use."

Chuckling, she accepted the glass of wine Christopher
had poured for her. Slowly sipping from his brandy, Christopher settled into a more comfortable position.

"I understand you and Father had a productive meeting.
He has told me you concluded some business."

"It went extremely well. Our first shipments should be
arriving within the week, and I look forward to learning
that they meet his approval."

"You really have no fears that they will not?"

"None. Had I doubts, I would not have concluded the
contracts, and I have gone out of my way in the past to insure that my cargo is only the best quality."

"He speaks of increasing your business together."

"That certainly is my wish. How long will your father be
away?"

"Until Tuesday or Wednesday. He has gone to Albany to
compare notes with a few of his political friends."

"He is not entirely satisfied with what our state govern-
ment is doing for us here in New York?"

"That I cannot tell you. His political maneuverings are
among the few subjects he never discusses with me."

"Interesting."

She swayed just slightly closer to him. "I know of another subject I would find *far* more interesting at the moment."

He returned her level look. "Oh?"

"You have never kissed me, you know."

"Yes, I *was* aware." A smile twitched at the corners of
his mouth.

"Have you never been curious?"

"I had a feeling we would get to it in due course."

"What a tease you are. Any other man would long since have taken advantage of the opportunity and had me in a passionate embrace."

"But I am not any other man."

"Quite true, which makes you all the more fascinating." Placing her wineglass on the nearby table, Rhea reached out and took the glass from his hand, setting it, too, on the table. Then she moved languorously across the cushions to close the small distance between them.

"Very well, if you will not make the first move, it is up to me to do so, is it not?"

Christopher was not unmoved by her nearness. And now as he felt her soft, satin-gowned body pressed enticingly against his own, his male instincts were warmly aroused. Yet, for the moment, he held himself in check. It suited him to see how the game would progress with her leading the play.

As he watched silently, slightly smiling, she lifted her hand to touch his cheek, her thumb gently rubbing over the cleft in his chin. Green eyes narrowing, she drew closer, until her red lips were only inches from his own . . . then brushing his . . . pressing more urgently as she felt his response, his arms closing around her back. Her kiss became more demanding, her lips parting, her tongue licking out.

Only then did he return her kiss with all the expertise at his command. He heard her throaty sigh; felt the heat of her breasts pressing against his chest, sending fire flashing through his veins.

Breathless, she pulled a few inches away, her mouth moving to his ear. "You are indeed quite a man, Mr. Dunlap."

The clean, gently perfumed scent of her hair was heady in the air about them.

"I have been waiting a long time for you to do that to me," she whispered.

"I know."

"What more can you show me?"

"Come here," he said quietly, drawing her onto his lap.

Her arms went around his neck; but this time he was the aggressor, his mouth seeking hers, burning with the intensity his temptress desired. The pressure of her hips on his loins fueled his growing need, sending hot waves of desire through his body. His hand moved to her breasts, caressing them across the bodice of her satin gown, then slipping beneath the low decolletage to touch her nipples; they were already hard. She moaned, dropping her head back against his shoulder, and his lips moved down over the column of her throat, his hand cupping her breast until his mouth found the sensitive peak.

"It has been so long since I felt like this," she sighed.

His lips still at her breast, he lowered his hand to draw the skirt of her gown up over her long legs, his palm gently gliding along the length of her thighs then drifting between them; and at her encouraging cry, his fingers sought out the heart of her pleasure, rubbing the tender flesh through the sheer fabric of her undergarment.

Her fingers began a descent from his shoulder, over his chest, across the hard, taut muscles of his abdomen, halting only at the rising bulge in his breeches, hovering there, gently touching. His breathing had become harsh and heavy; his heart was pounding. He wanted her; his body craved it.

"Your bedroom?" he whispered huskily, his voice constricted with desire as he brought his lips up again to her cheek.

"No . . . here. I want you now—this instant."

He needed no further encouragement. His fingers went to the buttons of her gown and hastily undid them. He eased the fabric off her white shoulders, over her waist and hips, down her legs. The sheer chemise and pantelettes she wore beneath gave little resistance to his eager fingers, and in moments her naked perfection was exposed to him. He ran his hand lightly down one side of her body, then rose to remove his own clothing.

As he undressed, she lay back on the cushions, an alluring goddess, watching him, her eyes bidding him to hurry. His breeches fell, and she reached out to grasp his swollen manhood, then moved her hands up and down its hard and heated length. He gasped with pleasure at her touch.

Her eyes were hazy, heavy-lidded. "You are quite irresistible, my love. Come . . . satisfy me."

Swiftly, kneeling between her spreading legs, he pressed his body over hers, not immediately entering. Her hips began to rotate slowly as her hands eased down his back to his buttocks, around to the base of his manhood, there to linger and caress. At her continuing touch, his need became so intense he knew he could wait no longer. He lifted his hips. The head of his staff sought her warm passage, found it. He entered her slowly, then thrust more urgently. Her back arched as she rose to meet him, press him deeper . . . deeper. Their bodies moved in an ever more frenzied rhythm as each sought out a greater pleasure, Christopher forgetting all but the aching ecstasy that was building, growing, bringing him closer and closer to release. He heard Rhea's excited cries, but he wasn't thinking of the woman beneath him. His mind was a blank that registered only his own physical sensations. When at last the climax came, he seemed to hang suspended. Then his breath was released in a heavy sigh, and a tremor went down his spine as his muscles slowly relaxed.

The room was silent but for the sounds of their breathing, hers softer than his but of the same tempo. As his mind cleared, he began to give thought to the woman still joined to him. There'd been no thoughts of Jessica this time; he had made love to Rhea knowing full well where he was heading. But although his body had reacted in passion, his mind had remained more dispassionate. He did not love Rhea . . . might never love her . . . but she offered all he was seeking at the moment in a woman.

She was the first to speak as he shifted to his side to remove the burden of his weight from her. "Beware, I may never let you out these doors." Her hair had become unfastened and now lay in a black veil over the pillow behind her head.

"That might necessitate some rather awkward explanations for us both."

Her hand lightly touched his cheek as she smiled.

"A pity, though, that Father does not travel more frequently."

"I am sure we can make some other arrangements for the time to skirt that barrier to our pleasure."

"Aha . . . your mind appears to work along the same channels as mine."

He only smiled as she brushed a few sweat-dampened tendrils of hair from his forehead. The room was still warm from the summer day's heat.

"You are a very mysterious man, Christopher," she whispered.

"Am I? I never thought of myself in that light."

"I do. Why is it you tell me so little of your past? You never speak of another woman, yet it is obvious you have known many."

"Yes, I have known many, but it was never a topic I thought to discuss with you."

"I have a feeling you are hiding something from me."

"That is not my intention." A deliberate lie, but Christopher would never tell Rhea about his relationship with Jessica; never even reveal that he'd known such a deep love. It was an experience sacred and beautiful, one that would only be defiled in the telling.

Rhea, finding she could pry out no secret truths, changed the subject. "Will you be going to your offices in the morning?"

"Since it is Saturday, and I have nothing pressing, I thought I might take a drive up the island, where it is cooler." He deliberately paused, knowing that she was awaiting an invitation. "Perhaps you might like to come along."

"I had only some shopping planned. That I can do another time."

Christopher chuckled. "Shall we say at eleven, then? I will have my housekeeper pack a lunch."

"And I will provide a blanket." A tiny smile played suggestively at her lips as she gazed at him.

"What might you have on your mind, madam?"

"No doubt the same as you have on yours."

The arm still circling her waist tightened for a moment. "For now I should be going."

"So soon?"

"Not that I wish to run from the pleasure of your company, my dear, but it is getting late and I have a long walk home."

"You could call a hack."

"The night air and exercise will do me good." Sitting up on the edge of the couch, he reached for his breeches and began to dress. Rhea slid across the cushions and reached for her own garments, continuing to talk easily as she dressed. "I received an invitation to the Van Helt dinner party next week. Did you as well?"

"Yes, and I will have to attend, much as I dislike late affairs on a weekday."

Lifting her hair from her neck, she turned her back to him. "Would you help with the buttons? I cannot reach them." He obliged as she added, "At least the company should be more stimulating than at this evening's reception. Since you are going, why do you not let Father and me pick you up in the carriage?"

He considered a moment as he moved to the mirror at the side of the room to adjust his neck cloth. "That would save me time. I may have a late night at the office. One of the schooners is due in midweek."

His tie in place, Christopher stepped back to the couch to collect his jacket. She came up to him and put her arms around his waist. "Ah, the suave gentleman once again. From your appearance, one would never guess at the delightful entertainment we enjoyed this evening."

He let his hand rest on the thick black hair flowing down her back. "I am afraid the same cannot be said for you, madam . . . though your present dishabille is quite bewitching."

Her soft chuckle was muffled against his jacket front. In a moment she lifted her head, stretching so that her lips were invitingly near his own. "A good-night kiss?"

"You make that a difficult proposition to resist." Pressing his mouth hard to hers, he released her only when he felt his senses quickening again. "I must go."

She made no demur as he stepped back and led her back
to the hall, where he donned his hat and gloves. "Sweet
dreams, madam."

"Never fear of that. Until eleven."

"Eleven."

As Rhea had well known it would, that evening marked
a transformation in their relationship that brought them
into continual companionship. For social entertainments,
hostesses were careful to include both of their names on invitation lists, and local gossips began to lift their eyebrows, wondering if an "important announcement" might
not be forthcoming soon.

Christopher drifted along with the arrangement. He had
no reason not to. The connection ideally suited his needs,
and there certainly was no one else in New York who interested him as much as Rhea did. Nor did it bother him
unduly that she was beginning to consider him her possession. Although he had never made any promise to her,
from their constant companionship she had good reason to
assume their relationship would eventually lead to a permanent attachment. Yet for the time he was content with
the status quo. He ignored the gentle pressure Rhea placed
on him to cement the ties between them, and she was too
wise to nag at him. Her father, too, though obviously well
satisfied with the course of events between his daughter
and Christopher, was careful never to interfere. He'd
known men of Christopher's caliber and independent
spirit before, and was well aware that to push the man toward a decision would be the surest way of sending him
running.

Through the fall the situation continued amicably for all
parties concerned. Aside from their social encounters and
afternoons spent driving or walking through the more
fashionable city streets, Christopher and Rhea found the
opportunity for secret trysts. Although he never brought
her to his town house—he did not care to have Mawson
learn the full extent of his relationship with Rhea—he and
Rhea did have private hours together at the Wilson mansion when her father was out of the city on business, which

he occasionally was, or discreetly in one of the well-appointed rooms of the City Hotel. A few bills passed under the counter to the night desk clerk assured Christopher a room and access to the back entrance of the hotel, where he and Rhea could enter and leave with no one the wiser.

Sexually, he had to admit, the lady did excite him. She was a seductress between the sheets, always ready for innovation, always able to please him highly without falling to the tricks of a paid whore. She had a way of holding a tiny bit of herself to herself, tantalizing him to discover what other secrets she might have in store. As sure as he was of her ultimate intentions—a solid and respectable marriage between the two of them—she never allowed him to feel he had her totally within his grip. She was one of the most sought-after women in New York for both her beauty and her fortune, and although she was never so foolish as to throw the fact in Christopher's face, he was ever aware of the not unconsiderable number of hopefuls in wait to capture her heart and assets should he not toe the line.

But Christopher, too, knew he held a trump card. Rhea was falling in love with him, although she never admitted it—her feelings were increasingly evident in her actions—but he remained safely untouched by any chord of that emotion. Though he felt no distaste at the thought of her as his wife and knew that they would deal well together, her rather calculating approach to life precluded his ever feeling for Rhea the soft, sweet, overwhelming passion he'd known for Jessica. There'd been no guile in the love Jessica had given him; and none in the love he'd returned.

In the rush to bring as much cargo into his warehouses as possible before the winter freeze closed up some of the local harbors, Christopher was often at his office desk long after the clerks had left and locked the door behind them. One early November evening as he sat working alone, he heard Robert Bayard's familiar knock at the street door.

"Ah—happy to catch you still in, Dunlap," Bayard called as Christopher released the latch and let him in.

"Good to see you, Bayard. Come back while I clear my desk. I was just getting ready to leave." They entered

Christopher's working domain, lit by a shaded oil lamp on the desk, a gift from Rhea. Christopher pointed toward the decanter on a table to the side of the room. "Pour us a glass, and we can sit and chat for a while, unless you are in a rush."

"No. That was one of the reasons I stopped by, as it has been a while since we talked and I am in no hurry to get back to my rooms." He handed a glass to Christopher. "I put in a bid on that Jennings cargo, and Hone is expected to auction off another lot of East Indian tea in his rooms tomorrow."

"So I heard at Tontines this afternoon." Christopher began to organize the papers on his desk and locked several in his top drawer. "We will be needing that cargo. I have orders booked for New Haven and Providence."

"Providence, eh? I thought the Providence men were bringing in their own goods."

"Several brokers up there are in short supply."

"Excellent. Perhaps we can build up a little continuing trade there."

"My hope exactly." His desk cleared and locked, Christopher took his glass and leaned back in his chair, propping his feet on the desk. "Ah, how pleasant to relax."

"I do not wonder. You have not given yourself a break in weeks . . ."

"I have no choice—these are important days if this venture is to be a success."

"Except for the times you are in the company of a certain lady," Bayard said, adding to his previous remark as if Christopher hadn't spoken.

"Yes."

"How are things progressing there?" Bayard lit up a thin cigar and puffed the tip to a glowing red.

"Well enough."

"So you will soon be coming to the point and making it a permanent arrangement?"

"There is no hurry."

"You begin to sound like Mawson." Bayard chuckled.

Christopher returned his smile. "I have thought that myself."

"How is Mawson, by the way? He's been out of my sight for several weeks. Work is progressing on the merchantman?"

"Very well. Mawson's built a model and has been scouting around for shipwrights and carpenters. He has already had a shipment of timbers and mast beams brought down from his old friends in Maine and expects to begin the framing up at Corlears within the month."

"I shall have to go take a look."

"If all goes according to schedule, we should have an ocean goer under our flag by spring." Christopher smiled with satisfaction.

"I have been putting together some information on markets abroad, also keeping an eye out for a good captain for you."

"There is one gentleman I have in mind. Fish is his name, although we would have to lure him away from the Griswolds."

Bayard's eyes fairly danced at the prospect. "There is nothing I would enjoy more. Those gentlemen have given me enough worry over the last years. I owe them a bit in return."

A half hour later both men were glad enough to start home for a warm meal, parting company at the corner of Pearl Street as Bayard headed across town and Christopher to the south.

"I shall see you in a few days," Bayard called, "with news of the auctions. Give my regards to the Lady Taylor."

"I would be delighted. I have often wondered if you had a light in your eye where the lady was concerned."

" 'Tis a bit late for either of us to be concerned about that."

But in fact Christopher saw comparatively little of Rhea in the ensuing weeks, socializing only at the weekends. She did not allow herself to slip too far from his thoughts, sending him cheery notes or having one of her servants deliver a basket of cheese, bread, fruit, and wine for his noon repast—yet she also managed to convey that she was less than delighted by his inattention.

The list of forthcoming holiday entertainments among the elite was a long one, and Christopher could spare himself for only the most important engagements. He felt pangs of guilt for neglecting Rhea and tried to make up for his absences by being particularly attentive when they were together, as was the case in early December as they lay snuggled together in a room at the City Hotel.

The remains of a delicious light supper and chilled bottle of champagne rested on the table beside the bed, brought up earlier from the hotel kitchens as Christopher's treat to Rhea. Beside the empty champagne bottle was a vase of blood-red roses, another gift from Christopher and a special luxury in wintery New York.

Warm beneath the down covers on the bed, surfeited with the food and drink and their just completed lovemaking, Rhea wrapped her arms tightly about his torso.

"I think I shall chain you to this bed, make you my prisoner so you will spend the whole of the night with me."

"Why such drastic measures, my dear?"

"It seems I must use drastic measures," she murmured. "I see so little of you of late—so when I do see you, I despise seeing the evening end."

"Then we shall stretch this one out as long as we can."

He felt especially guilty that evening. He'd been supposed to meet her at eight-thirty, but there had been problems with the unloading of one of his schooners, and he'd had to go down to the wharves himself to straighten things out. It had been close to ten o'clock when he'd arrived at the Wilson mansion, and the sparks had fairly flown from Rhea's eyes. He had explained, apologizing profusely, and she had forgiven him; yet he still felt more amends were due.

She cuddled closer. "When will all this business rush be finished?"

"Soon, I hope. With the cold weather settling in, it should ease."

"But not before the holidays."

He hesitated. "No, perhaps not."

He heard her disappointed sigh.

"I know it is difficult for you," he said quietly, "but I have been thinking of a way we might make it up. I received an invitation a few days ago to a weekend Christmas ball in Connecticut. It would give us several days all to ourselves." Even as he spoke, he wondered at the wisdom of his suggestion. Connecticut carried so many memories of his happy days with Jessica . . . memories that he held sacred.

But Rhea had immediately perked up. "We could travel up and back on one of your schooners," she said thoughtfully. "It would be a chilly trip, but you have a cabin on board, do you not?"

"I do."

She grinned. "Then what problem the chill weather? When is this ball?"

"The week before Christmas."

"Personal acquaintances of yours?"

"No. The invitation comes from the owner of a firm in Eastport with whom I do considerable business. I have never met the gentleman myself, having dealt strictly with a son-in-law, but if this gentleman throws a party with the same enthusiasm he runs his business, it should be enjoyable."

"Mmmm, business," she mused, sounding dubious. Christopher knew that she had already made up her mind; was sure of it when she took his hand and squeezed it. "Yes, I think I should like to attend. I have never been to Connecticut, and the promise of your constant companionship for several days is one I cannot let pass by . . . But will it not raise comment, the two of us traveling alone together for such a distance and so long a time?"

"You will bring your maid."

"Yes . . . but one wonders at the standards of these country gentry. I would not want it bandied about that I was a woman of loose reputation."

Christopher chuckled. "Such niceties do not now seem to bother you overmuch."

"You know perfectly well that word of these rendezvous of ours will never leak out. But openly to travel off with a man for three or four days . . ." She let him carry the thought to its completion.

For a few seconds he was silent, debating; then on impulse Christopher made a decision.

"Then you will tell them that you are my fiancée. Surely that information will assuage any gossip." It was a decision he'd known he would eventually make. He reasoned now that it really made no difference that he'd come to it sooner than he had originally anticipated. And perhaps it was better to have the tension relieved, the situation out in the open between them.

Although Rhea's last comment had been intended to prod him to such a commitment, she sat up now, almost afraid to believe what she'd heard. Her eyes were alight, her cheeks flushed.

"Do you mean it?"

"It would be highly dishonorable for a gentleman to make such a statement and not mean it."

"Oh, but how wonderful! Oh, Christopher, how I have waited . . . hoped . . ."

"I think you knew our present course would eventually lead to this point."

"But never was I sure. You are not a predictable man." She leaned over and kissed him warmly, then sat up again, brimming with excitement. "Ah, there are so many plans I shall have to make. And the announcement! When—"

He brought his fingers up to cover her mouth gently. "Rhea, as for the public announcement, I would prefer you wait until after the new year . . . until things have settled down a bit at the offices. As it is, I quite honestly do not have the time to give to all the festivities involved in an engagement . . . all the parties and whatnot. You understand, do you not? It is only another month."

Rhea was upset, but quickly wiped the frown from her brow. She had the good sense now not to be greedy. She forced a sympathetic smile to her lips. "Yes, yes, of course I understand. As you say, the time still is short enough, and we can tell our news privately to those who should know."

"Yes."

Again she snuggled up against him. "We shall have to begin looking for a house, although Father may offer us the Broad Way mansion. And set a date—I think late spring, perhaps May—ah, but there is time for all this talk later." Her voice dropped to a coaxing purr as she pressed her breasts against the hard breadth of his chest, ran her hand possessively down his back. "For now, my handsome fiancé, come make love to me."

As he pulled her tight in his arms and felt the silken softness of her skin under his palms, the full curves of her body melting into his, he forced away the uncertainty that had suddenly worked its way through his consciousness. Why should he have this unexpected, piercing doubt? He had done the right thing. Yes, of course he had—he was sure of it. What more could he ask in life with Jessica gone?

9

There were moments when Jessica could hardly believe so much time had passed; could hardly believe that she had survived as well as she had from day to day. It had been almost two years since she had found herself in the cottage on the Beard farm.

Kit was a sturdy toddler now, just having celebrated his second birthday, and was a joy to everyone on the farm. He was a well-behaved child whose energies and curiosity nevertheless often carried him into mischief, but there were plenty of loving nursemaids to keep him well supervised. Many a fall afternoon that year, Jessica would stand at the kitchen windows watching her son scamper across the backyard on Jeb's heels, full of childish questions, eager to give a not-always-helpful hand with the feeding of the animals. How much more like his father he looked the older he got! The resemblance almost startled her. Sometimes she felt Christopher's image should be dimming in her mind, yet when she closed her eyes, his features were there before her, sharp and clear as ever. She missed him no less with the passage of time, but now the pain had become an ever-present dull ache. Gradually she had learned to face the reality that she would never see him again.

Although they seldom spoke of it to her, all the members of the farm household presumed that when her husband hadn't returned after the announcement of peace the previous winter, he had been one of the casualties of the war; and those that had had suspicions that there'd never been a husband, kept their mouths shut in the face of Jessica's stoic strength. Her dignity shamed them—even Rachel, who had yet to relent and show Jessica any warmth or friendship.

Amelia Beard had persuaded Jessica to write to the Dunlaps' former address in New York. Since Mrs. Beard would give her no peace until the letter was posted, Jessica had complied, knowing full well, since she had invented the story of their living in New York, a letter would never reach him. And several months later the much handled envelope had been returned "Not at this address."

However sympathetic they were, Jessica knew from Molly's and Amelia Beard's unsaid words that they thought she should find another husband. She was alone, had a child to raise; she was young and attractive, and there were fine, hard-working men in the area who, given some encouragement by her, would have been delighted to offer her marriage. Still, she could not find it within herself to give up Christopher's memory or to actively seek another relationship.

At least her relationship with Elizabeth Beard had taken a step for the better. Though at times Elizabeth was still the spoiled younger daughter, she was gaining some maturity, making life a bit simpler for Jessica. Elizabeth had never gone to her mother after their argument over a year before; instead, there'd been a reluctant truce, Elizabeth realizing that she could not push Jessica too far. Then too, since the end of the war, social events had become more frequent. Elizabeth was in her glory and therefore less needful of antagonizing Jessica to relieve her boredom. She had beaux now—and one young man in particular, Terrence Day, the spoiled son of wealthy parents from a neighboring town. At the age of twenty-five, he was a skilled dilettante and, as far as Jessica could surmise, had never lifted a finger to an honest day's work in his life. Neither of the Beards fully approved of him, but Elizabeth was awed. He was handsome and charming and knew precisely how to play to her vanity.

Lucas, as well, was still a patient admirer of Elizabeth's, and since he'd bought out half-interest in the sawmill, she wasn't quite so condescending to him as she'd been before;

but he could come nowhere close to equaling the credentials of her other suitor.

Jessica was more than ever Lucas's friend and confidant. He never complained, but it was to her he mentioned his growing impatience with Elizabeth; his coming closer to a decision to let the whole thing go. Jessica's friendship with him was so relaxed and honest, they were so at ease with each other, that she couldn't help but wonder sometimes whether something might have developed between them if it hadn't been for Elizabeth. But it was a thought she quickly put out of her mind. Despite Lucas's impatience, he was still utterly enamored of the Beards' youngest daughter, to the exclusion of considering any other woman.

That Elizabeth knew this and used Lucas so pitilessly was one of the remaining sore spots between her and Jessica. Jessica would see red as she listened to Elizabeth recounting the events of a party she'd just attended.

"The Lathropes were there and Jeremy Stone, and Lucas, of course. You know how infatuated he has always been with me . . . he came right over as soon as I arrived—and you have to admit, he *is* handsome. I saw Corinne Smithe watching us, but Lucas paid not the least heed to her. I danced and chatted with him until Terrence arrived; there really was no one else the least interesting at the party."

"You underestimate Lucas."

"So you have told me. But really, Jessica, he can be such a rustic . . . particularly compared to Terrence. Terrence was wearing the most divine green evening jacket . . . the latest thing, he told me. He had his tailor in New York make it up after the new styles in London. Lucas looked so dowdy in that brown thing he has been wearing since before the war. And, of course, Terrence knows just *everybody,* and everything that is going on. He was telling me . . ."

And so Elizabeth's conversation went on, lauding Terrence to the skies, while Jessica inwardly seethed at Elizabeth's poor judgment. Couldn't the girl see that Terrence Day was only out for himself, and would accept only the wealthiest and best connected young woman he could catch? No wonder that the elder Beards were not overly delighted with their daughter's infatuation with the man! Of course, she was still their spoiled child, and they had difficulty in denying her her whims. But it was a shame Elizabeth herself was not more perceptive. Jessica had a feeling that the girl was in for a big letdown when Terrence eventually showed his true colors.

Mary Weldon was a frequent visitor to the farm. Now the proud mother of a darling little daughter, Anne, during the summer months she'd brought the then eleven-month-old up to Silvercreek to be doted upon by her delighted grandparents. Jessica's and Mary's liking for each other had grown into as close a friendship as was possible between servant and her employer's daughter, and Mary's visits gave Jessica a much-needed opportunity to talk to a woman of about her own age; to compare notes on their growing offspring. The two of them laughed one day to see Kit's suddenly very grown-up and protective manner toward Anne when the little girl eagerly began exploring all the interesting sights in the kitchen, moving rapidly on all fours toward the fireplace when the adults' backs were turned.

"No go there, Anne," Kit called out, kneeling down and grabbing her pudgy little hand. "Fire hot." As he dragged the reluctant baby away from the fireplace, he looked up at his mother. "We go outside. I show Anne Bessie."

Bessie was the new calf, penned into the small enclosure by the barn. "All right, Kit, but stay where I can see you from the window."

"Yes, Mama. Come, Anne. I walk slow," he said, holding her hand, and the little girl, just learning to maneuver on two legs with assistance, toddled along beside him toward the door.

Since the end of the war, the community had begun prospering again. The mills were working to full capacity to satisfy the local shipyards' demands for timber. Lucas claimed that he'd already more than earned back his investment in the mill, and because of the prosperous volume of business, Bertram Beard was considering expanding his store in town. He spoke of opening an office in New York. He'd made several trips to see a banker in the city and was more than his usual jovial self around the house.

With things going so well in business, he and Amelia had decided to throw a tremendous Christmas ball. They hadn't entertained to any extent since their oldest daughter's wedding, and the air of excitement about Amelia spread to the rest of the household as she bustled about preparing for the event. The house had to be cleaned from top to bottom, and all the extra guest rooms and the cottage prepared, as well as Jessica's and Rachel's rooms. They would be moving into Molly's room for the weekend, since every extra bed was needed. The Lathropes and several other neighbors would also put up overnight visitors, and any overflow would be directed to the inn in town.

Bringing out all the best china and silver, Jessica and Rachel spent hours washing and polishing and carefully stacking it all away again. The ballroom was aired, the crystal chandeliers lowered and washed pendant by pendant so that the resulting sparkle was dazzling. Chairs were brought down from the attic and set up along the ballroom walls, Christmas garland hung over doorways and mantelpieces. To help prepare the gargantuan amount of food that would needed, an extra kitchen girl was brought in—Nan Constable, from the neighborhood. Almost daily during the two weeks before the festivities, delivery wagons pulled into the Beards' driveway to unload cases of wine and champagne, whole hams, and other culinary necessities, as well as linens from Beard's Mercantile.

Amelia spent hours writing out invitations to personal friends, while a clerk of Bertram Beard's wrote out those to be sent to business associates.

Guests were being invited from as far away as New York and New Haven, and the Beards kept their fingers crossed that the mild winter weather would continue through the end of the month. In case snow should fall, however, Bertram made arrangements for the hire of several sleighs to transport guests—most of whom, if traveling any distance, would be arriving by packet into Eastport harbor rather than following the rough roads overland.

Of course, Elizabeth was in ecstasy over the forthcoming entertainment. Her altered disposition might have been termed sweet and accommodating, and if Jessica hadn't been left constantly frazzled by all the extra work in her daily schedule, she would have relished the change more fully than she then had the energy to do.

Nan Constable would stay on to help serve at the party, and two other local men would come in to act as footmen. Still, both Jessica and Rachel would have a full schedule, serving, taking wraps, and otherwise seeing to the guests' needs.

The morning of the ball was as frenzied as the rest of the day was destined to be. Jessica would be working rather than enjoying the entertainments, but still she found she was looking forward to the evening. The event certainly offered a break in the routine, an opportunity to see new faces.

That morning and early afternoon, she gave the guest rooms a last-minute dusting and straightening, laid the fires, and put out fresh towels; then she went to the kitchens to assist Molly, who was remarkably calm considering what lay ahead of her that day. Kit, content for the time in his playpen in the corner, though he had long since discovered how to escape over the wooden rails, was entranced with the toy wagon and horse Jeb had carved for him. He seemed to sense that the adults had urgent business on their minds and would only be short-tempered if he disturbed them. Rachel was in the laundry room ironing the tablecloths, and Nan had begun bringing out the silver, glasses, and dishes to the tables in the ballroom, where light refreshments would be served. A more substantial buffet would be set up in the dining room.

"Never thought to see so much food in this kitchen all at the same time," Molly said, laughing, as she and Jessica worked companionably together at the wide kitchen table. "Certainly nothing like it since Miss Mary's wedding, and even that didn't compare."

"The worst seems to be over, thank goodness." Jessica

smiled. "Though I don't know that I could have done such an efficient job as you."

"Nonsense, child. And look at all the help you've given me. But you'd best take it slow. You've a long night ahead of you."

"Yes. I planned to take a rest this afternoon . . . if there's time."

"The mistress will give you time—not to worry. Though I suppose you'll have to go up and help Miss Elizabeth with her dressing. Pity you can't be going to the ball like the lady you are instead of helping Rachel with the serving . . . prettying yourself up in a new gown, fixing your hair with all those curls like you do for Miss Elizabeth. You'd be the light of the party, you would." Molly shook her head emphatically.

"There's no point in thinking about it, Molly. I'll be putting on my new uniform, passing trays of champagne and food, and that will be that. Just the same, it will be pleasant seeing all those interesting new faces."

"Still say it's a pity—just wish certain others in this house could have your good nature."

Jessica chuckled, yet deep inside she did feel a pang. It had been so long since she'd dressed in a beautiful gown, pampered herself in a sudsy, fragrant bath, curled and fussed with her hair, or looked forward to an evening with nothing but entertainment, laughter, and dancing in store. She recalled so clearly that one wonderful evening when she and Christopher had danced together for the first time. How magnificent he was, twirling her about the floor to the strains of a Strauss waltz with all the finesse of the expert he was. She could remember the feel of his hand on her back, the soft words he'd whispered in her ear.

She shook her head to force the thoughts away. Tonight would bear no resemblance to that evening. There'd be no dancing for her . . . and certainly no Christopher.

Amelia Beard burst into the kitchen far from her normally coolly collected self.

"Oh, here you are, Jessica," she said breathlessly. "Are all the rooms ready? I have been supervising in the ballroom and have not had time to check."

"Yes, everything's ready, Mrs. Beard. I went over the rooms a short time ago."

"Good, good. And Molly, you appear to have things going along with your usual efficiency. Do you need any more help?"

"No, I'm just fine. Just finished up these pastries."

"The two men will be in about four to bring up the cases of wine and champagne. If you need them for any other heavy work, Molly, just let me know."

"Aye. Nothing I can think of at the moment, except to help the girls bring out the food for the buffet—they'll be wearing their feet off later with the serving."

"You all should take an hour this afternoon to rest. It will be a long evening."

Molly grinned. "Can't say I'd mind putting my feet up for a while."

"Since I am here, Jessica," said Amelia, still rushing over her words as though she had too much on her mind, "let me go over this evening's duties with you. I have told Rachel and Nan to look to you for directions. Just be sure all the serving dishes remain full. Perhaps one of you might want to be responsible for overseeing the buffet in the dining room, and the others can pass around trays of finger food in the ballroom. The two men will help in serving the glasses of liquid refreshment, but you will want to remove empty glasses and soiled dishes. Some of the overnight guests have begun arriving, so see that Rachel or Nan brings up hot water for their rooms—I have given them the three end guest rooms on the second floor, although eventually all the rooms will be used. I do not expect the majority of guests will arrive until about six or seven, and those staying elsewhere will be coming at eight. I will have one of the men in the front hall to collect hats and capes—but should any of the ladies need assistance, have one of the girls give a hand. As I told you, Mary will be bringing her nursemaid along to watch over Anne and Kit for the evening, so you need not worry about leaving the child alone."

She pressed her fingers to her brow. "Dear me, what have I forgotten? Jeb's brought in firewood?"

"Plenty," Molly nodded.

"Then I will expect you girls downstairs by seven."

"Of course," Jessica agreed, although she knew full well that in order to get everything accomplished, they would be at their posts long before that.

"Good. Mary will be arriving soon, and I do want to visit with her and the baby before the place is in too much confusion. I will see you all later then."

"If I might offer some advice, ma'am," Molly put in, "relax a bit yourself. Everything's going to go just fine, but you'll be worn to the bone if you keep aworrying."

"I know." Amelia smiled. "I shall give myself the same advice and try to heed it."

Jessica did get a chance to rest that afternoon. About three o'clock, she and the others went up to Molly's room. But as she lay back on the cot, her mind was whirling as she mentally previewed the evening ahead. She was far too restless to doze off, and supposed her aching muscles and feet would regret the lack of sleep by midnight.

She rose and dressed in her new maid's dress, its white ruffled collar and cuffs and its snowy apron set off against dark blue. Pinning her hair atop her head, she fastened over it a lacy mob cap. When she'd finished, she knew the result was attractive, though she certainly would not be mistaken for one of the guests. After two years she was truly tired of her subservient role. She tried to shrug away the streak of snobbishness, but she knew she was above the status of maid. She belonged out there with the guests, not waiting on them and serving them their refreshments. Yet she had no course but to resign herself with good grace to the hours ahead.

She went back downstairs at six, checking in first to say good night to Kit, who was settled with Mary's nursemaid.

"You be a good boy tonight," she smiled, giving him a hug and kiss. "Listen to Emma and do what she tells you."

"I will, Mama. I help take care of Anne."

"You do that, and I'll see you in the morning. I'll be working late tonight."

"You not sleep in here?"

"No, but I'll be right across the hall." She saw the mischievous twinkle in his eye. "And don't get any ideas, young man, about sneaking over. That would make Mommy very angry."

He nodded; she gave him one last hug, and went down to the kitchen. The guests who had already arrived were in their rooms, so the house seemed quiet but for the bustling servants. Molly was busy at her cooking, Rachel assisting, and Nan was running up and down stairs with buckets of hot water for the guests. Jessica went through the rooms checking to see that the various sconces and candlesticks were filled with the dozens of new candles that had been ordered in. At seven she would light them all, but now only a few brightened the interior of each room—enough to allow the servants to go about their tasks. The fires blazed in the downstairs rooms, however; the two fires in the ballroom fireplaces in particular were roaring in an effort to maintain the warmth in that cavernous high-ceilinged room.

Jessica was thoughtful as she made her way alone from the dining room, to the parlors, on to the ballroom. How lovely everything looked, immaculate and welcoming, the brasses and mirrors shining, the wood floors waxed, the carpets freshly swept, their colors vibrant. She could take pride in all this beauty, for her own hard work was partly to thank for it.

Jonas, a hired man, was polishing and setting out glasses at the table when she entered the ballroom. Behind him were stacked wooden cases of wine, and outside on the porch beyond the nearby French doors where they would remain chilled were the cases of champagne. Jonas looked up and smiled as she approached.

"Everything well under control here. You ladies need any help bringin' things in, you let me know."

"I will, Jonas, and thanks. Will you be in the front hall to take the wraps?"

"Naw, Marcus will be. Has more of a gentlemanly air about him."

Jessica laughed, moved across the room to check the wall sconces. She could hardly believe the transformation in this area that under normal circumstances was an

empty, echoing expanse. Now many dozens of chairs lined
the walls. In the far corner a velvet-draped wooden plat-
form had been constructed for the musicians—a string en-
semble Bertram Beard had hired from New York—who
would play throughout the evening. The chandeliers had
been lowered in preparation for lighting, after which the
men would pull those heavy weights back up to the ceiling
and secure them. She imagined how it all would look with
the room filled with laughing, chattering people, the music mellowly filling the air, the candlelight all but dis-
pelling the shadows. She would know in a few hours—
unless she found herself too preoccupied by work to notice
such details.

In the kitchen Molly's plump form was bending before
the oven doors. The woman turned with a baking tin full of
pastry shells to be filled with a mixture of diced and spiced
meat. Her face was flushed from the heat of the ovens, and
once she'd set down the tins, she wiped beads of perspiration from her forehead. "Rachel's just run to the cellar, but
she'll be back to fill these shells. If you like, you can start
putting out the food in the dining room. What'll keep is
ready there on the sideboard. What'll you be needing Nan
to do?"

"I thought since she's been running up and down stairs
with water for the last hour, I'd have her help Marcus in
the front hall. That will give her a little rest, Molly . . . unless you need her for something else?"

"No, no. Rachel will give me the help I need, and we've
got an hour or so before there's any need to start serving in
the ballroom. You and Rachel can handle that all right."

"As soon as I get down from helping Elizabeth dress."

Molly snorted. "You'd think that girl would take care of
her own dressing tonight, what with all the rest you have
to do."

"It's only to fix her hair. There's a particular style she
wants that she can't manage herself."

"Can't very well refuse, can you?" Molly frowned, and
Jessica went to the sideboard to begin bringing the filled
chafing dishes into the dining room; once there, lighting a
candle under each to keep the contents warm.

The next two hours went by in a blur. At seven she made the rounds of the rooms, lighting candles, adding logs to the fires; she spoke briefly to Rachel and Nan as they outlined the schedule for the evening ahead, then rushed upstairs at seven-thirty to Elizabeth's room. Although Jessica was on time, her mistress was fretting.

"I thought you would never come, Jessica, and I cannot reach all the buttons on my gown."

"Let me help you." As Elizabeth turned her back, Jessica easily fastened the three remaining loops, smoothed the royal-blue satin skirt, the front panel of which was split to reveal a lighter blue underskirt. The low neckline was trimmed with soft, creamy lace, as were the long, tapered sleeves. "What a beautiful gown." Jessica sighed.

"Do you think? I admit I am rather pleased." Elizabeth swirled before the mirror to examine herself. "And I am glad I decided on the blue rather than the rose. The color does more for my eyes."

"I quite agree."

"Ah, but let us start on my hair. You know the style I want . . . and do take a care, it must come out well. I want to make a particularly good impression on Terrence this evening."

As she sat at the dressing table, Elizabeth continued to chatter. She'd already removed the rag ties that had set her curls, and her blond tresses hung in ringlets around her face. Jessica carefully began brushing through the strands, pinning them up atop the girl's head.

"I am so excited about this ball." Elizabeth's reflection in the mirror was animated. "I have this *certain* feeling . . . Terrence will be making me an offer tonight. He has been leading toward that, telling me he has a surprise in store for me this evening. Papa makes all these noises about Terrence not yet having proved himself, but he really is being a bit fussy. Can Terrence help it if he has enough wealth that he need not trouble himself? He is *so* charming and well connected—and after all, it is *I* who will wed him . . ."

"Marry in haste, repent at leisure," Jessica whispered under her breath.

"What did you say?"

"Nothing. You must make up your own mind. Have you told Lucas that you would consider an offer from Terrence?"

"No, of course not. Why should I?"

"I think he deserves to know where he stands."

"Nonsense! Besides I do not want to give up Lucas . . . just yet. It is better that Terrence knows there are others who are interested."

Jessica could have said something more—something about using people—but what was the point?

It was close to nine before Jessica first entered the crowded ballroom. There seemed to be people everywhere —in the hallways, in the parlors and study, descending the main staircase. All were beautifully dressed, the men smart in dark, long-tailed evening coats and white breeches, the women in a multitude of elegantly fashioned gowns, the colors and fabrics of which were enough to take one's breath away. The room shimmered with the sparkle of jewels, the glint of crystal in candlelight; the air was scented with a fragrant blend of perfumes, masculine colognes, and fresh pine from the greens hung all about the room. Above the merry laughter and chatter could be heard the strains of a waltz floating out from the musicians' strings. Many couples were dancing, looking gay and graceful as they twirled over the parquet floors. There were more new faces than Jessica could absorb in the moment or two she had to observe; well over one hundred guests in the ballroom alone, making it difficult to pick out familiar faces. As she made her way to the refreshment table to collect the tray of food she would distribute, she saw no sign of the host and hostess, but they were no doubt circulating through the crowd. She did catch a glimpse of Lucas and Elizabeth on the dance floor; apparently Terrence had not yet arrived.

A large silver tray of tiny meat-filled popovers secure in her hands, Jessica stepped out into the throng, offering the tidbits to guests. The girls had divided their areas of responsibility into three equal portions of the ballroom, and Jessica's was the left side.

As she stepped amid the throng, some guests ignored her; others gave a curt wave of the hand as if they resented the interruption to their conversation; but most were pleasant, smiling as they either helped themselves or graciously declined. Some men were especially friendly, widening their eyes appreciatively as they noticed Jessica's face, but she'd expected that. It was not uncommon for certain men of the social set to take an interest in a serving maid and try to lure her off into a secluded corner. It was quite clear from Jessica's behavior that she was not of such loose-moraled inclination.

Jessica divided her time between the ballroom and the kitchen. In her journeys down the hallways she'd seen Terrence Day arrive and enter the ballroom, to be singled out immediately by Elizabeth. They'd talked and danced; but later, quite unexpectedly, Jessica had seen him again in one of the hallways deep in conversation with a pretty, dark-haired young woman. His usual charm was apparent, and the young lady seemed enraptured, intent on his every word. "I had once briefly met your father, the senator, at a gathering in New York . . ." Jessica heard him say as she walked past. She would dearly have liked to pause to hear more, for, often though she and Elizabeth were at odds, this was Elizabeth's young man, and what was he doing charming *this* young lady?

Later she saw him dancing with Elizabeth, but the look on that young woman's face wasn't all it might have been. Had that been anger in her expression? Jessica wondered as her view of the couple was blocked by others caught up in the rhythmic flow of dancers on the floor.

Not long after, Lucas stopped Jessica as she was passing about her tray in a crowded corner of the room. His normally easygoing expression was irate—brows down, lips tight.

"You have seen Elizabeth?"

"Briefly, a while ago."

"She was with the honorable Mr. Day . . . running to meet him at the entrance doors."

"I would not quite call it running."

"Yet you catch my point, Jessica. Suddenly I do not exist!"

"Lucas . . ."

"There is no sense in trying to ease the blow, my friend. I have been quite willfully dense these last years, but my eyes are seeing very well tonight. I have had all I can take."

"Lucas, I am sure she will see that Terrence is not worth her effort. She's still young enough that—"

"Not so young any longer that she should not have some wisdom. I have pretended for a long time that what I was seeing could be interpreted differently. But Jessica . . . she is making a fool of me."

"Not a fool—you'd never be a fool. She just doesn't appreciate or understand what she wants. And she needs someone like you, or she would have let you go long since; yet she has an idealized picture of being swept off her feet by a most eligible Prince Charming. Whatever Elizabeth has wanted, she has gotten. She's yet to realize that what she wants is in her hand."

"Jessica, I am sorry to be burdening you with this. Here you are, working yourself to exhaustion, and I come to you with my problems."

"It's all right, Lucas. We're friends; always will be. Who else to go to with your dilemmas? Though I admit it would be nice to be one of the company this evening."

"You should be, Jessica."

"I know. There was a time . . ."

They were interrupted by one of the guests coming over to examine Jessica's trayful of edibles.

"We will talk later." Lucas reached out a hand to touch her shoulder.

"Yes, I hope so."

Jessica moved on after serving the group. There was something in Lucas's touch. What did it mean . . . that tightened grip, that look in his eyes? Almost as though the vision of Elizabeth was no longer standing there between them. She shrugged it from her mind. She was tired, too busy imagining things.

She'd emptied her tray and picked up another to collect

empty glasses from the guests and side tables. Leaving the ballroom with the full tray, she came down the main hallway, passing Bertram Beard's study door. Suddenly a figure emerged from the doorway. There was no time for her to move out of the way. He walked directly into her, upsetting the tray. Glasses went spilling in all directions over the carpeted hallway.

"I am so sorry," a man's voice spoke. "Here, let me help you."

Jessica's cheeks reddened. It was bad enough that she had dropped a tray in front of a guest; but to have a guest offer to help . . .

"Thank you, sir. But I will be quite all right."

"No, it was entirely my fault. Instead of looking to see where I was going, I stepped directly into you. I am afraid I had a great deal on my mind . . . business matters. I was speaking with my host, and—" He lifted his hands expressively. "You see it does not pay to mix business with pleasure." He studied her.

Jessica quickly kneeled to retrieve the glasses. In a moment he kneeled beside her, and helped her set the scattered glassware on the tray.

"Please, sir, I wish you wouldn't. I can take care of this myself. It was only an accident. Enjoy the ball."

"Oh," he said, placing another glass on the tray, "I will enjoy the ball, though this is my most diverting moment yet. No, I do not wish to embarrass you, but I do not often find myself on my knees retrieving glasses with a charming damsel. It *is* a most pleasant diversion."

"I am Jerome Weitz, by the way," the gentleman added. "I handle Bertram Beard's banking arrangements in New York."

"How do you do." Jessica continued putting glasses back on the tray.

"Might I ask your name?"

"Jessica."

"A lovely name."

The glasses back on their tray, Jessica made to rise.

"I thank you, sir, for all your help, and I apologize for the interruption. I hope I haven't soiled your clothing."

"No, I am left with no scars—even to these damnable knee breeches—the price one pays for these otherwise charming parties."

Weitz stood.

"Thank you again, sir."

"It was my pleasure."

Jessica nodded, then turned to move down the hall.

He stopped her with a gentle touch on her arm. "I shall hope we will see each other again tonight . . . not so precipitously, perhaps. You understand I do not mean that as certain other gentlemen might. I speak only in friendship. You see, you remind me very much of my mother—long dead now—but a woman I admired greatly. When I was a child, she supported us by working as a servant, so I know the burdens of your occupation first hand—it is something I will never forget. And I sense that you, like her, were brought to this profession by some tragedy in life, not by choice."

"You are very perceptive, sir."

"It is not difficult to see your intelligence, and your spirit, despite your efforts at disguising both. Well, enough of this. I see that I *am* embarrassing you." He smiled. "I only wanted you to understand my motives were honorable."

"I do, Mr. Weitz. You are a gentleman."

"I try to be."

"Good evening, and thank you for your kind words."

He nodded his head, and Jessica moved off toward the kitchen feeling suddenly less wearied. Aside from Molly and Amelia, it was rare indeed that she heard such words of appreciation for the job she was doing.

She noticed Jerome Weitz later, on the far side of the ballroom in the company of a petite and pretty blond woman, but as she concentrated on efficiently serving the increasing number of guests, she had little time to observe him at length.

The musicians played without cessation as the glittering guests moved in a steady flow on and off the dance floor, circulated about the ballroom and through the other rooms of the house. About halfway through the evening, as

Jessica was leaving the ballroom with another loaded tray, Elizabeth Beard touched her hand.

"Jessica, you must come with me."

"Elizabeth, I have so much to do."

"I have caught my hem with my heel and it needs mending. Besides which I *must* talk to you." Jessica was startled to see that the girl's eyes seemed filled with tears.

"Please, Jessica, come now! Mama will understand."

Elizabeth took Jessica's arm and pulled her up the main staircase.

Elizabeth hurried into her room, and Jessica closed the door behind them. The girl was distracted, pacing.

"Show me where your hem is ripped," Jessica said, trying to calm her. "I don't have time to sew it, but we'll see if we can't pin it up."

"Here in the back. My heel caught it."

"Yes, I see. Please stand still. I can't fix it with you moving about." Jessica examined the tear, then reached for some pins on the dressing table. "Yes, I can pin it up to hold for the rest of the evening."

"I do not know what I am going to do, Jessica. This evening has turned out entirely wrong."

"Wrong? In what way."

"Terrence. He is ignoring me!

"But I saw you dancing together."

"Earlier. Then suddenly he seemed to be avoiding me, and I saw him with Serena Payton. Her father is a senator, you know, and the family is wealthy beyond reason. I have met her only once before. I do not know where Terrence made her acquaintance. I do not understand it at all. He was devoting his attention so completely to me . . . I thought . . . was so sure . . ." Her voice broke, and Jessica quickly stepped in.

"Perhaps you are misjudging the situation." She felt she had to give the girl some consolation even if she herself believed Elizabeth was correct in her assumption.

"He was actually rude to me, Jessica. I walked over, and he said, 'Must you follow me about, Elizabeth?' I wanted to die, but before I could ask him what was the matter, he moved off and began talking to some of the gentlemen."

"Elizabeth, I know you would rather not hear this, but do you think you may at last be seeing Terrence's true colors? You've said your parents have been cool all along about your connection with him. Perhaps they saw him for an opportunist. You say this Serena is very wealthy . . . and her father is a senator?"

"Yes . . ."

Jessica was silent, letting Elizabeth draw her own conclusions.

The girl dabbed the corner of her eyes with her handkerchief.

"I realize it is easy for me to say, but there are other men out there far more worthy of your attention, who would like you for what you are. Terrence is very handsome and charming . . . I can understand how you would be swayed. But outward appearance is often the least important characteristic in a person."

"I know . . . I know. Mama's told me the same, but I could not help caring about him."

"Well, the worst thing you can do is to let him see you so upset. Chin up and go back to the dance and have a good time—pretend you are, even if you are not."

"Yes, you are right. And there is Lucas. I will talk to him. He is always there when I need him."

Jessica inwardly cringed that Elizabeth might contemplate once again using her dear friend, but perhaps after this eye-opening experience, Elizabeth might finally begin to see Lucas in a new light. There was no sense worrying about it; she had done all she could.

"I have to go back. You'll be all right?" At the girl's nod, "Come, I'll walk down with you."

Jessica left Elizabeth at the ballroom door and, sighing with weariness, moved toward the refreshment table to prepare a tray. Another few hours and she could put her feet up. She saw Amelia and Bertram Beard near the end of the table involved in a conversation with a tall young woman whose black-haired beauty, accented by a deep-red gown, for a moment left Jessica startled. She couldn't help but overhear some of their conversation, the Beards making friendly inquiries into the woman's background.

"So you are a native New Yorker."

"Yes . . . resided in Washington after my marriage . . . my husband . . . killed in the war."

"So sorry . . ."

"There were many who lost loved ones."

"I understand your father is . . ."

"Do you know him?"

"I had the pleasure briefly . . . on a business trip to New York."

". . . you have business associations with my fiancé."

"Quite satisfactory, although we have not had the pleasure of meeting . . . had hoped to earlier this evening . . ."

"Yes, we were delayed in arriving . . . our apologies. Ah, but I see him approaching now. Let us rectify that."

Although sorry to have inadvertently eavesdropped, Jessica thought nothing of the conversation as she turned with her full tray to begin circulating the room. Looking out into the crowd to set her course, she suddenly stopped dead in her tracks.

Coming toward her—actually toward the group at her side—was a man in a superbly cut black evening jacket, his dark head standing out above the crowd. His swinging gait moved him with lithe grace, bringing him closer and closer. Those features, that cleft chin, those blue, blue eyes . . . It *couldn't* be!

She couldn't move. She found it impossible to do anything but stare in disbelief at what she was seeing. It had to be he; no two men could look that much alike!

He was making straight for the Beards and the young woman with them. The black-haired woman was motioning to him. Jessica saw him smile, a flashing-white grin, felt the tray start shaking in her hands. There was hardly any question in her mind now. How was it possible?

He took the woman's outstretched hand. "Ah, Rhea. I have been looking for you."

"I have been having a most pleasant chat with our host and hostess. Christopher, I do not believe you have yet met Amelia and Bertram Beard. Amelia and Bertram, my fiancé, Christopher Dunlap."

"A pleasure to make your—" Bertram Beard's words

were cut short by the very audible gasp that had just escaped Jessica's lips. The sound of her tray crashing to the floor silenced the conversation of the Beards' and their guests. They all turned—four pairs of eyes staring at a white-faced and shaking Jessica.

For an instant Christopher's features remained impassive. Then his eyes widened. He shook his head quickly; stared again, the color slowly leaving his face, to be replaced by uncertainty, then shock. He took a step forward; stopped.

They stared at each other. Jessica's lips slightly parted, wanting to speak but unable to. The others watched the strange interchange in confusion. It was happening so quickly and unexpectedly, they had no time to question.

Jessica's mind spun in whirling disorder. Christopher! Her Christopher . . . here . . . now!

He took another step forward; his eyes piercing, probing her every feature: her eyes, her lips, the brown hair nearly hidden by the mob cap covering it.

"Jessica?" His voice was a barely audible croak.

Beyond speech, she could only nod . . . nod again.

"My God . . . oh, my God!"

People around them in the ballroom were gaping. He was oblivious as he strode forward and stood over her, gazing down with pain and joy warring in his expression. "Tell me . . . tell me it is *you!*"

"It's me, Christopher."

"Jessica!" It was no more than a whisper, a sigh, as he reached for her hands, gripped them with a strength that almost pained her. She was seeing him through a blur of joyful tears, yet what did that matter—she was *seeing* him, in the flesh!

They stood with gazes locked, all else in the crowded ballroom nonexistent to them.

"I dare not believe," Jessica whispered at last. "Can you really be here . . . not just a dream?"

"Do you feel my hands? Flesh and blood—no illusion. How long I have searched every face I have seen, praying— yet so sure I had left you behind!"

"I never knew what to think . . . where you'd gone."

"Not far . . . not far at all, it seems." He moaned, then suddenly drew her against him. "To feel you in my arms again! Jessica . . . Jessica . . . my Jessica . . ." he repeated as his arms tightened across her back. Unaware of anything in the world save the woman in his arms, he sought the soft lips that were awaiting him. He pressed home a kiss of passion—almost of disbelief that Jessica was again with him—a kiss too long dreamed of and one he'd thought never possible again.

She swayed tight into the closeness of his arms, melting into his warm strength, returning his kiss with all the intensity in her being. He was here—at last he was *here!* Nothing else mattered except that they were in each other's arms again—nothing!

10

"Christopher! What is the *meaning* of this? *Who* is this woman?"

Jessica tensed. Christopher, suddenly aware of their surroundings, slowly, reluctantly released her, leaving one arm tight about her waist as he turned to face the accusing voice.

Jessica heard other exclamations from the crowd; saw the Beards' stunned faces. On the black-haired beauty's face, however, there was only cold fury.

Christopher looked directly at Rhea. His voice registered his shock, his total unpreparedness for what had just occurred. "Rhea, I would not have broken this to you in this way had I a choice. This is a woman I thought I would never see again in my life. This is Jessica Dunlap . . . my wife."

If the scene had been babbling commotion a moment before, it was now dead silence as eyes stared, mouths dropped. Then all was uproar again. There was the sound of shattering glass somewhere in the room. The Beards came rushing forward to Jessica, Rhea to Christopher.

Amelia came to Jessica's side, her voice low and concerned. "This comes as such a shock, my dear! I really do not know what to say. Had you no idea? No, of course, you did not . . . but the unanswered correspondence . . . my goodness . . . my goodness!"

Bertram Beard stared at Christopher, waiting to see how events would proceed.

But it was the angry comments of the black-haired beauty to which Jessica's ear was attuned.

"Your wife! What are you saying? I cannot believe this! How dare you so deceive me!"

"Rhea, it was not intentional. Two years ago Jessica and I were most unfortunately separated. I . . . I honestly had given up hope I would ever see her alive again. I should have said something to you before, but it was too painful a subject to me. Had I any idea—"

"Married! And to a serving maid no less—a weak moment in your youth, Christopher?"

"Rhea, I think this discussion would be better conducted in private. I am aware of your shock. Mine is as great."

"Shock? What of my embarrassment—the scandal that will be attached?"

"Please lower your tone! There are others witnessing this conversation, and you will only make matters worse."

Jessica stood listening, her stomach in a sick knot. She'd heard the woman describe Christopher as her fiancé, but only now was it sinking in.

"As if matters *could* be worse," Rhea cried. "You may be sure that when I am through, your name in New York society will be tarnished forever!"

"I am totally in the wrong for not having advised you of the true situation, but nothing is gained at the moment by airing this in public."

"Yes," she said sarcastically, "of course you would not want the details of this intrigue made too public—a melodrama of lost love that will tear at my heart strings, no doubt."

"You will know all in due course."

"Indeed. No wonder you were not anxious to have the announcement of our engagement made in New York just yet!"

Jessica felt her face growing paler with every word of their conversation. This could not be real! This reunion with the man she thought she would never see again should have been wonderful, joyous—not the cause of such a terrible scene. Was she not walking through someone else's nightmare?

Amelia saw Jessica's increasingly dazed expression and

knew it was time she stepped in. Leaving Jessica's side, she went to Rhea and spoke quietly but firmly.

"Mrs. Taylor, I do not mean to interfere. I fully understand your chagrin, but do you not think this discussion would be better conducted in another room where you might be alone? Please, there is a parlor down the hall where you will be away from all these listening ears."

"Yes, Rhea, please," Christopher added in the same reasoning tone. "I will come and talk to you shortly."

"You had best," Rhea hissed, her green eyes flashing, and she shot Jessica such a look of loathing, the latter wished she could make herself invisible. Rhea, her head held high, swept off with Amelia, the stunned onlookers parting mutely to make way for them.

Immediately Christopher turned to Jessica, his grip on her waist tightening. "Jessica, I am so sorry . . . so very sorry."

Jessica could only stare at him.

Bertram Beard intervened. "You both would like to get out of this crowd as well, I am sure. Come with me. You may use my study."

As they hurried from the room, Jessica numbly registered the sight of Elizabeth Beard standing to the side and staring in total astoundment, Rachel behind her with jaw agape, and near the door, Lucas, his expression set, his eyes questioning. Jessica had no time to analyze their reactions; she herself hardly knew what to feel. Here was Christopher, her Christopher. Yet what had she expected? That wherever he'd been, whatever he'd been doing for the last two years, he would have remained as faithful to her memory as she had to his?

Bertram led them to his study, checked to see that the room was empty, then motioned them in.

"No one will disturb you. I or my wife will be nearby should you need us."

"Thank you, sir," Christopher's tone was not as steady as before. "I appreciate this, and my sincere apologies to both you and your wife for the disruption to the party."

"There are certain things in life over which none of us has control. You are all right, Jessica?"

"Yes."

"Then I will leave you. You have much to say to each other. I might add that my wife and I would be most interested in hearing the details of the last years' events as well." The last was said in a slightly warning tone, as though he was imparting to Christopher his skepticism that a man living no farther away than New York had still lost trace of his wife for such a period of time. Turning, he stepped from the room and closed the door behind him.

For a moment neither Christopher nor Jessica moved, then he laid his hands on her shoulders, looked down silently, his eyes moving over every inch of her face. Those blue eyes so vivid had a well-remembered effect on her. She felt her heart beating faster. Still without a word spoken, he pulled her against him, one hand snatching away her mob cap so that he could bury his lips in her hair.

"Jessica, my God, what you must think of me! I don't know where to begin to explain . . . I was so sure I had left you and Kit in the twentieth century." Suddenly he lifted his head. "Our *son!* He is with you?"

"Yes . . . yes, he's here and he's fine—"

"Thank heavens!"

"But where have you *been?*" Her voice felt strangled by the warring emotions she was experiencing.

"In New York . . . only forty miles from here. When I came to my senses, I was in a shabby room on the waterfront. There was a calendar on the wall that told me the date and that I was in New York City. I think I knew before I looked that you and Kit were not with me. I could still envision you in our bedroom with our son in your arms, your hand reaching out to me. It seemed so clear that our hands *had* met, that I had grasped the warmth of your fingers. How I had hoped that contact would keep us together . . .

"I dreamed again and again of this moment—of seeing your face, holding you in my arms—so sure it would never happen . . . so sure I had left you in the twentieth century."

"All this time we've been so *close.*" Her voice was hushed in disbelief.

"You've been in Eastport all along?"

"Yes."

"Jessica, I have been to Eastport before now—in town, along the river! I was going to hire a hack to ride up here to where we used to live—but did not because I was so sure it would only bring me pain. If I had only known!"

"You had no way of knowing."

"You have been all right?"

"The Beards have been good to us."

"Did they not question your sudden appearance in their house? How did you explain?"

"I found myself in the cottage on the property, not the house. There was a new maid due to arrive from New York. They mistook me for her. Fortunately the real maid never came. I told them I had lost my luggage during the journey."

"And Kit—where is he now?"

"Upstairs, asleep."

His voice was trembling. "It has taken me so long to re-sign myself to never seeing you both again. Now you are here—and what have I done to you? My God, I feel a cad and a fool. There is nothing in this world I would do to hurt you, yet it seems I have succeeded quite well in doing just that!"

She drew away so that she could look up at him; saw the pain and remorse on his face. It touched her deeply, but she had to know the facts about him and the other woman.

"This Rhea—"

"Oh, Jessica. It hardly makes me look better to say this, but I do not love her; I never did. Until I met her, I saw no women in New York—had no interest in doing so. They weren't *you*, and you were all I wanted. In the beginning I was numb, only going through the motions of living. Maw-son, a man who befriended and helped me, found me a job at the docks. It was not until a year later that I made any attempt to start a business of my own. After I did, it occupied all my energies. My business contacts brought me out into the social world of New York. Still I had no in-terest in forming an attachment with any woman. Then about six months ago I met Rhea. We drifted into a relationship. She was attractive, and quite obviously interested in me. I knew what *she* wanted, knew, too, that a good marriage could strengthen my business standing, and I allowed us to slide toward that commitment. But I was doing it with the knowledge that I could never feel for another woman what I feel for you. Can you understand how it happened? How, despite it all, you and Kit were—would always be—closest to my heart? . . . Every word I have just spoken is the truth, if you can believe me."

Jessica was silent. Another man might spout words to rationalize his behavior and not mean a one, but it was not in the nature of the Christopher she'd known and loved to lie so blatantly. And there'd been such honest joy and wonderment in his expression when he'd known that indeed it was Jessica he'd found. It hurt her that he'd been so close to another woman, but she could understand how it had happened.

"Yes, I believe you," she said at last. "Those who were close to me here thought I should look for another man, too. There was the child to raise."

"But can you find it in your heart to *forgive* me—to truly believe I love *you* . . . have never ceased doing so and never will!" He hesitated, his voice tight. "Do you remember that first meeting of ours? Two people from two different worlds feeling awkward, not quite certain what to say or do? I feel that way now."

"After being without you for so long, afraid I'd never know real happiness again, all I want to think of is that we're together and have a new future."

He moved his fingers softly against her cheek. "If anything, you have grown more beautiful, both within and without. I will do anything I can to prove myself to you. Oh, Jessica . . ."

Gently he lifted her chin. Then his mouth was seeking hers, finding it, covering it, possessing it, coaxing alive in Jessica a fire she'd forgotten existed. As many times over the last years as she'd remembered the embraces she and Christopher had shared, this moment of feeling his lips on hers was a new experience—a wonderful one . . . warm, overwhelming!

"I have waited for so long to feel this way again." He pulled her closer as though he would mold her body to his own, prevent the chance of their ever again being separated.

"So many times I didn't know if I had the strength to go on," she cried. "If not for Kit . . ."

"Hush, I am here now, and pray God I will never be apart from you again! Come, sit down. You are trembling."

"Finally, Christopher . . . I'm finally realizing it's real."

He led her to the couch, and, drawing her down beside him, kissed her once more deeply; held her in a protective cocoon, his lips pressed against her brow, until finally she ceased shaking.

"You should know," she said quietly after a moment, "that when the Beards wondered at my arriving alone with a child, I told them that my husband was out to sea; that I had run out of money and taken this job, leaving word at our lodgings in New York where you could find me when you returned. After the war, when you never came and I never heard from you, they all presumed you were dead."

"For all the good I have done you, I might as well have been."

"You had no choice over that."

Christopher's arms tightened. "Still, how are we to explain my absence? We obviously cannot tell anyone the truth—yet they *know* I have been in New York all this time."

"We could say that when you returned from the war and went to our boarding house, the building had changed hands; the previous owners were gone, and the message I had left for you was gone with them. You talked to the neighbors and advertised in New York, but you had no idea to look for me in Connecticut. In the end you had to presume I'd died or, thinking you dead, I had left. Since you had to find another place to live, that would explain why the letter Amelia Beard made me send to New York was returned."

"Yes, it fits in nicely, though I feel it makes me look the cad for not having pursued you further." He smiled down at her. "As I most certainly would have done were that story the truth. Unfortunate that we cannot *tell* them the truth."

She fingered the pearl stud in his shirt front. "What are you going to tell . . . her?"

"The same."

"Do you think she will take it well?"

"No. I can only hope she will be calmer now."

"You were to go back to New York tonight?"

His color deepened at the question. "I have accommodations at the inn in town. She can spend the night there, and I will have my schooner bring her back in the morning."

"Your schooner?"

"Yes, one of the three I use for my business. He paused, shook his head. "There is so much I still must tell you . . . ask you . . ."

He was interrupted by a knock on the door.

"May I come in for a moment?" The voice was Amelia Beard's. "I must speak to you."

Christopher quickly rose, opened the door.

"My apologies for intruding, but Mrs. Taylor is asking for you. She wishes to leave. I have offered her a room, but she has declined, and would like to speak to you."

Christopher nodded, then turned to Jessica, on the couch. "Do you mind? I will return in a moment."

"No, go ahead."

"If you will point me the way, Mrs. Beard."

"Just down the hall, first door on the right. I will stay with Jessica."

"Thank you."

Christopher gave Jessica a long, apologetic look, then slipped out the door.

Amelia came to the couch. "This is a night of upheaval —to the rest of us as well—but I do want you to know how happy we are for you." Her eyes probed Jessica's. "You *are* happy?"

"Very." Jessica smiled, radiantly.

"Not that I wish to pry, but just what happened? There is this other woman claiming him to be her fiancé. Why is it he never contacted you from New York? But it is perhaps none of my business . . ."

"But it is. You and Mr. Beard deserve to know the details. He did not know I was here. Our old lodgings in New York had changed owners. The message I had left there for him had been lost—overlooked, perhaps, or even callously disregarded by the new people. He searched for us, but none of the neighbors knew anything—they moved in and out so frequently, I was never close to any of them—nor did he get any response to the advertisements he placed. After months went by with no word, he could only think we had deserted him . . . or died. But we have had so little time to talk . . ."

"I realize, my dear." She shook her head. "My, what a difficult situation!"

"I don't mean to keep you from your guests."

"They will doubtless not even miss me. I want to make arrangements for you and your husband this evening. I thought the Hayden girl could move in with Elizabeth, which would leave your room free."

"Please don't put anyone out."

"What, and send your husband off to the inn with that woman?" Amelia wrinkled her brow. "Society she may be, but not to my taste. And some reunion that would be for you."

Jessica had to smile. "Elizabeth may be upset."

"The child will survive. I have a feeling she may need some consolation this evening, in any case. That Terrence has been spending more time with a certain other young woman than he has with my daughter."

"Yes, Elizabeth spoke to me briefly. She was upset."

"I will talk to her. I fear we have sheltered her so much that she has not before had to face many of life's disappointments."

"Mrs. Beard, I realize how awkward this is for you and your husband, but I want to thank you both—for everything."

"One good turn deserves another. You have been good to us, a hard worker with never a complaint, and that son of yours has certainly been a bright light in the house. I only hope all works out well for you."

"It will."

Amelia patted her arm. "I will go talk to Elizabeth and have Nan move the Hayden girl's things."

"Oh—I forgot Rachel and Nan. They can't manage everything alone!"

"They can. Our guests will not suffer unduly if some of them have to find their own refreshments. You and your husband may go whenever you wish . . . no need to come back to the ballroom. I will explain to the others."

"Again, Mrs. Beard . . . . thank you."

Amelia rose. "Well, good night, my dear. We can talk further in the morning, but you have our best wishes."

Jessica waited another twenty minutes before Christopher reentered the room—twenty minutes during which she paced about, pondering the situation and her reactions. She wondered what was going on in the other room between Christopher and Rhea; not for a moment did she think Christopher was having an easy time of it. How far would this Rhea go in her anger? Had she meant what she said about blackening Christopher's name and reputation? Still, Jessica felt sorry for the woman, knowing she, too, would feel the anger of betrayal were their situations reversed.

Christopher had entered the room down the hall to find his former fiancée pacing the carpet. She swung on him at the sound of the closing door.

"Well, it is about time you came! I was wondering if your presumed honor had altogether deserted you. But, of course, you have much catching up to do with your newly found *wife!*"

"Rhea, I do not know how to begin to explain to you. I realize my behavior was deplorable, but I never thought I'd see Jessica or our son again."

"A son!"

"Yes, we have a son."

"As though it were not bad enough to suddenly discover

a serving maid wife in the background, you also have a child! What kind of man are you?"

"One who is very sorry at the moment for the embarrassment I have caused you. It was during the war, before I'd started my business. I had left Jessica and the child in the city." He went on to outline the story he and Jessica had concocted. "I did not know where to look for them, could only guess that they had died or, thinking *I* was dead, left to find another life . . ."

"Yes—and then your miraculous reunion this evening. A truly touching tale. Could you not have had the decency to tell me earlier at least a part of this?" Suddenly her eyes narrowed. "Or perhaps you were actually hoping you might never see them again? Your life has changed drastically since you connected yourself to this woman. Perhaps you realized you required a more sophisticated mate in your present circumstances?"

"Not so! Jessica possesses all the qualities I desire in a woman, and she has not always been a serving maid. That was a fate brought on by necessity."

"Was it indeed? What of her family? Why did she not turn to them?"

"She has none."

"The tale becomes more interesting all the time." There was a coolly calculating glint in her eye. She smiled, but without warmth. "Well, I am not about to make a fool of myself over this affair. You have already succeeded in doing that quite nicely."

"I am *truly* sorry. Never willingly would I have exposed you to this evening's events."

"You will be bringing her to New York, I take it."

"In due course."

"That should be interesting. Do not expect me to pave a smooth road for you."

"I would not expect that. I shall do whatever I can to make this as little embarrassing for you as possible."

"It is a bit late for that—and I am quite capable of taking care of myself, thank you. If I am not mistaken, that strength of mine is a characteristic that initially attracted you." She stared at him levelly. "There is nothing further

I wish to discuss with you, Christopher. At least not this early in our little game. I have a ride waiting to take me back to town, and I trust you will make your schooner available to carry me to New York in the morning."

"Yes, most assuredly."

"Then I will wish you good luck with this precious domestic endeavor," she said, her tones dripping acid. "Although I quite frankly wonder whether you may not soon be regretting the events of this evening, or finding yourself sadly bored and discontent. Do not be surprised if you discover, as most men do, that I am not all that easy to forget." She walked proudly past him, opened the door, and disappeared down the hall.

Jessica turned as Christopher came quietly through the door and came toward her where she stood by the fireplace. Without preamble he took her in his arms and heaved a sigh.

"She is gone—taken a carriage back to the inn in town. In the morning my schooner will take her back to New York. I will have to go to the dock tomorrow and give instructions to the captain."

"How did it go?"

"Not well. She was calmer, but hurt and angry . . . with just cause."

"Will she carry out her threat to ruin your name in New York? Can she?"

"She could make a good attempt, although, honestly, I do not know what she will do. We will face that when we come to it. The truth will come out in any event—whether from her lips or my own. Obviously, I would prefer my side of the story to be made known."

"I spoke to Amelia Beard while you were gone, telling her as briefly as possible the story we'd agreed on."

"Good. That should help appease the curious, though we are still bound to meet with skepticism."

"She's also set aside a room for us tonight."

He smiled down at her, his arms holding her more tightly for a moment. "Even better. Shall we adjourn there, where no one will interrupt us? But of course first I

must see our son! There were so many times in New York
when I would see a child Kit's age. How it tore me apart,
wondering how you both were."

"You shall see him. He's grown to look so much like
you." They began moving toward the door. "We'll use the
servants' stairs. No one will see us."

The winding stairs were well lit, and soon they were
walking hand in hand toward the end of the narrow attic
hallway.

"You won't believe how he's grown, Christopher. He's
such a good boy, and so bright. He amazes me sometimes."

"Any son of ours," he chuckled, "must be a bit ahead of
his time. Do you not agree, Mrs. Dunlap?"

"Unequivocally." Before entering the room, where
Mary's nurse was watching the children, she knocked
lightly on the door. "It's Jessica, Emma." She pushed the
door open and led Christopher in.

The nursemaid sat by the fire, her knitting in her lap.
She smiled. "He's sound asleep . . . a good boy, this evening."

"I'm glad. I would like you to meet Kit's father, Christopher Dunlap." Since Emma probably had no knowledge of
her background, Jessica explained no further.

"Pleased to meet you." Emma nodded.

Jessica was already walking over to the small cot where
Kit lay on his back, his chubby arms thrown over his head
on the pillow. She bent and gave him a gentle kiss on his
sleep-flushed cheek. He stirred slightly, but didn't waken.

His father now, too, leaned over the cot, and Jessica was
moved to the core by the expression on Christopher's face—
the joy, the pride, the amazement that this sturdy lad was
his son. Yet there could be no question of that. Jessica
could remember a portrait of Christopher at about Kit's
age that had hung in the gallery at Cavenly, and the child
was a mirror image of his father's younger self.

"Do you want to wake him?" Jessica whispered.

Christopher was still gazing down. When he spoke, his
voice was husky. "No, he is too peaceful. Tomorrow morning will be a better time for us to become reacquainted."
Smiling gently, he reached down and touched his fingers

to his son's cheek. "My dearest love, you have done a fine job. You and Kit make me proud . . . and humble, that you have had to do it alone."

"But you're here now."

He reached for her hand. His eyes, as he turned them to her, spoke volumes. "Yes, thank heaven."

Christopher was thoughtfully silent as they retraced their steps to the first door along the hall. He remained so as Jessica preceded him in and lit the candle on the night table. The room was warm, the fire glowing dimly.

"This is the room Kit and I share when there are no entertainments going on."

"It seems comfortable," Christopher said, looking around. "But I would have wished more for you than this."

"If not for the Beards, I dread to think of the situation Kit and I might have been in."

"I would rather not think of that. I owe them a debt of gratitude." He followed her as she went to the side of the room to hang her apron on the hook, and his arms went around her waist from behind. He pulled her against him and nestled his lips against her neck. Covering his hands with her own, she leaned back into his warm embrace.

"You feel so wonderful," he sighed.

"It feels wonderful to be here." She turned, still in his arms, and placed her own arms about his neck. Her eyes were bright with happiness, her mouth softly smiling. "I didn't realize quite how empty and aching I *was* . . . have been . . . until an hour ago."

"I know. How often I have tried to make myself forget how good things can be with the right person . . . will be again for us. We have so much time to make up for. There is so much I want to do for our son, for all of us."

She gently traced her finger down his cheek, over his lips.

He moaned, drawing her more tightly against him. Hungrily his mouth found hers, with a passion that was tender, speaking of a deep, overwhelming love. Their lips parted, their tongues touching, seeking. Their desire for each other rose quickly, welding them together. It was not only their bodies meeting and speaking to each other, but some part of their inner beings, too, making the two of them one whole.

Christopher's breathing was deep as he cradled her, his lips now against her cheek. "We have not talked . . ."

"There will be time."

"So much has been left unsaid . . . but I want you, Jessica. I need you."

"Yes . . . oh, yes."

His hands dropped to her hips, pressing her to him. She could feel his need, and his very tangible desire aroused her further.

His eyes were clouded with passion; his voice a husky entreaty as he spoke to her.

"Let me unbutton your gown. It has been too long since I had the pleasure of undressing my wife." His fingers slipped the buttons, then his palms were against the bare skin of her back, easing the material off her shoulders. She helped him, pulling her arms from the sleeves, and the garment slid to the floor. He turned her again as his hands went to the front lacings of her camisole. She heard his breath catch, saw his eyes widen with desire as the material separated and her breasts slipped free. But as though heightening his anticipation, he didn't touch her yet. His eyes remained on her breasts as his hands finished the work of drawing off her undergarment; then he turned his attention to the ties of her petticoat, loosening the drawstring so that it, too, fell to the floor, leaving her naked. He picked her up in his arms, and sat her on the edge of the bed, then pulled off her shoes and stockings. The sensuous touch of his hands on her bare calves and feet sent a tingle up her spine. Then he rose and, as she watched, began undressing himself: first the evening shoes and white stockings, then the fitted jacket, which he draped over the back of the chair. With controlled haste he pulled loose his neck cloth, unbuttoned his shirt and shrugged it off his broad shoulders. Jessica felt her excitement mounting to see his muscular, dark-haired chest again, his narrow waist. Her eyes were riveted to his hands as they went to the fastenings of his breeches. Her senses reeled as she viewed the

exquisite body she'd so often longingly envisioned in her
dreams, day and night, the last two years.

In a second he was stepping toward her on long, trim
legs, standing before her, reaching out his hands to take
hers and draw her up at arm's length from him. Only now
did he allow his hands to touch and caress her as they
moved with feathery lightness over the contours of her
waist and hips, up to her breasts. There they lingered, his
thumbs gently rubbing her aching, hard nipples, teasing
them and sending waves of pleasure down to her belly,
heightening her already trembling need for him.

"Yes," he moaned as her hand reached out. "Touch me."
He gave a long sigh as her fingers began to caress him. He
watched her, then he lowered his own hand into the moist
softness between her legs.

"Christopher . . ."

He circled his arms around her and brought her body up
against his naked flesh, then, with his hands on her buttocks, he lifted her. Her legs gripped him tight about his
waist; her arms slipped around his neck as he eased her
hips up and a few inches away from his own until the head
of his staff was touching her, ready to enter the welcoming
warmth of her womanhood.

"My love . . . oh, my love," she sighed when, for a moment, he held her thus, and they stared into each other's
eyes.

Then he gently lowered her hips, and slowly his manhood filled her.

"My God, Jessica . . ." He gasped. Briefly his eyes
closed. They opened again to passion-hazed slits. His
mouth sought hers, and as their tongues licked at each
other's, his hips slowly began gyrating, round and round,
side to side; his hands on her buttocks moving her with
him . . . lifting her so his staff slid the length of her pas-
sageway, then pressed home once more . . . over and over.

Jessica's senses whirled in delightful dizziness from the
pleasure he was bringing her. A muffled cry of joy escaped
her throat at the feel of his loving pressure within her. She
wanted the feeling to go on forever—never cease.

Then carefully, gradually, he was lowering her back

onto the bed. She heard him groan as his staff momentarily slipped from her body, but soon he was over her, lowering his weight, pressing deep within her again, molding his body into hers.

His ragged breaths brushed against her cheek as his movement stilled for a moment. She lay quiet beneath him, understanding the pause, holding her body motionless. Yet she could feel her own flesh throbbing from the contact, aching for an intensification of the sensation that left her quivering for him. They had waited too long for this union; suffered through too many unfulfilled hours, dreaming of being joined to each other just as they were at this moment. It could not progress slowly this time; it had to rage forth in an explosion of passion too long suppressed.

Without her conscious volition, her hips pressed up to him, began to slide ever so gradually side to side. Her hands on his lower back urged him ever closer, coaxed him. "Christopher . . . Christopher . . ."

At her breathless words, he shivered. The pleasure was no less for him. The sight of her lovely face, her sweet warmth beside him after so long, brought a fullness to his soul; a softness that was yet building to a crescendo that roared and crashed within him. He wanted to hold back as long as he could to prolong the pleasure for both of them, yet his body moved uncontrollably within her, pressing, then thrusting again and again. He couldn't stop the crescendo now. He felt himself being pulled closer and closer to sheer ecstasy, her responses heightening his tremendous excitement—until he was over the edge, crying out at the unfathomable intensity of his orgasm. With no other woman could he reach such heights: with no other would he ever want to try.

His cry was sweet music to her ears; a perfect accompaniment to her own responses and to the overflowing love she felt for this man. As she let her hands play over the still-tense muscles of his back, she could only think how right it was that they be together, as though nature had created each of them with this union in mind. She loved lying entwined with him, hearing his breathing in her ear, feeling the throb of his pulse where her lips touched his neck, sensing a mental bond between them as strong as or stronger than the physical one.

His lips were moving against her hair, gentle kisses; his voice, still laced with emotion, was whispering, "What you do to me, sweet wife . . . From now on I intend to love you until you cry halt."

"Beginning tonight?" she whispered with teasing suggestion. Her fingers caressed the thick hair at the nape of his neck.

He chuckled. "A promise I gladly make, if you will but allow me to recoup myself."

"With pleasure, my lord."

" 'My lord' . . . now there is a salutation I have not heard in a long time, my countess." His expression suddenly grew serious. "I have often wondered these last years what you would tell our son about my former life."

"The truth, when he was old enough to understand, and possibly believe. We agreed on that after he was born."

"I remember, but circumstances were different then. If we had not found each other, and you had been left alone, it might have been wiser to let the boy believe his father had led a more normal existence."

"There is still *my* past life in the twentieth century."

"The fear is always with me, Jessica, that what has happened before will happen again. Before this evening, I hoped that if I was again swept through time, the journey would bring me back to your side. Now, once more, I am afraid at the thought of separation from you."

"Don't talk of it! Not yet! Please . . . I have only just found you."

"What is life doing to us? Are we destined to live out our days in constant fear that each moment together may be our last?"

"At least we appreciate more than other people those moments of happiness we have, knowing how fragile each is and how swiftly it can be blown away."

"My wise, sweet wife. How I have missed you." Carefully he slid his weight from her. "Come, let us get beneath these covers, and then we must talk. I want to know everything!"

And with the quilt warm and snug about them, they talked, Jessica telling him of her life with the Beards, her work as a maid, the adjustments she'd had to make to living in his century, the desolation she'd so often felt, the gradual dying of the hope that she would ever see him again. And he told her about New York, his work on the docks, his friends Mawson and Bayard; how, through his knowledge of the future, he started a successful business.

"Did you ever think of going back to England?" she asked.

"The temptation was there. But we knew the future, knew that I never reclaimed my title. If I had gone back, it might very well have changed the course of events—something I could not risk doing. Better that I make another life for myself in New York. And if I had gone back, this reunion might not be taking place!"

She cuddled closer to him. "Where will we go from here?"

"I have a house in New York. I share it with Mawson, but there is more than enough room for all of us. I think you will like it, Jessica, for the time. Then perhaps, if we can find a nice piece of land, we can build a house for ourselves here in Eastport. I could easily oversee the business from here, and I would prefer Kit to grow up in the country."

"So would I, but can we afford something like that?"

He smiled. "You need not worry about money any longer. I intend to surround you with luxury to make up for these last two years of suffering."

"It hasn't been so bad. The suffering has been mostly mental, not physical."

He pulled her closer. "I wish to do something about the mental suffering as well."

Later, their questions for the moment answered, they made love again, more leisurely, completely; and finally, both content beyond measure, they drifted to sleep in each other's arms.

As Jessica woke that next morning to a room of bright

winter sunlight, she knew immediately that this day was different; and Christopher's arm resting in the curve of her waist gave proof of that. Through still-hazy eyes she gazed at his sleeping face, scant inches away on the pillow, and was filled anew with joy, with wonderment that he was with her again—that she could reach out her hand and touch his flesh, cherish with more than memory's eyes the well-loved features, from the wide brow, partially covered now by curling locks of dark hair, to the square chin accented by its deep, shadowed cleft.

As she lay there letting her mind slowly come awake, she heard a light tapping at the door, a child's tentative voice.

"Mama . . . Mama . . . you 'wake?"

Carefully, so as not to disturb Christopher, Jessica slipped from the bed, took her robe from the peg on the wall, and went to the door. Kit was standing just outside, expectantly. He thrust out his arms when he saw her.

"Kit, what are you doing here? Did you sneak away from Emma?"

"Mama, I missed you. You not come for me and I wait . . ."

Jessica knelt down and drew the two-year-old close. "Ah, sweetheart, I'm sorry. I didn't wake up as early as I thought I would."

The door at the end of the hall opened suddenly, and a worried-looking Emma peeped out. Jessica called to her. "He's here. I'll take him now, thank you."

"Stepped out so quick, I didn't even see him."

"That's all right." Jessica smiled, and Emma retreated.

"I have a surprise for you, Kit," she said quietly, again addressing the child.

" 'Prise?" The child's eyes widened. "What 'prise?"

"A very special one, sweetheart." She paused, wondering how best to phrase the news that could only come as a shock to the child. "You remember me talking about your father, don't you?"

Kit nodded. "He went 'way on boat."

"Yes. Well, the surprise is that he's back. He came last night."

The child only stared at her, not fully understanding.

"He is here, Kit . . . in the bedroom, and very anxious to see you again."

"Don't 'member father." The boy sounded slightly alarmed.

"No, you were much too young when he left. But he's a very nice daddy, and he loves you. You'll like him very much. Do you want to meet him now?"

His arms hugged her more tightly. "I want stay with you."

She laughed. "You will stay with me, but from now on your father will be with us, too. We'll all be a family again."

"Like Anne? She has daddy. They live same house."

"Yes, like Anne. Won't it be nice to have a daddy of your own to do things with?"

Kit's eyes told Jessica that curiosity was getting the better of the child now; but still he hesitated.

"Come, I'll hold your hand. You know there is nothing to be afraid of in meeting your father."

Jessica pushed the door open and led Kit forward. "He's still sleeping," she whispered.

Kit's eyes, wide as saucers, looked toward the bed, but he remained silent.

"I'll wake him up."

"He be mad."

"No, he won't. Come, I'll show you." Determinedly she led Kit forward, stopped at the side of the bed, and leaned down to kiss her husband's cheek. "Christopher?"

"Mmmm."

"Christopher, it's Jessica. Wake up. There's someone here to see you."

"Jessica?" he mumbled, his eyes still closed.

Gently she shook his shoulder. The blue eyes opened a slit, and peered up at her. She saw startlement in them for a moment, then a gleam of happiness. "Jessica! You *are* here," he said drowsily. "I thought for a moment it was only another dream."

"I'm here."

He reached out for her. "Why are you out of this warm bed?"

"For a very good reason. I have a visitor for you. Your son."

She drew the child closer to the bed, and Christopher, immediately alert, quickly sat up.

Father and son stared at each other. Then Christopher, smiling widely, reached out his arms. "My, what a fine, handsome boy you are! But what are you doing down there? Come up here on the bed with your lazy father so I can get a good look at you."

As Jessica watched, Christopher took his son's chubby hand. "Here you go. Jump up, and we will make a place for your mother, too."

Kit climbed up and sat cross-legged on the coverlets, cautiously facing Christopher, while Jessica squeezed herself in at the edge of the bed.

"I have been thinking very much about you while I was away," Christopher began, trying to put the child at ease. "If I did not know better, I would think you much older than two . . . are you sure that is all you are?"

Kit nodded solemnly. "Just had birthday."

"Of course you did. How could I have forgotten! And what does a grown-up boy like you do on the farm all day? Do you fish? I see you have a river near by."

"Sometime Lucas take me. Too cold now."

"Indeed. But when it was warmer, did you catch many fish?"

Kit nodded vigorously this time. "This big." He held out his arms indicating a catch almost as large as himself.

Christopher suppressed his grin. "My! I do not know that I have ever gotten one so large myself. And what else do you do at the farm? I remember when I was your age I had a lovely dappled pony named Gray Boy."

"Don't have pony. Ride Nellie."

"The farm workhorse," Jessica explained. "Though of course Kit needs a little assistance."

"Then we will have to get you a pony of your own, will we not?"

"Pony? Oh, yes! Keep in barn with Nellie. Can I, Mama?"

"Yes, though I don't know about keeping it in the barn here. We'll be getting a home of our own, which will be even better."

"But *I* like farm, and Molly and Jeb and Lucas and Aunt 'Melia!"

"I know you do, and we'll see them, but you're going to like where we're going, too. Your father has a house in New York, and there will be all kinds of new things to see and do, and someday soon we'll build a house here in Eastport."

"Wait until you see all the exciting things in New York, Kit," his father added quickly. "There are two forts—with real soldiers—and tall buildings and ships. I'll take you on one almost as long as this house, with two tall masts and sails—"

"Like boat in picture, Mama?"

Jessica brightened. "Yes, like the one hanging in the downstairs hall."

The child was now regarding his father with decided interest. "Big boat. When we go?"

"Soon. As a matter of fact, I can take you today, if you would like. I have to go down to Eastport to see my schooner off. Although we cannot go sailing today, I will take you on board."

Kit's expression grew eager, excited. "Yes?" He looked to his mother in question.

"You don't have to ask, sweetheart. If your father wishes, of course you can go. Would you like to?"

He nodded, glancing shyly at Christopher.

Smiling his delight, Christopher laid his hand on his son's small shoulder. "Then we will go. You will have to dress warmly. It will be cold on the water."

Something suddenly occurred to Kit. "You go, too, Mama?"

"No, I have things to do here, sweetheart. And this is a man's trip—for big boys, not ladies."

That information impressed the child. He nodded importantly and started to scramble from the bed. "I go get hat and coat."

Jessica laughed. "Do you think maybe first we should give your father a chance to get dressed and have his breakfast? But come on, I'll bring you to Emma and she **can** help get you into some warmer overalls and a sweater. Then we'll all go down and have breakfast."

"All right."

As Jessica rose and went to the small dresser to remove a few articles of Kit's clothing, the boy remained on the bed and, more courageous now, began asking his father questions about the "big boat."

Listening to their conversation, Jessica felt a throb of relief. The ice had been broken, the awkwardness between them all but banished. For all the days he would remember of his short life, Kit had been dependent on her alone, and she'd had her fears about his acceptance of a father he'd never known.

"Are you ready, young man?" she said now, at a break in their conversation.

Kit nodded and slid from the bed.

Christopher was still smiling, his eyes on Kit. "I will see you soon."

"Little while." Kit grinned and followed his mother from the room.

When Jessica returned, Christopher was up and already partially dressed.

"My, you are an elegant sight at nine in the morning," she teased.

"The Beards will forgive me, I hope, for this evening dress, but my luggage is all at the inn." He finished buttoning his shirt, then held out his arms to her. "Come here, temptress. You have yet to give me a good morning kiss."

Jessica gladly flew to his arms, and even more gladly raised her head for the warm pressure of his lips—a pressure whose passion grew quickly. He sighed. "Were it not for our waiting son, I would be most delighted to take you back to that bed, madam. However, I will save that pleasure for later."

She grinned up at him, then rested her head on his chest. "It went well with Kit, don't you think?" she said quietly. "He was so shy at first . . ."

"As could only be expected. After all, it was a very difficult experience for him to meet his father for the first time—what to Kit seems the first time—at the age of two. I am delighted with him, Jessica . . . more so than I can put into words. This is truly a beautiful morning."

"The first of many. It's good that you're taking him with you today."

"You do not mind being left alone?"

"It's better that you two have a chance to get to know each other."

"What a difference twenty-four hours can make! To think that such a short time ago my approach to life was little more than a matter of getting through one day and into the next. Now there is something really worthwhile to build for again."

When, a few minutes later, they arrived downstairs, their first order of business was to meet with Amelia and Bertram Beard. Christopher reiterated the events that had occurred over the last two years, explaining why he had not been able to contact Jessica before now. He told of their plans for the future, entailing a move to New York.

Despite Bertram Beard's initial skepticism, once he had heard Christopher out, he offered them what assistance he could; his wife, though she repeated over and over how they would miss Jessica and Kit, was bubbling with excitement. Later, at the breakfast table, Elizabeth's reaction could better be termed shock. All during the meal her eyes moved back and forth between Christopher and Jessica, her expression registering disbelief. Jessica could almost read the girl's thoughts—amazement that there *had* been a husband; a touch of envy that this handsome, articulate, well-established gentleman was he. Elizabeth was very subdued.

Immediately after the dishes were cleared, Christopher went to the front parlor to pen two letters to Willis Mawson and Robert Bayard, telling them what had transpired.

They would need and deserve to know the details when Rhea Taylor arrived in New York with her startling news, which she would waste no time announcing.

Christopher advised Jessica that while in Eastport that morning he would arrange for the schooner to return in two days' time to carry them all to the city. By then Jessica should have things straightened out with the Beards, and she and Christopher would have her belongings and Kit's packed.

Not until after Christopher and Kit left for the Eastport docks, Kit bundled and proudly sitting beside his father on the driver's seat of the carriage Bertram Beard lent them, did Jessica have a chance to talk privately with Molly. Of all the people at the Beards', it was to this kind, motherly woman that she felt closest.

As Jessica entered the kitchen, Molly held her arms wide. "Ah, child," she said, giving Jessica a hearty hug. "More happy for you I couldn't be. 'Tis just so wonderful . . . and he seems a good man, little I have seen of him. The mistress says he's a gentleman—and to see him and Kit—"

"I know. I'm happier than I can say."

"This calls for a cup of tea and a nice chat. You sit right there and I'll get us each a bit." She bustled off to the hearth and the steaming kettle, continuing to chatter as she prepared the brew in an old china pot. "I heard how he come back to New York and couldn't find you. Someone up there must've been watching out for you, to bring him here to the ball."

"It seems that, doesn't it?" Jessica smiled.

"And what an uproar you put this house in—not that it wasn't worth every minute. Rachel come back to the kitchen last evening looking as though she'd been struck. Can't say it wasn't fair return, after all her coolness to you." The pot now ready, Molly brought it and two cups to the table, sat down, and poured the tea.

"What're your plans now, child? We'll be missing you, but a far happier life you'll have."

"Christopher has a house in New York, and we'll go there for now. We'd like to come back to Connecticut even-

tually and build a house of our own. It will be better for Kit
to grow up in the country."

"Aye, and *that* news pleases me! Hate to lose sight of
you."

"I'd hate to lose touch with you, too. You've all been so
good to me, and I feel guilty going off so suddenly and leaving Mrs. Beard short staffed."

"That's the last thing you should be worrying your head
about. Mistress talked to me this morning. She'll be bringing Rachel up into your place—that ought to bring a smile
to the girl's face for a change—and taking on Nan full
time. It'll work out well, though Rachel'll never have your
way of things . . . then again, I shouldn't be prejudging the
girl."

"Maybe this is the chance she needs."

"Aye. Miss Elizabeth's going to be missing you, too,
much as she'll never admit it. Heard she and her young
man friend had a tat last evening. Nan says Miss Elizabeth hung close to Lucas the latter part of the night. Now
there's a fine man. Maybe her eyes are finally opening to
the fact."

"I hope so. I've felt sad for Lucas. I do hope I'll have a
chance to say good-bye to him before we leave."

"Often wondered if something might develop between
you two. Not that I should be talking—and better now it
didn't. But like I said, we're going to miss you."

"We'll be here to visit. We won't lose touch . . . I promise."

By noon, the last of the overnight guests had departed
and the house returned to a more peaceful state. Jessica
had a long talk with Amelia Beard over the new household
arrangements and, despite Amelia's protests, gave a hand
to help with the post-party cleaning. She needed an outlet
for her happy excitement, and not by nature or experience
was she one to sit by and watch others work. As she moved
from ballroom to kitchen clearing away dishes and silver,
a silent smile stayed on her lips; nothing could displace her
tranquil glow.

Nan came to her to say there was a gentleman in the

front hall who wished to see her. She went out to find Lucas, hat in hand, staring unseeing at one of the paintings.

"Lucas," she called, hurrying forward, a bright smile on her face. "You must be reading my mind. I wanted to speak with you before we left."

He turned, took her extended hands, held them for a moment, studying her expression, but his face was serious. "You're happy, then."

"How could I be otherwise? Yes, I'm very, very happy."

"Elizabeth will be down soon, but I wanted an opportunity to talk to you." His tone rested on the same serious note as his expression. "I thought perhaps you and your husband would want privacy today."

"Christopher and Kit have gone down to Eastport to collect his luggage."

"I have to be honest in saying I am concerned for you. It all happened so suddenly last night—and that other young woman . . ."

"I know, but it's all been settled. She's gone back to New York. You see, he'd given up hope of ever finding Kit and me, Lucas."

"Still . . . strange, to say the least, that he had already formed such an attachment."

"I have to believe him, Lucas. And I do."

"I'm sorry. I don't mean to seem a black cloud. It's only that I think so much of you that I am concerned about your future happiness."

"Everything will be fine. He's a good man, Lucas, and he loves us."

At last he hesitantly smiled. "I must wish you well then. I understand he has a business established in New York."

"Yes. We will be going there temporarily, but would like to come back here and build a home."

"Needless to say, we would all like that." As he studied her face again, Jessica felt the intensity of his gaze; saw in his expression an emotion she had tried in the past to pretend she was imagining. But she wasn't imagining anything now, as Lucas placed his hands on her shoulders, bowed his head. "I am going to miss you." He sighed. His lips loomed ever closer, then suddenly instead he hugged her against him, dropping his cheek to the top of her head.

Perhaps it had been the flash of warning in her eyes that had made him change his course; made him realize that a kiss between them now would forever destroy the pretense that only friendship had bound them.

When he spoke his voice was constricted. "I must say good-bye . . . but not good-bye forever, I hope." He gave her one last squeeze, then, releasing her, let his arms drop to his sides. "Take care of yourself, Jessica."

"And you, Lucas. Take care . . ."

"Having your friendship has meant a great deal to me, although there is no need for me to tell you that."

"No; and the feeling is mutual." Her voice was soft. She sensed that he was thinking as she was—that things might have been very much different between them.

"Well, good-bye."

"Not forever, Lucas."

Then, as though holding a deeper emotion in check, he turned quickly and disappeared through the doors into the parlor.

By the time Christopher and Kit returned from their excursion, Christopher smiling and carrying his overtired son in his arms, Jessica had bathed and dressed in her most becoming gown. Wrapping her cloak about her, she hurried down the back walk to greet them as they descended from the carriage.

"Did you have a good day?"

"Excellent," Christopher beamed. "When Kit is more awake, I am sure he will tell you all about it. We seem to have given life to a budding seaman."

"And the rest of the day's business?"

He grew serious. "I spoke to Rhea. I left Kit in the care of one of my crew while I went to the inn. Rhea's fury has not cooled. She left me with the parting words that I will hear more of this when we arrive in New York . . . and no doubt we shall. I sent off a letter to her father this morning, too, explaining my side of the situation. He is a fine gentleman whose respect I do not wish to lose. . . . Well, enough of that. The good news is that Kit and I are on our way to becoming fast friends.''

Kit stirred now, having regained some of his energy. ''I walk, Daddy. Big boy.''

Jessica lifted her eyebrows at Christopher. ''You *have* made progress.''

Christopher lowered Kit to the ground. ''You may walk, my boy, but after a snack in the kitchen, I think a nap may be a good idea.''

''Not tired. 'Wake now. I saw *big* boat, Mama . . . my daddy's boat. I steered, climbed ropes, Daddy show me where I sleep when we go New York. Where you sleep, too.

''My, it sounds like you had a busy day.''

''Go tell Molly . . . right?''

''Yes, go ahead. We'll be right in.''

When he was gone, running ahead on eager little legs, Jessica took her husband's arm. ''I haven't seen him this excited in a long time.''

''It is such a wonderful feeling for me to be with Kit—to teach him, guide him, hear his boyish questions—as wonderful as having you again.'' Suddenly he cast her a mischievous look. ''You know I, too, feel quite worn from the day's adventures. I wonder if it would be possible for mother and father to sneak away for a bit of a nap.''

''I think that can be arranged.'' She laughed.

''I do not intend to let you sleep, you know.''

''All the better.''

11

A cold, damp breeze blew off the river as they stood bundled on the deck of the schooner, Kit on tip-toes, gripping the rail; his mother and father behind him, each with a hand on one of his shoulders. Despite the cold wind, the sky was clear on that December day, the weather still warm enough that the river was not ice-locked; and in the distance beckoned lower Manhattan Island, clearly etched. It was a picture very different from the one Jessica had viewed in the twentieth century—far more tranquil than the future scene of sky-tickling structures and all-encompassing blocks of brick and stone; but to Kit, who'd never seen such a concentration of buildings and activity, the sight was awesome, as evidenced by his gaping jaw and his efforts to hike himself farther up the railing for a better view. "Careful, sweetheart." Jessica tightened her grip on his shoulder. "I don't think you'd care to go swimming today."

"He will be all right." Christopher said proudly. "We have talked of safety on the ship. So what do you think, my love? Quite a difference from what *you* last saw."

"I almost like this better, but then you know I've always enjoyed things of the past."

"Myself included, I trust." He laughed.

"You in particular, though you're making yourself sound like a relic."

"As long as I do not behave like one."

"Far from it, though I'll be sure to increase your ration of vitamins should I notice any symptoms."

He lowered his voice for her ears only. "Vitamins have not yet been invented, my dear."

"Then cod liver oil. I'll dose you with Kit's tonic."

"An excellent incentive to stay young. Over there"—he motioned with his hand—"just below Trinity Church steeple, is our humble abode. You cannot see the house from the water, although you will be able to see my business offices when we dock."

"Daddy, Daddy!" Kit was tugging on Christopher's coat sleeve, then enthusiastically pointing downriver. "Look! 'Nother boat!"

"Ah, yes, and a fine one. A merchantman, and from her direction, just putting in from overseas. Wait until we dock, Kit, I will walk you and your mother along South Street and you will see more ships than you will be able to count."

They were coming in closer to the docks now, the schooner's captain shouting to the crew. On this occasion Christopher had left the sailing of the vessel entirely in his captain's competent hands.

"How do you think your friends will react to Kit and me?" Jessica was slightly nervous about the upcoming encounters.

"Though the news had to come as a shock to them, they will accept you. Both Mawson and Bayard are good men . . . good friends, and they will like you, if that is what is troubling you—but then again, how could they help but like you?"

"I believe you are prejudiced on that account."

"A shade. But you have nothing to worry about. I hope you will be happy in New York, Jessica. It's far different from the life you are used to, but our stay here is only temporary."

"I'll like it—I am sure of that already."

They stayed on the schooner's bow until the heavy mooring lines were cast over the side to be secured to the dock pilings. Only then did they move midships and descend to the wharf. Their luggage would be brought up in a while by the crew and strapped on to the carriage Christopher had instructed the first mate to hire for their trip to his house. As they moved up the wet wooden planking of the wharf, Kit's chatterings were silenced as he gazed, eyes wide, from one scene to the next, from the line of three-story brick buildings facing South Street, to the tall, trimmed masts standing proud along every wharf and slip. Christopher acted as a tour guide, pointing out the various importers' offices and those of the well-known shippers; and he directed Kit's eyes to some of the finer vessels. Despite the clutter of stacked cargo, and the smell of tar and animal droppings and other litter in the gutters, which even the brisk salt scent in the air could not disperse, Jessica was charmed by the cobbled street; the many-paned front windows of offices; the excitement of errand boys running by; dray wagons rumbling to collect goods; the seamen, off-vessel for a night's revelry, winding their way toward the nearest tavern; the prosperous businessmen, shipowners, and merchants in tall beaver hats and caped greatcoats moving through the crowd, pausing by a vessel or stack of cargo to converse with ship captains and agents. It was all so invigorating.

She wouldn't have minded walking farther, but Christopher reminded her that by now their carriage should be waiting. He turned them back, scooping his son up into his arms as he directed them through the busy crowd, off South Street onto Burling Slip.

"My offices are right up here, Jessica. The carriage should be waiting out front. There is not time to take you through today, but I will bring you and Kit back soon for a tour."

She'd already seen the gilded sign, C. D. Enterprises, hanging over the next doorway. "I didn't realize your offices were so big. You have this whole building!"

"Yes. The upper floors are the warehouse. I do not mean to boast, but it is going quite well."

"I'm proud of you."

"Thank you, my love."

The carriage stood at the curb, the driver next to the horse's head, looking out for them. But before they could approach, a well-dressed man stepped out of the door of

Christopher's office and looked up and down the slip. Seeing them, he waved, his face breaking into a grin.

"Dunlap! I have been waiting for you to pull in. They told me at the schooner that you were out walking."

"Good to see you, Bayard. You received my letter, I take it."

"I did indeed!" Bayard closed the distance between them and took Christopher's outstretched hand. "And quite a surprise. I see you made it home safely." As he spoke, his eyes flashed between Jessica and Kit, curiosity evident in his expression.

"A pleasant trip. I apologize for any shock I caused you. Had I any idea of the events that would come to pass, I would not have kept you in the dark for so long. But let me introduce you. Robert—my wife, Jessica. Jessica, my very good friend Robert Bayard."

Jessica smiled as Bayard took her hand. "How do you do, Mr. Bayard. It's a pleasure to meet you."

"Robert, please, and the pleasure is mine. Your husband has indeed been keeping secrets . . . but charming ones. Allow me to welcome you to New York—welcome you back, I should say. I understand you and your husband once resided here."

"Yes, and I am glad to be back."

"And this, Robert," Christopher continued, a wide smile on his face, "is our son, Kit. Kit, shake hands with Mr. Bayard."

The boy, still held in his father's arms, shyly complied, and Bayard grinned. "I must say, Dunlap, the resemblance is remarkable. How do you do, young man. This must be quite an adventure for you."

Kit, timid with the stranger, only nodded his head affirmatively.

"He quite enjoyed himself on the trip over," Christopher put in. "Had his sea legs right from the start."

Bayard chuckled. "An admirable trait in a son of yours, who will no doubt be in the shipping business one day."

"Have you spoken to Mawson?"

"He came by my office yesterday as soon as he'd received your letter. Your news had taken him off his pace a bit, although apparently you had once mentioned to him some painful episode in your past."

"So I did; I had forgotten. I went into no detail at the time."

"Well, with work going well on the vessel up at Corlears, he will probably be on hand at the house to welcome you. We both realize you all will want time to settle in, but I did think I should come down today to greet you and your refound family."

"That is very kind of you, Robert. Our carriage is waiting to take us home. Why do you not come along to the house with us—or do you have other business?"

"If you do not think I am intruding, I will be delighted to ride with you, but only to your door, then take my leave."

"Come along, then."

In a moment they were all seated in the closed carriage. As Christopher turned to call through the sliding window behind him to tell the driver to proceed, Bayard looked over to Jessica.

"Although your husband says my intrusion is not minded, are you sure you do not object? I realize you must be tired from your journey."

"I do not mind at all. I'm delighted to have you with us, in fact. Christopher's told me what a good friend you have been to him."

"I am flattered that he should think so—and also eaten up with curiosity. Your husband's letter, though detailed, still left my head spinning with unanswered questions. Tell me, this was truly a chance encounter? You have been living with a family in Connecticut, thinking your husband lost at sea?"

"Yes, it was utterly by chance that we . . ."

Jessica and Christopher took turns filling in the gaps in Bayard's knowledge during the following minutes; he from time to time shaking his head in amazement, posing another question.

"Quite incredible," he remarked at the end. "It is a story many would find difficult to believe. Which reminds me of some news I have on another front." The last was said almost to himself.

"What news is this, Robert?"

"I should not have spoken. This is neither the time nor the place to discuss it. Perhaps if I dropped by your house tomorrow?"

"You may speak. Jessica and I have no secrets."

"That may be, but what I have to say will not brighten the mood. Tomorrow would be a better time, and also . . ." Bayard glanced significantly at Kit, who might have been glued to the window, so absorbed was he in the passing scenery. He seemed not to be paying the slightest heed to the adults' conversation.

Just the same, Christopher agreed with the need for caution. "Perhaps you are right. It would be better to finish this discussion later. In any case, I believe I have an inkling as to your news. Pertaining to a warning in my letter?"

Bayard nodded.

"Has Nathaniel Wilson had anything to say?"

"Not to my knowledge, although it might be wise to speak to him at your earliest opportunity."

"I had intended to. I shall call tomorrow." The carriage slowed; stopped. "Well, here we are, Jessica, Kit . . . your new home."

Jessica looked eagerly out the window at the respectable brick dwellings lining the road. Though not an ostentatious area, it was obviously a well-kept one, the sidewalks unlittered, the front doors bearing a clean coat of paint.

Bayard jumped out first, followed by Christopher, who reached up to give Jessica a hand, then lifted his son to the curb.

"This is our house, Daddy?" Kit said excitedly. "Big house . . . but no grass. No trees."

"You will find a nice little yard in the back for play; it boasts a tree or two. And your mother and I will take you to the park, where you will have grass and trees galore. You are sure you will not come in for a moment, Robert?"

"No, I thank you. You will have enough to do without a guest underfoot. Let us speak tomorrow . . ."

"Then thank you for greeting us, my friend."

"My pleasure. Jessica, your husband is clearly a most

fortunate man. I hope you will number me among one of your friends in New York."

"Without question. You'll come and have dinner with us soon?"

"I would be honored."

Christopher grasped his friend's hand. "You and I will talk tomorrow then, Bayard."

"Yes. The three of you, do have a good afternoon." And with a tilt of his hat he set off up the sidewalk.

"Well, my love," Christopher smiled. "Let us get inside before we become chilled."

Christopher unlocked the front door and swung it open, motioning Kit and Jessica into the small front hall; the driver followed on their heels with the luggage. When Christopher had paid the driver and closed the door after him, he turned to pick up his son and put an arm about his wife's shoulders. "Here we are at last, all together in our new home. 'Tis a good feeling." He hugged them both. "I guess Mawson is not about after all . . ."

"Ayuh, I'm here, and good to see you, man." The words were spoken by a husky, dark-haired man who stepped in from the doorway to the right of the hall. "Sure set me back a peg or two with your news." His brown eyes were frankly staring at Kit and Jessica. "So this is your family. Would appear to be one to make a man proud."

"And that it does. Willis, I would like you to meet Jessica . . . my son, Kit."

"Pleasure," Mawson said, extending a large hand to Jessica. "Your husband's sure a tight-mouthed one, keepin' secrets from us all."

"I can imagine you were a bit surprised." She laughed, immediately liking the man and his straightforward honesty.

"Can't say I'm not happy for you—just takes a bit of getting used to." He now went to Kit, still in his father's arms. "Fine lookin' lad. How d'ya do there, son? Mind shakin' a hand as big as this one?"

It was the right approach, and Kit grinned.

"Got the parlor all warmed up for you," Mawson motioned. "Should be nice and cozy by now."

"Then why are we standing here in the hall? Let's go sit down. Jessica, I am sure you would like some hot tea, and what about you, Kit? You are no doubt hungry. I do not know if we have such a thing as a cookie in the house, but I believe Mrs. Hart can find something for you in the larder." Christopher led them forward into the front parlor, its furnishings and color scheme of a masculine aspect. "Ah, there you go, Kit. Let your mother get you out of your jacket and hat, and I will have a word with Mrs. Hart about some refreshments."

He removed his own outer clothing and laid them over one of the chairs, "Mawson, I know you will keep my wife and son entertained." He winked, then departed toward the back of the house.

"Your husband's just funnin' me 'bout my social graces," Mawson explained as Jessica removed Kit's coat. "Pay him no mind."

He again turned his attention to Kit, who was standing in the middle of the room looking about uncertainly. "Got somethin' here, son, I think you might enjoy." He reached up to the mantel and brought down an unpainted wooden model of a ship. "You like boats, I'll bet, like all lads. Brought this one out specially when I heard you was comin'. Copy of the one I'm buildin' for your dad. You come sit down on the carpet here by the fire, and you can play with it."

The boy eagerly took the model with both hands and plopped down on the floor to examine it. "Nice boat."

"What do you say, Kit?" Jessica prompted.

"Thank you."

"Welcome, son. And don't worry about harmin' it. I've no need for it anymore."

Mawson sat down in a chair near Jessica. "That was good of you," she said.

"Always like little ones," he answered shyly, "and figured there wasn't much in the way of play things in this house, bachelor's quarters as it is—beggin' your pardon, was."

"Willis, I hope we haven't inconvenienced you by moving in like this. I realize you share the lease with Christopher."

"Be good havin' you. Kinda quiet 'round here with just two men. And I'm happy for Dunlap . . . haven't seen him in this good spirits since I've known him. The man's been sufferin' . . . wouldn't talk 'bout it, but I always knew there was some sad happenin' he was tryin' to forget. Put all his heart into his business, but a man needs more'n that." He paused. "You and the lad been havin' a hard time of it, I gather, workin' as a household servant."

"It hasn't been all that bad. The worst was the fear that I'd never see Christopher again. It seems almost a miracle that he should have come to that party."

"Know he feels the same. Well, don't worry about me, and movin' into the house here. I'm out more'n I'm in . . . got a lady friend I'm kinda partial to . . . and there's plenty o' room in any case."

"Thank you. Christopher told me how you came to his aid two years ago."

"Kinda thing any decent man would do. Now I know what was troublin' him, makes more sense his tyin' one on that evenin'. Had a bit on his mind."

Christopher stepped back into the room then. "Refreshments will be up in a moment. I also suggested to Mrs. Hart that she might want to come with us full time. She seemed agreeable, and you will need the help, Jessica. So, have you and my taciturn Yankee friend become acquainted?" He grinned.

"We have. Willis was nice enough to give Kit a model ship to play with."

Kit had risen at his father's entrance and was now happily displaying his new toy. "See boat, Daddy. I be careful not break."

Christopher knelt beside him. "I am sure you will. Did you thank Mr. Mawson?"

"Yes."

"Then you go ahead and play while we adults talk, and you will have your snack in a moment." Christopher rose and went over to sit on the couch beside Jessica. "That was good of you, Mawson. That was your working model, was it not?"

"Don't need it anymore. Work's progressed beyond that."

"Excellent. You have been busy."

"As anxious to see this vessel finished as you. First time I've designed one all myself."

"Well, you have done a fine job, and the work is going a lot faster than I ever expected." Christopher reached over and took Jessica's hand. "Tired, my love?"

"Surprisingly, not much, and even less once I have had some tea. I like the house, Christopher, what I've seen of it."

"Do you? That is heartening news." He laughed. "Mawson and I did what we could, but we are neither of us decorators."

"Ain't that a fact." Mawson chuckled. "More a matter of luck the way things ended up." He stretched, began to rise. "Well, I'll say good day to you both. I'm off to Abbey's for dinner."

"There's no need for you to rush," Christopher protested.

"You'll want some time alone, and Abbey's waitin'." Stepping across the room, he went to pat Kit's head. "So long there, tyke."

"Bye, sir."

" 'Twas good speaking with you," he said, looking, still shyly, at Jessica. "And good to have you in the house."

"Thank you, Willis, and good day."

"I'll see you out," Christopher said, and started toward the door with his friend. "I have some questions for you."

After Christopher had seen Willis off, and they had their tea and Kit his snack, Christopher took them on a brief tour of the house—to the kitchen below, through the dining room and study on the first floor; upstairs to his larger bedroom and the smaller one behind that could be given to Kit. The other front bedroom was Mawson's. Everything pleased Jessica, and although Christopher informed her that she should feel free to make any changes she wished, she saw no need, except to find more youthful draperies and a bed cover for Kit's room.

Back in the parlor, Christopher poured them each a glass of wine. Kit, weary now, snuggled up on the couch beside his mother and was soon nodding off to sleep.

"Shall I move him?" Christopher whispered, a soft look on his face.

"No, let him be. With everything so new, he'd rather be with us for the time."

"So what do you think of my friends? I believe they were both highly impressed with you."

"They're both very nice. I can see how you've formed close attachments. Christopher, this news that Bayard spoke of . . . I've been wondering about it. It has to do with Rhea, doesn't it? She's begun talking."

"I am afraid so. When I took Mawson aside before, I asked him if he had heard anything. Robert had told him that the talk is spreading like wildfire and already is all out of proportion to the truth, as is the way with gossip. It would seem I must go talk to Nathaniel Wilson, her father, as soon as possible—tomorrow morning if I can get an appointment. I had wanted to show you and Kit a bit of New York."

"That can wait. This other is far more important. Do you think she can really do you damage?"

"I can answer that better tomorrow."

"But does she really have grounds? I've heard of these breach of promise actions . . ."

"There was no formal engagement, only the verbal commitment between the two of us. It would depend, I suppose, on how far she wishes to press the matter, but why she should wish to do that either, I know not. There is little she could gain. What a foolish mistake I made even to consider—"

"Please, Christopher; there's no need for you to say that. What's done is done. Had we not found each other, I would someday have had to consider marriage again, too."

He took her hand, held it in both of his. "Bayard is right—right beyond measure—about my being a fortunate man. I often think of that special day at Cavenly, when we walked through the park and sat under the trees in that favorite boyhood place of mine. I had just discovered the evidence that seemed to prove I was not going back to my nineteenth century life as the earl of Westerham. We were so sure that the future was safe, that we would be together in the twentieth century for the rest of our lives. I knew that day—as I held you in my arms on lands that once had been mine and would never be again—that none of what I had lost mattered. Just having you made me the happiest man on earth. I still feel the same. Let us pray that this time the future *will* be safe."

"Yes, let us pray."

"I was thinking about the house we will eventually build in Connecticut." He spoke thoughtfully now, staring out across the room. "How would you feel about modeling it after Cavenly? It would have to be much smaller, of course, but of the same stone and similar architectural details . . . perhaps on a piece of land overlooking the Sound."

"Oh, yes! Yes, but could we manage such a project?"

"On a simpler scale, I believe we could."

Jessica was picturing the magnificent structure of Cavenly as she'd first seen it, rounding a curve in the drive on that spring morning two and a half years before. There it stood, verdant green parkland to either side, the graceful gray stone facade rising three stories, the many-paned windows reflecting the sunlight streaming across their surfaces; every line of the house perfect beauty, from the imposing porticoed entry to the fountain that played in the center of the half-moon drive curving before it.

"There is no other home in which I would rather live," she responded simply.

"Then we will plan it. I can draw up the rough designs myself, and we can begin looking for a piece of real estate; perhaps even break ground in the spring."

"Do you think that might be rushing it too much?" She was as enthusiastic as he, but concerned. "If this talk of Rhea's undermines your business . . ."

"Many of the men with whom I do business are out of

town, and I would prefer to look at the optimistic side. You and I have lost two years already."

And they talked of their plans, Jessica letting caution fly away, until Kit began to rouse, and shortly thereafter Mrs. Hart peeked in to announce dinner.

12

Christopher's first mission of business the next morning was to call on Nathaniel Wilson, and he was not entirely pleased with the course of the proceedings. Although willing to hear out Christopher's version of the story, Wilson was tersely cool and disapproving.

"I admit, sir, that my daughter has been a shade out of hand in her comments. However, she has every right to be undone by the whole affair," he stressed. "You were not behaving in an aboveboard manner to neglect advising her of your marriage and the loss of your wife and child. There may have been no formal announcement of your engagement, but you gave Rhea your word as a gentleman. This you yourself admit."

"Yes, I did tell her she could consider herself my fiancée. I realize how wrong I was, and I take full responsibility. I do not wish to make excuses for my actions, but the loss of my wife and child had remained a subject most painful to me—one I did not confide to even my closest friends."

"My daughter has suffered much pain in the past herself. She has lost one husband, and those wounds are barely healed. To be confronted with this second shock when she had implicit faith in you—it is a wonder she has stood up under it all as well as she has!"

"Again, my deepest apologies."

"The fact that you have come here personally to speak to me impresses me; I respect a man who does not hide from unpleasantries. However, that does not excuse your behavior, nor does it make my daughter's situation any more bearable. Since I have never believed in allowing my emotions to interfere with my business sense, our two firms will continue to trade together, although I will be honest in saying that your actions have left some serious doubts in my mind."

"As is only understandable. As much as I would try to assure you that what occurred was not premeditated, or even imagined possible, you have been more generous than I have a right to expect."

"Good day then, sir. I will inform my daughter that you came to speak to me."

Christopher rose. There was nothing further he could do, but at least he had made the effort. Now, only time would tell the damage done to his standing in the realms of business and society. He could stand the slurs to himself; it was for Jessica he feared. She was an innocent bystander in the tangle and deserved not the slightest ostracism. Yet much though he sought to shield her from any cuts, he realized they could not hide themselves away until the storm blew over, if it did at all. Their only course was to get out into society as soon as possible, holding their heads high and confronting the scandal face-on, without shame; otherwise it would appear there *was* something to hide.

Christopher came home disturbed from his meeting, and as he and Jessica sat together over tea, he told her what had occurred.

"I dislike so intensely having to put you through it, my love, but I feel we should make our social bow here in New York as soon as possible."

"I understand, after what you have told me, and knowing the gossip Rhea's spreading." She fingered her teacup, waiting.

"Before I left for Connecticut, Jessica, I received an invitation to a private exhibition of artwork—a charity affair hosted by John Richardson and his wife, with the price of the tickets going to the Trinity Church Orphanage. Only the most prominent in the city have been invited to attend. I believe we should go." He paused, obviously discomfited. "I should warn you that Rhea Taylor will undoubtedly be among the guests. As important as it is that we show our faces, I shall understand if you do not wish to be in the same company as Rhea just yet."

"Since when have I been a coward?" She smiled slightly to take the serious edge off her words. "No, Christopher, maybe I'll be a bundle of nerves, but we'll attend—that is, if the host and hostess don't bar their doors to us."

"The Richardsons—at least Mr. Richardson—would not do that. From what I know of his wife, Celia, she delights in gossip, and although I know her to be a friend of Rhea's, she would be only too pleased to have us make our first appearance together at her reception."

Jessica took her husband's hand and squeezed it. She frowned in thought, then made a decision. "It's settled, then. But I'll need a new gown. Nothing I have is even close to being suitable."

"I was going to suggest that a new wardrobe be one of your first priorities. To see you in these plain, worn gowns," he said, touching the fabric of her skirt, "reminds me too sharply of all you have suffered these last two years. I want the best for you, Jessica, to try to make up for—"

"There is nothing to make up for. You had no more control than I over what happened to us—and you suffered, too. I only mention a gown because I don't know a seamstress; I don't even know if there will be time to have a gown made."

"Mrs. Hart might be of assistance to you. I seem to recall her mentioning a friend of hers who is a dressmaker."

"I'll talk to her before dinner . . . speaking of which, have you eaten?"

"My conversation with Nathaniel Wilson has not enhanced my appetite."

"In all justice, he had reason for what he said, Christopher. If you were in his position, and your daughter was involved, wouldn't you act the same?"

"Most certainly. I do not fault the man. As a matter of fact, I still admire him greatly. *I* am fully at fault for not having told Rhea something of my past, although I do not have to tell you what a ticklish subject *that* would have been." He smiled sheepishly.

"It still amazes me that I never slipped at the Beards, never gave away some information about the future." She shook her head. "Being with you again makes me feel, somehow, that such worries are gone. Of course, they're not. I've realized, these past two years, just what an adjustment you had to make when you arrived in the twentieth century. Since I've been here in the nineteenth century, I've wished so many times for your advice, tried to remember all that you told me—"

"Now I am here to help you."

He laid his other hand over hers. She studied the long, finely shaped fingers, the square nails, the dark hairs across the back of Christopher's hand—a strong hand. How good it was to see that hand on hers again after so many months of her longing to feel the touch of him again. She sighed.

"You might begin your lessons by telling me what to expect at this reception. What will it be like? What should I do?"

"To the last question, do nothing but be your attractive, charming self. We will greet our host and hostess as we enter and will most likely be directed to the drawing room, or wherever the artwork is displayed. There are going to be curious looks and comments directed toward us—that I can guarantee—although I do not believe anyone will go so far as to cause outright embarrassment. I will be at your side, remember, should there be any awkward moments. Also remember that these people are going to be so caught up in their examination of us as principals in the rumored scandal that they will not have time to question you too deeply. You will make a most positive impression. Aside from your beauty, you are intelligent, and speak well; believe me, my love, you have nothing to fear. If there is any nastiness at all, it will be directed toward me, and at the moment I feel very much equal to the battle."

She chuckled. "When you say things with such gritted teeth, I can almost see you drawing swords, or at least pulling a matched set of pistols from a velvet-lined case."

He smiled, for the time relieving his features of their tension. "Twenty or thirty years ago, perhaps; not now.

And I do not really want to risk my life, to lie dying in a field, when I have just been reunited with the one woman who can help make that life worthwhile."

After talking with Mrs. Hart, Jessica found a dressmaker who could have a new gown ready for her with a day or two to spare before the reception. What with fittings, organizing her new household, shopping, and running other errands, Jessica's first week in New York was a busy one indeed.

Christopher had taken them on a tour of the city that first weekend, and Kit had been wide-eyed as they stood on the Battery promenade and his father pointed out the stone fortifications of Castle Clinton and Castle Williams, and the busy traffic in the harbor. Jessica, too, enjoyed the sights, summoning up her impressions of the roaring, rushing street noise and the soaring concrete of twentieth century New York and comparing that remembrance to this quaint and very personable old city.

She was able to put aside her nervousness about their social debut, until the arrival of that evening itself, when she and Christopher were dressing.

He helped her with the buttons of the high-waisted green silk gown delivered from the seamstress the previous afternoon. She turned before the long mirror above the dressing table.

"Do you think it looks all right?" Critically, from all angles, she viewed the lines, the fall of the silk.

"You look marvelous—beautiful! You will have every other woman swooning from envy."

She laughed. "I'm not so nervous that you have to exaggerate." As she spoke, she swung around toward him, and caught such a soft, loving expression on his face that her heart melted.

He stepped across to take her hands. "I do not exaggerate."

"Thank you. And you look remarkably handsome yourself."

His deep-blue, tailed evening jacket seemed molded

across his shoulders; cream-colored breeches clung to his long, slim legs.

"Do you remember," Jessica mused, reaching out to finger the finely woven blue cloth, "that you were wearing a jacket of just this color the day we met?"

"I have not forgotten. I remember well, too, the dress you wore—dotted, and exposing far more of a lady's leg than I had ever seen in public."

"A bit shocked, weren't you?" A grin warmed her face. "And that *next* day, when you first saw me in a pair of jeans!"

"As I recall, that was quite a *pleasurable* surprise. I immediately began to feel that my journey to the future was going to be far more interesting than I had anticipated."

"You tease. As I remember it, your brows lifted nearly into your hairline, though you laughed at me, all the way down the stairs, when I replied that jeans were far less revealing than the dampened muslin gowns that were the rage in your era." She slipped closer into his arms, rubbed her cheek against his lapel. "How long ago all that seems. So much has happened."

"Do you regret any of it? Your life would have progressed far more simply had I not popped into it."

"I regret nothing . . . and never will. What an empty existence it would have been without you."

"But if fate had not crossed our paths in the way it did, neither of us would have known what happiness . . . or tragedy . . . might be ours." He was silent for a moment, lost in thought; then his lips touched her hair. "Well, my love, if we are to make our entrance at this party with any promptness, we had best be leaving."

"You'll stay close by?"

"I would not think of leaving your side."

As they entered the Georgian town house on State Street, a butler and a maid were on hand to take Jessica's warm cape and bonnet and Christopher's cloak and top hat; and they were motioned toward John Richardson, a thin, graying man with a quiet smile, and his wife, Celia. Jessica quickly studied her hostess. A fading blond,

dressed to the height of fashion in a style more appropriate
to a woman in her late twenties than to one in her early
forties, Celia herself was busy assessing Jessica, her sharp
eyes sweeping over her, and the look did nothing to calm
Jessica's already strained nerves.

Celia smiled and greeted Christopher, but her attention
was given over primarily to Jessica. "Good evening, Mrs.
Dunlap. So pleased that you could join us this evening. Allow me to welcome you to New York. You are enjoying our
city?" Her voice was conventionally pleasant, though Jessica sensed the pleasantness was provoked more by curiosity than by warmth.

"Indeed I am. You understand it takes a bit of time settling into a new household, but I am delighted with it all."

The woman was clearly surprised at the educated tone of
Jessica's speech, but hid that surprise quickly. "How nice
to hear. You do not find the city somewhat awesome in
comparison to the Connecticut countryside?"

"Not at all. My husband and I resided in New York for a
brief while some years back, so it is not totally unfamiliar."

"True. And you have a son, I understand. How is he adjusting?"

"Beautifully. I believe he has inherited some of his father's love for the sea. All he can talk about is going down
to the Battery or to South Street to watch the ships."

"And how old is he?"

"Two."

"Yes, an inquisitive age. Well, I hope you will enjoy
yourselves this evening." From the sly turn of her lips, it
was obvious she was skeptical about that being a possibility.

"We shall." Jessica smiled and nodded to the woman as
Christopher led her forward to the drawing room.

He leaned down to speak in her ear. "You handled that
extremely well, my love."

"The real challenge is surely yet to come—but she *was* a
pompous boor, wasn't she, waiting for me to make a slip?
How I wanted to set her back on her heels—and just a few
words of truth would have done it so nicely. 'Yes, the earl

and I are very happy,' or, 'Actually, I find this New York rather rustic and unsophisticated in comparison to the one I used to know, but then you are *years* behind.' "

"And at that I would have loved to see her face!" Christopher didn't try to disguise his laughter. "Never fear, someday you will have your revenge for all this."

As they entered the drawing room, a quick perusal of the room told Jessica that Rhea Taylor was not there. Her apprehension eased a bit—but not entirely, as she noticed the stares directed their way by other guests.

Christopher, too, observed. "Remember I will remain at your side," he whispered.

Although the bulk of the Richardsons' artwork was displayed in the adjacent gallery, several paintings hung on the drawing room walls, and Christopher led Jessica in that direction. As they paused before a Vandyke on loan from the collection of John Astor, Christopher spoke quietly. "I see several businessmen here whom I have spoken to since our return to New York, so I do not think we will be ignored."

"Thank heaven for that. I'm a stranger, but most of these people know you, and to have them act as though we were both invisible . . ."

"To give them the benefit of the doubt, their reticence may be due in part to their momentary shock at seeing us together."

Jessica gave him a wry smile.

As they moved on to view the next masterpiece, Jessica glanced to the doorway just in time to see Rhea Taylor entering—on the arm of none other than Jerome Weitz. Instantly remembering her accidental encounter with Weitz at the Beards' ball and the kindness he'd shown, Jessica found her shock doubled, seeing him escorting Rhea Taylor. Rhea looked magnificent in an elegantly simple gold satin gown that would have attracted attention on its own merits, without the enhancement of the woman who wore it.

"Well, it would appear Rhea has wasted no time in finding another suitable connection," Christopher remarked in a dry tone. "Although I did not realize she and Weitz were well acquainted."

Jessica only nodded, too surprised and disconcerted by the entrance of her husband's former fiancée to think to mention to Christopher that she had met Jerome Weitz.

"A step up for her, actually," Christopher went on to clarify. "Weitz is easily one of the wealthiest men in this city—a banker of some repute."

She heard her husband's words, but her attention was riveted on Rhea as the lovely young woman and her escort moved from the doorway toward a group of acquaintances, who greeted them warmly.

"Their reception is a bit different from ours," Jessica remarked. "It seems the guests have already taken sides."

"Relax. It is early yet." Christopher placed a reassuring hand over her cold fingers where they gripped his arm.

"I know. I feel foolish getting so upset, but seeing her enter that doorway . . . she seems so utterly self-confident, Christopher."

"I have a feeling some of that confidence is only a facade. She has to be feeling as much strain as we are."

"Do you think she will come over?"

"Under the circumstances, I seriously doubt it, and if she should, there is nothing in such an encounter that you are not fully capable of handling."

That Rhea had seen Christopher and Jessica was evidenced by the sly glances in their direction made by the people with whom Rhea was speaking; yet Rhea never looked their way or gave any acknowledgment. Jerome Weitz, already deep in conversation with another gentleman, was not a party to the activity around Rhea.

"Come," Christopher spoke then with almost a sigh of relief. "I see Robert Bayard has arrived. Let us go speak with him and take your mind off the other."

In fact Bayard was already walking toward them, a wide smile on his face. "Ah, my friend, and his beautiful wife —so good to see you." He took Jessica's hand, his appreciation evident in his eyes. "I cannot tell you how delighted I am to see you both here this evening." The full meaning of his words escaped neither of them. "A wise decision on your part, Dunlap, although a trifle uncomfortable, I would suspect."

"A trifle, but I thought this our only course."

"Indeed. And how is everything going with you, Jessica?" he said, turning slightly to face her. "This evening apart, you are still favorably impressed with this city of ours?"

"Very much so."

"And the boy? How is he adjusting? It is easy to imagine that the move and the events leading up to it might feel a bit tumultuous to a child his age."

"Actually, he seems right at home. He is so thrilled to have his father with us again."

"I would say his father himself is rather thrilled."

"Am I that obvious, Robert?" But Christopher winked and drew Jessica closer to his side.

As the three chatted together, at last they were approached by others who were not of Rhea's circle. The first were the business acquaintances Christopher had mentioned, towing somewhat hesitant wives whose curiosity had gotten the better of them. As stiff and forced as her smile felt to her own lips, Jessica did her best to be charming and polite to those to whom she was introduced. There was no overt rudeness toward her, although the tension in the air was almost palpable, and Jessica could read the unasked questions in the women's eyes, particularly as they tried so obviously to skirt around the glaring issues that were foremost in their minds. How had husband and wife come to be separated to begin with? What was a man of Christopher's caliber doing married to a serving maid? And who *was* this serving maid, who obviously possessed the social graces? What was the unspoken mystery in both their backgrounds? Most important, whose story should they believe? Rhea Taylor's accusations that the man had acted without principle? Or the Dunlaps' own story of tragic separation and joyous reunion? The Dunlaps certainly gave no appearance of having something to hide; their happiness with each other seemed obvious, and their actions demonstrated no guilt or shame.

Rhea never approached them, for which Jessica thanked

her lucky stars, and Rhea's social manners were too polished to allow her, by any outward sign except ignoring them, to display her fury and chagrin at encountering Christopher and his wife socially when, no doubt, she'd hoped fervently that all doors would be shut to them.

Rhea was having some success in her mission, however, in that the crowd now seemed equally divided: those in Rhea's circle, who ignored them; and those who had made gingerly overtures.

When Bayard left them and they were, for the moment, alone, Christopher seized the respite to lead Jessica toward the adjacent gallery. Nearly alone together, they slowly strolled and studied the fine paintings adorning the walls.

In the solitude, with her husband's arm in hers, Jessica finally began to relax a little.

"It has been a difficult few hours for you." Christopher placed his arm around her waist and drew her against his side.

"For you, too," she sighed. "I'm so glad Robert came over to us. It seemed to break the ice."

"As I am sure he intended it should. We need only stay a few more minutes, then we can politely take our leave. I believe we have accomplished our mission."

"Do you think? Even the people who did approach us—with the exception of your business friends—were not particularly warm."

"But they came and spoke to us; that is the important part. We have not been ostracized, although there may always be those who turn their backs. We do not need them."

"You're right; and at least now you don't have to fear for your business interests."

"I was just as concerned about you. I did not want to see you isolated. We have plans for building a home in Connecticut, where you have many friends, but until then you will need some contacts in New York."

She snuggled her head against his shoulder.

"Have you seen enough?" he spoke quietly.

"Yes. I only wish I was in a better state of mind to appreciate all this art."

With a gentle pressure at her waist, Christopher turned her back toward the drawing room.

"Let me just go freshen up before we face that crowd again."

"Shall I wait for you here, or in the drawing room?"

"The drawing room's fine, as long as you don't get lost in the crowd."

"I promise not to."

Jessica made her way down the hall from the gallery to the bedroom she'd been told had been set aside for the women guests. The room was empty but for a maid who sat in a chair to one corner. Jessica went to the mirror, straightened a curl or two of hair, resecured a pin, then pinched her cheeks to bring some color to her face. The previous few hours of tension had left her pale. She smoothed her gown one last time and moved to the door. Just as she reached for the handle, the door swung open.

She stepped back quickly to get out of the way, then froze in her tracks. There stood Rhea Taylor; and it was clear her surprise was as great as Jessica's. Then a slow, derisive smile touched the woman's lips.

"My, my, of all people to bump into—the eminent Mrs. Dunlap."

For a moment Jessica was too stunned to respond.

"What a quiet mouse you are. Have you nothing to say? But then I forget. With your country ways, you are probably quite awed by New York society."

"As a matter of fact, quite the contrary, Miss Taylor. If you will excuse me." Jessica made to step by Rhea, but Rhea stood firmly in the doorway.

"No need to run away. As long as we are face to face, I might as well say what is on my mind. I was quite surprised to see you and Christopher here this evening. I must give you credit for courage, in any event. Were I you, I do not know that I could hold my head up. Everyone here is well aware of his behavior during your separation. Of course, he believed you dead . . . is that not the story?"

"As well as the truth."

"Deceive yourself as you will, but I must warn you, you are playing out of your depth."

"You do not know me well enough to make a statement like that; nor am I afraid of your threats."

Rhea lifted her brows airily, although she was obviously irked by Jessica's ability to defend herself. "That is not a threat but a statement of fact—and one wonders what *you* were doing these last two years. You have certainly played up this woeful tale of being forced into service. Perhaps a few inquiries might bring out a far more interesting story."

"Feel free to inquire, if you care to waste your time. I certainly have nothing to hide. If you will excuse me, Miss Taylor, I really *must* go. My *husband* is waiting for me."

With head high, Jessica stepped past Rhea, and forced her steps to remain measured as she moved down the hallway toward the drawing room. She knew Rhea was watching her, and she knew she should not let the woman's words bother her. She had expected a confrontation, and realized that anything Rhea said was prompted by a vindictive anger. As Jessica gave her head a light, quick shake to force her doubts away, she saw Christopher standing just inside the doorway of the drawing room.

As she approached him, she had her next shock when she saw that he was standing with Jerome Weitz.

Christopher looked up, and motioned her over. The look he gave her told her that his conversation with Weitz had been nothing but casual. "Jessica, let me introduce you to Jerome Weitz. Jerome stopped to speak to me a moment about some mutual business interests we have."

Weitz smiled, taking Jessica's hand. "But your wife and I have already had the pleasure. Of course, I am delighted to meet you again in a situation far more suited to your charms."

Christopher frowned. "How is this?"

"Mr. Weitz and I met rather precipitously, as I recall his putting it, at the Beards' ball," Jessica explained. "He bumped into me in one of the hallways while I was carrying a tray of glasses, and I managed to spill everything on the carpet."

"An accident caused entirely by my carelessness," Weitz added.

"In any case, he was kind enough to assist me in clearing up the glasses, and introduced himself."

"Had I only known at the time, Dunlap, the identity of the fair Jessica," Weitz said seriously, "I might have saved you that later awkwardness."

"Yes, it was certainly an evening to remember." Christopher was looking at his wife, the frown still marring his brow.

"And," Weitz continued, "if I am to prevent a further awkwardness this evening, I had best be off. Good to speak to you both. Dunlap, I will have those papers I mentioned delivered to your offices during the week. Jessica," he said as he bowed. *"Always* a pleasure."

When he'd departed, Christopher spoke quickly though quietly to his wife. "What is this? You have met Weitz? Why did you say nothing to me earlier when you saw him and Rhea arrive together?"

She was startled by the anger in her husband's tone. "It didn't seem important at the time. With all the tension . . . all I had on my mind . . . I'm sorry—"

"It would seem of importance to me. I even went on to describe who he was—and you said not a word."

"All I could think of at the time was that *she* had arrived. I didn't deliberately not tell you Mr. Weitz and I had met."

He saw her dismay, and immediately his expression softened. "Oh, Jessica, what is the matter with me? As if you have not been through enough this evening without my chastising you—and over such a foolish thing. I am sorry."

"Your nerves are as short as mine."

"You will forgive me?"

She nodded, paused. "I just had a run-in with Rhea."

He was instantly alert. "Oh?"

"She met me as I was coming back to the drawing room. I'm sure the meeting was an accident. She seemed as surprised as I was."

"What had she to say? You look pale . . . or did my words cause that?"

"She was rude . . . made some comment about my being a country bumpkin and not used to New York society."

"That sounds very like her."

"I think I came out of it well enough, considering how surprised I was. I conveyed that I did not find New York society at all beyond my depth. She also said she was surprised to see us here—that it must have taken courage. Then she returned to making purely snide remarks. I excused myself and left."

"If I only had been with you when you encountered her! But of course then she would have said nothing."

"Better the air was cleared. After tonight, knowing I'm not afraid of her, perhaps she'll let things die down."

"That is to be hoped." He took her arm, smiled gently. "You know how very much I regret having put you through all of this—but I *am* so proud of you."

"Did Jerome Weitz make any comments to you about us or Rhea?"

"No, it was strictly business, although under the circumstances I must say I was surprised when I saw him approach me. However, he seemed intent on avoiding all personal issues. Perhaps he was trying to make up for Rhea's actions, although I do not know him well enough to say for sure."

"Well," she sighed, "the night is nearly over."

"Shall we go home to bed?"

"Yes, I'd like that."

With their social bow behind them, they returned to day-to-day life with lighter souls. A pleasant coziness was settling in on the house on Beaver Street. Christopher was off every weekday to his offices, and Jessica and Kit spent comfortable days organizing things at home or taking the carriage out to the shops where she selected some fabrics for the redecoration of Kit's bedroom, and other materials to be made up into new gowns for herself. Although Jessica had Mrs. Hart to tend to the cooking and housework, she insisted on helping out; she would have been bored otherwise. Never had she played the lady of leisure, and her system refused to be geared to it now. She took pride in the house, and although there was no need for major changes, she enjoyed rearranging the furniture, adding a painting here and there—all of which gave the rooms a more welcoming look.

When he was about, Mawson was a great companion for the child, bringing him home bits of wood blocks from the shipyards, kneeling down with Kit on the carpet as they constructed forts and bridges. When Christopher arrived home from the office, he was only too delighted to join in the fun, surprising his son with a set of miniature soldiers to man the forts.

The scene of domestic tranquility seemed to aid in inclining Mawson's thoughts to his own personal affairs. He was often out of the house to visit Abbey, and at Jessica's prompting brought her to dinner one evening, an informal family affair. Kit sat perched in a high chair at the table, feeling very proud to be included with the adults.

As they finished the main course and coffee and dessert had just been served, Mawson glanced nonchalantly around the table.

"Got an announcement to make."

"Oh?" Christopher, although suspecting what the announcement might be, played innocent.

"Ayuh. Abbey and me, that is."

Abbey, sweet and fresh-faced, a dappling of freckles across her nose, had none of Mawson's Yankee reserve; she sat beaming.

"We'll be gettin' wed," Mawson finished. "Thought early this summer."

"Well, congratulations!" Jessica exclaimed. "That's wonderful. I'm so happy for you both."

"As am I, my friend," Christopher echoed. "I have been wondering when you would come to the point, and I am sure Abbey has been, too."

Abbey giggled. "You know Willis cannot be rushed, but we have talked about it for some time."

"What're you sayin', girl?" Mawson, too, was grinning. "Gettin' impatient, were you?"

She blushed. "I would not want you any different."

"That so? Myself, I was afraid there'd come some handsome, charmin' fella put me to shame and snap you right out from under my eye."

"Now you know that would never be the case."

"Just teasin'." He winked, and turned again to Jessica and Christopher. "We've been thinkin' on June. Saw a nice little house uptown a bit we've got our eye on, leave me close enough to get back and forth to work. Wonderin' if you'd stand with me as best man, Dunlap."

"I would be honored, as you should know."

"Thought I'd ask; never know. You'll be busy on your own 'bout then makin' plans for that place you want to build in Connecticut."

"But never too busy for an occasion like this. And I know a few others who will share my sentiments."

"Didn't think I'd do it, eh?" Mawson smiled broadly, took his bride-to-be's hand. "Got a girl like Abbey, man'd be a fool not to know a good thing."

At those words, Christopher's and Jessica's eyes spontaneously met, and his soft smile told her his feelings for her were no different.

By early March, Christopher had scouted out a piece of land in Eastport that he felt would be ideal. He'd found fifteen acres on a low rise of land facing out toward Eastport Harbor, secluded enough for privacy, yet close enough to the town and docks for convenience to his business. The following weekend he brought Jessica and Kit up to see the land. From the moment she stood on the crest of the hill and looked down the sloping bank to the blue waters of the Sound, there was no question in Jessica's mind that this was the perfect spot for their home. As Christopher turned this way and that, motioning with his hand, showing her where the house would stand to get the best view, where they'd put the stable, where to cut in the drive, she felt with certainty that they belonged here together. Forever. Everything that was dear to both their natures was manifest in this piece of ground; it seemed the land itself was welcoming them, calling out to them to settle there.

"So you are happy with it, my love?" Christopher stood with his arm about her shoulders as they watched Kit scampering through the greening patch of meadow before them.

"Nothing could be more right for us."

"My thought exactly. When we drive back to town I will put a deposit with the owner." He rested his cheek against the top of her head. "We will be happy here. Kit already seems to sense that."

"I sense it, too. I can picture the house already standing."

He chuckled. "We will see what we can do to satisfy that whim of yours as soon as possible, Mrs. Dunlap."

While they were in Eastport, they went to Silvercreek to visit with the Beards. It was a warm and happy reunion; Amelia and Molly rushing out into the yard, hugging Jessica and Kit, exclaiming how wonderful she looked and how the child had grown. Bertram Beard shook Christopher's hand, and the two began a friendly chat. Christopher and Jessica's news of their recent purchase was greeted with jubilation.

"Delightful!" Amelia exclaimed. "Now we can all visit together."

During their short visit, Elizabeth was out at a house party with Lucas. The two were getting along well, Molly confided to Jessica when they had a moment alone. It would seem the girl was at last taking a serious interest in Lucas, and this wasn't just a case of her running to him until the next beau appeared on the scene, or using him to get over her last heartache. As happy as Jessica was for Lucas—after all he'd been waiting so long for Elizabeth to return some of his affection—she felt strangely disquieted at the news. Was it that she was afraid Elizabeth would one day revert to her old tricks, and Lucas would be hurt again?

Molly bubbled over, too, with news that affected her own future. Jeb had asked for her hand, and they would be wed within the month.

"Oh, Molly, I am so happy for you!" Jessica exclaimed.

"Pretty happy myself." Molly blushed. "We'll be stayin' on here at the farm, which pleases me, too."

"I wish you every joy." She hugged the older woman. "Both of you."

On their return to New York, Christopher put all his extra energies into moving their building plans forward. With an architect's assistance, he scouted for building materials; hired laborers to break ground, masons and carpenters to begin construction. If all went well, he said, early winter would see them in their new home.

As they sat one evening with their after-dinner coffee, Jessica studied his weary face; knew that as soon as his coffee was finished, he would go to his study to pore through papers until bedtime. "Isn't there something I can help you with?" she questioned.

He glanced up at her. "Help me with what, my love?"

"The building plans. I have time to spare on my hands. While you're busy at the office, surely I could speak to the architect or help you with the paperwork . . . or something."

He grinned. "And what do you know about building?" He said it teasingly.

"Well, admittedly not a lot, but I could learn."

"Thank you for the offer, but it is easier if I take care of it myself, and I should think you'd have plenty to occupy you between Kit and running the house."

"Physically, but not mentally, and Mrs. Hart is so efficient."

"I notice we have been receiving more and more invitations. It seems you have struck up a few friendships with these women—Alfred Harrison's wife, for one. I know she is active in some charities."

"Yes, I was at one of her charity meetings last week. They get together every two weeks to sort and mend used clothing for the poor."

"A worthy endeavor."

"Oh, I don't argue that. Lucy Harrison is a sweet woman, as are most of the others, but they haven't an intellectual thought between them. Or if they do, they certainly keep it to themselves."

Christopher had finished his coffee, and pushed back his chair. "You will have to remember that none of them have had your education. Give it time, my love. You are still adjusting, and I am sure you will shortly be more comfortable with life here." He stepped over and dropped a kiss on her brow. "I will be in my study. See you in bed, my love."

She knew Christopher was right; it would take her time to adapt to this new way of life. But that knowledge didn't ease the vague sense of mental isolation she felt now.

Still, in the weeks that followed, more and more society ladies were paying a brief morning visit to the house on Beaver Street, showing their social acceptance of the Dunlaps, and Jessica's hours were more fully filled. The name Rhea Taylor was never mentioned, although Jessica knew from comments Robert Bayard had passed on that a tight circle of her friends still supported Rhea in her desire to see the Dunlaps ostracized. This fact alarmed neither Christopher nor Jessica; they did not need Rhea's friends. But every so often, the remarks that Rhea had made on the night of Jessica's social introduction with Christopher flashed through her mind. She tried to force the thoughts away. She could not allow that woman's vindictive words to upset her.

That May, in 1816, Jessica discovered she was pregnant. The knowledge brought a satisfied, happy glow that she was sure Christopher would remark on. Yet she held back telling him the news until there was no doubt in her mind about her condition, finally broaching the subject one evening as they lay together in bed, reading.

"Christopher."

"Mmmm. You know that flue construction I was concerned about? I believe I have found the answer here—a similar plan . . ." The book open before him was an architectural and building guide, and he was immersed in it.

She smiled to herself. "I'm glad we decided on that extra bedroom. We'll be needing it next February."

"Yes . . ."

"When the new baby arrives."

"Yes, new—new *what?*" He was staring at her, almost afraid to believe what he had heard, or thought he had heard. "Jessica, did you say new baby?"

"I did. I'm pregnant."

"Are you sure?"

"As positive as I can be without having a doctor confirm it."

He threw the book to the floor, gathered her up in his arms. "Oh, my love, that is wonderful, marvelous news. I had been hoping myself that it would not be long before once again . . ." Tenderly he cradled her against his bare chest. "You are feeling all right?"

"As well as can be expected. A bit queasy in the mornings, and tired, but that will pass."

He smiled to himself. "I am dense. It is not like you to doze off on the sofa as you have the last week or so."

"You've had a lot on your mind." She leaned back so that she could look up into his eyes. "You are happy? There are so many other things going on right now . . . the house, your business."

"As if any of that could take precedence over our having another child! Of course I am happy; I am delighted." There was a flash of concern in his eyes. "But are you?"

"Completely."

He relaxed. "Good."

"And it's time for Kit to have a sister or brother."

"I was afraid myself that he might be lonely, particularly in the country." He drew her back against him and tangled his fingers in the dark hair cascading down her back. "We will have to find a good doctor. Only the best for you, my love."

"I was going to ask Mrs. Hart's advice."

"I will do some investigating myself."

"Though perhaps a midwife would be sufficient. With what I know of medicine, I'm better versed than most of these nineteenth century doctors in diet and exercise."

"I still want you to see a physician." He spoke firmly. "I would not be comfortable otherwise. Yes, I know what you think of the archaic practices of medicine in this century, but we have nothing else to turn to."

"I have already had a child, Christopher; I know what to expect. And you were there with me—as you'll be this time, too. There's no need for some strange man to be in attendance to tell me what I know perfectly well myself."

"Jessica," he warned.

"A midwife and I will manage everything very well."

"I will not hear of it. You are too precious to me."

"We'll get a reputable woman, of course, and you have to admit a female is better acquainted with childbirth. I would be more comfortable, too."

"There are many very reputable *physicians* in New York."

She sighed, and in order to pacify the nervous father, at last agreed. "All right, I will see a doctor, but only on an advisory capacity. Don't expect me to heed every dictum if I think it unwise, and don't expect me to let him rule the birth. You may have him near by, but I will not have him interfering."

Despite the seriousness of the discussion, Christopher chuckled. "It would appear I will never be allowed to forget what a modern woman I have married—and quite literally yanked back into the past."

"I can't forsake the knowledge I've been fortunate enough to acquire."

"No, you cannot, and I love you all the more for it. My stay in your time was so brief in comparison to the whole—I need you to remind me not to be complacent, to think of what I learned and remember how much man can and will achieve. If you will see a physician, I will be sure he does not step beyond your bounds. Then again, he can prescribe whatever vitamin tonics are available, disguised under another name, of course." His hand lifted her hair, and gently he stroked the nape of her neck. "I am going to be a nonconformist, too, in that I do want to be present at the birth of our second child as well."

"I'd hoped you would, Christopher."

"How could I wish otherwise? I would feel I was missing something. This is *our* child. I want to see it take its first breath of life as much as you." He sighed contentedly. "This news makes our reunion very complete, does it not?"

"Very complete." She ran her hand up the length of his arm, let him draw her down beneath the covers.

Yet later, as they lay warm and satisfied from their tender lovemaking, their old fears came creeping in, and they fell silent. Though neither spoke, each suspected what the other was thinking. Could it happen again? Could they be separated? It had been shortly after Kit's birth that fate had interceded in their happiness. No, life could not repeat itself so terribly, they both prayed separately.

13

With the birth of their second child to look forward to, Christopher forged ahead on the construction of their home, often traveling to Connecticut through the spring and summer to supervise the masons and carpenters. He wanted his family in their new home when the baby arrived, and would do everything he could to reach that end. Although it was still too early to begin making purchases toward furnishing and decorating the house, Jessica scouted the shops, making lists of the china, glassware, linens, and drapery fabrics she wanted. Christopher had yet to ask her assistance with any of the building plans, but the preliminary hunting helped her feel she was part of all the excitement. Her journeys from shop to shop filled her afternoon hours, and she'd arrive home satisfyingly weary only a short time before Christopher's own return from the office. When he returned home several times to find her rushing to change before dinner, he commented.

"Jessica, don't you think you are overdoing it a bit? You need your rest."

She laughed. "I feel fine. You know the doctor gave me a clean bill of health, and I've been eating properly and getting plenty of rest. You notice I've been sleeping in of recent mornings."

"Yes. Which is one reason I am concerned. Perhaps you are pushing yourself too much. Mrs. Hart can run some of these errands."

"But I *like* to get out of the house. I need something to do besides make social visits and oversee household affairs."

"Very well, but I intend to keep a careful eye on you myself. One hint of shadows under the eyes and I will force you into a nap every afternoon, Mrs. Dunlap." He grinned, though she sensed he was quite serious.

She went to him, put her arms around his neck, and ruffled his hair. "You'd better be careful yourself. You're turning into an overprotective father-to-be."

"Do you blame me?"

She pressed her cheek against his chest as he held her close. "No, I suppose not."

Yet Jessica continued her shopping forays. Weeks before, to appease Christopher, she'd made an appointment with one of the most reputable physicians in New York. The doctor had told her nothing she hadn't already known herself. She knew her own limitations, but in fact couldn't have been in better health. Her morning sickness a thing of the past, her pregnancy troubled her very little except for a voracious appetite, which she resolutely kept in check. She found she needed physical and mental activity.

One exciting event late in June broke up the work schedules of husband and wife—Mawson's wedding. Calm and composed right up to the day of the wedding, Mawson went about his business without letting Christopher's good-natured teasing bother him.

But the morning he was to meet his bride at the lovely little neighborhood church a few blocks away, he fell apart. Jessica noticed his changed state at the breakfast table that morning when the man reached for the salt dish and poured a heaping teaspoon of the stuff into his coffee. She giggled.

"Willis, I would advise you to drink that cautiously." She grinned as the man lifted the cup to his lips.

"Eh?"

"That was salt you just helped yourself to, not sugar."

"You don't say." Bashfully, Mawson set the cup down. "Guess I'm a bit fuzzy yet. Your husband kept me up till all hours, carousin'."

"Here, let me get you another cup." Still grinning, Jessica went to the sideboard as Christopher picked up on Mawson's comment.

"How else to bid good-bye to the holy state of bachelor-hood—a long overdue celebration on your part, I might add. And you know I had you home promptly by midnight. I had to talk you out of a visit to the Ship's Tavern."

"Wanted to drop by to pay my respects to the old crew. Don't know when I'll be stoppin' in that direction again."

"For the sake of your marital happiness, I would suggest it not be for some time, if ever," Christopher laughed.

"Ayuh. Truth in that. Good bunch, but a bit on the wild side."

"An understatement."

"Well," said Mawson, pushing back his chair, "best be gettin' up and readyin' myself."

"Don't you want your coffee?" Jessica slid the fresh cup in front of him.

"Time's gettin' short. Can't have Abbey waitin'."

"You have over three hours to the ceremony!" Christopher tried unsuccessfully to hide his smile. "And I have never known you to waste more than twenty minutes in dressing."

"Still, best check out them new duds. Not used to doin' myself up in all that paraphernalia. Labor in itself."

"You haven't even touched your breakfast, Willis," Jessica pointed out to him as he started to rise.

"Stomach's a touch uneasy this mornin'. Dunlap, you'll come up in a bit and make sure I got my vest on proper?"

"I will, but first I intend to eat a good meal."

"See ya, then." Mawson wandered from the room in a daze.

When he was gone, Christopher laughed outright. "It would appear his Yankee composure has left him at last. I had better keep an eye on him or we will find him arriving at the wrong church at the wrong hour."

"The poor man. I don't remember your getting such an attack of nerves on our wedding day; or else you hid it well."

"If I recall, I was rather calm throughout, except for the marriage license we almost left behind. But then our situation was rather different."

"Yes," she smiled softly, remembering as well as he the

very private vows they had exchanged, becoming husband and wife in their own eyes alone, long before circumstances had permitted them to make their marriage legal.

Christopher did manage to get Mawson neatly attired and ready to step out to the waiting carriage exactly twenty minutes before they were to present themselves at the church, Mawson fairly much in possession of his wits except for a last-minute scurry through his room searching for the rings he'd forgotten he'd given to Christopher the day before.

The wedding itself was lovely. Jessica felt tears misting her eyes as Mawson and Abbey said their vows. There was no lack of confidence in Mawson's voice now—only strong purpose and a depth of love as he placed the smooth gold band on his bride's finger.

Later they all gathered at the bride's parents' house, the rooms overflowing with people, to refresh themselves with home-cooked delectables and to toast the beaming bride and groom with champagne. Robert Bayard approached Jessica during the festivities, champagne glass in hand, a broad smile on his face.

"Another of our trio of bachelors has met his fate."

"Which means you must be the next."

"Perhaps. The lady of my life, however, has yet to come knocking at my door."

"There must be some fortunate woman in this city."

"Once I had aspirations, but she was taken by another." For an instant his expression grew wistful. "We shall see."

Later, when bride and groom bid their guests good-bye and moved toward the carriage that would carry them to the Hudson docks and the schooner that would take them on their honeymoon journey up the Hudson, Mawson paused beside Christopher. The two men quickly embraced.

"Much happiness to you, my friend." Christopher's voice was husky.

"Ayuh, and same to you. Haven't told you before how glad I am for you and Jessica. Fine lady you have there, but you know that."

"I do."

"I'll miss the little one . . . miss you all, in fact. You've been a good friend to me. Won't be forgettin' it."

"Nor will I forget all you did for me—but Mawson, the friendship is not ending here, only taking a different course. We will expect to see you and Abbey often."

"And you will come up to see our place?"

"As soon as you are settled in."

For a spell of several weeks that summer, New York City broiled: a humid wave of heat hugged the narrow streets like a blanket, with nary a breeze off either river to stir it. The sun beat down day after day on cobbled pavements, sending up shimmering currents of warmth that even the darkness of night wouldn't dispel.

Jessica drifted listlessly through her days, watching the grass in their small back garden turn brown, the leaves on the maple tree become limp and dusty. The upstairs bedrooms were like infernos even with every window flung wide, making sleep nearly impossible. Everyone in the house grew cranky and short of temper—Kit less so, since he could indulge in daily splashings in a water-filled tub in the backyard; but because Jessica did not want Mrs. Hart lugging pails of water upstairs in the heat, Jessica and Christopher made due with a cool evening bath in the tub in the washroom off the kitchen. Yet the evening baths brought only a brief respite.

Jessica, waking one night from a fitful sleep, looked over to find Christopher lying on his back beside her, awake and staring at the ceiling, his thin covering sheet kicked to the floor.

"This is terrible." She sighed, tossing her own sheet aside. "I can't sleep at night, and spend all day walking around in a daze."

"I know." He shifted on the sheets. "Do you think it is any different for me? And I have a business to run. The staff is sluggish, the work is piling up."

"If only a storm would come through to break this heat. If only for an air-conditioner!"

"This is *not* the twentieth century, Jessica."

"But how I wish it was!"

He looked at her sharply in the dim light reflected from the street lamps outside. "Are you bemoaning the fact that we are in this time and not your own? I should have thought you would have learned to make do by now."

"I try, but there are certain conveniences it is difficult to forget. And these terribly hot long skirts, and all the underwear! How much more comfortable to put on a pair of shorts—"

"You would not seriously consider such an action?"

She flinched at the sharpness of his tone. "No, yet how much more sensible to dress for comfort than for the conventions of fashion and modesty. . . . Actually, I *might* consider it, if I was sure none of the neighbors would look in the windows."

"Jessica," he warned.

"Christopher, you're leaving tomorrow for Connecticut. Can't you take us with you?"

"You know I am only going for a few days to see how the building is progressing."

"But I would like to see it, too. I've seen nothing yet but plans on paper."

"And there is nothing for you to see now but wall partitions. With all the work going on, it is no place for a woman and a child."

"We would stay out of the way. Kit and I could go down to the water—it would be heaven! And stop off to see the Beards."

"I realize you would like to see your old friends, but this is not a pleasure trip."

"Well, I could forgo visiting Silvercreek, but I do want to see the house, even if it is only partitions—and perhaps I could make some suggestions."

"Suggestions?"

"Yes, for convenience's sake. You and the architect have done a wonderful job of duplicating Cavenly, but I noticed in the plans that the kitchen could be updated, and the laundry room, and we could be more inventive in the bathrooms. I realize indoor plumbing is a thing of the future, but—"

"Jessica, I am doing all in my power to see that this

house will be everything it should be! That is my responsibility as a man."

"I'm not criticizing you, just making suggestions. Shouldn't I have a part in the building of this house? Isn't it going to be *my* home, too? All along I've felt left out. You never ask my opinions. You've gone along and done exactly as *you* thought best—it's as though my ideas aren't important. You never used to feel that way, and now you won't even let me share your excitement in seeing the house take shape. You leave me cooped up in this house with no stimulation at all!"

"You *are* getting carried away. I have never implied that your ideas are not important." He lifted himself on his elbows. She could see the gleam of perspiration on his forehead. "You will have plenty to do when it comes time to begin decorating. That is a woman's responsibility, and I will gladly turn it over into your hands."

"Since when are we breaking everything down into man's and woman's responsibilities?"

He looked at her in exasperation. "Because that is the way it is."

"Yes, here—in the nineteenth century!"

"You also seem to forget that you are pregnant. I have been very lenient thus far, but I am sure the doctor would not approve of your jaunting up to Connecticut."

"With his old-fashioned ideas, he probably wouldn't! But if you'll remember, while I was carrying Kit I was very active. When we started the horse farm in Connecticut, I was right there beside you, hammering up stall partitions and shoveling hay—even manure. It certainly didn't hurt me. In fact, I was healthier because of it, and so was the baby. I am not some hothouse flower that has to be wrapped in gauze."

"I did not say you were; but *you* should remember that things are different here. As you are always so quick to remind me, we do not have available the ultimate in medical skills should anything go wrong. Aside from which, you are beginning to show. I do not want you climbing over the construction site with all the workers goggling at you."

"Christopher!" She was so stunned by his words, she could only stare at him.

"I do not know why we are even discussing this. You should know yourself by now what is proper. Women do not behave now as you were used to behaving, and you will have to learn to adjust—just as *I* had to learn to adjust in your world! No, you and Kit will remain here in the city."

Perhaps it was the heat, perhaps her disbelief that these words could be coming from the lips of her beloved Christopher, but she burst into tears. Even as the sobs came, she felt a foolish and weak woman, as though she were trying to gain her own ends by resorting to crying tactics.

Frowing, Christopher sat up. "What *is* the matter?"

She shook her head mutely, then forced out a response. "How . . . how can you say such things to me? How?"

"Jessica." His expression grew worried. He reached for her, drew her against him. "I am sorry. I should not have spoken so sharply. It is this heat. We would not be arguing otherwise, and you would not break down like this. Shhh, stop crying now. Here, let me get you a damp cloth." Releasing her, he slid from the bed to wring out a cloth in the washbasin, and returned in a moment to sit beside her and dab her face. Her tears were subsiding. He continued quietly. "I can understand how this weather would affect you even more than the rest of us. All right, you and Kit may come with me to Connecticut. Tomorrow morning have Mrs. Hart pack your bags. We will be leaving in late morning. Perhaps the trip away from the city *will* pick up your spirits."

She nodded, too choked up to speak. She'd gotten what she wanted; she was going to Connecticut. But he'd made the concession for all the wrong reasons. She'd wanted so much for him to see her as he used to; to see her as a partner in all this, to share all of the plans of the house with her, not to shunt her off in a corner, expecting her to be content with "women's work." Yet at that point she was too tired and upset to argue further, and knew nothing would be gained by it.

"Are you all right now?" Christopher whispered.

"Yes." Her voice still trembled from her recent outburst.

"Why don't you lie back now and try to get some sleep? You will feel better in the morning." He gently fluffed the pillow behind her and, as she leaned back upon it, pressed his lips to her brow. She watched him in the dim light as he rose to return the wet cloth to the washstand. His naked body had lost none of its tone or supple grace. The sight of it, as always, had the power to move her—not, this evening, to physical desire—but she was reminded anew of how much she loved him, and how that deep love made their argument that evening that much more painful to her.

The mattress sagged under his weight as he returned to his side of the bed. He didn't immediately lie back, but rested his weight on one elbow and studied her silently for a moment. Then he reached out to touch his fingers to her cheek. "Good night, my love. Try to sleep."

"I will. Good night."

He rolled to his back and closed his eyes; only some minutes later did she close her own. Her thoughts were still churning, but she was exhausted, and it wasn't long before she fell off into a troubled sleep.

Yet late the following afternoon, as Christopher drove the rented carriage off the roadway and onto the newly cut drive of their future home, Jessica forgot for the time their argument of the evening before. She absorbed the beauty of the building taking form at the crest of the hill above them. Christopher had done a fine job, and the resemblance of this house to Cavenly, his beloved birthplace and ancestral home in England, was so startling it nearly took her breath away. Yes, this house was of a far smaller scale, yet small by no means; and it stood on a dramatic rise, whereas Cavenly was reached via a long curving drive through lush parkland. Still, the stone structure, rising two and a half stories, its window openings still blank, its roof beams still going up, bore such a resemblance to the elegant simplicity of that magnificent structure, seat of the earls of Westerham for hundreds of years, that Jessica's throat constricted.

All she could see from their vantage point, Kit squirming on her lap in excitement, was the front of the building. The drive curved up the hillside, then made a semicircle before the imposing front doors, where wide steps would lead down to the drive. To the sides of the steps were the beginnings of the stone pedestals that would hold the entry lanterns. To the back, Jessica knew, three wings stretched out to form the house in the shape of an E, but those wings weren't visible to them as the horses' hooves scrambled over the rocks and dust of the rough drive. To their right, beyond the roughly mowed meadow that would one day be lawn, stretched the length of Long Island Sound, now giving off beautiful impressions of blues and greens and golds as the setting sun dipped over its western edge.

"Oh, Christopher, I love it!" Jessica's words were spontaneous, coming from her soul. She sat farther forward in the seat, hauling Kit up higher on her lap.

"Mama," he protested, "I can sit seat."

"I know, but the drive is bumpy, so let me hold you. Look, Kit—what do you see?"

"This be *our* house?"

"It most certainly will," his father answered. "Do you like it, my son?"

"Yes . . . ooh, yes."

They continued up the drive, around to the front of the house, where they were forced to stop before the workman's sawhorse that blocked their way. It was after six, and the workers had left for the day, but the midsummer light would continue until nine; they had plenty of time to explore. Christopher pulled up the horses and, jumping down from his seat, tied them to one of the sturdier workmen's forms—a heavy wooden scaffolding that reached up to the third floor, where the roof timbers were being laid.

He went back to the side of the carriage, reached up and took his son down, then raised a hand to help Jessica.

Husband and wife were silent for a moment as they stared at what was before them. Christopher spoke first.

"You are happy with it?"

"It's more than I ever dreamed."

"I am pleased."

"This reminds me, Christopher, of the day you first brought me to Cavenly. I'll never forget my impressions, any more than I will forget today's. Driving through those huge stone gateposts, down that long, curving drive, I couldn't believe such a lavish place had once been your home. The azaleas were blooming and there were swans on the pond in the front parkland, and mares and foals scampering in the new grass in the pasture behind. And the house itself, with the sun glinting off all its windows—I'd never seen anything so lovely!"

"Jessica." She saw a suddenly pained expression on his face. "How could I forget that day, or my feelings—but the old Cavenly is behind us. The new one is here at hand."

Through that fall and early winter, as Christmas approached, affairs at the house on Beaver Street fell into a busy but peaceful state. Everything was going smoothly with the new house and Christopher's business, and his lighthearted mood reflected his success. And although the remembrance of Christopher's comments to her on that hot summer night four months before occasionally caused Jessica a pang of disquietude, there were no more arguments between husband and wife. Jessica directed her thoughts to the new house, and the new baby. She did slow her pace a bit. Her pregnancy was making her more awkward, and she was tiring more easily, but although other society women in her state of expectancy would probably at this point have confined themselves to their homes, Jessica would not be confined. There was so much still to be done in preparation for their move, articles to be purchased for the baby, Christmas gifts to be selected for Christopher and Kit and their friends in Eastport. She went out almost daily, rationalizing that her winter cloak substantially hid her condition. She met with no protests—until the afternoon she encountered Rhea Taylor in the dry-goods store. Since they were walking toward each other down a narrow aisle, a face-to-face meeting was impossible to avoid.

"Well," Rhea smiled, a turn of lips lacking any sincerity. "If it is not Mrs. Dunlap. I see you have not been idle in the months since we last ran into each other." Her eyes in bold appraisal drifted down over Jessica's cloak-en-shrouded but obviously pregnant form.

Jessica ignored as best possible the woman's rude stare. "Good afternoon, Miss Taylor."

" 'Miss' Taylor again—really! It is *Mrs.* Taylor . . . or did you not realize I was a widow?"

"I did not. My husband never informed me." As soon as the words were out of her mouth, Jessica knew she had erred.

Rhea quickly caught her up on it with another slow, sly smile. "Did he not? But, then again, I imagine there are a great many things about the two of us that he did not see fit to confide to you."

"That may be. I was never particularly interested."

"No? Perhaps you should have been."

Jessica forced herself not to react to the innuendo in Rhea's voice as she sought for an equally biting response.

Rhea, however, knowing her thrust had hit its target, gave Jessica no time for response. She coolly began to move past. "I know you will excuse me. I have a thousand things to do. Always a pleasure seeing you." Her languid movement giving the impression of leisured boredom, Rhea turned and moved away, leaving Jessica fuming, aching to call out after the retreating figure. She did not, knowing any such remark would only lower her to Rhea's level. But oh, the woman was impossible! And she had obviously not yet given up her mission of igniting a spark of dissension between husband and wife. Again Jessica determined not to let Rhea's remarks get under her skin; there was nothing about Christopher and Rhea Taylor she needed or wished to know. At least that was what she told herself as she forced herself not to dwell on the encounter. But she could not know what would be said to her at the dinner table that evening.

Since his arrival home Christopher had seemed to have something on his mind. Now he spoke.

"I ran across Rhea Taylor this afternoon as I was leaving my office. She told me you saw each other in one of the shops today."

Jessica looked up sharply. "Yes, I saw her at Parker's. It was not a pleasant meeting."

He didn't ask why, but continued with his train of thought. "She was quite shocked to see you out."

"Oh?" Jessica frowned. "Why?"

"That should be obvious. In your condition, you should not be jaunting about in public. With all that is on my mind, it never occurred to me that you have been going out as frequently as ever. It is an embarrassment."

"An embarrassment to whom?"

"To those who see you . . . and to me. I certainly did not enjoy having Rhea come to me remarking on your behavior."

"And what business is it of hers what I do?" Jessica felt a knot of anger begin to tighten her stomach. "I am certainly not doing anything unrespectable. Having a child is a natural and beautiful part of life. Why should I hide my condition? Rhea is well aware, I presume, that children are not delivered down the chimney by the stork?"

"Your sarcasm is not necessary. We have been through all of this before."

"Well do I recall. But am I to be a hypocrite?"

"No, I only expect you to do what is proper."

"Yes—hide myself away behind closed doors as though there were some shame in my pregnancy."

"Is it so much to ask that you seclude yourself for a while? We will be leaving the city soon. Jessica," he pleaded, "I have tried so hard to make life happy for you and Kit here in New York, provide everything you have needed. Is it not enough that we are together again? Should we not be cherishing each day instead of looking for arguments?"

The response Jessica would have made was prevented by a knock on the dining room door as Mrs. Hart stuck her head in.

"Excuse me, sir, ma'am, but you have a visitor. Mr. Bayard."

"Robert!" Christopher called.

Mrs. Hart swung the door wide to usher in Robert Bayard.

"You see," Bayard spoke to the woman, "I *am* interrupting."

"Do not be silly, Robert." Christopher motioned him forward. "We have given instructions that you are always to be shown in when you call." He smiled. "Come, have a seat. Have a glass of wine while we finish, then dessert and coffee with us."

Bayard came forward as bid, unaware of the touchy discussion he had just interrupted. He gave Jessica a warm greeting, then took the chair Christopher offered. As he and Christopher started chatting about business matters, Jessica sat in silent chagrin, the words that had been about to come off her tongue when Bayard was announced lying frustrated inside her. Why should she seclude herself? What right did Christopher have to ask that of her? More important, why was he listening to his ex-fiancée? Why was he letting that woman's opinions influence him?

Jessica gritted her teeth and made polite conversation through the balance of dinner, hoping Bayard would soon excuse himself and leave; but he seemed in a mood to have a long chat with Christopher, and Christopher did not put him off. As the coffee was being cleared away, Christopher rose.

"Jessica, you will not object if Robert and I retire to my study for a while? There are some things we must discuss." He touched her arm absently. "We may be awhile, so you go on upstairs. You need your rest."

Since any protest from her would have seemed rude, she nodded her head.

"Good night, Jessica." Bayard smiled as he, too, rose to follow Christopher. "And I promise not to keep your husband too late."

"Good night." Her voice sounded disgruntled even to her ears, but neither of the men seemed to notice as they stepped out of the room.

By the time Christopher came up, much later that evening, Jessica had already fallen asleep, so there was no chance to finish their discussion that night. And the fol-

lowing morning he was off early to the office, not even
waking her before he left. She was left with her questions
and arguments still spinning in her mind, to be left unanswered again that evening: Christopher did not come
home from the office until very late. By the next day, pick-
ing up the thread of their conversation seemed impossible.
Christopher's mood suggested that he had forgotten all
about it and thought everything was as it should be, and
Jessica's own temper had cooled enough for her to think
back and remember Christopher's last comment about
cherishing what they did have and not looking for arguments. Was she asking too much? *Wasn't* it enough that
they were together again? Still, no more could she erase
the feeling that Christopher had been wrong in accosting
her than she could forget that it had been Rhea Taylor who
had instigated the dispute. Although in the next weeks she
let the subject lie, it wasn't one she could put blithely from
her mind.

Despite all, their Christmas holidays were happy ones,
Christopher going overboard with gifts for Kit, and the
child dancing about the house on Christmas morning in
ecstasy, filling the rooms with laughter. There'd been a
surprise visit from Mawson and Abbey late in the afternoon, and they'd stayed to have a cup of good cheer, Mawson sliding down on the carpet beside Kit to assist with
Kit's new building block set.

Not until their guests had left and Kit had fallen exhausted into an early bed did Christopher and Jessica exchange their own gifts for each other before the fireplace.
Jessica had noticed Christopher's curious eyes surveying
the large tissue-wrapped gift in the corner several times
that afternoon, and now, as he tore away the wrappings,
she knew from the expression on his face how deeply he
was touched. In his hands he cradled the three-foot-long,
perfectly detailed scale model of his newly launched merchantman that, with Mawson's technical advice and some
purloined plans, she'd had a local craftsman create. Christopher looked up at her as the ship was fully revealed; then
his eyes went back to the model. Studying every inch of it,
he ran his fingers carefully over the string rigging, the

miniature barrels on the deck, the captain's cabin, and last, over the gold embossed nameplate on the bow. When he set the model on the carpet and came to her, he seemed almost too moved to speak. He only took her in his arms and, gently, hugged her as close to him as her swollen girth permitted.

"Thank you," he whispered. "You always seem to know the perfect gift." He paused for an instant, composing himself. "For yours, you will have to let me go into my study, where I hid it from inquisitive eyes. Wait here—no peeking."

"I promise." After seeing his happiness with her gift to him, Jessica needed none other for herself; yet she was curious, watching the door for his return, wondering. Jewelry, perhaps? A gown? Or perhaps even a fur?

She heard him call before he came in sight of the door. "Cover your eyes, and do not sneak. Are they covered?"

"Yes."

"If I catch you looking, I will turn around and hide this until next year."

"I promise . . . I won't look."

She heard his footsteps, muffled by the carpet. He seemed to be going toward the couch. She restrained her overflowing curiosity with an effort through seemingly endless minutes of silence.

"All right. You may look now. No, turn around—face the other way." As he spoke he came to her side and put his arm about her shoulders.

She turned. There, propped on the couch, facing her head-on, was a life-size framed portrait of their son, so alive she almost jumped. Kit was seated at the edge of a chair, in his best attire, yet ready at any moment to bound off the chair in search of adventure. Everything about his young personality was there—the impish, happy smile, the dancing blue eyes, the inquisitiveness. She couldn't believe it.

"Christopher, how . . . when did you get this portrait painted without my knowing it? It's marvelous! It's Kit. Oh, I love it—I love it!" She turned to grip him about the waist.

He laughed. "Well, it was not easy. Mrs. Hart and I had a little conspiracy. We worked out an arrangement with a good portraitist in town, that whenever there were moments available, he would come here, or Kit would go there, usually when you slept in late in the mornings or went upstairs for an afternoon nap. It was rather a rushed affair, particularly to finish this up. I think that is why it seems Kit is falling off the end of his seat."

"No, that's Kit completely. Have you *ever* known him to sit full and still in a chair for more than a few seconds at a time? The artist was excellent to have caught him so well. Who is he?"

"A total unknown. I saw him painting on the docks one day. He seemed to have a great deal of promise, and after he had shown me some of the work he had done, I hired him. I do not regret the decision."

"Nor do I." She reached up her head to give him a kiss on the cheek. "We have no other pictures of Kit yet. I really cherish this because it catches him at a perfect age. In watching him grow up, I've really missed having photographs to look back at."

Christopher sighed, and Jessica knew instantly that he was feeling dismayed about her missing yet another twentieth century wonder. She didn't want him to think that way, and quickly tried to turn his thoughts from disappointment.

"Where shall we hang it?" she asked excitedly. "Here? In the living room?"

"I was thinking of it more as something to be hung in our new home, although we certainly shan't hide it for the time we have left here. I was thinking of the front hall, although that is rather out of the way except for visitors. In the drawing room over the fireplace would be better, do you think? Or would you prefer our bedroom?"

"The drawing room. As much as I would like to look at it every morning when I rise, I'd like our guests to see our family, and we won't have a portrait gallery at the new home like you had at Cavenly. In time, perhaps . . ."

"Most likely after we are long dead," Christopher

chuckled, "when there has been time to collect family portraits."

They pulled a little closer in each other's arms as she looked up to the vivid blue eyes watching her. "I am really so thrilled with my gift."

"And I."

"It's been another wonderful Christmas. Thank you, Christopher."

"Thank *you*, my love." He cupped his hand under her chin. "And soon we will be in our new home, our second child will be born. I am so very happy, Jessica."

"So am I." She couldn't mention to him then the twinges of discontent that had come to her from time to time. This was Christmas; let them have this untarnished moment of joy. She only smiled at him, the warm love that came from deep inside her glowing in her eyes as his lips met hers and they shared a long, sweet kiss.

By mid-January Christopher informed Jessica that the house in Eastport was ready for them. There was still some minor work to be done, but with Jessica's due date approaching, he did not want to postpone the move any longer. It was a sentiment with which Jessica agreed wholeheartedly.

It was a joyous moment for them all as they rounded the curve of their newly graveled drive on that clear but cold day and saw the graceful outline of their new home on the rise ahead, its mellow stone walls proud in the slanting afternoon sunlight. From its appointed spot, at the center of the half circle the drive formed before the front doors, rose the not yet completed fountain. The Sound waters in the distance, across what in the spring would be a stretch of green lawn, were a sort of outsized facsimile of the swan-filled lake on Cavenly's grounds.

Kit's hand in his, his other arm around Jessica's shoulders, Christopher ushered his family up the front steps and through the wide double front door held open by one of the two maids Jessica had hired in New York. Because of close family ties in that city, Mrs. Hart had reluctantly decided not to come with them to Connecticut, but had accepted the housekeeper's position with Mawson and Abbey instead. Christopher's mood was ebullient as they stepped into the high-ceilinged front hall. Ahead of them a graceful staircase curved upward, the railings branching off on either side along a small balcony from each end of which halls led off to the eight bedrooms in the house. To the right of the marble-floored hall in which they stood was a large drawing room, a smaller replica of the main salon at Cavenly; beyond that was a cozier sitting room. To the left of the front hall was an anteroom, which Christopher referred to as the smoking room, and beyond that the spacious dining room, taking up the whole west corner of the house. Behind the main staircase a long corridor stretched the length of the house, and off it ranged three short wings, giving the house the shape of an E, in the first of which were the kitchen and servants' workrooms; in the second the family breakfast room; in the last, Christopher's study.

"Well." Christopher grinned. "You have not seen it in several months. What do you think? Have the decorators followed your instructions?"

"To perfection, from the little I can see. It's so wonderful to be in our own home. It *is* like Cavenly—particularly now that I see it finished. It brings back so many memories. Happy memories, Christopher."

"Yes . . . I am sure you are right," he said wistfully. For a moment they were both thoughtfully silent, then Christopher hugged Jessica's shoulder and turned to the waiting maid. "Clara, will you see that tea is served in the drawing room in about twenty minutes? Milk and cookies for the boy. The fires are lit in there?"

"Yes, sir."

"Good." He smiled to his wife. "I thought we might celebrate this first afternoon in our new house. Shall we go up to see the bedrooms and freshen up?"

Kit, who had been silent until now, perked up. "Yes, want see my room, Daddy. All my toys come yet?"

"They should be here, unpacked and waiting for you, young man."

In his eagerness the child began pulling his mother and father toward the stairs.

At Christopher's prompting, Jessica had hired a real English nanny to watch over Kit and the new baby, but she would have nothing to do with Christopher's idea of a third-floor nursery, much though he had protested that it was a true tradition and one that he had been brought up with. She did not want her children set apart from Christopher and herself. Instead, Kit would have the room across the hall from theirs, and they brought him there now.

Kit had already met his nanny, Mrs. Bloom, in New York, so there was no awkwardness as they bustled into Kit's room, where she was finishing the unpacking of Kit's things.

"Well, good afternoon to you, Master Kit," the affable gray-haired woman said warmly. "And to you, sir and ma'am. Welcome to your new home."

"Thank you," they responded simultaneously, Jessica adding, "The room looks lovely. You've done a fine job."

"Only try my best. And such a nice room to work in, plenty of sunlight."

Kit was casting significant glances between his mother and the toys piled along the bedroom shelves. Jessica gave him a nod, and he was soon pulling down his favorites.

"We will be back in a moment to collect him, Mrs. Bloom," Christopher said as he led his wife to the door. "I have a feeling he will not miss us."

"Not for the moment, it would appear." Mrs. Bloom beamed down on her fully occupied charge, and Christopher and Jessica stepped across the hall to the master suite. Their bedroom had been modeled after the room Christopher had occupied at his beloved Cavenly.

As Christopher swung the door wide, Jessica looked excitedly about the interior of the room. "It's marvelous," she cried, her eyes sweeping the large bedroom with its impressive canopy bed, jewel-toned oriental rug, finely crafted dark wood wardrobe and nightstands, framed hunt scenes on the walls, armchair placed cozily before the marble-trimmed fireplace. "They have put everything where I told them to, Christopher. Did I remember it correctly? I saw the original room only so briefly when we snuck up the hidden back stairs that day."

"Your memory is accurate indeed. I almost feel I had stepped back three and a half years in time. Unfortunately, I did not incorporate the hidden stairs in this house."

"Just as well, or we might lose our son in those dark passageways." She stepped quickly about, examining everything, running to the windows to see the view that faced the Sound, adjusting the placement of a bud vase on her dressing table. Grinning ear to ear, she returned to her husband, who stood inside the doorway watching her every movement.

"Oh, Christopher!" She ran into his waiting arms. "I'm so happy!"

"Yes." His voice was deep, full of feeling. "Another new beginning . . . and this time nothing will mar our happiness."

"Yes. Everything will be better for us here." Suddenly she felt her worries in New York could be forgotten. Now that they were in this house, everything would be all right.

14

On a snowy February afternoon, Jessica's labor began. The snow had begun as a light flurry about noon, but now it was coming down heavily. She stood at the window overlooking the snow-covered drive waiting for the return of Jim, the caretaker. If he wasn't back soon, she'd never get a message through to the doctor they'd made arrangements with in town. And where was Christopher? It seemed he was away on business so much of the time lately. Knowing his wife's due date was only a few days off, at least he'd gone no farther than his Eastport offices that day; but with this storm, wouldn't he have left for home by now?

She tried to push the worries from her mind. She did not need additional anxiety now. She forced her mind to more pleasant thoughts, of their first weeks in their new home.

They'd settled into the house so quickly, it was as though the house was an old and welcome friend. The staff she'd hired in New York was a good one, and Mrs. Bloom was a jewel with Kit. Jessica sometimes saw the woman as a replacement for the grandmother with whom Kit had not been blessed.

They'd had visitors since their arrival. Bayard and Mawson and Abbey surprised them one Saturday afternoon, chancing the weather and coming up for the weekend—and what a merry weekend it had been, the three men catching up on news, none of them able to talk fast enough; Jessica and Abbey watching and smiling. They'd all stayed up too late, then cleared their heads the next morning with a brisk walk across the frozen grounds as Christopher proudly gave them the grand tour.

Of course, their friends at the Beard farm had also visited. While Amelia and Bertram exclaimed over the main rooms, Molly checked the kitchens and Jeb the stables. Mary and Roger Weldon delighted them with the news that they were expecting again that coming fall. Mary and Jessica had a long chat, comparing notes on their growing families. Now that Jessica was no longer a servant in the Beard household, all barriers to friendship with Mary were removed.

The most startling news, however, came from Lucas and Elizabeth as they stood smiling before Christopher and Jessica and made the announcement of their engagement. Christopher, knowing none of the past circumstances surrounding Lucas and Elizabeth, immediately offered his congratulations, which Jessica quickly echoed. Yet in the back of her mind, she couldn't stop herself from thinking, "So soon?" Yet actually, it wasn't that soon. Almost a year before, Molly had informed Jessica that the two were seeing each other regularly. Why, then, should this feeling of suddenness strike her?

As she took Lucas's hand, wishing him well, their eyes met for a long moment and a silent message passed between them. No words were needed to tell her that there would always be a special feeling between them; nor did Lucas need words from Jessica to note the disquietude their announcement had brought her. As they dropped hands quickly, awkwardly, realizing their contact had gone on longer than convention warranted, Jessica saw the frown of puzzlement on Christopher's brow. He hadn't missed the clasp of her hand and Lucas's, the long look exchanged between them. Afterward he had remained strangely thoughtful for some time, finally coming to her when they had a moment alone.

"You know this Lucas St. John well?"

"He was a very dear friend to Kit and me while we were at the Beards'."

"Was he?" He'd said nothing more, but during the balance of the afternoon she'd seen his gaze rest several times on Lucas.

Now, as she stood before the window, another pain gripped her stomach. She took deep breaths until it passed, then gazed outside again. Kit would be fine. Jessica had told Mrs. Bloom an hour earlier that her time might be near, and the nursemaid would keep Kit well occupied. But where was that caretaker? And oh, if only Christopher would come home! She wanted him with her when the time came. Second babies almost invariably came much faster than the first. She wasn't sure how to gauge herself. A birth this evening? In the early hours of the morning? Not that she felt the urgent need for the doctor to be at her side, but only the cook and maids were with her in the house, and she didn't know if any of them had the presence of mind to aid her through her delivery. Mrs. Bloom would surely keep her head, but Jessica already knew that the woman had never attended a birth.

Dusk began to fall, and still no caretaker, no Christopher, in sight. Jessica felt her anxiety grow to the point where her fears could no longer be put from her mind. The snow swirled in dancing whirlwinds; a foot of it covered the drive, and drifts blew up against the house. She went to the kitchen and had the maid light the covered oil lanterns from the storage room, and place them on the hitching posts outside the front and back doors. The light was meager, but perhaps would give some guidance to the men returning home in the storm. The pains were coming more frequently now, and she knew she had to stay busy to keep her mind from dwelling on them. Nervously she rechecked the linens that had been carefully wrapped and set aside in the master bedroom wardrobe, in preparation for the birth; she refolded the blankets in the cradle she'd set beside the bed a week before; she stopped in to see Kit, busy at his dinner. Concern was evident in Mrs. Bloom's eyes, but Jessica said nothing to her of her own worry. She returned to the kitchen, where the cook was in the midst of preparing dinner.

"Some blow out there," the woman commented.

"Yes."

"Maybe best Mr. Dunlap stayed in town."

Jessica couldn't find her voice to answer that. She only nodded and left the kitchen, walking to the front windows of the house to watch the drive again. The whiteness on the ground still reflected the tinest bit of light left of the day, but the lines of the landscape were deceptive. Was that a shadow she saw—there at the curve of the drive where it turned off into the trees to meet the road? No, just another gust of blowing snow. She blinked her eyes. This time it was clearer. A man on horseback . . . or was it? . . . Yes, she was sure now. He was having a difficult time, his horse plodding through the drifts, hesitating, moving forward again. She ran to the front door and threw it open, oblivious of the flakes of snow that swirled in and stung her cheeks.

She could see him now, faintly, as he made his way up the drive.

"Christopher!"

"Jessica!" His voice sounded muffled. "Yes, it is I. Get inside! I must take the horse around to the stables."

She quickly shut the door against the storm and hurried through the candle-lit hallway toward the kitchen. She rushed through to the back door, startling both maids and the cook.

"Mr. Dunlap is coming," she said in breathless explanation. Even as she spoke, another pain gripped her abdomen, deeper this time, more severe. She took deep breaths and hid her discomfort from the others.

"Wonder he's gotten through," the cook commented. "We'll have a good meal for him when he gets in."

Jessica watched through the glass, saw her husband dismount, pull wide the stable door and enter, leading his horse. It seemed an eternity later when he emerged to trudge through the drifts toward the back door. Again the cold blew in on her as she pulled open the door and he came stomping into the room.

"What a night! Thought I would not make it. My love, you have been worried." He took her hand with his snow-covered glove.

"Yes. Terribly."

"Had I known it would turn into this, I would have left the office sooner." He was removing his hat now and muffler, shaking the snow from them, then began to unbutton his greatcoat. "Come, let us go into my study. I feel in the need of a warm dose of brandy."

They moved briskly out of the kitchen and down the hall, Christopher shrugging out of his coat as he walked. "Remind me to bring this to Clara. It will need a bit of drying." Behind his study door, the draperies closed, the room was warm from the fire that had been lit earlier. He threw his coat over a chair, kissed his wife, and went to the decanter on the sideboard to pour himself a small dose. He tossed it down. "Ah, that is better. I thought for a while I would never know warmth again." He came toward her, drew her against him. "And you are a welcome warmth, too."

She rubbed her cheek against his jacket. "I'm so glad you are home! Christopher, my labor started this afternoon."

He tensed.

"I was afraid you wouldn't be here in time."

"You are sure?"

"Yes."

"You have sent for the doctor? He is here?"

"No. Jim left just before noon to run errands. He hasn't returned. I couldn't send a message."

"Then I must ride out now."

"No! How could you make it to town, let alone bring the doctor back?"

"But, Jessica, I must! There is no one here who knows what to do."

"You and I."

"I only watched Kit's birth. I took no part in it!"

"Christopher, if you go out in this storm, I'll be left with only the cook or maids to help me."

Anxiety and indecision were written on his face. "But if anything was to go wrong . . ."

"It won't. We can't think of that."

She gasped as a sharp pain caught her unexpectedly, nearly doubling her over.

"Oh, my love! How far apart are the pains?"

"About five minutes," she whispered when she could breathe normally again.

"You should be upstairs."

"In a minute. Promise me, Christopher, you won't go out."

"I cannot leave you like this—but I feel so helpless! You are *sure* there is not time for me to go into town?"

"If you could even *get* into town. You barely made it home. If you left, I'd have not only our baby and myself to worry about, but my husband, too." Her voice was pleading, and he nodded in agreement to her logic.

"We'll be all right, Christopher."

"We have no choice, do we?" He took her arm, began leading her from the room. "Let me get you upstairs. And then what else can I do?"

"One of the maids should stand by in case we need anything. Clara, I think is the most level-headed one. I haven't said anything to them of my labor."

"I shall speak to her." When they reached the bedroom, Christopher pulled down the bed covers. "You will want to get into a nightgown."

"That white one in the corner," she said, motioning as he went to the wardrobe. When he returned, he carefully helped Jessica from her dress and undergarments, and slipped the gown over her. "Let me help you to bed."

"I'm better off up and about for a while. The time will go faster if I'm not lying on my back waiting for each pain."

"I know there is more that must be done . . . other things we will need." He spoke distractedly, rubbing his hand across his brow. "My mind does not seem to be functioning."

She placed her hand on his arm. Now that he was home, she suddenly found a calm strength flowing through her. "Relax. There is time. I have linens ready here in the wardrobe. I'll need some warm water to wash, but other than that I feel much better now that you are here. Go get yourself some dinner. It may be a long night."

Husband and wife began their vigil. The next hours passed slowly. Christopher left Jessica's side only to place another log on the fire, or wring out a damp towel to wipe her perspiring brow, or send Clara, who was seated nervously in a chair beside the door, for more water. He'd removed his jacket and tie and sat beside her with his white shirt rolled up to the elbows, his face pale as he watched Jessica bear each increasingly severe contraction; but he was there, with a comforting hand, a soothing word, quiet conversation, until Jessica suddenly gripped his hand hard.

"Christopher, the pain is changing. I feel the need to push. Help me move up, and put more pillows behind my back."

He acted with alacrity, and when she was settled, again took her hand in his as several more contractions came and went.

"Are you all right?" His blue eyes were clouded with worry. "Is this the way it was before?"

"The pain is more in my back, but everything seems normal."

With each of the next few contractions, Jessica pushed with all her strength, Christopher ready to help as she'd instructed him. She felt the pressure of her child's head, a tearing, ripping pain that brought an involuntary cry to her throat.

In a moment she heard Christopher's awed, yet excited tone. "Jessica! The head is free . . ."

"One more contraction," she groaned, and pushed again as the pain of the contraction overwhelmed her.

She forced her eyes to remain open, watching her husband and the joy and fear on his face. She saw his hands reaching to gently grip the baby, pull if from her straining body. The absolute rapture on his face, beautiful to behold, relieved the last of her anxiety. Then he was holding their child up in the air; a wet, bedraggled, red-faced, but beautiful little infant.

"A girl, Jessica! A girl!"

Tears of happiness sprang to her eyes. "Put her on my stomach. Let me touch her."

Gently he placed the already squalling baby on his wife's belly. As Jessica laid her hands on her child, the baby immediately began to quiet, the tender touch of maternal love already making itself felt through Jessica's hands. Though faint from weariness, Jessica's face was radiant, her eyes drinking in and memorizing her newborn daughter's every feature. Christopher, too, was beaming, although he was concentrating on the cutting and tieing of the cord and the delivery of the afterbirth.

Jessica continued to soothe her child, as milder contractions sent the afterbirth out of her body. Clara went to fetch the small gown and blanket folded in the cradle. The cord cut and tied, with Clara's help Jessica laid the child on the bed beside her and, taking a warm cloth from Clara, began to wash her, then dressed her in a tiny diaper and the infant's gown. When the baby was snug in Jessica's arms, Christopher leaned down and tenderly laid his cheek against his wife's. "I love you," he whispered, "and I am so very proud of you."

"I'm proud of *you*. You were wonderful. I knew we could do it."

"I am going to lift you and the baby from the bed for the moment, so Clara can change the linens. Then I will bathe you and get you into a fresh gown."

She smiled. "I could get up on my own. I may be a bit wobbly . . ."

"I would not hear of it." He kissed her brow as he slipped his arms beneath her. "Tonight you will have nothing but complete pampering and rest."

"What time is it?" she said, suddenly dismayed. "I forgot to look at the clock when she was born."

"But I did not. She was born at precisely twelve-oh-one. A beautiful beginning to a new day."

She hugged him as he lifted her and carried her to the chair near the fire, where she placed her child in the cradle beside her. When Clara was gone with the soiled linens and the bed was freshly made, Christopher bathed his wife, helped her into a lacy, soft blue gown, carried her to the bed and rested her back against the fluffed pillows. In a moment he brought their blanket-wrapped daughter to her. Jessica eagerly took their child in her arms, cuddling and cooing to her as Christopher undressed and slid into bed beside them.

He smiled, studying the features of his sleeping daughter's face. "Such a tiny little thing. Ours."

"Shall we call her Mary, Christopher, after your mother?"

"If that is what you really wish. You liked the name Jennifer, too."

"Yes, but I think it would be nice to follow tradition this time."

"Then Mary she is. Mary *Jessica* Dunlap, welcome into our lives."

Little Mary Dunlap thrived during her first weeks of life, and through February and March contentment reigned in the Dunlap household as the radiant parents treasured each hour in their new home with their growing family. Jessica was so pleasantly busy, she did not even mind the inclement weather that prevented her from driving into Eastport in the carriage for shopping or to visit with Mary Weldon in town or the Beards in Silvercreek. She pushed from her mind even the smallest twinges of discontent at her comparative isolation. Instead, while Mrs. Bloom watched the baby, Jessica took brisk walks with Kit across the grounds, or sat and played with both her children for hours before the blazing nursery fire. While Kit romped on all fours over the carpet with his set of toy soldiers, Jessica held Mary in her lap, delighting in her daughter's gurgles and the alertness the infant exhibited.

Christopher's adoration of his little girl was equal to Jessica's. Unlike many fathers, intimidated by the smallness of an infant, Christopher felt no qualms about holding her, carrying her about to show her off to friends who dropped by the house with their congratulations.

Each evening when he arrived home from his newly established Eastport offices, he joined the family gathering; first kneeling down beside his son to take part in some game, then rising to lift his daughter from his wife's arms and hold her as he and Jessica sat and discussed the day's happenings. All was as it should be, he thought happily; he was blessed with a beautiful wife contentedly immersed in overseeing a well-kept home and two lovely children; his business was prospering; and at last he and Jessica had the joy they deserved.

It was a business visitor of Christopher's from New York, invited to spend the night with them, who brought the influenza into the house early in April. Jessica had noticed the man's repeated sneezing at the dinner table, and frowned worriedly at his feverish look as he left the house the next morning. Because Christopher and Jessica were in excellent health and not likely to be susceptible to infection, and the children had not been in contact with the man, both husband and wife put their worries aside until Clara came to Jessica two days later with chills and fever. Immediately Jessica sent the young housemaid to bed, but now she was worried. She took all precautions available to her to protect the children, keeping them in their own wing of the house, being sure she stayed out of contact with Clara, sterilizing Kit's eating utensils. But knowing she had already been exposed to Clara's illness, her greatest fear was that she herself carried the germs. If she became ill, she could not feed Mary; arrangements would have to be made to bring in a wet-nurse.

For a week all went well. Clara, although very ill for a stretch, seemed to be on the road to recovery, and no one else in the house was showing any symptoms. Then one morning Mary woke fretful. Jessica was not concerned at first; all young babies had their moments of disagreeableness, and although Mary was a good and happy baby, she occasionally suffered bouts of gas that made her cranky. Jessica said nothing to Christopher as he left for his Eastport office that morning, but as the day progressed and Mary grew worse instead of better, Jessica became afraid. She sent the caretaker into town for the doctor. While she waited, she laid cool cloths on the infant's brow to alleviate the fever that had begun to make itself felt, and when the baby refused to nurse, spooned a sugar and water solution down her throat. Fresh fruit juice was unavailable, as was even an aspirin to help break the fever. When the doctor arrived, he could advise no further remedy. He told Jessica to protect the child from drafts, and wait out the influenza. Yes, he knew such an illness was a serious thing in a child that age, but there was nothing else he could do. He would stop by each day to see how the baby was progressing.

When Christopher arrived home that evening and heard the news, he ran up to their room, not even pausing to remove his coat. Jessica was seated by the baby's cradle, gently rocking the infant.

"How is she?"

"Sleeping. The fever has knocked her out."

He paced across the room to gaze down at his daughter's flushed face. "Poor child. They tell me downstairs that the doctor was here."

"Yes, but he could do nothing. We must wait it out, he said."

"How long?"

"Several days . . . perhaps more." Jessica's worry was showing in the paleness of her face.

"You look exhausted. You have not left her all day, have you?"

"The maid brought me a tray at noon."

"Well, go and get something to eat now. I will stay with her."

Through the night they took turns watching the child, who woke frequently amid alternating fever and chills. Jessica forced more sugar water into the child to ward off dehydration and changed the baby's garments whenever they felt damp.

There was no change by morning, and Christopher remained home so that Jessica could get some much needed rest. The doctor came and examined the child.

"Give it another day. We may see some change by then."

But on the third day, although the chills were gone, the fever was still present, and now the baby was wheezing.

The doctor's expression was grave when he visited, but his words told Jessica nothing that she had not already suspected: Mary was developing pneumonia. The doctor's diagnosis filled the still air of the room like the voice of doom. Christopher and Jessica could only stare at each other, each knowing Mary's chances for recovery were now slim. But neither of them would admit to the possibility that their child would not recover. Round the clock they worked, applying hot plasters to the baby's increasingly congested chest, forcing liquids down her throat. Mary could nurse very little, and Jessica's breasts were sore and aching. She was forced to drain them daily to keep her milk flowing. A kettle steamed constantly over the fire, spewing out soothing vapors, but the additional moisture in the air was still not enough to ease the child's breathing.

As three days passed and Jessica watched her child literally dwindling away before her eyes, saw the bluish cast to her lips and fingers that indicated lack of oxygen, her frustration and anger knew no bounds. Her daughter's suffering was the fault of this archaic medical knowledge of the nineteenth century. If only she could obtain for her offspring the antibiotics or penicillin that would soon have Mary on the road to recovery! Yet all the drugs that would cure her daughter were beyond Jessica's reach in time.

"Why, Christopher, why?" She sobbed that night in his arms. "I feel so angry! Especially when *we* know there is a cure. We know how to help her—if only we had the tools. This can *not* be happening!"

There were no words of comfort he could give her; her frustrations were his own. As much as this was his world and he was accustomed to witnessing the cruel toll of infectious disease, he knew of the progress that would be made in the next one hundred and fifty years, of the miracle drugs that would save so many. His pain was as great as Jessica's.

Despite all, Jessica still could not allow herself to think that her daughter might die. She would save Mary, if by sheer force of will alone. She labored constantly at her daughter's side, sleeping little during the ensuing forty-eight hours, until there was a gray pallor to her face and Christopher began to fear for his wife's health, as well. He tried to comfort her, to get her to rest.

"It's my fault, Christopher," she cried, so overtired she

was no longer thinking coherently. "I was the one in contact with Clara. I brought the germs . . ."

"My love, stop . . . please! No one is to blame. You did all you could to prevent this and are doing all you can now."

"And to so little good! I can't stand it. I can't stand to see her suffer, and be able to do nothing to help her!"

"Oh, Jessica . . . dearest love." Gently he rubbed his hands over the weary muscles of her back. "I know how you feel . . . I know. Come, lie here for a moment on the bed. Rest. I will watch over Mary. It will do you no good to waste all your strength now and be ill yourself when Mary is better." He stayed with her until her eyes closed and she fell off into a troubled sleep that she had too long denied her body.

Later that night Jessica took her turn, watching the baby while Christopher rested. Gently she lifted the two-month-old child from the cradle, and listened in agony to her wheezing, rasping breaths. Tenderly she hugged her child close against her breast as she rocked her and crooned to her. For a short time it didn't register in Jessica's mind that Mary's labored breaths were coming no longer; that there was a terrible stillness to the infant in her arms. When it did, she stared at the tiny pale cheeks, the closed eyes, the minuscule mouth, terrified of comprehending the truth, refusing to believe what she feared the most. The tiny child in her arms was so still, the face so serene, the fragile chest unmoving, wearily having given up the battle for life-giving air.

"No!" Her cry echoed across the room, reverberating against the walls. "No, Mary, you cannot die! I won't let you! Breathe. Breathe!" In desperation she placed her mouth over the child's in an effort at artificial respiration . . . not thinking, only instinctively trying to force the needed breath into her child.

Her cry pulled Christopher from his sleep. He came bounding out of the bed to his wife's side. He saw his child's still form, his wife's attempts at revival; saw from the expression on Jessica's face that she was going into shock. He quickly knelt at her side, his fingers pressing to feel for a pulse in the baby's neck. There was none.

"Jessica, please . . . my love, that will not help."

"I can't let her die! My baby . . . my tiny baby . . ."

"Jessica, I know, but it is more than just her breath that has stopped. My love, she was weak, tired. Her heart has given up."

"Don't tell me that! I won't listen to you." She clutched her baby closer.

"Do you think I do not feel the pain?" Tears were running down his cheeks unheeded as he himself felt the finality of Mary's death. "We did all we could . . . but the disease was stronger than we were. It is too late."

"I won't let it happen!" She dropped her head again to the baby's mouth. She was too torn with grief, too bent on her mission to save her child, to realize that her efforts were gaining no response. The color was all but drained from the baby's lifeless form. Even the bluish tinge was fading, being replaced by an awful white.

It was more than Christopher's heart could bear. Roughly he shook his wife's shoulders. "Jessica, stop!" he sobbed. "Stop! She is gone!"

Despite all her efforts, deep within herself Jessica knew the truth. Now a racking cry shook her body. All her anguish, her grief, her hatred at the unfairness of it all came out in one cry. Christopher held her and the now peaceful infant close to his chest.

"Oh, Jessica . . ." There was no peace in his own voice as he tried to comfort his wife. How could there be peace? This daughter he had helped bring into the world was dead. Was that justice? Was much of anything that life had done to him and Jessica in the last three years *justice*? They were together again, yes, and Kit was alive and healthy; but what of those years of separation, and now the death of their second child, the still-uncertain future looming before them?

"Christopher!" Jessica sobbed.

"I am here."

"I couldn't bear to have you leave, too."

"I will not." He didn't even try to brush the wetness from her cheeks or from her own.

"I loved her so much."

"I, too . . . Jessica, let me take her from you . . . put her in the cradle."

Again Jessica sobbed. "How can I let her go? . . . I don't need to cover Mary anymore to try to keep her warm, do I?" She spoke from dazed shock.

"Do not talk like that . . . please. We need to think that she is at peace now . . . and she is."

"She was suffering so."

Almost without Jessica's understanding what he was doing, he took the baby from her arms, placed her gently in the cradle, and covered her. He brought the blanket up nearly to cover her face, but couldn't; that sight would be more than either of them could bear. Though grief was tearing him apart, he tried to hold himself together. He went to Jessica again, drew her away from the immediate sight of the baby. There was a gentle rapping on the door.

"Sir. Ma'am." A soft voice, hesitant. "Not to disturb you, but I heard the cries. Is there anything I can do?"

"Mrs. Bloom?" Christopher answered.

"Yes."

"Kit is asleep?"

"He is."

"Then come in."

The gray-haired woman entered cautiously; saw Christopher and Jessica standing in the middle of the room, the child in the cradle by the fire.

"The babe?" the woman asked, her face registering her deepest fear.

"Yes," Christopher whispered. "She . . . died . . . a few moments ago."

Mrs. Bloom shook her head, stifled her own cry. "My dear Lord," she sighed. "A sad night . . . a sad night indeed." For Mrs. Bloom, who also loved the infant, there was a painful tightness in her throat to think that the child was gone. She had lived through a lot of sadness in her fifty odd years of life, and that experience came to her aid now. She looked toward Jessica, whose face was pressed against her husband's shoulder; saw Christopher's glassy, disbelieving eyes, and called up her reserve of strength. "What can I do for you?"

"We will need the doctor . . . to certify. Send Jim. And my wife needs something to restore her . . . a brandy? I do not know . . ."

"I will see to both. But, sir, wouldn't it be best if you both left the room?"

"The baby . . ."

"Forgive my saying it, but there's not much good you can do for her now, and your wife's not in a good way."

"We will wait for the doctor."

"Then I will go take care of the rest. Master Kit will be all right. He didn't hear a thing, and I won't say a word to the child."

"Thank you."

It seemed an interminable time before the doctor arrived, although less than thirty minutes had passed. The brandy had brought some color back to Jessica's cheeks and Christopher's, but they were also gaining a sharper clarity of their loss.

The doctor's examination was brief before he signed the death certificate. He was an older man who'd seen much, yet he sighed as he handed the document to Christopher, and took him aside.

"My deepest condolences. With pneumonia there can be no sureties."

"I realize."

"Your wife has taken it very hard." He glanced toward Jessica, now seated on the bed with Mrs. Bloom's arm about her.

Christopher nodded.

"I would prescribe a laudanum sedative tonight." He peered up at Christopher. "And for yourself as well, sir. I will leave a small dose." He paused. "Best to get her with child again as soon as possible. A new baby will help to ease the loss of the last."

Christopher heard his words, but didn't respond. It was too soon to be thinking of that. He bid the doctor good-bye and returned to his wife. As Christopher administered the laudanum, distracting Jessica's attention, Mrs. Bloom quietly carried the baby from the room to one of the empty guest rooms.

Two days later, on a rainy April morning, Mary Jessica Dunlap was buried in the newly consecrated family plot on the grounds of their home. Christopher, who in the previous days had gone about the sad tasks of making all the necessary arrangements and notifying their closest friends of their loss, stood at the graveside beside his veil-shrouded wife. As the first shovel of dirt was cast over the minute casket, Christopher could barely keep his pain in check; yet his wife remained silent and white-faced beside him, watching the shovel being lifted, listening to the clergyman's words. Her silence disturbed him. After the night of Mary's death, when she'd broken down and cried, she'd walked about a somber-faced introvert, seemingly contending with her loss; but Christopher knew that she wasn't bearing up at all—only pushing the deepest pain aside. He wished she could give into her grief. Open grief was healing; it would not make their loss any less, but it would not leave all the pain inside, to fester there.

But Jessica did not break down again. He watched her go through the ordeal of meeting sympathizers at the house after the service, accepting their condolences, her facial expression immobile, devoid of emotion.

He had no way of knowing that his wife's silence masked a deep depression. She had been through so much pain and fear in the last three and a half years—losing Christopher; having to learn to cope with a strange, unfamiliar world, always fearing for her son's and her own well-being; never knowing if she'd find Christopher again—suddenly she could take no more. Mary's death had brought home to Jessica just how great were the hardships of this nineteenth century world. Until then, having Christopher back again, her family together, had been enough; she had made it enough. After Christopher's admonitions months before, she had forced herself to overlook the inconveniences of everyday life, avoid thinking about the misgivings in the back of her mind. Most of the time, she'd been able to put aside her feeling of isolation, of being cut off from the mental stimulation that had been her mainstay in the world she'd once known. Now she could no longer pretend that she didn't miss her own world. Mary would not have died in the twentieth century! There would have been medication to save her. Instead of lying beneath a gravestone in the cold ground, she would have been a laughing, healthy baby!

As the weeks passed, Jessica looked at the world as though through gray-tinted glasses. Everything was obscured by a haze, and nothing around her could break through it. She would stand at the windows of the house and gaze out toward the Sound, knowing the beauty that nature was displaying for her there, yet unable to appreciate it. Nor could she respond to her husband's efforts at cheering her.

Christopher's arm would come around her in the night. She'd feel him pulling her close to his warmth as his hands softly caressed her, telling her of his love. Once they'd been moments she'd cherished; but now, much though she wanted, deep inside, to respond with the same uninhibited ardor as he demonstrated to her, she was like a puppet, mechanically going through the motions of lovemaking.

Afterward, one night, as they lay in each other's arms, his fingers tangled in the thick length of her hair, he gave a deep sigh of pain. Her pretense at participating in the act had not fooled him—not the man who knew her so very well.

"Oh, my love," he whispered. The desperate tone of his voice, the touch of his hands were telling her so clearly of his efforts to reach out to her. Still she could not respond; could only lie inert in his arms. Soon the gentle caress of his hands ceased, and she could sense the tension in his body as he fought for sleep that wouldn't come.

She didn't want to do this to him. She hated herself for it, but was unable to free herself from the mental turmoil that gripped her. What was the matter with her? She *wanted* to laugh again, to feel a soft peace and contentment, to appreciate the good things she did have. If only the dark clouds in her mind would go away!

Still, in the weeks that followed, there was little change in her state. She couldn't stop the self-destructive onslaught of her depression. In a modern world a psychiatrist could have helped her, but here there was no one who could ease her onto a brighter path.

In her listlessness she let the overseeing of the household slide. Clara came to her late one Saturday morning with a tentative dinner menu from the cook that needed Jessica's approval. Jessica was seated at the desk in the morning parlor, sorting through some correspondence; trying, and failing, to summon enthusiasm to frame her responses. She took the menu from Clara's hand and glanced over it without really seeing what was written.

"I'm sure it is all right, Clara. Tell cook to prepare whatever she likes. Her judgment is never lacking. I need not be consulted." Jessica handed back the handwritten menu and turned toward the window; she missed the sad shaking of the maid's head.

"Is there anything else, ma'am?"

"No. Go ahead, Clara. Cook will know what to do."

"Very well, ma'am."

As the maid left, Jessica continued to stare out the window, lost in her own dreary thoughts. She didn't hear footsteps approaching until she felt a hand come to rest lightly on her shoulder. Gasping, she swung her head around.

"I did not mean to startle you, Jessica." Christopher's eyes were full of concern as he gazed down at her. Then he stepped over to pull a side chair from along the wall, and sat down in it so that he was facing her.

"I overheard your conversation with Clara just now."

"Yes?" Her voice was flat, lacking any intimation of curiosity about what he was going to say.

"It is your responsibility to approve that menu. You cannot leave everything in the cook's hands." Despite the words, his voice was gentle.

"What does it matter?" She shrugged weakly. "You know she will always put a good meal before you."

"It mattered to you once. Once you wanted to know every detail of what was going on in the house."

"I suppose."

"My love, you are the mistress here. People look to you for supervision."

"They are running things very efficiently."

"And if you continue to take no interest in things, soon they will be running the house according to their tastes, not yours." He reached out and took her hands. They laid limp within his. "Please, Jessica. What can I do to snap you out of this? You must begin to take an interest in things again. We will take a ride in the country. It is a lovely day. Just the two of us? Or bring Kit along? If you would prefer, I will plan a few days' trip and take you into New York for some shopping."

"No. I don't really want to go anywhere, Christopher. It's too soon . . ."

"I know you mourn Mary. So do I—deeply. But life goes on."

"Yes, I know." She turned her face from his, back toward the window. "Give me time, Christopher. I need time . . ."

"I will. But will you promise me to try to take a stronger hand with the servants?"

"Yes."

"Look at me, Jessica," he pleaded.

She looked, her green eyes caught by the intensity in his blue ones. As she did so, she knew she loved him; knew he was trying to help her. Why did she feel so dead inside? It was a question she couldn't answer.

As though sensing that he could press the issue no further, Christopher squeezed her hands and rose. "You are sure you do not want to go for a drive?"

"Yes."

"Then I will be in my study for a while, going through some papers. Come get me if you change your mind?"

She nodded.

And Jessica tried to be more active in the next few weeks. Remembering Christopher's words, she took a firmer hand with the servants, but even as she checked on the details of the household, she knew her effort was forced, not spontaneous. She was going through the motions of living, but the zest and sparkle were not there, and no amount of pretending on her part could deceive those around her. She realized that because of her inability to go to Christopher and talk with him about what was troubling her, a chasm was widening in their day-to-day relationship, just as it was in their bed at night.

There was something else troubling Jessica, too, that June. For several weeks she'd suspected; now she was certain. She was pregnant again, and the knowledge filled her with more fear and confusion than ever. What if Mary's fate should befall this child, too; this bit of human who was barely more than a seed within her womb? She wouldn't be able to stand another loss; she would completely lose her sanity.

She held off telling Christopher, pushing through each day, forcing herself to find some activity to occupy all the idle hours and assuage the worries of those around her, who were always watching and wondering when she would become herself again.

She'd settled herself to the task of cleaning the drawers and closets in the master bedroom—the personal compartments she had never let the maids touch. She was going through a drawer in her dressing table—a bottom drawer, rarely used—when her hand pulled forth a tiny lace bonnet, and an envelope on the front of which was written in her hand, "Lock Mary's Hair Two Weeks." As she held the articles, staring at them, her hands began to shake. She could remember, now, putting them there, a temporary storage place until she could get together a scrapbook for Mary as she had done for Kit. Mary had been lying in the cradle, gurgling; an early spring sun shone in through the windows. Jessica had just clipped the half-inch lock of her daughter's hair as a remembrance of that fine, baby softness, then looked at the mantel clock and realized she only had a half hour to get herself and her daughter ready for a visit from Amelia Beard and Mary Weldon. She'd quickly dropped the lock of hair into an envelope, sealed it and dropped it into the bottom drawer of her dressing table, where her daughter's first, tiny cap already rested.

She'd forgotten about both until that moment, but now the sight of the precious mementos filled her with such grief and pain, the tears flowed unheeded down her cheeks.

No, Jessica's mind cried. *No!* The sobs came uncontrollably. She heard the door open; heard Christopher's voice.

"Jessica, whatever is wrong!"

She couldn't answer, even as his arms enfolded her and pulled her up from her kneeling position on the floor.

"Tell me. Tell me." He tried to pull her hands from her face; succeeded in doing so only to have her bury her face against his chest as the sobs continued to come. He held her tightly, waiting for her crying to subside. Then he saw the envelope on the floor and the words written on it. His heart froze. Was this something she'd just accidentally discovered . . . or something she'd been cherishing unhealthily for months?

"Jessica," he whispered in a moment, "I know what is wrong, but you have to stop grieving for Mary. She is gone."

"Don't you feel any of the pain of her death!" Her anguished voice was still muffled by the front of his jacket.

"I do, I do, but we cannot bring her back."

"She wouldn't be dead if it wasn't for this horrid, backward world."

"My love, we cannot change that either. Pull yourself together. There is a future. We have Kit . . . and there can be more children."

"Yes . . . more children. I'm pregnant now."

It took a moment for her words to register. He felt himself tense, then relax. This was the answer to Jessica's problems—a new child to fill the void. He buried his lips in her hair, rubbed his cheek against it. "But Jessica, what wonderful news!"

"So we can have another child die."

"Don't talk like that!" Her words had brought his head up straight. "Because one died, it does not mean our next will. It was a freakish illness! Our next will be fine. Kit is fine—is not he an example?"

"He was born in the twentieth century."

"With no complications—and no medical man even interferred in the birth. You did it yourself. Can that not happen again? And he has not been ill, despite living in this world for three years, since the age of one month. Is that not evidence enough to you?"

"I couldn't stand to have another child die—I couldn't!"

Her reaction was utterly the opposite of what Christopher had expected. He'd thought—prayed—that the anticipation of a new baby would be just what she needed to help her get over Mary's death. That apparently wasn't the case. But perhaps it was too soon? Perhaps the reality of her pregnancy hadn't settled in. Perhaps when she felt the first stirrings of life . . .

For now, he knew he had to get her out of that room and away from the reminders of their lost child. He would have Clara come and clear away the bonnet and the envelope after they were gone. He took Jessica's shoulders and forced her sobbing face away from his chest, then wrapped his arm about her waist.

"You are coming downstairs with me to my study for a brandy."

"I don't want one."

"However, you will have one. Come." He led her toward the door, forcibly. "We will talk."

"There is nothing to say."

"There is a great deal to say, if only you would let me hear the words you are holding inside you. But whether you will talk or not, we are going downstairs."

He led her through the door, out into the hall. Was her acquiescence a result of her numbness of soul? Or was the reason in her mind finally listening to him? He didn't know. He was only thankful that she was following.

She accepted the brandy he made her drink, and it did calm her—but only so that she withdrew into herself again. Christopher did not know how to pull from her the words and feelings that would release her inner anxiety. He did his best, holding her, talking soothingly to her.

"Jessica, I know it is early yet, but you will see—this new child will make the difference. I am so very happy with your news, and there is nothing to fear, my love. Our next child will be fine and healthy. There will be no more tragedy." Silently he prayed, "Please, Jessica, please be yourself again."

For all Christopher's prayers, Jessica's state of mind did not improve as her pregnancy progressed. Now it was not only her past grief that consumed her, but also her anxiety over her own health and that of the child she was carrying. She *must* get enough exercise, she *must* get enough rest; in lieu of vitamins, she *must* eat all the foods that would give the baby and herself the nutrients they needed. She didn't pause to think that while she had carried Mary she had taken more than adequately good care of herself without being obsessive, and the child's death had in no way been caused by her negligence.

As hard as he tried through comforting words and understanding, Christopher could not reach her. To escape his growing feeling of helplessness, he devoted more and more hours to his business, traveling frequently that summer to New York. After a journey of several days in early August, he was particularly anxious to be home; could barely wait to pull into their drive and view the handsome house on the hillside.

At the first sign of the carriage coming up the drive, Kit came bounding out the front door and down the stairs. He waited at the edge of the drive until Christopher pulled the team to a halt, then scrambled up into the seat beside his father to bestow a mighty hug.

"Daddy, Daddy, I missed you!"

"And I missed you, too." Laughing, Christopher held his son in one arm as he jumped down and secured the horses' reins to the hitching post. Automatically he looked toward the broad sweep of front steps, half expecting to find his wife standing there, eagerly awaiting him as she used to do. He forced down his disappointment at finding the stairs empty.

"Come, Kit." He placed his son on the ground. "I think we might find something in the back of the carriage for you."

"Present, Daddy?" The boy started doing an excited jig.

"Just a little something. Close your eyes." As his son complied, he reached into the boot of the carriage and withdrew a small package of sweetmeats which he placed in his son's hands. He knew Jessica wouldn't approve, but the candy was a special treat for the boy, and as Kit opened his eyes and saw what rested in his palms, his pleasure was evident.

"Thank you, Daddy! Not have candy since Christmas."

"I know, so do not go and eat it all this afternoon and get a bellyache."

Christopher also removed another small parcel from the boot, a gift for Jessica. It was a newly published history of New York, and Christopher's effort at trying to waken his wife's mind. Once she had read voraciously, particularly books of history; now she rarely touched one.

With Kit's hand in his, he climbed the stairs. "How is your mother, Kit?"

"She sad a lot. Why she so sad, Daddy?"

"She still misses your sister, Mary."

"But new baby coming. Mama tell me."

"Yes, and let us hope that will help make her happy again."

As they entered the front hall, Jessica came out of the drawing room toward them. She presented her cheek for Christopher's kiss.

"Welcome home. You had a good trip?" Her smile was perfunctory; it didn't reach her eyes, which, Christopher noticed to his deep dismay, were still listless and empty. He reached for her and squeezed her about the waist, hoping to evoke a response.

"The trip was excellent, my love, but I have missed you both."

Jessica said nothing.

He cleared his throat. "I brought something for you."

"Oh?"

"Yes. Knowing how you always enjoy history, I found this new publication about the history of New York." He handed the volume to her.

She flipped it open and briefly examined the title page and contents. "That's very sweet of you, Christopher. Thank you. I haven't been reading much lately."

"I had noticed." He smiled. "I hope this will change that."

"I'll try." She lifted her eyes to his face.

He waited for a bright smile, a hug—some expression similar to what she would have done in the past to let him know she was touched.

Her weak smile was distracted as she dropped her eyes again. "Well, you must be tired. I've told Clara to bring tea into your study. I'll join you there a little later, after I speak to the cook about dinner." She glanced down at her son. "Kit, isn't it time for your nap?"

"But Daddy just get home!" he protested.

"Yes, all right, I suppose for today you can skip it." She started to move off across the hall in the direction of the kitchens, paused and looked back over her shoulder as if in afterthought. "And thank you again for the book, Christopher." She turned her head and was off, leaving her husband and son standing alone.

At least there was no warmth lacking in Christopher's greeting from his son, who was now tugging on his father's coattails.

"Have lots to tell you, Daddy."

Christopher looked down, some of the sad disappointment leaving his eyes as he saw the bright face gazing up at him. "Do you indeed? Shall I give you a piggyback ride into the study so you can tell me everything?"

"Yes!"

As Christopher knelt, Kit quickly climbed up onto his shoulders, laughing merrily as his father rose, jounced Kit playfully, and jogged down the hall.

15

It was late summer when he ran into Rhea Taylor again at a dinner party in New York. They had not seen each other since Christopher and Jessica had moved from the city, and Christopher experienced a strange discomfort now as he looked across the room and saw the woman, as beautiful as ever, standing and chatting with some of the other guests. If she saw him, she gave him no indication, and at dinner they were seated at opposite ends of the table. Later, however, in the drawing room, she approached him. He felt uneasy as he saw her walking in his direction, not sure what to expect. But her smile seemed unaffected as she paused by his side.

"Hello, Christopher. It has been some time, has it not?

"It has indeed. Good evening, Rhea."

"I sense some hesitancy in your tone," she said.

"Justified on my part, would you not say?"

Her eyes studied him. "Yes. We have given each other reason to be wary in the past. That is why I stopped to speak to you tonight. I believe you must know how hurt and angry I was when our engagement was severed so shockingly. I wanted nothing more than to get back at you for the pain and embarrassment you had caused me." She paused, bit her lip. "It has taken me time to realize that I reacted too harshly . . . certain of my actions were unjustified, and I would like to apologize to you. I *am* sorry."

He stared at her, amazed. This was not like Rhea—to offer an apology? "I think if you owe anyone an apology, Rhea, it is my wife. She was the innocent party, who could have suffered the most as a result of your actions."

"I understand that and was going to ask you to convey these sentiments of mine to her."

He was silent, thoughtful. He could not see that Rhea had anything to gain by trying to placate him now. She must be sincere. Still, he was cautious. "Very well, I will relay your apology to Jessica."

"Thank you." She sighed. "It will soothe my conscience greatly to know that you would be willing to let bygones be bygones."

"It is not for me alone to forgive. Though, for myself, I have no desire to nurture old bitterness—as long as there is no repeat of previous occurrences."

"There would not be. My anger has long since been spent. I have come to understand that it was never your deliberate intention to hurt me."

"No, it was not."

Her smile was tentative. "Then might we begin again —as friends? We did have a pleasant friendship once."

"If you are sincere in what you have just said, I am agreeable."

"You have taken a burden off my mind, Christopher. Thank you."

He nodded. "And I appreciate your apology."

"You are in New York on business?"

"Yes."

"I understand from the talk about town that you are doing very well."

"I certainly have nothing to complain about in that respect. The purpose of my trip, as a matter of fact, is to lease some additional warehouse space."

"My congratulations." Her fingers toyed with her ivory-boned fan. "And how is Connecticut? You must have a new addition to your family by now."

Christopher's brow creased in pain. It was a moment before he answered in a tight voice. "Our daughter died this spring . . . of pneumonia."

Rhea's eyes widened in startlement; it was clear she had not heard the news. She lightly touched his arm. "Oh, I am so sorry. I had not heard."

"It has been difficult."

"I can imagine. . . . And your wife?"

"She has taken it hard."

"Understandable. You will give her my sympathy?"

"I shall."

"Well, I will not keep you. I know there are others here with whom you wish to speak. But I am glad we had this opportunity to talk . . . and very happy to have those past difficulties settled between us." Again she touched his arm. "I am terribly sorry about your daughter. Should you ever need anyone to talk to in New York, you know where to find me." And she was gone, gliding across the crowded drawing room.

He stared after her, not knowing fully how to gauge his reaction. He was pleased, he supposed, that Rhea was at last willing to bury the axe, although now, after all this time, that hardly seemed important. Far more important to him at the moment was his wife's continuing depression and his desperate wish to pull her back into the life stream.

He went home from New York with that objective in mind. He cherished no great expectations for the morrow, only a hope that from day to day, in little ways, Jessica would come alive again.

As the summer days drifted behind and fall colored the landscape, there were moments when he thought his prayers were being answered. One warm Indian summer afternoon he looked out the windows of the house to see his wife and son on the front lawns scrambling through the newly fallen leaves. Jessica was laughing—actually laughing. He could barely believe his eyes, but a warm surge of thankfulness rushed through him. He longed to hurry from the house, down to the lawns to join them, but knew that such a response might break the spell. He contented himself with watching as his wife and son gathered up a huge pile of leaves, and Jessica picked up Kit in her arms and tossed him gently into the pile. He came scrambling out, giggling, begging for more, and they continued the game, Christopher lovingly watching the two of them at play until a half an hour later, when they both came into the house.

But Christopher knew only deep despair when, a few nights later, he reached for Jessica in their bed. He'd been very careful and considerate about their lovemaking, never forcing or pressuring her, but it had been days and days since he had made love to her, and that night he particularly needed her warmth and closeness. She was half asleep as he pulled her close and gently began to caress her. She seemed responsive, lying relaxed in his arms, sighing sleepily, and his own desire rose to a burning passion. He rolled over her, his lips tracing a course up her neck to her lips. Suddenly he felt her tense.

"No, Christopher, no! The baby!"

"Jessica, my love, I will be gentle. Our loving will not hurt the child."

"I can't! Stop!" Her hands pushed at his chest.

He rolled away; he had no choice. Her body was steely and resistant beneath him. To have forced himself on her would have been tantamount to rape.

As he took a deep breath and lay there trying to control the ache in his heart, he thought he heard a whispered, "I'm sorry, Christopher." But it was so soft, so barely discernible, it could just as easily have been his imagination hearing the words he wanted to hear. When he turned his head to look at her, her face was turned slightly away, her eyes closed. In the darkness he didn't notice the tears that dampened her long eyelashes.

Soon afterward he saw Rhea Taylor again in New York. It wasn't surprising that their paths crossed since they attended so many of the same functions. Rhea made no advances; she behaved in a purely friendly manner, and he found that her witty conversation and solicitousness were a salve to his loneliness. She understood him perfectly and went out of her way to entertain him and lighten his worries. Although she said nothing to him, he sensed she knew there was a rift in his marital life, but he was careful to divulge nothing that would confirm this to her.

Throughout the balance of the fall and through the winter, they encountered each other many times when

Christopher traveled to New York, and since the relationship seemed no more than casual friendship, Christopher felt no qualms. Jessica was always in the forefront of his mind, and for the rest, he drifted with the tide.

Their daughter, Jennifer, was born that March of 1818. The birth was uncomplicated, both Christopher and a doctor in attendance, and the child was the picture of good health.

Christopher breathed a sigh of relief as Jessica held the baby in her arms and, for the first time in many months, a genuine, unforced smile sprang to his wife's lips. His relief was short lived, however. Although Jessica lavished love on her new offspring, she made no attempt to heal the breach between herself and her husband, and seemed not to realize that anything was wrong. All her energies now were channeled into protecting their new child. Visitors were screened so that no unsuspected diseases were brought into the house. She saw personally to most of Jennifer's needs, exhausting herself with the child's care, leaving Mrs. Bloom only Kit to look after. If Jessica had gained a new awareness of her surroundings, of her husband's needs, of life bubbling in her veins, Christopher could not detect it in the overtired woman who ran his household and stumbled into bed each night. Even then there was no closeness between them; she immediately dropped off into exhausted sleep, only to be wakened a few hours later by the baby in the cradle by her bedside, hungry for her next feeding.

And when the child outgrew her need for night feedings, Jessica did not relax her hawklike vigilance, keeping the cradle in their bedroom, rebuffing Christopher's advances with the excuse they might wake the child.

Not until Jennifer was three months old did Christopher's temper finally boil over.

"Jessica, this has got to stop!" They'd just sat down at the dinner table, the only hour of the day when they were entirely alone. But Jessica sat as usual, distracted and withdrawn, her thoughts preoccupied with her child. "For over a year now I have lived with a shadow. First you could think of nothing but your own grief. I could understand that; I suffered, too. But now when you have another child to comfort you, still I see no smiles. Jennifer is a healthy child. There is no need for you to hover over her as though she cannot take a breath without your being at her side! Give a thought to the rest of us in this house!"

"I do."

"How? When? Certainly not while I am here to witness it. Lately Kit sees more of Mrs. Bloom than he does of you, and if not for him, I do not think my absence would even be noted in this house. When I talk to you, you seem not to hear me, and otherwise answer in monosyllables. And do you realize it has been two months—two *months*—since you allowed me to make love to you? My patience is at an end, Jessica!"

She stared at him. In no way had she been prepared for this outbreak on his part; nor, she felt certain, had she been as insensitive as he seemed to think. "You've never understood what Mary's death did to me—why I fear so much for this child. Do you think I could go on if anything happened to Jennifer? And before that, did you ever care when I was unhappy, when I felt cooped up and stifled, pushed into a mold? Do you care now? Or is it just your own happiness you're concerned about?" Her tone became derisive. "Be a good little wife, Jessica. Don't think of yourself. You are only a possession. Do what will please your husband, like all the other good little wives. Then your husband will smile, and everything will be all right." It was though a dam had broken—the words flooded out of her without her fully realizing what she was saying.

"Have I been that inconsiderate? I hesitate to believe it!"

"No . . . not totally," she admitted.

"I should think not! And if I am not mistaken, it is you who have disrupted this household with your depression the last year."

"I know. It did not make me happy, either, but it was something I had no control over."

"You have control over it now? Or is it the reason for this sudden and unwarranted outburst of yours?" He spoke more sharply than he wished, but he was still smarting from her biting and, he felt, uncalled-for comments.

At his tone, Jessica became furious. Yes, she'd been wrong at times. Yes, she had been depressed, and everyone in the house had suffered as a result. But it was not deliberate. She had not set out to bring discomfort on anyone. Yes, now perhaps she was a little overprotective of Jennifer, but he should be able to understand how she felt as a mother. In any case, what interest had been left to her but the children? *He* had his business to occupy him. And she had *not* been neglecting Kit, no matter what he thought. "You don't seem to care anymore what I am feeling . . . just as long as I fill the role of wife and mother and insure that everything is perfect happiness for you. Once upon a time, you respected me for my intelligence and opinions, understood that I needed stimulating outlets."

"I still respect your intelligence. Have I not encouraged you in reading and expanding your mind? *You* have been the one who has lost interest. Do you remember that history book I bought you months ago? I doubt you have yet to read a page of it. What other outlets do you expect me to provide for you? This is not the twentieth century. I know you have had an adjustment to make—I know what you are facing, for I faced much the same in learning to adjust to *your* world! Did you hear me continually bemoaning all I had lost—my fortune, my position, my estates? No! I realized I had no choice but to make do in a world where my ignorance of its customs often made me look and feel the fool!"

"At least I tried to help you . . . understand what you were facing. I never tried to change you into something you were not."

"What do you expect from me? I have tried to do everything in my power for you. All I have asked is that you behave like a respectable woman and conform to the standards of the time. You cannot go back to your world—you will have to learn to live with things the way they are!"

"Yes—learn to live with and conform to a set of constricting and unfair conventions! As a woman I must learn to see myself as a second-class citizen, a chattel. I am not allowed to grow as you did in the twentieth century. Instead I am asked—*expected*—to throw away all I have learned—to regress!"

"Come, Jessica, it is not as bad as that!"

"No? How would you know? You are out there in this man's world as one of the rulers. Do you really have any idea what it's been like for me? Do you really *care?*"

"I do not understand you!" Roughly he pushed back his chair and began to rise, his face white with anger. "I have bent over backwards trying to be patient. Yet you seem to think you are the only one who has suffered. Can you not appreciate that I, too, have had a burden to bear, that I live with worry—the fear that I may again lose my family and—for a third time—everything else that I have worked so hard to achieve?"

Leaving his unfinished dinner on his plate, he stormed from the room.

"Christopher!"

The only response she received was the slamming of the dining room door behind him.

Jessica sat in shocked silence after his departure and stared unseeing at the door. What had happened to them? How could they, who had once been so close, have drifted so far apart? Could this unfeeling man be the Christopher who'd once been so close to her she'd felt they were one being? Could her buried discontent and recent depression have brought them to this? No. She wasn't so lost in her listless misery anymore that she could accept all the blame.

Christopher did not go up to bed until late that night, and the next morning left at dawn for a few days in New York. He knew that he was running away from his problems, but he had to escape the atmosphere in the house. He could not understand what Jessica wanted. Wasn't he the injured party? Hadn't he put up with her depression without complaint for longer than most men would have? What did she need to make her happy? Why couldn't she accept that she was no longer in the twentieth century? Why couldn't she be content with a life any other woman would find satisfying?

He went out to a reception in New York that evening. He hoped the interaction with other people would be enough to force away his confusion and dim his anger.

He suspected Rhea would be there—and she was, looking elegant and beautiful. She greeted him with a wide smile.

"Just the gentleman I was hoping to see this evening." She took his arm. "I believe I have found a very lucrative new business contact for you."

"Have you indeed?" He had been in the company of this vivacious woman for but a moment, and already he was beginning to relax.

"Yes, a friend of mine from Savannah has interest in opening some trade with New York, and I have heard you mention your desire to expand your outlets."

"I would be delighted to meet him."

"Come along then." Rhea drew Christopher across the room and introduced him to a gentleman of about his age. She remained at Christopher's side as the two men spoke briefly and made an appointment to meet later that week.

"I thank you, Rhea," Christopher said as they stepped away through the crowd. "This opportunity shows much promise."

"As I thought."

He handed her a glass of champagne from the tray being passed around the room, and took a glass for himself. It was not his first; he'd had several glasses already in the hope that the effervescent beverage would float his troubles away.

Rhea studied him as she took a sip. "You seem pensive and tense this evening. Is something troubling you?"

"You might say."

"Come, we are friends. You can speak about it, and perhaps would feel better getting it off your chest."

"This is not the place."

"We could find somewhere else to talk. Come to the house for a nightcap."

"Thank you, but that would not be seemly. I understand your father is away from home."

"True, but we are both adults. There was a time you would not have been disturbed to learn Father was away."

"My situation has changed considerably since then."

"Who is to know you are there? And you clearly do need to talk to someone."

He swallowed down his champagne in one gulp. He knew it would be unwise to be with her alone, but because of his mood, he agreed. "Very well. I have some farewells to make here before I leave. I will meet you at your father's in half an hour."

Forty-five minutes later, settled comfortably on the sofa at Rhea's, brandy glass in hand, Christopher let go of his doubts about the wisdom of his being there. There could be no harm in talking to this woman, and no one would know he was there. Rhea could not speak of his visiting her alone that evening lest she cast a shadow on her own conduct. She sat on the sofa next to him now, watching him lazily with her green eyes.

"This is better, is it not? I can see you are more relaxed already."

"Yes."

"So what is it that is troubling you?"

He began to talk quietly, staring at the wall opposite him. As he continued, describing the events that had occurred since his daughter's death, he felt an immense relief at being able finally to talk freely to someone about the burden he had struggled with silently. Rhea refilled his brandy glass, rested a compassionate hand on his shoulder.

When he was finished, she sighed. "It is such a pity this is happening after all you have already suffered. She certainly is being unjust."

At another time Christopher would have reacted negatively to such a comment made about his wife. It was one thing for him to be critical of Jessica; quite another for him to countenance anything less than praise of her issuing from the lips of others. But now he only said mildly, "It is good that you have let me talk to you, Rhea. My spirits have improved considerably."

"I only wish I could do more." As she spoke, she moved up beside him on the couch; her hand, as though by accident, brushed his thigh.

At her touch, he remembered in a flash the nights he and Rhea had shared little more than two years ago, the passion this woman had once aroused in him. He'd become so accustomed to Jessica's indifference to his advances, it was a heady sensation to realize that this woman beside him would show no such indifference; quite the contrary.

"I *could* do more for you if you would let me," she whispered, her voice a soft invitation. "It is not as though we are strangers to each other."

"Far from it." The alcohol he'd consumed was hazing his mind, but heightening his senses. He knew he wanted and needed a woman—one who would respond enthusiastically to him.

"A man like you should not be denied the warmth he needs." Her fingertips caressed his cheek. "And you do need it, do you not?"

"Yes . . . that I will not deny."

"Come upstairs to my room."

"Rhea, I cannot. We must consider our actions."

"We are both adults. Why should we forgo the small comfort we can bring each other?" She was already rising, taking the empty glass from his hand.

Her inviting words were taking hold in his mind. The touch of her hand, the movement of her full lips . . . Rhea's many enticements were arousing a physical desire that needed little further encouragement. It was, after all, only for one night. And Jessica assuredly did not desire him or make any effort to satisfy his frustrated yearnings. He made his decision, rose; followed Rhea from the room.

Once they were in her elegantly decorated bedroom, she turned toward him, and Christopher drew her to him. Up to the moment Rhea's lips pressed against his, he'd held on to a shred of reason; but with that hot, sensuous pressure, all logic left him. He sighed deeply, tightened his arms

around her as she arched her back to put her hips in closer
contact with him.

"Ah, Christopher," she murmured. "Such a man . . .
like none I have met before, or will again."

His mouth greedily captured hers again, his tongue
seeking as his hands worked loose the fastenings of her
gown and began exploring her velvet flesh. Within minutes they were undressed, their naked bodies sliding together on the satin covers of the bed; their legs and arms
sought one another, entwining; her hungry caresses skill-
fully roused him further until he was aching for her, wanting nothing but to bury himself deep within her. He forced
Jessica from his mind; thought of nothing but the physical
moment as Rhea's hand gently gripped him and directed
him into her waiting body. As he entered, his mouth fastened to her breasts, and she cried out softly.

"More, Christopher, more . . . let me feel you . . .
deeper . . ."

Acceding to her wish and his own overwhelming need,
he gave himself up to the pulsing waves of pleasure. With
each of his thrusts, she moaned, pulled him tighter against
her, moved her hips, until he, too, was gasping, holding
back until it was impossible to do so any longer. As his orgasm crashed over him, she continued to move urgently,
soon gave a throaty sigh and shuddered beneath him.

"I had forgotten . . . tried to forget . . . how wonderful
you are," she whispered a few moments later when heartbeat and breath had returned to normal.

He knew only a great weariness. He'd slept little the
night before, and now, his long-frustrated physical needs
satisfied, a desire for sleep washed over him in smothering
waves.

She spoke again, but he barely heard her, only felt the
warmth of the covers being drawn up over his chest. He let
his mind drift off; tomorrow he would think of all the
things he knew he had to think about . . . whatever they
were . . . Immediately he fell into a deep sleep.

It came as a shock to him that next morning when he
opened his eyes to a strange room and Rhea's black tresses
spread out on the pillow beside him. It took him a moment

to remember, and when he did, a sick knot clenched at his stomach. What had he done? How had he allowed himself to take such a foolish step? The throbbing in his temples—the aftermath of his overimbibing the night before—did not help his state of mind as he thought of the repercussions that might ensue from this one evening of folly. He knew Rhea too well; she would not let it go with just this one night. She would expect more, and he had no one to blame but himself. And Jessica—for all their misunderstanding, did she deserve this? He'd always thought himself more of a man than to behave so childishly, so spitefully.

He sat up in bed, feeling an urgent need to be out of that house. He must get dressed, leave. As he swung his legs over the side of the bed, his head throbbed miserably—a hangover of grandiose proportions. He couldn't seem to get his mind to function clearly.

At his movement, Rhea stirred and woke. He felt the palm of her hand on his back, heard her sleep-misted voice. "Good morning. Did you sleep well?"

"Yes." He barely recognized the croak that came from his lips.

"But why are you getting up? It is early yet; come back here where it is warm and cozy."

"I must go."

"There is no rush. They will not miss you if you are an hour late at your office."

"No, Rhea." He stood, paused a moment to let the pressure in his head settle, and walked to the chair where his clothing had been flung the evening before. He reached for his breeches.

In an instant she was out of bed, quickly slipping into a lacy and nearly transparent robe. She had been wily the night before, pressing on him all the alcohol he could consume, but drinking lightly herself. Rhea knew he was confused now, while her own head was clear, and she went up to him as he began to button his shirt. Her expression was sweet, her manner coaxing and innocent.

"Well, if you must leave, I will not keep you, but why not let me ring for coffee before you go?"

"Best your servants not know I spent the night in the house. I will slip out the side door."

She smiled, careful not to let her irritation show. "As you wish. We will see each other soon, in any case."

He'd been waiting for those words. "I think not."

"Oh?"

"Last evening was a mistake. I do not blame you, but I cannot see you again, Rhea." Oh, his blasted head. If only it would stop aching!

"You are being rash, don't you think? We have spent an evening that brought us both pleasure, and we are civilized adults."

"What you do not understand, Rhea, is that despite our misunderstandings, I love my wife. I would not wish to hurt her so."

"It is a bit late now to think of that—and you would not have come here last night unless, deep inside, you wanted to."

If he'd been thinking more clearly, he might have come back with a rebuttal, but now he could only shake his head in confusion.

She saw him weakening; made her final point subtly. "What harm can there be in our seeing each other on those occasions you are in New York? It will, after all, be our secret. No one else need ever know."

"We shall see." He couldn't argue with her any longer. He had to get out of this house; prayed sanity would return when he reached the city street.

But she was satisfied with his response and let the subject rest. As he made for the door, his dressing complete, she only smiled. "Have a good day, Christopher."

During the next few days, as he finished his business in New York, his guilt plagued him. He stayed far from the social scene, instead spending what free time he had visiting with either Robert Bayard or Mawson and Abbey. But even with these old friends he could not relax, knowing all the while he talked with them just what they would have thought of his meeting with Rhea a few nights earlier. His guilt was further aggravated by an offhand comment made by Bayard.

"I must say I am glad to see more of you than the last time you were in the city. I was a trifle concerned when I heard the talk that you and Rhea Taylor were again striking up quite a friendship."

Christopher reacted quickly. "Just casual meetings. I was bound to run across her. She only wished to inform me that her past bitterness had been laid to rest."

Bayard nodded, and Christopher changed the subject.

The next day he returned to Eastport, looking forward eagerly but anxiously to the sight and presence of his own home, his waiting wife and children. What reception would he receive from Jessica? Had she been thinking through the argument that had precipitated his sudden departure for New York? Had anything of what he had said gotten through to her, or had he only succeeded in turning her further from him?

As he strode through the front door just before dinner, Clara informed him that Jessica was upstairs feeding the baby. He was not certain what to do: wait downstairs until she came down to say hello, or go immediately up to their room. He went to his study, had a brandy, paced in indecision, then finally went up. As he stepped down the hall to their bedroom, she was just emerging, the baby in her arms. She turned and watched him come toward her.

"Hello, Christopher. Clara told me you'd arrived home."

Was there reproof in her tone that he hadn't come up immediately? Was his guilt so evident on his face that she read it?

"She told me you were feeding the baby."

"Yes." She paused. She was regarding him so intensely, he felt she was seeing right through him. "You had a good trip?" she finally asked.

"Passable."

"You left in such a rush that morning."

"I did not want to wake you."

"I see."

In the next seconds' silence, he sensed she was waiting for something—some comment from him about their argument? Now when he was feeling such pangs of remorse, realizing how much he still loved her, should have been the time to try to talk to her. But he was afraid to talk; afraid he would give himself away. If only she would bring up their recent argument. Was that what was on her mind as she looked at him so levelly?

The silence seemed to drag on. Finally, Jessica spoke. "Well, I must bring Jennifer to Miss Bloom for her nap. I will see you at dinner?"

"Yes."

She hesitated, her eyes still on his face. "Welcome home." Then she turned toward the children's room, across the hall, and disappeared through the door.

Jessica waited during those first days of his return for some sign from him that he was ready to make amends; that he'd thought over their last harsh words to each other and regretted what he'd said; that they could talk again, this time with patience and understanding. But she saw no sign, and felt too timid to broach the subject herself. She tried on several occasions to talk to him of relatively casual matters, hoping the conversation might lead in the direction of their recent argument. As they were finishing dinner a few evenings later, she spoke mildly.

"I received a letter from Abbey today."

"Oh? And how are she and Willis?"

"Very well. They hope to come up and visit us a few days this summer."

"Excellent."

"She said they haven't seen all that much of you in New York . . . you've been very busy, I guess."

His throat tightened. "Yes, I have." Had Mawson and Abbey, like Bayard, heard of his renewed friendship with Rhea? Had Abbey mentioned it in the letter to Jessica? . . . No, had that been the case, they would have said something to him when he last saw them. Still, the mere thought of Jessica's finding him out put him in a cold panic.

He said as little to her as possible, adding to the barriers he had already put up to hide his guilt, keeping all soft feelings from her.

"What week shall I tell them to come?" Jessica questioned.

"It makes no difference. Whatever you wish." He found he couldn't concentrate.

"But I want to work it around your travel plans." She gave a small smile. "I don't want them to be here and you in New York."

"Could we talk of this another time? I am very tired, Jessica." And he was tired. The worry on his mind, compounded by the weariness of a full day's work, left him exhausted.

But his words closed Jessica off. "Very well," she said tightly.

"I am going to my study for a few minutes, Jessica. I will be up to bed early."

"You don't want your coffee?"

"Not this evening, thank you," he said with all the politeness of a perfect stranger.

By the time Christopher went upstairs that night, he was feeling remorse for his shortness to her at dinner. He wanted to make amends.

He came to stand behind her as she sat at the dressing table brushing her hair. "Jessica, I have been thinking about Willis and Abbey. Why not tell them to come the last week in July?"

"All right." *Her* tone was short, now. She'd spent the last two hours nursing a feeling of hurt and rejection; she couldn't suddenly smile and push her anger away. "I'll write to Abbey tomorrow."

Christopher stood there indecisively a few seconds longer. He wanted to step over and place comforting hands on her shoulders, hold her, but Jessica was staring rigidly into the mirror on the dressing table, giving him no encouragement. Finally he shrugged, turned, and went to prepare himself for bed.

The situation between them went from bad to worse, and it was not long before Christopher began to wonder why he should be feeling any guilt at all. Once again he began longing for an escape back to New York, away from the stifling tension in the house.

He did not deliberately seek out Rhea; it happened more by chance, although he made no effort to avoid situations where he might run across her—as he soon did, at the theater. It was so much easier this second time to persuade himself that he was being wronged at home and needed the outlet of her companionship; so much easier to let one thing slide into the next and again share her bed. Still easier was it the morning after to rationalize that he was only behaving as would any other man of his day and stature in enjoying a small liaison outside his marriage when his needs were not met by his wife at home.

Unfortunately, he could not deceive himself completely, and in the back of his mind he knew the wrong of his actions; yet he allowed the situation to continue. Much as when he'd first met Rhea, he let himself be pulled along. His trips to New York again grew more frequent. Rhea and he shared their secret hours, but he was exhausted by the double life he was leading. At times he found himself wishing to forever dissolve the illicit relationship.

But Rhea, now that she had him trapped so firmly, had no intention of letting him go. Realizing Christopher was troubled, and fearing he would decide to end the affair, she let slip a thinly veiled threat to the effect that should he decide to leave her, she would have no qualms about seeing that word of what had been going on got back to his wife's ears.

Christopher could not bear to have Jessica suffer the pain of discovering his infidelity. He was truly caught in a trap; damned if he did, and damned if he did not. It was precisely what Rhea had planned from the start. Christopher was in her grip again, and would remain there.

16

The sunlight flooded the bedroom, slanting across Jessica's face and coaxing her eyes open. Instinctively she reached across the bed to where Christopher lay, only to find what was becoming more the rule than the exception, an empty space. She remembered he was off again on a business trip to New York and would not return until tomorrow. Then, as her mind lazily came awake, she recalled the shattering event that had occurred the afternoon before.

She'd been at a tea in Eastport, sitting with Mary Weldon, the two of them chatting about their respective families and other local news, when during a lull in their conversation, the would-be-hushed comments of two elderly matrons seated behind them had reached their ears.

"Such a pity," said the first woman in what emerged from her lips as a stage whisper. "On top of all the tragedy poor Jessica Dunlap has experienced."

"Yes," said her equally hard-of-hearing companion. "Bad enough a man is unfaithful—but to take up with his former mistress!"

"I was at that ball at the Beards' two years ago. A more brazen-faced woman than that Taylor creature I have never met . . . always thought she would make a move to get him back."

"Indeed a pity . . ."

The cup had begun shaking in Jessica's hand. She was forced to rest it on her lap so others wouldn't notice. It seemed impossible to believe. Christopher was seeing Rhea again. All those trips to New York—yes, it made sense. Why hadn't she considered the possibility before? She'd felt a knot of cold anger and pain closing her throat; had wanted to get up and rush from the room, scream out her anguish. Only Mary Weldon, who had also heard the comments and was looking over anxiously at her friend's white face, had forestalled Jessica's flight. Mary had remained silent, giving her unspoken sympathy, as Jessica had fought for control and composed her features.

And Jessica had remained in shocked control. It was not until late that night, when she'd climbed into bed, alone again, that the sobs had come—racking cries as she'd flung herself against her pillows and wondered how, why, things had come to *this*.

She'd literally cried herself to sleep, and now, as she touched her eyelids, she felt their puffiness. She rose quickly from the bed and went to her dressing table mirror. She stood before it and stared coolly and objectively at the image of the woman reflected there—at the red eyes, the disheveled hair, the shapeless sack of a cotton nightgown—good heavens! left over from her servant days—the chapped and unmanicured hand that was pressed to her pale cheek. It was her hands, perhaps, that made the most startling sight. She used to have such beautiful hands; long, smooth, slender fingers tipped by immaculately kept almond-shaped nails. How could she have let herself go like this? And her hair! She'd always washed and brushed her hair frequently and arranged it so that it shone in artfully placed curls atop her head. Now it was pulled sharply back, a few straggling ends fallen unkempt across her cheeks. The red-rimmed eyes were only a temporary result of her crying the night before—but where was the life in them? A listlessness and lack of interest were apparent, too, in the set of the well-shaped mouth that, once, had more often been poised at the edge of a smile. And again, that washed-out gown with its high, prim neck: it was not just her old maid's gown; it was an old-maid gown.

No! How could she have let this happen? Had her despondency really been so deep that she could have neglected herself to this extent? It had been months, a year, since she had given a thought to her appearance or the impression she was making on other people. She'd been too immersed in her inner self to think of the outer one.

Suddenly she was seeing herself with a clarity that had been lacking since her daughter's death, and she certainly wasn't happy with what she saw.

She went to the washstand and splashed cold water on her face, easing the soreness of her swollen eyes; then she went to the wardrobe and flung open the doors. Her hands flew as she flipped through hanger after hanger of gowns, most of them worn and out of fashion; not a new one added since her shopping spree in New York right after her reunion with Christopher. My God, she thought to herself, and I have walked around in this dreary fare day in and day out! I am only thirty-four years old, not some faded matron. What have I been thinking of?

She ran to the bell-pull and tugged it urgently to bring Clara upstairs. When the maid arrived, Jessica was already in her undergarments, at the dressing table vigorously brushing her hair.

"Clara, I will want breakfast up here this morning—something light—as soon as possible, and tell Jim to get the carriage ready. As soon as I have eaten I will be going into Eastport. I will be gone for several hours, perhaps more. While I am gone, go through my wardrobe. Any gown that is darned or the least bit worn, get rid of. Take them for yourself and the other staff, but I do *not* want to see them again in this closet."

Clara was staring at Jessica with wide eyes. Not in well over a year had she seen such force and purpose in her mistress. She could barely believe her ears and eyes, but she nodded vigorously. About time the mistress got rid of some of those old things!

"And I'll want to see Mrs. Bloom before I leave," Jessica continued without pause. "Tell her to come now if it is convenient."

"Yes, ma'am."

"That is all." Jessica was still wielding the brush with a vengeance on her long locks. "And quickly, Clara."

"Yes, *ma'am!*"

An hour later Jessica was seated in the back of the carriage, Jim at the reins. She was wearing the best-preserved dress in her wardrobe, one of only four she'd found that she did not want to discard immediately. Under the small, feathered hat on her head, her shining red-brown hair was softly waved and pinned. Her cheeks glowed from an application of cream and the vigorous pinching she'd given them and her eyes flashed like greenish jewels in their bed of dark lashes. She folded her glove-covered hands in her lap and sighed; thought back over this miraculous morning. What truly had caused her to awaken? Was it the shock of discovering the news of Christopher and Rhea? Or was it the shock of looking at herself clearly for the first time and seeing what she had let herself become? She was remembering, too, the woman she'd been before she'd met Christopher, and then on through all their days together in the twentieth century, when she'd not been afraid to stand up and fight life's battles.

A cold fury boiled inside her at the thought of Christopher's infidelity; yet the fury sparked her forward. She knew she was much to blame for his going elsewhere; she saw now how her introversion and despondency since Mary's death had turned him away—but could he not have persevered a little longer, given her more understanding and more time to recover? She thought of all she had gone through and yet remained true to him—living and surviving in a century that was not hers with nothing but her own wits to stand her aid; providing for Kit; waiting for two long years, never knowing what had become of the man she loved; coping with Christopher's increasing dominance; then, worst of all by far, their daughter's death. Yes, he, too, had gone through much, and she would be the first to admit it—but he had had no more to endure than she—certainly not enough to justify his running to his former mistress's arms.

Then the terrible thought struck her: did he love Rhea? No, she wouldn't allow herself to think that.

Rhea was not going to have him! As angry as Jessica was, as hurt, she loved Christopher and intended to get him back. If it meant swallowing a little pride, so be it. She had no intention of telling him of her discovery; but she

would see to it he started looking at her with new eyes—
and toward doing that, her first step was restoring her appearance. Her immediate destination in Eastport was the
dressmaker's. Then she would visit the hat maker, then
the chemist to replenish her dwindled supply of beauty
aids. Before the week was out, there would be a new and
revitalized Jessica confronting her husband.

In the days and weeks following, the transformation in
her was amazing. Suddenly she took every means to see to
her husband's happiness—dressing herself with care so
that her physical beauty shone forth, seeing that his favorite dinners were prepared, inviting in neighbors for evening entertainments to lighten the previously gloomy
atmosphere of the house. She listened to her husband
now—to his every word.

One evening when he arrived home late from his Eastport office, instead of letting Clara bring his dinner tray
into his study, she brought it herself. He glanced up in surprise when he saw his wife carrying the tray. She looked
lovely in a flowered gown, her hair softly shining in a new
style. Not blind to the change in his wife, he was very curious indeed to know the whys and wherefores of it. Yet because of the inner turmoil that held him in a viselike grip,
none of this showed in his manner.

"Why did you not let Clara do that?" he said.

"Because I wanted some time with you. I barely see you
anymore."

"I have been busy at the offices."

She placed the tray on the tea table beside his chair. "I
know. You're having some problems?"

"Not problems, precisely, but the business is expanding,
and I need to keep my eye on it."

"Yes, it seems you've been doing a great deal of traveling to New York."

Here was a subject he wanted to avoid at all costs. "The
trips are necessary," he said shortly. He took the rolled
napkin from the tray and reached for the fork.

"Kit misses you." The soft tone of her voice and the look
in her eyes told him that she did, too.

In a spasm of self-loathing, he dropped his own gaze to

his plate. This was a sentiment he'd been longing to see in her for over a year, and now he found it impossible to respond with the warmth she deserved. "I hope to be able to eliminate some of the New York trips in the near future."

Although Jessica had known when she'd instigated the conversation what his reactions might be, she still felt a sinking sensation in her stomach to have her worst fears confirmed.

From his withdrawn attitude, she realized it was pointless to try to carry the conversation further. She rose. "Well, I will let you finish your dinner. I have to go up and put the children to bed."

He nodded quickly.

As she moved away toward the door, she didn't see the painfully torn expression that creased his handsome features, nor did she see him return his fork to his plate and push the tray away, his appetite destroyed.

Despite the crushing hurt inside, Jessica was willing to be patient; it would take more than a day or two to repair a breach of over a year's duration. But from now on she was not going to let him slip away to enjoy his affair as easily as she had in the past.

Not long after that came the words Jessica had been awaiting.

"I shall be going into New York for a few days, Jessica," he informed her mildly when he returned home from work one evening. "Have Clara pack the usual things I will need."

"I was wondering if I might come along with you this trip? It has been so long since I have been away, and I do miss the excitement of the city. Jennifer is old enough now that I can leave her for a few days."

He glanced up at her, unable to disguise the panic in his eyes. "It will be a business trip, Jessica. I will not have the time to take you about town. Surely you would be bored."

"I do not need you to accompany me everywhere, and I do need to do some shopping."

She could see he was searching for some further excuse, but she gave him no time to find it. "Please, Christopher. My coming cannot interfere with your business meetings, and it will be a little holiday for me. I can easily be ready by morning." She paused a moment, looked at him seriously. "You have complained of my listlessness. Give me this chance to get out in the world again."

There was nothing he could say to contest the point, but he did not look directly at her. "Very well. If you really wish it. You are sure the children will be all right?"

"In Mrs. Bloom's efficient care they will not even miss me."

"Then pack for four days."

Jessica nodded. When he was gone from the room, she smiled grimly to herself. She imagined Christopher had some thinking to do that evening, wondering how he was to manage with his wife and mistress in the same town. Let him stew, Jessica thought. It was the least punishment he deserved.

They took rooms at the City Hotel. Jessica was truly delighted to be back in New York. She realized now how much she missed the excitement and bustle of the city after the quiet of her days in Eastport. Their first afternoon in the city, Christopher checked in at his offices, and Jessica took a hired carriage uptown to pay a short visit to Mawson and Abbey. In the evening, Christopher had at first wanted dinner sent up to their rooms, but she would have none of it, and coaxed him downstairs to the hotel dining room. As she'd expected, they saw many of their old acquaintances at tables about the room, people who'd extended hospitality to them two years before but many of whom Jessica had not seen since. She saw Christopher's eyes scanning the room—looking for one particular face, she was sure. Jessica also glanced about, but saw that Mrs. Taylor was not present.

During dinner several gentlemen stopped by the table to speak to Christopher and give Jessica messages from their wives with invitations for this or that event. Christopher appeared very reluctant to accept, hedging, refusing an invitation to a reception, another to a large party, before finally giving his acceptance to two smaller dinner parties at the homes of close associates of his.

Jessica fully understood. He was trying to keep her out of sight of Rhea, and at the smaller dinner parties there was less chance of their running into her. Well, she was not going to play along with his plans so easily and allow him to hide her away from his mistress. Let Rhea see husband and wife out together socializing; let her know that Jessica was not giving up the battle without a fight. When the next invitation came, to a large ball that Saturday evening, Jessica responded before Christopher could get a word out of his mouth.

"That would be lovely, and how kind of you to ask us. My husband, determined though he is to devote all of his time to business, does need some respite. We would be delighted to come."

Christopher cast her a sharp, angry glance, but under the circumstances there was little he could say without embarrassing both Jessica and himself. In their room after dinner, however, he had a few terse words for his wife.

"I would appreciate it in the future, Jessica, if you would allow me to decide whether or not we will go out. I told you clearly before we left Connecticut that I would have no time for entertainments."

"You cannot work all the time. You do need to get out and enjoy yourself occasionally—and what business can you conduct on a Saturday evening?"

"Just the same, you might have consulted me about the decision to accept."

Jessica almost snapped back: "I did not notice you consulting me about your refusals." But she held her tongue and casually continued with her undressing. An argument with him now did not fit into her plans and would only turn him that much more quickly toward his mistress's arms.

Jessica took extraordinary pains with her appearance. Her new gowns were in the height of fashion and extremely flattering. Her complexion glowed, and with her hair done in a new, softer style, she was radiantly beautiful.

Few gentlemen at the dinner parties they attended failed to cast admiring glances her way. Both the men and the women with whom she conversed were impressed with her, and Jessica made every effort to be at her best; witty, laughing, drawing others out in conversation, responding with charm to their questions, discussing current news and politics with intelligence, yet not presenting herself too strongly.

Although Christopher at times appeared oblivious of the attention his wife received, Jessica knew perfectly well he wasn't. She'd seen the tiny frown on his brow that evening at the dinner party when he'd overheard the compliments extended her by several of the attractive gentlemen present. She knew that his seeming distraction stemmed instead from the worry uppermost on his mind: his near panic that Rhea and Jessica should meet face to face. He was constantly glancing toward the entrance as guests were being announced, and his relief when Rhea Taylor did not walk through the door was visibly apparent, at least to his wife.

In fact, Christopher was keenly aware of his wife; of the color and fabric of every gown she wore, of the way its lines clung to her graceful figure. He was altogether too aware of the sparkle in her eyes, of her radiant smiles and gay laughter. He listened to other men flattering her, saw how truly charmed they were, and felt sharp twinges of jealousy. It should have been toward him alone that her charm was directed. At last she was herself again—vital, lovely— but because of his own deceit and fears of being found out, he could not open his arms and heart to her to show her his joy, could not tell her of the love he felt and was cherishing more and more as each day went by. If only he were not trapped in this tangle; if only he could wish his involvement with Rhea into nonexistence!

Rhea had to be aware by now that his wife was with him, and she would not be happy. He was terribly afraid that in her anger she might react rashly, somehow get word of their affair to Jessica. He couldn't risk that, yet he hadn't dared send her a written message.

It was almost with relief that he saw her carriage passing outside his office door at lunch the next day. An onlooker would think their encounter accidental. Christopher knew otherwise. She hailed him with a smile.

"Well, what a coincidence. I was just passing after delivering a message for Father."

Despite her warmly casual tone, he saw from the look in her eye that she knew about his wife and was not pleased. He stepped to the side of her carriage and spoke to her through the open window.

"Good day, Rhea. This is indeed a pleasant surprise."

"A surprise, yes. You are on your way to luncheon? Let me give you a lift."

"I have already eaten, thank you. I just thought to stretch my legs for a moment."

"You have just arrived in town?"

"Several days ago," he responded, although they both knew perfectly well that she'd known of his whereabouts.

"How disappointing that I have not seen you."

"I have been quite busy."

Her green eyes penetrated his; he fought not to turn his gaze away. "Some problems, Christopher, with your business? You usually find *some* time for relaxation."

He inferred her meaning very clearly. "I imagine my schedule will ease up in the next few days."

She smiled. "Yes. I shall hope to see you then." From her tone, the casual remark could be interpreted only as "I had *better* see you."

His mind was whirling: how to appease Rhea without Jessica discovering him? He could not simply ignore Rhea; she would not allow that to happen. "I am sure we shall see each other," he said finally, although he had no idea how or where.

"Good. I understand the Fishes are having a ball Saturday evening."

At her words his heart sank. Jessica and he would be attending the party. Nothing could be worse.

Seeing his expression, she smiled. But full satisfaction would come only from Christopher's forsaking his wife and coming to her. She would be patient, though; she would eventually get what she wanted—perhaps sooner than expected.

"Well, I see I am holding up traffic. It was good to speak with you, Christopher. Our conversation has *certainly* made my day."

17

Jessica knew of the emotional turmoil her husband was going through since they'd arrived in New York, but as far as his feelings for her were concerned, she was in the dark. She wanted so much to believe that he was beginning to look at her with new eyes; that there was love in those eyes. But she knew that what she thought were signs of change could just as easily be her imagination. Although fairly positive that Christopher had not seen his mistress —Jessica and he had spent every evening together—she did not for a moment believe Rhea would give Christopher up easily. The woman was crafty, and Jessica had no doubts that she would stoop to almost any means to reach her ends. It was Jessica's intention to outfox the vixen this time. She hoped that when Christopher and Rhea finally did meet, her husband would be so firmly intrigued with his newly revitalized wife, that he would have no desire to look elsewhere.

Yet as she dressed for the Fishes' party, she wondered if she had been totally overoptimistic. She glanced to the other side of the room, where Christopher was completing his dressing, the fabric of his white lawn shirt stretched tight across his shoulders as he gazed into his shaving stand mirror and adjusted his neck cloth. He was so tall he had to bend slightly to peer into the glass. She studied his reflection—his strong, even features, his deeply cleft chin, his dark-lashed blue eyes, narrowed now in concentration as he manipulated the folds of white cloth at his neck, one unnecessary wrinkle or crease in which would ruin the effect he was trying to create. At thirty-eight his handsomeness had not diminished; if anything it had been enhanced by age.

She sighed inwardly. How she loved him, in spite of what he was doing to her! It was a warm, overflowing feeling that in that moment of silently watching him nearly took her breath away.

Even as he doggedly continued dressing, she knew from the tension in his bearing that he was not looking forward to this evening. He'd made that obvious, yet there was no way he could gracefully back out unless the suggestion came first from her lips. His attitude left Jessica little doubt that Rhea Taylor would be there, and in her fear that his thoughts were even now on that woman, she called out to distract him.

"Do you like this dress, Christopher?" She twirled before him, the sea green of her skirts catching the lamplight.

"Very much so. I do not recall seeing it before."

"You have not. I bought it since we arrived in the city. I paid a visit to the seamstress I used to patronize. She'd done it up as a sample, but when I saw it, I knew it was right for me."

"Indeed it is. You will be the belle of the ball." But his response was so distracted that she wondered if he was really even looking at her.

He was quiet and introspective during the drive to the Fish home, his head averted as he stared through the carriage window to the street. His aloofness increased her own nervous anxiety, but Jessica did not know how to break the silence; not knowing what to say, in the end she sat with glove-encased fingers knotted in her lap.

Eyes turned as they were announced by the footman. Since Christopher had procrastinated so in his dressing, a great number of guests were already assembled, and in any event, such an attractive couple was bound to cause attention.

She saw him force a smile to his lips as he led her forward and they gave their greetings to those they knew. Such was the crush of glitteringly dressed, perfumed bodies that Jessica had difficulty in seeing across the room.

From his greater height Christopher had an advantage over her, and she knew when she felt him suddenly stiffen that her adversary was somewhere present. She strained her eyes in the direction of his gaze; at first could see nothing. Then the crowd shifted and she had a glimpse of Rhea's face, her features accented stunningly by the lustrous black hair arrayed regally atop her head in a coronet of thick braids. Seeing the woman's singular beauty again, she could understand why so many men were captivated by her, her husband included.

When Christopher had spied Rhea, his smile had disappeared. Now he forced it back to his lips as he made an effort to bring his attention back to the conversation going on around him, but there was an increased tenseness to his movements and his voice.

Whatever Rhea's reaction was at seeing Christopher with his wife, she let none of it show in her expression as she moved about speaking to this one and that. Witnessing the woman's self-containment and confidence, her vibrant beauty, Jessica felt a sudden stab of uncertainty. How wise was her decision to force Christopher into attending this party? Had she miscalculated? Instead of opening his eyes to her own charms and graces, would bringing him face to face with his mistress in his wife's company have just the opposite effect, forcing a comparison at Jessica's expense and drawing Christopher even further into the other woman's web?

From the look on his face now, Jessica feared that was precisely the case, and to combat her own misgivings, she placed her hand on her husband's arm. He turned to her, smiled. For an instant the tension in his face softened; then a mask came down over his features, and he turned away to respond to a comment made by the gentleman standing next to him.

Fortunately their movement about the room never brought them in contact with Rhea, although Jessica saw her watching when Christopher took his wife to the dance floor. There was a wicked gleam in Rhea's eyes that Jessica saw revealed when Christopher's back was turned, and her spirits sank further.

Rhea wasn't the only one watching them. Jessica had seen Jerome Weitz come in earlier alone. Now he stood at the side of the floor, his glance going to Christopher and Jessica, then sliding over to where Rhea stood. Jessica puzzled over it; wondered whether the reason for his interest was that he and Rhea had once gone out socially together. Had he, too, been cast aside when Christopher and Rhea had resumed their affair?

Jerome smiled to Jessica when he caught her eye, and later, when Christopher was drawn off by several other men, he came over.

He took her hand and formally bowed over it. "My, but it is good to see you again."

"And you as well. It's been quite some time."

"It certainly has. Well over a year, if I am not mistaken. You are looking as lovely as ever."

"Thank you."

"I was wondering if you would do me the honor of joining me for the next dance—or will your husband object?"

"I would be delighted."

"Excellent."

She discovered as he took her in his arms for the next waltz that he was an extremely proficient dancer, light on his feet, leading her confidently.

"I had heard you were in town with your husband," he said in a moment. "It is good to have you back among us. Apparently you have been enjoying your home in Connecticut."

"Oh, yes, though it's wonderful to be in New York again. I've missed the excitement."

He lifted his brows. "Myself, I would occasionally find the country life a welcome relief."

She laughed. "Are you saying that you are overworked, or only that your social life is too hectic?"

"From time to time a bit of both."

Jessica longed to bring up the subject of him and Rhea and inquire about his observation of them all earlier, but knew she couldn't be so bold. She hoped instead that he would volunteer some information.

But his conversation stayed wide of any potentially

touchy subject; and Rhea Taylor could definitely be described as a touchy subject.

As Jessica looked out over Jerome's shoulder, she saw Christopher on the sidelines, watching them. Yet when Jerome led her off the floor and remained to talk for a few minutes longer, Christopher had again moved across the room and was engrossed with a group of men. He did not immediately return to Jessica when Jerome stepped away, and in the interim Patience Fish, their hostess, came up to speak to her.

"My, you are looking lovely this evening, my dear. It is so good to see you and your husband out in company again. Although we see your husband occasionally, we have missed you."

"That's kind of you; and I have missed New York."

"It is a pity your husband does not bring you with him more often."

"Now that our daughter is a little older, I hope that will be possible."

Part of Jessica's mind was on their conversation; the far greater part on the scene being enacted on the other side of the room. Rhea Taylor was moving determinedly toward the group of guests with whom Christopher was conversing. Jessica froze; then in a moment sighed silently when Rhea's progress was halted by an older man who came over to speak to her. Jessica turned her mind back to her hostess. "It was so good of you to invite us this evening."

Patience Fish had not missed the momentary expression of anxiety on Jessica's face. She had heard certain rumors in the past months, but only said: "It is our pleasure—and do not be such a stranger to New York in the future." The last comment was more than just a simple pleasantry, and Jessica did not miss the underlying meaning of her words.

Christopher, although he danced with Jessica, became more and more taciturn as the hours progressed. Jessica felt only one brief spark of hope, when he came over and commented, "What has Jerome Weitz to say to you? He seems to find it impossible to leave your side."

"Do you think? I think perhaps he is making a special effort to be pleasant because you have been pulled away so many times in conversation with others."

"As you say," he said shortly, and in a moment was gone again. Although he seemed to be avoiding Rhea, Jessica could only think that with his wife there to witness his every move, what other choice did he have? Had he and Rhea, either much earlier or through an intermediary at the party, already exchanged some message for a later assignation? Or is fear feeding my imagination? she chided herself.

It was not until close to eleven o'clock that Jessica discovered her husband missing from the drawing room. She wanted to think nothing of it; perhaps he'd gone into the dining room for refreshments. But as her searching glance told her that Rhea Taylor, too, was missing, her stomach lurched. Hoping she was imagining things, she again perused the room, her eye going over every face in the crowd. There was no mistake—neither was there.

Struggling to hide a feeling of desperation, Jessica circulated through the crowd in the drawing room, trying to avoid other guests' attempts at conversation.

"Yes, it is a lovely ball, is it not? . . . Oh, thank you Mrs. Griswold—the gown was made here in New York, as a matter of fact. . . . If you do not mind, Mr. Pershing, I will take that dance later this evening."

Escaping the crowd, she went out to the dining room; still she did not spot the two faces she was seeking.

As she was passing down the hallway to return to the drawing room, she noticed the open doors leading off the hall onto a small balcony beyond. The doors were wide, and the evening summer air was scented with earth and flowers from a back garden, a distant salt scent from the bay drifting in.

Jessica stepped out onto the narrow railed expanse, her heart beating rapidly in trepidation. At first she saw nothing; then she looked to her left.

The lamplight from the garden below cast their figures into relief. Their backs were toward her, but their conversation carried clearly to where she stood a few yards away.

"I thought we would never find this chance to get

away." Rhea reached out her hand and rested it on his arm. "It has been a long week. I had hoped for some word from you."

"My wife—"

"You need say no more. I understand."

She moved closer to him, her arm about his waist. "Surely you can get away tonight for an hour or two. Father is out . . ."

"I do not think so."

"Please." She slipped into his arms, as comfortably as though she'd been there many times before. "Tell her you must meet with some business friends. She will not suspect. I have missed you."

"Rhea . . ."

She lifted her head, her lips pressing to his as if she owned him. "Mmmm. It is so wonderful to be with you."

From Jessica's vantage point, she could not see Christopher's response. All she saw was that this other woman was in his arms, and he was not pushing her away!

The pain, the humiliation, the anger that coursed through her made her dizzy. She had to get away— somewhere. She couldn't watch for one more moment; her pride couldn't bear it. And she couldn't bear even the thought of seeing him later; couldn't bear to be forced to listen to the intricate excuses he might make, when she knew they would all be lies.

She spun on her heel, still undetected, and rushed blindly out into the hall. At the end of the corridor she paused for a moment to pull herself together. What was she to do? She could not let the others know her state of mind. She must say good night to her host and hostess; plead a headache. Back at the hotel room she would pack and leave immediately for Eastport; pray there was a late packet running from the city to the coastal towns. . . . Perhaps she should have confronted Christopher when she first learned of Rhea—had it out then and there. But hindsight did her no good now—and would it have made a difference? Would he have stopped seeing the other woman? He certainly hadn't been deterred from meeting with her tonight, even with his wife present!

It took Jessica all her willpower to get through her fare-wells to host and hostess without giving herself away.

As she hurried from the room to collect her wrap, she paid no heed to those watching her rushed departure; to Jerome Weitz, whose eyes were following her every move. Nor did she see that he came to stand in the drawing room doorway, then followed her down the hall as she went to the front door and requested the footman to wave down a hack for her; nor that Jerome, too, collected his hat and left the party for his own carriage, which he signaled to follow hers in its direction toward the City Hotel.

Although Weitz had remained silent on the issue, he'd known for a while of Dunlap's return to Rhea Taylor's favors.

His discovery had been accidental. He'd been passing the Wilson mansion one evening as he found his carriage stalled in traffic. Glancing out the window in boredom at the delay, he'd seen Dunlap slipping down the walk to-ward the side door of the house. There was no mistaking the man for another—the street lamp had clearly illumi-nated his features. Was the fellow a fool? If not a fool, then a total cad? There could be no question of Dunlap's mis-sion: had he been paying a purely social call, he would not be making his entrance by sneaking down a side alley. Weitz had been furious at the discovery, not because of his own onetime involvement with Rhea Taylor—that had been of short duration once he had realized that Rhea was only using him to get over her anger at Dunlap. Most of the contempt he felt stemmed from his respect for Jessica Dun-lap. She deserved better than this.

Since his first meeting with Jessica, he had admired her. She might have been working as a serving maid, but it was apparent that she was a woman out of the norm. Then, so quickly, had come the startling news that she was Dun-lap's long-missing wife. From the start, Weitz had sensed something not quite right, yet in their later meetings Jes-sica had seemed happy with her state. Jerome had thought no more of it . . . until he'd seen Dunlap making his sur-reptitious entrance into the Wilson mansion.

When he'd first seen Jessica that evening, he'd been surprised by her air of relaxed happiness. Was it possible she knew nothing of her husband's activities? Either that or she was a supreme actress! But then as the evening had progressed he'd noticed the interplay between husband and wife, husband and mistress; saw the increasing tension, although he had to give Dunlap credit for his comparative coolness under the circumstances. Still, Weitz had no doubts that some kind of confrontation was in the offing. As he saw Jessica rushing alone from the party, he knew his fears were realized; knew he had to follow the woman.

Jessica's carriage stopped before the City Hotel. As Jerome watched, Jessica rushed in through the great front doors. Some instinct told him to wait. After seeing her expression as she'd fled the Fish residence, he feared she might do something rash, and this was not a city in which a woman was safe alone.

His instincts proved correct. Not thirty minutes later, Jessica reappeared through the hotel doors, a porter at her heels carrying luggage. The doorman waved her a hack—she was leaving. But for where, at this hour? Was she going to a friend's to take refuge? She wouldn't attempt to leave the city tonight for Connecticut! But then again, with her spirit, she might . . .

Again he told his driver to follow as Jessica's hack set off down the Broad Way, turning off onto side streets leading in the direction of the South Street wharves. She *was* going to try to get home; incredible. But the woman had pride, and he should have expected no less of her. At least he was there to watch over her, be her guardian angel in disguise if need be.

Her carriage pulled up at the packet berth. Her driver jumped down from his seat and disappeared inside. There were other pedestrians milling about the wharf.

In a moment the driver emerged and opened the door for her. Then he removed her luggage from the rack and carried it to wharfside. She paid the man, then disappeared into the ticket office.

How Weitz longed to get out of his carriage and go to her aid; but unless it came to the worst, he knew he could and should do nothing. He sat anxiously waiting instead, watching her board as a crewman loaded her luggage. He waited until the last passenger was aboard, the lines cast off and the ship slipping out with the tide.

There was nothing he could do for her now but to pray that she would arrive home safely.

18

Jessica left New York in such haste and fury, she'd thought no further ahead than getting away from the city, as if in running away she could block out the image in her mind of her husband and Rhea . . . the two of them in a hot embrace. In her anger she hadn't considered the dangers of traveling alone at night; of arriving in Eastport without transportation to the house.

She would have walked if she'd had to, but was fortunate enough at the Eastport docks to find an elderly farmer of her acquaintance who had been on the same packet and, asking no questions, gave her a ride in his wagon to her door.

There she stormed upstairs to her room. Her long-term plan of action had not been formulated until she'd stood at the packet railing and finally let her seething thoughts settle. She'd been so sure she would succeed in winning back her husband's interest. In truth, she'd never dreamed —never allowed herself to believe—his affair with Rhea had progressed so far. Now that she'd been forced to remove all the blinds from her eyes, her shock and pain were even greater than when she'd first overheard the gossip about them. She didn't know how to deal with what was facing her; whether she could forgive him; whether if she offered forgiveness, he would want it. All she did know was that she was not ready to face him.

He would come looking for her; that was certain. She'd left no message for him at the hotel or the party, but of course, when he found her gone, his search would lead him first to Eastport. She didn't want to be worn down by excuses, swayed by reassurances that would mean nothing in the long run. It was time she considered her own needs and where the future was leading her . . . and whether that future would include him.

Her decision had come with a surety that equaled its suddenness: she would take the children and leave temporarily; stay away until she could put all her confused thoughts in order.

Reaching her room, she set about packing the clothing she would need in addition to the two already packed bags she'd left below stairs. Then she stepped across the hall to wake Mrs. Bloom. She did not want the rest of the staff alerted to her plans, but she would need this woman's assistance in getting the children out of the house.

The nanny woke quickly at Jessica's soft call, sat up abruptly. "Mistress—you're back! Something is amiss?"

"Shhh. Do not wake the children. Yes, you might say something is amiss. I will need your help." Briefly Jessica described the events of the evening, her problems of the last months, her decision to be away for a while with the children.

Sympathetic though Mrs. Bloom felt toward the troubled—justly troubled—young woman, she felt it her duty to point out what a drastic measure the mistress was contemplating.

"To leave with the children like this . . . it is a sometimes cruel world out there. Would it not be wiser first to try to sort this out with your husband?"

"I know, Mrs. Bloom," Jessica said quietly. "I have considered all that, but I feel I have no other choice. All I ask of you is that you help me prepare the children and their things. I have a destination in mind where we will be safe. You may tell my husband what you wish when he returns; tell him I spirited the children out without waking you. I'll leave him a note, and I will be returning, once I have had time to sort all this—"

Mrs. Bloom interrupted her. "I cannot in conscience let you go alone. If your mind is made up, I will come with you."

"I don't want you to involve yourself so deeply in my problems."

"But I am already involved," the woman pointed out kindly. "Your husband will never believe I slept while you took the children and their belongings. He'd turn me out on my heel for not stopping you."

"Yes, you are right, I suppose. Very well, come along—but we must hurry. We must be gone before the rest of the staff are up."

By the time dawn was beginning to streak the sky, the women and two children were out of the drive, heading down the road toward Eastport, Jessica at the reins of the carriage.

The destination Jessica had in mind as they turned west onto the Post Road was a quiet and respectable country inn two towns away. She'd seen it during a drive with Mary Weldon; it would serve well as a safe hiding place until she'd come to a decision about what to do.

Although they traveled less than ten miles, it took two hours over the rough road to reach the inn. During the trip Jessica could not stop glancing back reflexively over her shoulder, so afraid that someone at the house had seen their departure; that Christopher might already be in pursuit. She let out her breath in relief as they finally pulled off the Post Road into the quiet and empty inn yard. Of course, there was always the possibility the innkeeper would not have any available rooms; in her rush to get away she hadn't considered that.

A livery boy approached, and held the horse's head as Jessica went inside. Though it was only shortly after seven in the morning, the innkeeper was at his desk. He glanced up at the travel-worn but still elegant woman before him. Before leaving Eastport, Jessica had changed into one of her most subdued traveling gowns; had pulled back her hair and disguised it beneath a veiled bonnet, powdered her face to leave it pale and make her look older than she was; but there was an aura of wealth and dignity about her.

"May I be of service to you, madam?"

"Yes. I will need two rooms—a suite if one is available, otherwise two adjoining chambers. For a period of a week or two."

The innkeeper continued to study her. "Well, I do have two rooms available, adjoining, at the back of the inn. How many in your party?"

"Myself, my maid, and two children. And I will need stabling for my horse and storage for the carriage."

He nodded. All types traveled this road and inquired for lodgings, although few women traveled without the company of a male. But his concern for respectability was appeased by Jessica's demeanor and her mention of a maid. "The charge is two dollars for the week per room, twenty-five cents extra for linens and maid service; stabling one dollar a week." He motioned to the book on the desk top. "If you'd like to sign in . . ."

"Yes; and I will pay you now." Jessica took the pen and wrote clearly, Mrs. William Franklin, Hartford, Connecticut—the name and address she'd decided upon during the drive. She then reached into her purse and counted out payment for two weeks.

The innkeeper inspected her signature. "Hartford, eh? On a bit of a journey. You're out traveling early this morning."

"We spent the evening with friends not far from here," Jessica said as she handed him the money with a smile. She blessed his curiosity; it gave her a further opportunity to steer away anyone who might come asking questions. "We are on our way back to Hartford, actually, bringing my niece and nephew for a visit. We thought we would rest here until a friend joins us to accompany us the balance of the way."

"Well, you should be able to rest here with no trouble. We run a nice quiet place. None of them carryings-on and carousing like the establishment down the road."

"I am delighted to hear that. In fact your establishment was recommended to me for precisely that reason."

The innkeeper stepped around the desk. "I'll just tell the boy to get your baggage, then I'll show you to your rooms."

Jessica followed him outside and spoke quietly to Mrs.

Bloom, who nodded and handed Jennifer down into Jessica's waiting arms, then climbed from the carriage. Kit, who'd already been informed firmly to say nothing and ask no questions, followed after her, still dazed by sleep. Never before had he been spirited off in the middle of the night, but he had no fears. With his father so often away, he was accustomed to his mother making plans for them—and this trip had all the makings of a high adventure.

The innkeeper led the four of them into the inn and up the stairway to two rooms that faced a rear yard.

"This will be excellent," Jessica said, looking over the interiors.

"Breakfast is set out in the front parlor till ten. The conveniences are to the back of the yard."

"Thank you."

"Keys are in the door. Let me know if you need anything further."

"I shall."

"Enjoy your stay."

When he was gone, Mrs. Bloom, who'd been carefully inspecting their new quarters—one large bedroom she and the children would share, and a smaller, adjoining bedroom for Jessica—gave a brisk nod. "Decent rooms, and clean, and I can make up this cot for the baby." Then her eyes went to Jessica, who stood with Jennifer in her arms, staring out the back window. Mrs. Bloom gave a soft sigh, thinking, I do hope you have made the right decision, my dear.

19

Christopher fervently hoped never to relive that night. It was not until well after seven in the morning that he rode up the drive to their Eastport home; she *had* to be here. Where else could she have gone? Anxious, exhausted, eaten up by fear and guilt, he prayed only that if she had left New York the evening before, she'd made the trip safely.

When he'd returned to the drawing room the evening before, he hadn't known what to think or say when his hostess had come straight to him to commiserate on his poor wife's headache.

"I do sympathize with her," Patience Fish had said. "I know others who suffer from these headaches—terrible things—and she did look so peaked when she left."

He'd tried to keep his amazement from showing on his face. Jessica was gone . . . was ill? But she'd said nothing to him, had no complaints a few minutes earlier, and she definitely was not prone to headaches.

"Yes, it is a shame," he'd answered, though he'd scarcely known what he was saying, "and I think I will be leaving, too, to see that she is all right."

"Of course, I understand."

He did not like the almost condemning look in Patience Fish's eyes, but did not have time to analyze it. A far more terrible fear gripped him. Had Jessica . . . *could* she somehow have seen him and Rhea in the garden? No; he'd been careful to see that no one observed him when he left the drawing room.

It had been against his better judgment to talk alone

with Rhea, although he'd already made up his mind to do
so at the first opportunity in order to break off his relationship with her. He'd at last resolved to risk everything—to
tell Jessica the truth before Rhea could. Admitting his
guilt was a great risk; he had no guarantee that Jessica
would forgive him. He would be asking a great deal of her,
but he had no other choice. He loved her; he wanted with
all his heart to work things out between them. Most of all,
he didn't want to hurt her any longer.

Seeing Jessica those last days out in company again—
sparkling, beautiful, alive—had reawakened him to just
what an extraordinary woman she was. Each hour of those
days he was torn into indecisive pieces. As he'd watched
Jessica dressing, brushing out her long hair, serene and
beautiful in her ignorance of his infidelity, he'd felt a desperate longing for the closeness they'd once shared. At the
dinner table as he'd listened to her converse with others,
saw their impressed reactions, he knew a swelling of pride:
this woman was his wife . . . *his.*

He remembered so clearly his conversation with Rhea—
how she'd coaxed him out into the garden, and he'd gone,
deciding to use the opportunity to tell her of his decision.
When she'd snuggled up against him in a manner that in
the past had always been so persuasive, encouraged him to
join her at her father's house, he'd felt the bile of self-
disgust rising in his throat.

Only moments later, he'd pushed her away. His words
had been emphatic: "No, Rhea. Not tonight—not any day
or night in the future. It is over."

"What do you mean?"

"I mean precisely what I said. I will not be seeing you
again. I love my wife and intend in the future to be the husband she deserves."

"You do not know what you are saying!" she'd gasped.
"It has been an uncomfortable evening for you; you are
overreacting."

"I know full well what I am saying, and it should have
been said long past."

"I will not allow you to do this!"

"You have no choice in the matter. It is my decision."

"You are a fool. You wish to spare your wife, but she shall find out what a 'loyal' husband you have been—that I can assure you!"

"Yes, I am sure you will waste no time in running to tell her the worse, and I have lived with that threat of yours long enough. It means nothing to me now, and I do not give a damn what you do. My wife will already have learned the truth from my own lips."

"Ah, the remorseful husband," she sneered, "bowing at her feet, baring his soul."

"And I only pray she will forgive me!" With determined purpose he turned and began to move quickly away. Her voice stopped him.

"You will live to regret this, Christopher. You left me once before only to find it impossible to stay away. We have something between us that is not going to be so easy to forget. You will be back."

"Good night, Rhea."

All he'd wanted at that point was to get away from her. It was done; at last he'd ended it. He'd hurried back to the drawing room to find his wife. He'd take her back to the hotel room, and there would tell her the terrible truth, beg her forgiveness. Already he was composing the words he would say to her.

Then, to his great shock, he'd found her gone from the party. He rushed to their hotel room, sure she was there, only to find she'd left with all her luggage. She'd written him no note. All the doorman could tell him was that he'd called Mrs. Dunlap a hack about forty-five minutes earlier.

Christopher knew then that Jessica had witnessed part or all of his meeting with Rhea. Either that or she had in some other way learned the truth and in anger and pain had run off, perhaps to their friends in New York. He set out immediately for Bayard's and Mawson's. Bayard was out, and Mawson said they had not seen Jessica since the day she and Christopher had arrived in New York. Unable to answer Mawson's and Abbey's anxious questions, he told them only that there'd been some misunderstanding. Christopher returned quickly to the hotel to check out, then headed to the docks. One of his schooners was in, but could not be made ready to sail for several hours, during which time he paced the wharf, ready to tear his hair out, worrying, wondering, cursing at the wasted time. What if Jessica had not returned to Eastport? It would be hours before he could continue his search elsewhere.

Now, with his front door beckoning, he spurred his horse up the drive, hastily dismounted, and, fastening the reins to the hitching post, bounded up the stairs into the house. He found the house quiet, the servants obviously occupied in the kitchens and unaware of his entrance. He raced up to the second floor and into their bedroom. The bed was made and showed no evidence of having been slept in; the room was in perfect order—except that Jessica wasn't there. But perhaps she was already up and gone downstairs?

Then he saw the folded white note propped on the night table. He stepped over and reached for it quickly. His hands trembled as he unfolded it and read.

I have left for a while with the children, and Mrs. Bloom. I have a great deal of thinking to do. There is no point in looking for us, but I promise you we will be safe. I have known for some time about you and Rhea Taylor. I've tried to be patient, knowing what you went through with my depression after Mary's death. I hoped you would give her up, but after seeing the two of you rendezvousing in the garden last night, I realized my efforts were futile. I need time to decide what I must do. When I've reached a decision, you will hear from me. After all we have shared together, Christopher, I have prayed it would never come to this.

> Jessica

He stared for a long while at the missive, his eyes glazing with pain as her words sank in. Gone—and with the children! She had known all along about his affair and been suffering with the knowledge. What had he done to her? What had he done to himself? He wanted to scream, to pound his fist against the wall. The only thing keeping him at all in control of himself was the conviction that he must find her! Perhaps all was not lost yet. He would not give up hope.

Christopher began his search. He questioned the remaining servants, who stared at him blankly and shrank back from his wrathful voice. They had not even known the mistress had come and gone; had not realized Mrs. Bloom and the children were not in their rooms. It was only shortly after seven in the morning; Mrs. Bloom never sent for the children's breakfast until eight. The caretaker came rushing back from the stables to inform him that the carriage and horse were gone. At least that gave Christopher some clue: the women had a fairly speedy conveyance. But in which direction did they head? Where would Jessica possibly consider going? The Beards'. Of course. Her closest friends in Eastport, who wouldn't hesitate to give her refuge. But when he arrived at their door and confronted a confused Amelia Beard, he realized that Jessica would not have chosen such an obvious hiding place. Still he didn't want to believe Amelia's repeated assertions that Jessica and the children were not there, nor had she heard from them. He hadn't the courage to tell Amelia the full truth of why Jessica had left, responding to her worried and probing questions only that there had been an argument. Finally, however, he accepted her offer to send her husband to aid in the search as soon as she could contact him.

Christopher returned to Eastport, to the office of the local constable. He did not want to bring the public authorities in, but what else was he to do? A force of two, even three men alone could not cover the area. Giving the constable full descriptions and asking the man's discretion, Christopher set out again, combing Eastport inside and out, checking at every inn and boardinghouse. He had his caretaker go in another direction; ordered one of his crew members to check every outgoing vessel's passenger list, every stage passing through.

In the afternoon he was joined in his search by Bertram Beard and Lucas St. John, who met him at his house as he stopped in to see if there was any news. Both men were terribly concerned, although Bertram kept his thoughts to himself. He took in Christopher's frantic, disheveled look and thought it wise to say as little as possible.

From Lucas St. John, however, Christopher received a piercing stare. Christopher was so distraught that he might not have noticed had Lucas not taken him aside before they all set off on their renewed search.

"What really happened, Dunlap?"

"What do you mean?"

"I know your wife well. Jessica would not fly off with the children unless she had some very pressing reason."

"And how would you know my wife so well?"

"You must be aware that we were friends while she was working for the Beards."

Christopher suddenly remembered a look he'd once seen Lucas and Jessica share; remembered how disturbed he'd been at the time.

Lucas was still speaking. "I know that she went through some bad times after your daughter's death, but that tragedy was in the past, and I do not believe her running off was prompted by it."

"As I told Amelia Beard, we had a disagreement."

"Quite a disagreement, apparently." Lucas lifted a skeptical eyebrow. "No, there is more to it than you are telling us. From the moment you appeared in Eastport two years ago with a fiancée on your arm, I have felt unsettled about Jessica's happiness."

"And might I ask what business our personal affairs are of yours?"

"I speak from deep concern." Lucas studied Christopher unflinchingly. "You have a wonderful woman in her, Dunlap. I pity you that you cannot better appreciate that fact."

"How dare—" But Christopher's angry retort was wasted. Lucas was already mounted and heeling his horse off to pursue the search.

Although furious, Christopher thrust his anger aside. There was a far more urgent matter on his mind—finding his wife and children. In a moment, he, too, was mounted and galloping down the drive. Still, he could not put Lucas St. John's words from his thoughts.

Their first day's efforts brought nothing. Bertram Beard reported to Christopher his and Lucas's lack of encouraging news, advising that they would both continue the search in the morning. Christopher, unable to sleep himself, was out again before dawn, searching farther afield, up and down the Post Road. Everywhere he stopped, the answer was the same. No one had seen two women and two children fitting the description Christopher gave them.

The men met again that evening, Lucas St. John visibly cool to Christopher. Given his own increasing anxiety, Christopher barely noticed. Exhausted, they stayed together only long enough to decide on the following day's plan, then went off to their homes.

By the end of the fourth day, Christopher was beside himself; possessed. He'd eaten little and slept less, yet he was driven on by an inner force that superseded his physical needs. He must find them; he must explain everything to Jessica; tell her how much he loved her; beg her to come back! Every hour that he did not find her increased his nightmarish fears that some accident or misfortune had befallen them; that he would never see them again. God— that he himself might die first!

His state of mind was not helped by the unexpected arrival of a visitor on his doorstep. He had returned to the house only briefly, for a change of clothing and to check on the progress of the search efforts, and was at first annoyed when the maid informed him there was someone waiting in the drawing room. Then he'd felt a surge of hope, thinking perhaps it was the constable with news. His surprise and dismay were evident when he saw Jerome Weitz rise from the armchair and step across the room.

"Good day, Dunlap. I hope you do not mind the intrusion, but I was in the neighborhood on business and thought to stop by and pay my respects to you and your wife." Weitz knew immediately that something was wrong. Dunlap was visibly drawn and shaken; his redveined eyes gave the appearance of his not having slept in days. Weitz had made the journey to Eastport impelled by the strong, instinctive feeling that there was trouble and he should investigate.

Dunlap's voice was curt, irritated. "Unfortunately my wife is not here, and I have to go out almost immediately on business."

Weitz sought for some way to prolong the conversation long enough to get answers to the questions in his mind. "Your wife is well?"

"Yes." There was a decided flash of pain on Dunlap's face.

"I am sorry I missed her. As a matter of fact, I have a message from Patience Fish for her, hoping that she will see you both in New York before long."

"I do not know. Perhaps she shall. If you will excuse me, Weitz, I really must be on my way."

That decided Jerome. If he wanted information, it would have to come through blunt inquiry. "You will pardon my straightforwardness, Dunlap, but I have been concerned about your wife's welfare since I saw her leave the party in New York and followed to see her board the packet for Eastport."

Christopher's face went whiter, if that was possible. "You *saw* her?"

"Indeed I did. I am also aware of her reasons for running off as she did. I have known of your relationship with Mrs. Taylor. Your personal affairs are none of my business, but I happen to like and respect your wife, and her well-being is important to me. I have been deeply concerned whether she made it to Eastport safely. From your obviously distraught condition, I gather she did not."

"She did . . . but she has left." If not for his mental exhaustion and his shock at hearing of Weitz's knowledge, Christopher would never have said so much.

"Left! Left for where?"

"I do not know."

"What are you saying, Dunlap?"

"She left that night with the children before I arrived here. She left a note saying they would be safe."

"What! And you have not found her? It has been four days! What have you been doing?"

"Searching for them! What do you think! And going out of my mind with worry."

"Nothing that you have not brought on yourself."

"You think I am not aware of that? And I will thank you to keep your opinions to yourself. This is none of your concern!"

"I am making it my concern! Their lives may be at risk—have you considered that?"

"Damn it, what kind of a heartless fool do you think I am, Weitz!"

"A man more concerned with his dalliance with a strumpet than with the feelings of an altogether remarkable woman!"

"Get out of my house!" Christopher moved toward him, ready to lay the man level with his fists. "We have nothing further to say to each other!"

Weitz was already striding toward the doorway. "No, we have not. But be well warned, I am taking up this search on my own, and if anything has happened to that woman, I shall hold you personally accountable!"

"Get out!" Christopher followed after him, his blind fury evident in his fists clenched tightly, his nails biting into his palms. But before he could reach Weitz, that man was already out the door, slamming it behind him. Christopher crashed his fist into the ungiving wood panels, smashing his knuckles so badly they began to bleed. He did not feel the pain; it was no match for his inner torment. If Lucas St. John's accusing comments a few days earlier had not been enough, Weitz's interference now had been sufficient to snap Christopher's self-control completely. What right did these men have to interfere? What had gone on in the past between St. John and Jessica, that he should claim to know the workings of her mind so well; feel he had the right to make accusations? And what was there now between Jerome Weitz and Jessica that had prompted the man to come to Eastport to check on her? Was Weitz part of the reason Jessica had left him? Was it not only his own indiscretions that had sent her off, but the lure of another man, as well?

Tired and angry though he was, he knew he had no justification for such suspicions, although he'd been so wrapped up in his own worries these last months, many things could have been going on without his being aware. He only knew that on top of his anxiety for Jessica and the children, he was suddenly consumed by a white-hot jealousy. He could not bear the thought of Jessica with another man! Was this to be his punishment for his dalliance with Rhea? To discover how much he loved his wife, only to lose her to another? She'd known for some time about him and Rhea. Had that knowledge sent her into another's arms?

Yes, he'd been a fool to get involved with Rhea again; but he was also beginning to see that his and Jessica's problems went back before that . . . before even her depression. He was remembering the times in New York, before Mary was born, when she'd tried to tell him of her unhappiness, her boredom, her feeling that he was forcing her to be something she wasn't; the time he'd berated her for going out in public in her obviously expectant state; and their terrible argument a few months ago when she'd finally told him of the depth of her discontent, and he'd still been unable to understand or sympathize. Yes, looking back now, he could see how their relationship had changed—how *he'd* changed—from the man who had once treated her as an equal partner into a husband who now made all the decisions, set their course and expected her to follow along without complaint, like the wives of all his friends. So quickly had he forgotten that Jessica was not of this century; that she was a woman grown beyond submissiveness—and a far finer woman for it! Why did it take the fear of losing her again to make him realize all this? Why hadn't he seen it sooner?

He swung from the door, his long strides carrying him quickly across the hall. First he must find her; then he must pray that it was not already too late.

The first two days at the inn, her anger still boiling and her crushed pride aching, Jessica had no doubts about the wisdom of leaving Eastport. This escape was for the best, giving her time to think and Christopher something to worry about. She knew revenge was unworthy, but something base in her wanted to see him suffer as much as she had. She ignored Mrs. Bloom's worried frowns, Kit's irritability at being closed up in confined quarters for so long. Those first days she'd wanted to take no risk of discovery and had kept them all in their rooms, telling the innkeeper the children had come down with slight colds, and having their meals sent up. The few times she did leave the rooms, she was careful to have her disguise in place, completed by a dusting of powder on her hair to give it a graying appearance.

But as the days ticked by and nothing happened, no innkeeper came to tell her that a gentleman had come by asking about two women and two children traveling alone, she began to wonder whether Christopher *was* worrying . . . or even searching. She could not believe him that callous. He *would* search for the children, if not for her. When he'd found her gone from the hotel in New York, he must have come back to Eastport; must have read her note telling him she'd left with the children. What had he thought? What had he felt?

No matter how angry she'd been, how determined to remain undiscovered, in her heart she'd held tenaciously to an image of Christopher pounding up to the inn doors in search of her. Now, with that vision unrealized, her determination began to sag, her hopes dwindle.

Nights alone in her room, after the children were asleep, she cried her heart out, but she could not go back to Eastport to confront him—not with her spirits so low. They sank lower still as she forced herself through days that dragged tediously by.

Almost two weeks had passed when, one morning, foresaking her usual caution, she left by the front door of the inn to cross the street to the chemist's for a cod liver tonic for Kit. She hadn't bothered with the powdering of her hair or face, only tied the veiled bonnet over her head and hurried out. She was in the middle of the dirt road when she heard a loud call.

"Jessica!"

She froze, then turned to see two horsemen only a few yards away. She couldn't believe her eyes. Her first instinct was to flee—but there was nowhere to go. The men had already recognized her, had urged their mounts forward and were now gazing down at her from a distance of only a few yards.

Silently she stood her ground as they hurriedly dismounted.

"It *is* you!" Lucas St. John was the first to reach her. His arm stretched forward as though to touch her and prove her reality, but he halted the action in midair. "We have been worried sick, Jessica. Do you know how many have been searching for you?"

She couldn't speak to acknowledge him; her shock was too great at being so unexpectedly discovered. Her gaze swept to the second figure, and she was totally confused. Jerome Weitz? But what was he doing here with Lucas when, to her knowledge, the two men had never met. And why was he searching for her?

Realizing her confusion, Jerome spoke quickly. "I saw you leave the Fishes' party that night and followed you, saw you board the packet." He hesitated, sought for a tactful way of phrasing his next words. "I knew for some time of your husband's activities. I was concerned for you; realized what you must have discovered that evening. A few days ago I came to Eastport and confronted your husband, who told me you were missing. I began to search for you on my own, and at one of the stage stops, overheard St. John asking the clerk questions about you and the children. Realizing we had to be on the same mission, I introduced myself, and we joined forces."

Jerome's explanation confirmed that Christopher *had* returned home. But where was he now? What did Jerome mean by taking up the search on his own? Was he implying that Christopher was doing nothing? The thought brought Jessica a spasm of pain, and her pride would not allow her to ask the question aloud. She took a deep breath to steady herself. "So, you have found me."

Lucas stepped closer. "Jessica, it is for the best. You cannot remain hidden away. I know you are resourceful, but you are a woman alone. Think of the rest of us, too, who have been worried to death, afraid some accident had befallen you."

"We are all safe."

"Where have you been staying?"

"Here at the inn."

"All along? But I have passed through here before."

"I've done what I could to alter my appearance, and used a false name. And we have stayed close to our rooms."

He was frowning at her.

"I know you do not approve of what I did."

"From what Weitz told me, you had more than just cause. But Jessica, why did you not come to your friends? We would have given you protection."

"I didn't want to involve you, and the Beards' would have been the first place he . . . he would have looked."

"It was."

So, Jessica thought, the smallest shred of hope returning to her, Christopher *had* looked for them, and a visit to the Beards' would explain why Lucas was involved in the search.

Curious pedestrians were beginning to stare in their direction. "Perhaps it would be best if we finish this discussion in a more private place," Jerome suggested, taking her arm. "The inn has a parlor where we will not be disturbed?"

"Yes."

"Then come."

Jessica held her ground, gave both men a level look. "I am not ready to go back."

"We are not going to force you to do anything," Jerome said.

"I have your word?"

"You do."

Jessica looked from Jerome's face to Lucas's; he nodded his agreement.

She followed them as they tied their horses to the hitching post outside the inn's door and proceeded up the stone steps and inside. The innkeeper was not at his post in the front hall, so there was no one to observe their entrance into the parlor. Jessica gave a sigh of relief, and Jerome directed her toward a table in the furthest corner,

where the light from the windows did not penetrate brightly.

As Jessica fought for control over her whirling emotions,
the two men sat quietly. This was not at all what she had
expected. The dream she'd held on to of her husband arriving at the inn doors and joyously finding them was a hard
one to let die. She cared deeply for both these men, but to
have them—and not Christopher—discover her brought a
terrible disappointment.

She heard Lucas speaking and pulled herself from her
sad contemplations. "Where are the children?" he asked.

"Upstairs. Mrs. Bloom, their nursemaid, came along
and is watching them."

Another moment's silence, then Jerome cleared his
throat. "We have promised not to coerce you into returning home, but what *are* your plans? You cannot remain here indefinitely."

"I can."

Both men stared at her. "We realize you left Eastport
in anger," Jerome continued, "but it is not prudent or
healthy for you to stay cooped up in this inn. You must
have some plans. Are you going to communicate with your
husband? Are you leaving him for good?"

"I haven't decided. I came here to think. You see, I've
known about him and Rhea for some time. Eventually I
will have to talk to him, but I'm not ready yet."

"Jessica." It was Lucas who placed a gentle hand over
her clenched ones and forced her to look up from her blind
stare at the table top. "I sympathize with you, completely.
We have known each other for some time and been good
friends. I am furious when I think of all you have been
through, the burden you have carried, only to have him
treat you as he has done. But much though I dislike the
man, I cannot in good conscience let you remain here and
not advise him—tell him at least that you and his children
are safe."

"St. John is right, you know," Weitz added. "Since I took
up this search entirely on my own, I do not feel as bound to
the honorable course, but Lucas would be behaving with-

out principle if he were to keep your whereabouts a secret."

His words nearly brought Jessica to her feet. "You won't
do this! You promised not to coerce me, yet that is precisely
what you both are doing. This is a problem between my
husband and myself, and it is up to us to resolve it."

"When you disappeared, you made your problems the
concern of all who care about you," Lucas said mildly.

"I appreciate that concern, but I am perfectly capable of
handling my own affairs."

"You should communicate with your husband," Jerome
persisted, "if for no other reason than to tell him you are
not returning to him."

"I've told you: I have not made up my mind what I am
going to do."

"Then for your own safety."

"I see no reason to fear for our safety here. Why must
you interfere?"

"Please, we are only thinking of your well-being."

"I'm sorry." Suddenly Jessica sagged back into her
chair. "I know you mean well, but you don't understand. I
have to be prepared before I face him; have to know exactly
what I am going to do." She paused, forced out a question
her pride hadn't permitted her to ask until that moment.
"What has he to say?"

"He is worried and anxious. There is no question of
that," Weitz said honestly, "although I have not seen him
since the day I arrived in Eastport and we exchanged some
very harsh words."

She looked to Lucas, who was frowning. "I have not had
personal contact with him either these last few days. Considering my angry feelings, I thought it best to avoid him
and have let Bertram communicate any news to him."

"Bertram Beard is involved in the search?"

"Of course. Amelia enlisted us both when your husband
came to the farm looking for you."

Jessica sighed, then looked at the two men with pleading eyes. "I understand how you both feel about my remaining hidden, but please give me a few more days. By
then, if I have not reached a decision as to what to do, you

may tell him where to find us. We won't leave. But to see him now . . ."

Jerome shook his head, his mouth set in a tight line. "Very well," he said finally. "I will not disclose your secret. I know what my gentlemanly duty is, but my sympathies lie with you, and I know St. John will be near by should you need him. I will return to New York—but I will expect you to keep me informed. Otherwise I will be back here interfering in your affairs again posthaste."

Jessica smiled weakly.

"I do not think, however, that St. John agrees with my decision."

"No, I agree. For the same reasons as yours. But only a few days, Jessica," he reminded her.

"In the meantime I will check in on you every day. Is there anything you need now—anything at all? You have money?"

"I brought sufficient funds, and the rooms here are inexpensive."

Jerome reached into his breast pocket, withdrew a card and handed it to her. "Nonetheless, my addresses in New York—the bank and my residence. Do not hesitate for any reason to get in touch with me should you need money. I obviously have the bank at my disposal."

Jessica took the card. "I do not think I will need the help, Jerome, but should something unforeseen arise . . . thank you."

"My pleasure. Might I order us some refreshment?"

"A cup of tea would be wonderful. Let me just speak to Mrs. Bloom so she doesn't worry."

Jessica found the woman knitting, the two children asleep in the room with her, and told her that she would be downstairs having tea. It was not the time to go into the story of their being found.

Mrs. Bloom peered up over her spectacles. "Fine, my dear. You enjoy. It is time you got out of these rooms."

"Would you like me to have something sent up for you?"

"No, no. I've a kettle boiling on the fire, which is all I need until the children wake. You go ahead."

Still, Jessica felt a pang of guilt as she left the room. She knew Mrs. Bloom did not approve of their extended seclusion, yet she'd been a rock of patience and understanding since their hasty departure from Eastport, asking little, providing a steadying presence for the children.

Lucas looked up as she approached. "Is everything all right upstairs?"

She nodded. "The children are asleep."

A pot of tea was already on the table, and a maid appeared with a tray of simple small sandwiches.

"Will there be anything else, sir?" she inquired of Jerome.

"No, thank you." He waited until she was out of the room before speaking again. "Lucas and I have discussed our course of action. After this refreshment, we will leave you." He gave Jessica a steady, probing look. "We do have your promise that you will not streak out for another hiding place."

"You have my word."

"I will be by tomorrow to see that all is well," Lucas added, "although I have never been an actor and hope that in the meantime I don't give away to the others my knowledge that you are safe. Amelia and Molly are very worried about you."

"I wish I could let you tell them the truth, but Amelia couldn't keep such a confidence from her husband—and her husband would tell mine."

He was silent.

"How is Elizabeth?"

"Good, although worried for you, too. We have purchased the house across from the mill, and she is busy furnishing it."

"Your wedding is in two months."

He nodded.

"And I have put a blight on the festivities by involving you all in my problems."

"No. Please let that be the least of your worries. You have enough on your mind at the moment."

Despite the men's supposed desire for refreshment, the plate of sandwiches lay untouched on the table. Jerome began pushing back his chair. "I must go now or miss the last packet to New York." He rose, paused by Jessica's side, took her hand. "I hate to leave you in the midst of your dilemma, but I know there is nothing further I can do for you here. My thoughts will be with you, and remember, I am a friend in waiting should you need me for anything at all."

"I don't know how to thank you, Jerome."

"I shall be waiting to hear from you." His eyes were on her face; then he lifted her hand and pressed his lips softly to the back of it. "Take care of yourself."

In a moment he moved over to Lucas, who had also risen. The two men shook hands firmly. "St. John, a pleasure working with you. I believe our paths will cross again."

"I believe they shall."

"You will keep your eye on this lady."

"Most definitely."

"Good, although I will not be fully at ease until all of this is settled. Even then—well . . ." He shrugged. "Good day, St. John. Jessica." Jerome bowed to her. He studied her briefly once more, then turned and left the room.

When he was gone, Lucas spoke. "I honestly do not feel right about leaving you here."

"We will be *fine.*"

"You know to come to us in Silvercreek if you have any problems."

She nodded, hesitated, then asked quietly. "How much did Jerome tell you?"

"Substantially all, I believe, of what has been going on the last few months," Lucas said tactfully, "although I had my own suspicions right from the start, as he was already engaged to be married to that woman."

"In fairness to him, Lucas, he thought he would never see us again. He hadn't stopped loving us, and up until recently he's been good to me, particularly when I was so despondent after Mary died."

"Granted, I am only seeing one side," he said; but his tone was dubious.

She turned her head away to avoid Lucas's watchful gaze. Her voice was muted, sad. "Perhaps I will find it impossible to forgive him, too. I'm afraid that what has happened would always stand as a barrier between us . . .

even if he never sees her again. Lucas, do you know . . . did Jerome say . . . whether Christopher was still in touch with her?"

"Weitz said nothing to me, and even I hesitate to believe your husband could be quite that much the cad. He *is* terribly concerned about your absence."

"Mine or the children's?" she said, unable to stop herself from voicing the doubt aloud. She expected no answer from Lucas, and he gave her none.

He took her hands instead, and squeezed them lightly. "I will be going. I will be back tomorrow."

Jessica had gone up to her rooms shaken, more confused than ever. She repeated to Mrs. Bloom the events of the previous hour and told her that for the time, the secret of their hiding place remained safe. The woman only shook her head.

"My dear, it is not my place to criticize, but the children are suffering from this confinement. They need their home. 'Tis unnatural to keep them and yourself hidden away like this."

"Tomorrow we will take them on an outing in the carriage, perhaps bring a picnic lunch."

" 'Twould it not be better to return home and speak to your husband, my dear? Nothing can be settled until you talk to each other."

Jessica closed her eyes for a moment, then moved toward the windows, away from the well-meaning nursemaid. "Not yet, Mrs. Bloom. Not yet."

She herself was not sure why she was so opposed to an immediate encounter with Christopher; why she continued putting off that inevitable. Was she afraid that her worst fears would be realized—that the man who greeted her would be cold and unresponsive and turn her away? Such treatment would be far worse than the anxiety she was suffering now.

Lucas arrived at the inn in late morning the following day, and he and Jessica talked for a while in the parlor. Since Jessica did not want Kit to see Lucas, feeling that the sight of a familiar face would only make the child more homesick and discontent, Lucas made his visit a short one, and after he had left, Jessica took the children and Mrs. Bloom on the promised excursion into a nearby, yet private, bit of field and wood. Kit was ecstatic with his new-found freedom, and Jessica was able to forget her troubles for a while as she romped with him through the golden fall meadow. Even Mrs. Bloom seemed happily exhausted as they returned in late afternoon to the inn for an early dinner and bed.

The next day, however, Lucas would not be satisfied with a brief visit. He was upset that she had not yet come to a decision; begged her, if she would not relent and notify her husband, to come and stay at the Beard farm.

"You are being unreasonable, Jessica."

"I am not."

"If you are not concerned for yourself, think of the worry you are causing others."

Afraid that the argumentive tone of their voices would reach other ears, Jessica said softly, "Can we go for a short walk, Lucas, and finish this discussion?"

"Very well."

Choosing the back entrance of the inn for their exit, she led him onto a seldom used country lane. As they walked, she thrust back the veil of her bonnet—the only remnant of her disguise that she had bothered with that day—and let the fresh air brush her cheeks.

"You are not afraid of being recognized?" he questioned.

"I've walked this back road before. It dwindles into a track and is not a route anyone would use unless they lived along it."

"Part of the reason you have eluded your searchers."

"I've been cautious." They walked on at a brisk pace, the tension of their disagreement still standing between them.

Jessica spoke first. "You haven't let on to anyone at the farm that you've found us."

"No, although my conscience suffers greatly to hear Bertram recount his own fruitless efforts. He tells me that your husband is in a very bad way, too."

Jessica studied the contours of the rutted lane beneath her feet. Her voice was strained with suppressed emotion when she answered. "In what kind of a bad way?"

"Distraught. He sleeps and eats little. Your staff quake when he is about the house, his temper is on such sharp edge."

At the side of the road was a small orchard, and they stepped off between the rows of fruit-laden apple trees.

"Jessica, don't you think it is time you did something?" She saw his frustration as he pulled his fingers through his thick blond hair. "Your husband's infidelity infuriates me, but I have to have some sympathy with him. It has been over two weeks, and he has no idea whether you and the children are safe or have come to harm. If I were in his shoes, after all the searching that has gone on, I would be fearing the latter."

He paused, looked over to her silent form. Reaching out, he took her shoulders and turned her to face him.

"You know I care about you . . . a great deal more than I have ever told you."

"You've been such a good friend, Lucas, I—"

"More than a friend." His eyes bore into hers; she could not draw her own away. "All those months while you were with the Beards and counseled and bore with me over my infatuation with Elizabeth, I walked around like a blind man holding on to a dream. One day I woke up and realized it wasn't the pretty little lady who played so merrily with my feelings that I loved most . . . but you. I wanted to tell you. I wanted to ask you to marry me, but you didn't seem ready to accept that declaration. You were still in love and holding out hope for the return of a husband the rest of us were sure was dead or had deserted you. I was willing to wait and be patient. I had already realized the fruitlessness of my pursuit of Elizabeth, and was going to tell you all this the night of that Christmas ball. But we were interrupted, and before I had a chance to speak to you again, Dunlap appeared. I knew then that I no longer had a right to say anything to you about my feelings. You seemed so happy, and I tried to push aside my misgivings about your husband—although I admit, after that scene on the ballroom floor, I would gladly have put him in a cannon and shot him off into oblivion.

"It was that night, too, in all my disappointment and misery, that Elizabeth came to me as though, after years, she had suddenly realized my worth. Please, do not misunderstand. I love Elizabeth and will be a good husband to her. I would not have asked her to marry me if I felt otherwise. But the feeling I had . . . still have . . . for you is something that perhaps only comes once."

As Lucas spoke, Jessica's eyes had grown misty. She was remembering that time almost three years ago—remembering so well the warmth she'd always felt when Lucas was around, brightening her otherwise dreary days; the frequent, flitting thoughts that had caused her to wonder what would happen if there were no Elizabeth; and later, the strange sense of loss and melancholy when she'd learned he and Elizabeth were engaged. She'd tried to convince herself that her melancholy had been caused by her fear that the young woman would hurt him again. She knew now that it had been more.

His voice was soft, gentle. "I have wondered, ever since, how things would have turned out if your husband had not returned . . . have thought that perhaps you would now be *my* wife. Was I wrong? Am I? Could you have loved me?"

A choked cry escaped her lips. "Yes—yes, I could have . . . but it's not to be . . ." His words brought such upheaval! She tried to cover her tear-streaked face with her hands, and felt herself being pulled against his chest.

"Jessica, I am sorry . . . I should not have spoken."

Several moments passed before she whispered into the cloth of his jacket. "It's all right, Lucas. One day these things had to be said."

"I only told you now because I wanted you to understand just how much I care about your happiness. We cannot go back. I have long since resigned myself to it—nothing beyond friendship can ever be fulfilled between us. I know that you love your husband and that no other man could hope to attain such a place in your heart. On the other hand, I could not bear to see him hurt you again. I would see him dead first."

"Lucas!"

"Strong words, perhaps—but true."

"I don't know what to say to you. Yes, I do love him. We have gone through so much together. I suppose even if he turns his back on me now, I will go *on* loving him. It's the kind of feeling that anger and pain can't seem to kill." Jessica drew a little away from him, gazed up at his fine, strong face; she saw the furrow of regret on his brow, the whiteness of pain about his sensitive mouth. "Do you think me a fool?"

"Not a fool. I am only regretting that I did not meet you first. There must be some great tie binding you to him, that you can love him still, even after this . . . but I have to respect a love that deep."

Lucas realized, as he gazed down at the woman he might have loved to an equal depth, that there was nothing else to say. There was nothing he could offer her but his friendship; she would accept nothing else. He tried to smile. "We have been gone awhile. They will be wondering what happened to you."

She nodded.

"I will walk you back."

But before they left, she took his hands, brought them up to her face and held them there. Her eyes, the lashes about them still damp, looked into his. "Thank you, Lucas . . . dear friend."

The feeling in that simple statement went far beyond the literal meaning such words usually conveyed.

For three days thereafter, Lucas paid his brief daily visit. Though their talk that day in the orchard was still searingly fresh on both their minds, they said nothing of it to each other; it was better that way. Lucas only asked if all was well, if there was anything she needed. She didn't tell him how, with each day, the hurt and confusion within her were growing, or that because of the pain that increased with each day her husband himself did not arrive and find them, she was only going through the motions of living. The longer she waited, the greater her doubts that she and Christopher could work things out; the greater her fears of returning to Eastport. She had no guess as to her reception. He might be so thoroughly enraptured with Rhea that he would turn Jessica out in the cold.

Worse still, he might whisk the children away and never again let her see them. Wasn't that the way it worked in the nineteenth century when a wife willfully left her husband?

To keep her mind occupied, she began taking the children farther afield for their airings, driving them over some of the more remote country lanes. Yet even with the respite of getting out of the inn, she knew she could not continue this way much longer.

Lucas tried his best to be patient and not press too hard in his persuasions that she give up her vigil and accompany him to the Beard farm or send a message to her husband. Finally that patience snapped.

"Enough is enough, Jessica," he told her emphatically. "If you continue to insist on doing nothing, then I must take action."

"No, Lucas, please." She knew he meant it this time, and she knew he was right; yet she felt more afraid than ever.

"I have no choice. To see the growing despair in everyone's faces and know the secret I am hiding from them! Jessica, have a thought for other people's feelings, too."

"I do, I do. It pains me to know I'm hurting them, but please, one more day—only one."

His expression was grim, undecided. Finally he acceded, sighing heavily. "All right. But only one. Jessica, no matter how much I care for you, no matter how much I try to want for you what you yourself want . . . if you have not made up your mind by tomorrow afternoon, I am sending a message to your husband."

As Jessica waved him good-bye a few minutes later, she was overcome by a numbing sadness, a heaviness in her heart. Was he right? Was it time to talk to Christopher? She could not remain at the inn forever, but was there any hope at all of repairing the breach between Christopher and herself? What future did she have to look forward to? Her pride would never allow her to remain with a man who didn't love her, who actively saw a mistress on the side. But what laws governed a sundered marriage in this age? What of the children?

She didn't know. She simply did not know what to do.

20

The early fall day was unusually mild, and with the sun warm and bright in a cloudless September sky, Jessica took the children to a small pebbled beach in a cove not far from the inn. Today was the day her decision was due, and that unsettling thought was foremost on her mind. While Mrs. Bloom rested in the shade, Jessica let Kit remove his shoes and stockings to splash barefoot through the shallows. She carried her daughter down to the water's edge, out of range of her brother's frolics, to let the baby dangle her hands in the lapping water. Jennifer was at first startled by the cool, ever moving waves, but her curiosity was soon aroused by this new form of water that did not lay complacent in a bathtub, and in no time she was reaching out with chubby little fingers to catch the wave crests.

It was Miss Bloom who first noticed the horseman approaching down the dirt road that led off the main Post Road.

"Rider coming," she alerted Jessica. There was always a need for caution that close to the Post Road, where ne'er-do-wells traveled as frequently as respectable citizens.

Jessica looked up, stood. Her daughter protested at being lifted out of reach of the water, but Jessica's eyes were riveted to the solitary figure. Although the rider was yet too far away for her to make out his features, there was something familiar in his seat, the set of his shoulders. In a moment he urged his horse into a trot.

Mrs. Bloom was now at her side. "Trouble, you think?" she said nervously.

"No . . ." Yet Jessica's voice, barely above a whisper,

was filled with trepidation. She knew now who the rider was.

It seemed to take a very long time for him to approach, each second increasing Jessica's anxiety. Then he halted before them. His eyes were only for Jessica; hers for him. They said nothing as they stared at each other. She noticed the tired lines on his cheeks, the reddened eyes, the furrow between the brows, the first hint of gray in the dark waves at his temples.

As though the scene was moving forward in slow motion, he dismounted, stepped forward warily, and stopped. Jessica made no move. Even the baby had ceased fidgeting in her arms, sensing something of the importance of the moment.

The spell was broken by Kit, who came racing out of the shallow water toward the man with arms wide, a child's uninhibited smile of joy on his face.

"Daddy . . . my daddy!" The boy flung himself into the waiting arms of his father, who lifted him high in the air, then clutched the small body to his chest.

"I missed you, Daddy . . . so much."

"And I missed you . . . more than I can say." Christopher's voice was choked, his eyes blurred by the wetness that sprang to them.

"I wanted to come home, Daddy, but Mama said we have to stay here for a while."

"Your mother had her reasons, Kit."

"But we come home now!"

"I would like that very much." As he spoke, his gaze fixed on his wife. Seeing the longing and need in his eyes, Jessica felt her heart surge; but still she stood unmoving, her eyes on his.

"Jessica . . . to have found you—" His voice broke. He swallowed. "There is so much to say. Will you hear me out?"

Something inside her was crying out in happiness to see him; something else was holding her back. So many impressions of the moment were whirling in her brain—of his haggard look, his obvious joy at seeing them, his uncertainty over what his reception would be; yet much else had happened between them. It wasn't something to be sorted out with an instant's decision.

"I will talk with you, Christopher." Her voice sounded strange in her ears.

"Now?"

"Yes."

"Can Mrs. Bloom take the children?"

She nodded, then turned to the woman and spoke quietly to her. "My husband and I want to talk for a moment. Will you watch Kit and Jennifer?"

"Of course, ma'am."

Jessica handed her the baby while Christopher lowered his son to the ground. But Kit's hand had grasped his father's coattails, and would not let go. "No, Daddy. I will stay with you."

His father's voice was its most reassuring. "Your mother and I must talk alone. You go along with Mrs. Bloom. We will follow soon—I promise."

The child gave him a fearful, wide-eyed look. "You won't go away?"

"We will be right here."

Reluctantly Kit allowed Mrs. Bloom to take his hand and lead him off. He cast a long look back over his shoulder, as though afraid to let his father out of his sight.

When the children were gone, Christopher and Jessica faced each other uncomfortably.

"I have been searching for you for weeks." His voice was hoarse with feeling. "I have been over every inch of this road—and every other road for miles and miles. I had nearly given up hope when a rumor came to me today that a woman of your description had been seen in the area." His wearied, beseeching eyes told her of his anguish. "Where . . . where have you been?"

"At the inn up the Post Road."

"But I have been there! And to every other inn and rooming house for miles around."

"I took precautions that we should not be recognized."

"You went to such lengths?" His blue eyes darkened further in pain. "Why did you run off? Why have you not sent some word to me?"

"You know why I ran off, Christopher; and I did not send word to you because I needed this time alone."

"You must have known what my anxiety would be, to find you and the children gone and have no idea where to look for you!"

"Under the circumstances, I did not know."

Under her steady stare, he lowered his eyes.

"I had a great deal of thinking to do," she added.

He immediately looked up again. "Is that the only reason you stayed away? To think?"

"I was hurt and angry. Did you expect me to feel otherwise?"

"Indeed no. . . . Jessica, I am so sorry," he choked.

She remained silent. She needed to know far more before she would have any forgiveness to offer him.

"I have been afraid," he continued unsteadily, "that there was more to your leaving than what occurred that evening in New York. Jerome Weitz paid me a visit—"

"Yes, I know. He and Lucas St. John found us . . . which made me wonder why you had not."

"Lucas St. John!" Astounded, he stared at her. "Then why did he not tell me? I saw Bertram Beard only this morning. Why did St. John send no message?"

"He wanted to. I forbade him."

"Why, Jessica, why? Was this your way of punishing me for what I have done? Or was it more? Have you stopped caring? I know your friendship with St. John in the past was a more serious thing than I ever suspected . . . and now Weitz . . ."

"No, Christopher! Jerome and Lucas have been no more than friends in their behavior toward me. It was purely by accident that they found us."

"Then why have you not at least given me some chance to explain? I know I have been wrong, terribly wrong, and have cursed myself and suffered for every second of my foolishness and deceit! Could you not have waited to hear my side?"

"I am listening."

"My God, have things come to this between us—that you must talk to me like a stranger!"

Jessica forced back a sob. "What do you expect, Christopher? Am I supposed to come running back into your arms as a loving wife when I know you have been lying to me, deceiving me, making love to another woman—when I *saw* you in New York in the arms of your mistress?"

"That is over—believe me! It was over that night in New York." He reached for her hands, gripped them desperately. "If only you had not rushed from that party, not left the hotel, you would have known then. I was on my way to explain to you . . . to tell you the whole truth of my infidelity and to beg your forgiveness, ask you for another chance . . ."

"That is easy for you to say now."

"It is the truth! Believe me! If you had remained to witness all of that scene in the garden, which I can only presume you did not, you would have heard me tell Rhea that it was over, that I no longer wanted to see her again—no longer cared about her threats of exposing our affair to you—that I intended to admit everything to you myself. And that *was* precisely my intention, but when I returned to the party, you were gone, and gone from the hotel. As soon as my ship could sail, I went to Eastport and there found your note. I cannot describe to you the anguish I felt—how I have hated myself these last weeks, known I had no one but myself to blame!"

"This is all fine and good," she cried, "to say how sorry you are now—but why did you do it? Why did you ever start up with her again? Did you think of my feelings then? Did you care about anyone but yourself?"

"Jessica, please. I was utterly wrong. I will not attempt to make excuses for myself. I thought at the time I had cause. It was after Mary's death, when you were so remote, that I saw Rhea again. No, the affair did not begin then; we chanced to meet at a gathering. I tried to hold her at arm's length, but then when you got pregnant and still seemed to want nothing to do with me . . . well, once again our paths crossed in New York, and one thing led to another. Yes, I felt guilt. I wanted nothing more than to come back home and hold you in my arms and try to make up for what had just occurred; but you turned me away. I felt I was living with a stranger. After that it was easier to succumb. I rationalized that if my wife did not want me, why not find what I needed in another woman? Wholly selfish of me; totally the wrong way of thinking, as I realized later. But it was done. When I wanted to get out of the relationship, Rhea threatened to expose my duplicity to you. I couldn't endure the thought of your discovering, so I stumbled on with it—another weak and spineless thing to do. It was during those days we were in New York together that I finally realized just how much I hated myself for what I was doing; I didn't care about Rhea. I loved *you*, only you! I made up my mind to end it; and I did, that evening . . . too late." His eyes had never left her face; their piercing anguish bore through to her soul. "If you cannot forgive me, Jessica, I can understand, but in these last weeks of soul-searching I have come to realize even more just what a wonderful love we have shared together. It is something too special to be lost. I need you . . . must have you."

She was silent, yet still so filled with doubt and pain. It was not easy to wipe from her mind the image of the man she loved making love with another woman; not easy to forgive his actions or to understand why he had been drawn to another woman in the first place. No matter how much she loved him, wanted to forgive him, wanted to be back in his arms, it was so hard to dismiss the memory that he'd lied to her, gone behind her back, and hurt her to her very core. And despite all his avowals to the contrary, might it happen again? She felt so torn; knew that she'd been wrong, too, in pushing him away when he'd needed her. But did that justify what he'd done? Couldn't he have stood by her side a little longer?

"Jessica, I mean every word I've said."

"I'm beginning to believe that."

"Then will you please let us try again? If nothing else, these past weeks have forced me to look at myself very critically, to ask myself why any of this ever happened. I thought back to the way we used to be before Kit was born. I thought about what a wonderful partnership we'd had; how we had shared everything. I began to realize that we were not sharing anymore; that I was making all the decisions for both of us; that I was not letting you be the woman you were meant to be—the woman I fell in love with and have loved with all my heart ever since. When you tried to tell me you were unhappy, I did not understand. *Now I do.* Let us go back to the way we were, Jessica, in the beginning . . . in your world. I know, after learning the hard way, that I do not want a meek and compliant wife. I want *you*—the way you are." He clenched her hands more tightly, as though with the pressure of his fingers he would transmit the feeling in his heart.

"I won't pretend that I can forget the hurt that quickly," she said quietly. "I will try . . . but the memory will always be there. Every time I think of you and Rhea together, I'll turn cold inside. I hate her; I despise her. I never want to hear her name or see her face again! I can't condone what you did, but I know I've been wrong as well. I've hated you these last weeks for what you'd done to me; but I couldn't stop loving you, too—and I've made an effort to do that." She stopped, her eyes going over every inch of his worried face, a face that showed so much of what he'd been through the last weeks. "If you mean all of what you've just said, Christopher, then I am willing to try again."

"Oh, Jessica, I mean it—I have never meant anything more in my life!" The sincerity in his voice was unmistakable, even were it not aided by the desperate stare that bore similar testimony to his seriousness. "Does this mean you will forgive me?"

"Forgiveness comes in small stages," she said softly. "I can't forgive everything with a snap of the fingers. But I haven't been perfect, either. I forced you to suffer through my depressions." Pausing, she looked deep into his eyes. "We've been through a lot, haven't we?"

"And we have a lot further to go, you know."

"I'm looking forward to it."

He smiled, still unsteadily. Then he was drawing her close, tight into his arms. It was a closeness she'd been longing for, dreaming about; she welcomed it, cherished it. Those strong arms about her back, the feel of his hard chest against her cheek, the thick curls of his hair tangled in her fingers as she caressed the back of his neck; the unperfumed scent of him, of his sweat from hard riding and worry. And she welcomed his lips, in a moment coming gently down on hers; then pressing more firmly as each sought for—and found—the soul-filling warmth and passion they'd too long denied each other.

When they drew apart, he brought his fingers up to trace the curve of her cheek. "You will come home with me now?"

"Have I your promise that she is gone from your life— our life—forever?"

"You have."

"Then I am coming home."

He lifted her off the ground in an exuberant embrace. "We should go tell Kit."

"He'll be happy. He's missed you."

"Is he the only one who will be happy?"

"No, hardly the only one."

21

It was a joyous entourage that left the inn an hour later, so very different from the sad group that had arrived two weeks earlier. Jessica again was at the reins of the carriage, but this time Kit—smiling, fairly bursting with pride and excitement—rode up on his father's saddle. While Christopher had helped Mrs. Bloom pack the carriage, Jessica had written Lucas a quick note, to be left with the innkeeper, telling him that they were on their way home, explaining briefly the reconciliation she and Christopher had made. Though she knew that Lucas would be relieved to learn she had finally left the inn, she doubted he'd be pleased over her so hasty forgiveness of her husband. Only time would prove her faith justified; and of that she now had no fears.

The staff at the house, on the verge of desertion after living with Christopher's volatile temper for weeks, ardently welcomed the return of Jessica and the children, and Jessica was thrilled to be back. She hadn't realized until that moment just how much she had missed her home.

Shortly after they celebrated their homecoming over a gay lunch, Mrs. Bloom appeared and took her young charges upstairs for a nap. Christopher came around the table to his wife with a twinkle in his eye. Putting his arm around her shoulder, he grinned down at her.

"My love, I wonder if you might accompany me upstairs to the bedroom. There is an urgent matter I must take up with you."

"Is there?" she said innocently. "If it's so urgent, we can discuss it here."

"It was not a discussion that I had in mind."

She lifted her brows. "No?"

"Madam," he laughed, "we are wasting valuable time. Come." With a quick movement, he lifted her in his arms and began striding from the dining room.

"What are you doing?" she giggled. "I *can* walk."

"Ah, but is this not so much more romantic a beginning to our second honeymoon?"

"We never had a first, if you'll remember . . . at least, we didn't travel anywhere."

"And we will not be traveling far this afternoon, although I promise you immeasurable enjoyment."

Carrying her as though she were a feather in his arms, he lengthened his strides, moving them swiftly up the main staircase.

"Christopher, what if the servants should see us?"

"They would be delighted that our reconciliation is going so well."

"You're impossible." Tightening the grip of her arms about his neck, she pressed her lips to his cheek. "But I love you!"

The moment they were inside the bedroom, he kicked the door shut behind them and carried her toward the bed. Only as he laid her down on the mattress did his expression and tone become serious. "And I love you . . . you do believe that, Jessica? Believe, too, that I will never hurt you again."

"I believe it."

"I want to show you just how great my love is."

His eyes stared deeply into hers as he leaned forward and pressed his mouth tenderly to her lips. In a moment his tongue sought eagerly for hers.

Gently, as their kiss grew deeper, his fingers unbuttoned the front of her gown, unlaced the camisole beneath. Lifting his head so that he could look down at her, he slowly pulled the fabric wide and drank in the sight of her soft, full breasts. Only when she was tingling with expectancy, aching to feel his touch on her flesh, did he let his hand brush against her skin, allow his fingers to move over her with a feathery, arousing gentleness; over her midriff, up and around each breast, circling ever higher until his fingertips rubbed across her taut and waiting nipples.

She moaned, closing her eyes in pleasure.

"Yes," he whispered. "I have been longing for this, too."

With his fingertips still caressing one breast, his mouth sought the other, his tongue and the gentle nibbles of his teeth taking over the pleasurable work of his hand.

Jessica felt her desire growing in a series of delectable waves that rippled through her body, even to her toes. She longed for him; longed for him to continue his exploration, tasting and touching every inch of her. When she thought she could stand no more of the longing to have him a part of her, he lifted her shoulders and drew off her gown and camisole, sliding them off her arms and down around her waist. Then he pressed her back against the mattress, his hands gliding over the newly found skin. Slowly, tantalizingly, he caressed lower, below the waist of her gown, his palm swirling, pressing against her abdomen, teasing ever closer to the heart of her desire. She felt his fingers in the soft triangle of hair; moaned again as with leisured purpose he sent his fingers to explore the throbbing spot between her thighs. With light, tender pressure he touched her again and again.

Then the delightful touch was withdrawn. Her gown was being pulled down over her hips, along the length of her legs. Only when her nakedness was absolute did his hand come back to resume its delightful journey, drifting so softly and delicately up her legs that she felt they might have been made of silk; lingering on her sensitive inner thighs, ranging oh so slowly upward, inward, until his fingers were caressing again amid the soft, curling hairs, bringing her higher and higher . . . and her whole consciousness was consumed by the ecstasy he was bringing her.

She was gasping as he brought his lips up to her ear. "Let it come, my love . . . let it come. I want so much to take you all the way like this, give you that joy."

His coaxing words swelled the crescendo already building within her, drawing her closer and closer until she was overwhelmed by a wave of such utter and complete pleasure, she was left writhing and trembling.

"My love . . . oh, yes," he whispered. His kisses covered her flushed face; her forehead, her cheeks, her eyelids, her lips.

As he leaned over her, she was conscious of the heat of his own need pressing against the constriction of his trousers, burning into the skin of her thigh. She reached for him, her hand rubbing softly over the hard, hot bulge, eager to give him the pleasure he'd just brought her. He moaned, his hips straining toward the contact of her hand.

Then he was rising quickly, casting off his clothes. Her eyes swept over his tall frame as first his jacket was discarded, then his shirt. She reveled in the sight of his broad chest, with its thick mat of softly curling hair that tapered down over his firm belly. She watched as his hands went to the fastening of his breeches, her breath frozen in her throat as he slipped the garment down over his hips, revealing the full evidence of his desire. And hers was equal as she waited for his undressing to be complete. He came to stand beside the edge of the bed and gazed down at her, his blue eyes hazy with love and passion, his sculpted body silhouetted in the golden glow of the mid-afternoon sunlight cast from the partially curtained windows. Then he slid down beside her, and she welcomed his warm strength in her arms, gloried in the feel of his flesh touching hers. She held him close, smoothed her palms over his firm skin, over the muscles of his back. Their lips met hungrily, their tongues seeking and touching. As his arms cradled her ever more tightly, she felt the warm staff of his manhood pressing between her thighs; craved a wholeness that would not come until they were one with each other. Gently she brought her hand down to encourage him, massaging him until his breathing was harsh and heavy.

"Jessica, I need you . . . I want you."

"Come . . . come to me . . ."

He moved over her, his body tense with aroused passion. She knew a thrill of anticipation as she waited for his warmth to enter her, a thrill that was heightened a hundredfold as he slowly pressed forward, joining their bodies into one being.

She wanted nothing else but this man; no other could ever fulfill her as he could do, bring the ecstasy he was bringing now as he moved within her, deeper and deeper, until her senses were spinning, reeling, and they were merged together in a space where nothing but them and their loving existed.

The movement of their bodies became ever more urgent and intense.

"You feel so wonderful!" she cried.

He was beyond answering. Enveloped in her warm softness, his every nerve registering only the greatest ecstasy, he felt his senses pitching ever upward toward that ultimate, overwhelming release. The sensations of his body blocked out all other reality, except that this was his beloved wife in his arms, bringing him such pleasure. Then he gasped as his climax was upon him with a shattering explosion. "Jessica . . . Jessica!"

She pulled him closer still, knowing his joy; feeling that same joy within herself. She held him thus, treasuring his sweat-dampened skin, the thud of his heartbeat against her breasts, the scent of his sweet breath gusting on her cheek, until his tense body began to relax; until his lips gently touched her ear.

"What you do to me, sweet wife," he breathed softly. "I have told you that before."

"What you do to *me.*"

"I love you so very much, Jessica."

"I love you, too . . . always . . . forever."

He sighed with contentment, rubbed his cheek against her hair, their bodies clinging together, still joined.

The world was as it should be, she thought happily. Their love was destiny.

In the weeks that followed, they sought fervidly to make up for all the pain they'd given each other and suffered; yet there was no conscious effort in the loving looks they exchanged, the touch of a hand across a table, the soft sighs in the night and the arms reaching across to hold the other tight, the gentle, half-awake lovemaking in the morning. They communicated their love, their sense of the oneness of their being, continually to each other, often without a spoken word.

Christopher took more time from his business, and in those early fall days, as the leaves began to turn, brought his wife and children for drives in the country. He and Jessica began schooling Kit on his new pony, Jessica nervously clasping her hands as the fearless child attempted a low jump; Christopher shouting his proud encouragement as his son went flying over and exuberantly asked for more.

In the evenings Christopher no longer holed himself up alone in his study, but asked his wife in to join him, and as they sipped a brandy together, they talked as they used to, of politics, what was going on in the world; they talked of their lives, their meeting across centuries, the possibility that they yet might be separated by time. It had been many months since they'd discussed that uncertainty; they had been too concerned about their day-to-day problems. Now, in their happiness, the specter was there again.

"I would want the children to know," Christopher mused one night, "about how we met, who you are and who I am, my travel to your time and then yours to mine, the three of us arriving here from the twentieth century. They should be prepared should the worst occur and we be separated again."

"I don't want to think of that possibility." Jessica reached for the security of his hand.

"No more than I; but we must."

"I wonder if they will believe us."

"They will no doubt find it very strange, as would any sane person. And although Kit was born there, he cannot remember his days in the twentieth century."

"It seems so odd to hear you say that and know it's the truth." She was silent for a moment. "How terrible if the children should be separated from us before they're grown!"

He looked at her. "Yes, terrible . . . but we have many good friends who would care and fend for them in our

stead. Far more terrible if we should be separated again
from each other."

To celebrate their refound happiness, they decided to
throw the house open for a fabulous party. They would invite everyone, make a weekend celebration of it. The house
and grounds were certainly large enough, and they'd entertained so little until now. Christopher was as excited as
Jessica as they drew up the invitation list, planned the
first evening's ball, the following day's activities for the
guests, the concluding dinner and chamber music.

"We will make it like a London fete." Christopher
chuckled. "At last, after all these years, I will get to show
you a bit of that society as I knew it."

"Then I will let you take the lead in all the arrangements," she laughed, "for you, my earl, are the expert."

In the days just before the party, the household was
aflutter with activity, and Jessica threw herself wholeheartedly into the preparations. She wanted everything to
be perfect, from the linens on the guest room beds to the arrangements of fall flowers distributed about the house.
She went over every detail of the menu with the cook,
hired in extra help to assist Clara, a temporary butler to
answer the door. As she went through the rooms the afternoon before the party, feeling a proud glow at the beauty of
their home, she was reminded sharply of a day, almost
three years before, when she'd made a similar inspection
of the rooms in the Beard house prior to their Christmas
ball. Things were so different now. She was not the meek
servant surveying the results of her own physical labors,
but the mistress of this incredibly beautiful home. She was
not that lonely young woman, aching and empty from the
loss of a husband she feared she might never see again.
Now she was blissfully reunited at his side. Standing in
the drawing room, running her hand over a gleaming table
top, gazing out through the front windows at the magnificent expanse of the Sound, she smiled, then laughed aloud
in her uncontainable joy. This was happiness—true happiness.

The guests were lined up in the front hall that clear mid-
October evening, waiting to proceed up the grand main

staircase to the ballroom on the second floor. The magnificent room, a smaller duplicate of the room that had taken up the whole third wing at Cavenly, had been Christopher's one great extravagance, and it had remained unused until this evening.

Carriages were still pulling up into the drive as Christopher and Jessica stood at the head of the stairs greeting their guests.

"Like your parties at Cavenly, my lord?" Jessica leaned over to whisper in his ear.

He grinned. "Precisely, although I have not before now had the pleasure of my countess standing at my side."

The orchestra they had hired from New York was already playing in the ballroom; from the excited chatter of the guests, Christopher and Jessica knew the anticipation of those gathered and had overheard that evening various remarks on the magnificence of the house that many apparently had longed to have an opportunity to see.

"Ah, Mr. and Mrs. Griswold." Jessica smiled. "We are so delighted you could come. Do enjoy yourselves."

Christopher was already speaking to the next arrivals. "Ezra . . . and this is your wife, Margaret. My pleasure. Welcome to our home." As Christopher bowed and, in truly courtly fashion, brought to his lips the hand of Margaret, wife of Ezra, that woman's cheeks were suffused with a blush of delight.

"Christopher, look who's here!" Jessica exclaimed as the next guests on the staircase approached. "Willis, Abbey—how good to see you!"

"Ayuh." Mawson grinned, giving Jessica a huge hug. "Would've been here sooner but ran into a bit of congestion down there at the docks. Schooner had to hold out at anchor a couple hours. Would've rowed in, but Abbey didn't want her finery mussed."

"And I don't blame her." Jessica laughed. "Someone's brought in your luggage?"

"Your man down there at the door, though from the angle of his nose, he seemed to think himself a bit above it. Gettin' yourself up kinda fancy out here in the country, eh, Dunlap?" Mawson winked broadly. "Brit butler and all."

"We must keep up the appearances," Christopher replied with mock seriousness, "particularly with such honored guests as yourselves."

"Can't argue that." Willis chuckled as he took Christopher's hand. "Good to see ya."

"You, too, my friend. And Abbey—my, you are looking lovely this evening." He brought her hand to his lips, and Abbey dimpled.

"Ought to. Cost me near a week's wages to outfit her."

"And well worth the expense, I would say."

Mawson's turned his eyes appreciatively toward his wife. He grinned. "She *is* lookin' fine. Well, we're holdin' up the proceedings. Best move on. Talk to you later, Dunlap."

"Assuredly."

It was not until a few minutes later, as Jessica looked down the still-long line of arriving guests, that her breath caught in her throat. She nearly gasped. Rhea! There was no mistaking that raven-tressed head. What was that woman doing here!

She cast one quick glance toward her husband. He, too, had seen her: the smile had been wiped from his lips. He turned to Jessica. The surprise and confusion in his expression were enough to tell her that he'd had no foreknowledge of Rhea's appearance. With guests waiting to be greeted, it was impossible for husband and wife to talk, and it was not until Rhea passed farther along the reception line to them that they understood how she had come to be at their party. She was in the escort of one of Christopher's more important contacts, William Jeffries, who was new to the New York scene and unaware of Christopher and Rhea's past liaison.

It took all of Jessica's powers as a polite hostess not to order the woman then and there to leave her house. As it was, her greeting bordered on rudeness, but Rhea seemed not the least bit perturbed. Christopher only cast Rhea a lethal glare, but he, too, was unable to say what was on his mind in front of the other guests, and in a moment Rhea and her companion were moving off into the drawing room.

As they departed, Christopher quickly leaned over to speak in his wife's ear. "I am so sorry, Jessica. I had no idea."

"I know."

"Shall I ask her to leave? It might be awkward since she is in Jeffries's company."

"No. I know you value Jeffries's business. Let's see what happens." She was forced then to turn her attention to their next guests. "Good evening Vivian, Charles . . ."

The next surprise in the otherwise smoothly flowing festivities came with the arrival of Jerome Weitz, long after Christopher and Jessica had gone to join their guests in the ballroom. Husband and wife had discussed the invitation sent to him. After his last encounter with the man and knowing Weitz's affection and admiration for his wife, Christopher was not the least disposed to include him, yet he knew Weitz was a business tie he could not readily afford to sever, and Jessica assured him repeatedly that she and Weitz were no more than friends; they owed the man some consideration for the assistance he'd offered her at the inn. But since Jerome had made no acknowledgment of the invitation, Jessica had assumed he would not attend.

Now as she saw him enter the crowded room, she felt uneasy about what words might pass between him and Christopher tonight. But Jerome did not come in their direction; instead he moved farther away to speak with a group of New York guests.

Christopher said nothing to her about Jerome's arrival until they were dancing, and then there was no anger in his tone. "So, the evening should prove interesting. You will not object if I do not go over and greet Weitz with open arms."

She smiled. "No. I will be too busy keeping an eye on a certain other party."

"There is no need." He tightened his arms about her, dropped his cheek to the softness of her hair. "I will never stray again."

"It is *she* I don't trust."

But all went smoothly, despite some guests' obvious concern that it might not. Their hostess associated any shocked expressions she saw among them with Mrs. Taylor's appearance at the party; Robert Bayard and the Beards seemed particularly disconcerted, Jessica noted as she paused to speak with them during the evening. Of course, everyone was too polite to comment, but she had no trouble reading the thoughts going through their minds. She was almost glad that Lucas was out of town and had therefore declined his invitation to the party. There was the animosity Lucas still felt toward Christopher; and then, too, he would not have stood silent when he saw Christopher's former mistress appear. It was Christopher's own behavior that went the furthest toward waylaying harmful gossip as he stayed close to his wife's side, his arm often about her waist, his whole manner that of a man very much enamored of his spouse and having no desire to look elsewhere. And Rhea—Jessica watched her closely—made no move toward Christopher. She remained at the side of Jeffries displaying her best social behavior.

Jerome Weitz, too, kept his distance. It was only as Christopher stepped from the room for a moment that he spoke briefly to Jessica.

"It is very good to see you again."

"And you, Jerome."

"Though I admit to being a trifle surprised when I received your invitation. I debated about coming." He smiled. "Curiosity got the better of me. I hope my being here has not made you uncomfortable."

"Not at all. You're most welcome."

"I received your note after you returned to Dunlap. Thank you. All is going well for you?" he asked, sounding as though he found it difficult to believe that possible.

"Very well, Jerome. I think we have finally sorted things out. I am happy."

"I . . . I could not help but note a certain lady's presence here. That was not planned, I take it?"

"Far from it. Jeffries brought her. He didn't know."

"Hmmph." He fingered his lips. "Some people will go to any ends. Take a care, Jessica."

"I shall. I believe I know how 'the lady' operates, having had some experience with her."

"Well, there is no more I dare say on *that* subject. What I don't mind repeating is that I am very happy to see you again . . . and to see you looking so well. And remember, if you should ever need me . . . as a friend . . ."

"Thank you, Jerome. That will always be understood between us."

The guests, extravagant in their praise of the entertainments, the refreshments, the lovely home the Dunlaps had designed and built themselves, did not begin to make their departures until well after one in the morning. Their closest friends and the most prominent of Christopher's business associates and their wives would be staying in the guest rooms in the house. Others who had traveled in from out of town had taken rooms in Eastport and would return on the following afternoon for the rest of the entertainments and the dinner following.

By two-thirty in the morning, as the last of the houseguests departed down the staircase, Jessica was dead on her feet, but happily so. She had planned to wait for Christopher, to talk over with him the success of their first large party, but he'd been dragged off to his study by Bayard and several other gentlemen for a business chat, and she had no idea when the men would call it a night. Too tired to wait any longer, she went up to their room, undressed quickly, and crawled into bed, sighing contentedly at the soft comfort for her weary muscles. Within seconds she was asleep.

The following afternoon, the almost expected storm began to brew.

Jessica woke from a brief nap. The rest of their guests would begin arriving again soon to enjoy wine and light refreshments out on the lawns while many of the men, and some of the more energetic among the women, competed in an archery contest, lawn tennis, or other, less demanding, activities. Later, dinner for fifty would be served, with cards and the chamber music following. She'd not wanted to leave her houseguests to their own devices, but Christopher had insisted she go up and rest for a while in preparation for the evening ahead, and he was right—she was tired. He'd slept later than she that morning and had more strength in reserve. She slipped from her robe and went to the washstand to freshen up.

It was then she saw the envelope laying on the polished floor, just inside the door, as though it had been slid beneath; perhaps something Christopher or one of the maids had dropped. But as she knelt to retrieve it, she saw her name written on the front. She took it to the bed, sat down, and broke the seal.

The note inside was unsigned, but written in an obviously feminine hand.

Perhaps I go beyond myself in addressing this message to you, but I felt you should be aware. I can understand the trials you have faced being wed to such a handsome and charming man and have thought very highly of you for having held your head up in society in the face of his numerous past affairs. It is an example which gives the rest of us courage. And for you to persevere still, when even last evening, in your own home, your husband dallied into the wee hours with one of your guests, takes strength indeed. It is a terrible shame some women cannot be gotten out of a man's system, but it is a situation most of us have faced at one time or another, although some of us do not have the spirit to stand up beneath it as well as you have done and continue to do. This note is meant to let you know that you are not alone and that you are much admired for your determination to keep your house and home together.

Jessica read the note again and yet again, scarcely believing her eyes. Who would write something like this to her? Was it some kind of joke, albeit in incredibly poor taste? She rose, ready to crush the note into a ball and consign it to the fire, when her eyes again caught on the line: "And for you to persevere still, when even last evening, in your own home, your husband dallied into the wee hours with one of your guests . . ."

No, it couldn't be possible! Someone was trying to plant

seeds of doubt in her mind. But who would be so cruel? She could think of only one person, but Rhea had not spent the night in the house—Jessica was sure of that. Jeffries had not been one of the overnight guests, although he'd been invited to today's festivities. Could Rhea have returned to the house? Had Christopher slipped out? It seemed preposterous. Jessica was letting her imagination run away with itself for pondering even the possibility.

But then, she *didn't* remember when Christopher had come to bed; she'd been sound asleep and hadn't wakened. She only knew that he'd been beside her this morning, quietly snoring. She'd let him sleep on, presuming that once the men had got to talking, they'd kept him up quite late. But perhaps it hadn't been the *men* who had kept him up. Was it possible he had spent a good part of the night elsewhere? . . . She could find out by asking Bayard how late the men had remained in the study. . . . But since she had no idea what time her husband had finally slid into bed beside her, would that necessarily tell her anything? No, no! She refused to contemplate it. Just the thought of Christopher and Rhea together brought a fury that left her hot and cold in the same instant!

Deep in thought, she strode to the windows. She was being ridiculous. She had nothing to worry about; the note was either some sick practical joke or another of Rhea's ploys. She would talk to Christopher about it at her first opportunity. She refolded the note, lifted her head and looked out the window.

There, on a path to the side of the front lawn, she saw her husband; and beside him, elegant in a flowered afternoon dress and cape, Rhea Taylor! The two were involved in an animated discussion, seemed oblivious of anything but each other. In a moment they disappeared, hidden by shrubbery, around a corner in the path. It was all Jessica's confused mind needed to see. He'd *promised* never to talk to that woman, never to see her alone! So what was he doing taking a solitary walk with her, just when he was sure his wife was safely napping upstairs!

She wanted to scream, but forced herself to be calm. Suddenly the note didn't seem so ridiculous anymore. Still, she must remember that it was possible she was misconstruing the situation. Rhea might have confronted him and left him no alternative but to talk to her. Despite the fury that raged within her, she had to keep her faith in Christopher. He had promised . . . promised!

At dinner she was tense, alternating between silence and nervous chatter. Jerome Weitz, seated beside her, immediately sensed something was wrong and tried to draw her out or, that failing, to divert her thoughts from whatever was troubling her. That he didn't succeed on either count worried him further, but there was little he could do except to continue with milder conversation. To bluntly ask her what was on her mind as they sat with the other dinner guests would be unheard-of behavior.

Christopher, at the opposite end of the table, was very much aware of his wife's intense conversation with Weitz, and he looked their way as often as he felt he could without drawing unwanted attention.

Jessica, consciously avoiding looking at her husband, was unaware of his discomfiture. She feared that if she did glance over to him, she would discover his eyes resting on Rhea, who sat halfway down the length of the table, beside William Jeffries. She did not want her deepest dread confirmed.

After a sumptuous dinner, which Jessica barely tasted, she rose to lead their female guests into the drawing room, while the men remained for a time in the dining room over their port. Amelia Beard came to sit beside Jessica and immediately engaged her in conversation. Out of the corner of her eye, Jessica noticed Rhea going to the far corner of the room to examine the curio cabinet there. The woman seemed to have few female friends among the guests; but that was not entirely surprising.

Amelia didn't miss Jessica's quick glance. "Perhaps it is none of my business, Jessica, but why do you not just throw her out of your house?"

"She came with an important business associate of Christopher's. It would be extremely awkward."

"And the situation is not now awkward? I am not doubting your husband, but that woman has put you through enough."

"Yes, I know, I know, Amelia." And perhaps Rhea isn't finished yet, Jessica added silently; then, excusing herself, rose to see to her other guests.

As the men entered the room, Jessica's tension redoubled. She had one eye on Rhea, the other on her husband; but Christopher came immediately to her side. He wasn't smiling when he spoke. "Is everything all right?"

She was startled by his question. "Yes. Yes—why shouldn't it be?"

"I was only wondering. You seemed distracted at dinner . . . seemed to have a great deal to say to Weitz."

"Jerome? Well, yes, I suppose, but then he *was* seated next to me. Just chitchat."

"You are sure?"

"Why, yes; of course."

He went off to instruct the servants to set up card tables, but that terse conversation had reassured her that it was not Rhea who was uppermost in his thoughts. She began to relax a bit, circulating to make small talk with the guests who had chosen not to play cards, but to mingle with one another to the accompaniment of the string quartet playing in the background. As Jessica paused to exchange news with Abbey Mawson, she saw Christopher, after some prompting, take a seat at one of the tables to be dealt in for a few hands. She knew from experience that he was an excellent card player. She was not disappointed when, a few minutes later, she heard a mumbled oath from one of Christopher's opponents. "Should have known you were holding that trump aside, Dunlap."

Jessica smiled as Christopher and his partner took the first hand, the cards were shuffled and redealt, and the play continued. She heard Christopher laugh at some comment; glanced over and saw the frowns of concentration on the other players' brows. It wasn't until the hand was nearly played that she looked over again to the table to see the woman who had just come to stand behind Christopher's chair. Dear Rhea.

Jessica reminded herself that her husband hadn't beckoned the woman over—nor did he acknowledge her now. Still, Rhea was obviously making a move, and Jessica did not like it one bit. She would have acted herself, gone over to make her presence very definitely felt at her husband's side; but Clara came from the kitchens to whisper in Jessica's ear that there was some small problem—the cook was having an argument with one of the serving girls. Jessica had no choice but to tend to it.

When she returned to the drawing room, Christopher had left the card table and was now in conversation with some men at the other side of the room. Near by was Rhea. It had become apparent that her interest in William Jeffries had been only of sufficient duration to get him to bring her to the party, for she'd paid little attention to him since; the woman's eyes were only for Christopher.

Jessica resolutely turned her attention toward the others at the party. Her eyes met those of Jerome Weitz, who was walking toward her. Remembering her husband's earlier comments, she subtly shook her head. Too much was on her mind already this evening; she did not need further complications. Jerome understood her, and changed his course.

Not long afterward, Jessica saw Christopher leave the room. Within seconds, Rhea followed.

That was it! Jessica was not going to stand by and watch any longer. Her anger boiling over at the woman's audacity, Jessica went in pursuit. She saw neither of them in the front hall as she left the drawing room. She quickly stepped through the other downstairs rooms; the smoking room, dining room, breakfast room, Christopher's study, the small parlor, her anxiety growing with each minute. Then, her mouth dry in fear of what she might discover in one of the bedrooms, she went upstairs. Nothing.

She breathed a sigh of relief, but it was only very temporary. She had not found them, and she had to know where they'd gone. She was hurrying down the hallway from the back stairs en route to the drawing room, hoping they had returned there, when she saw Rhea Taylor entering the other end of the hall from a side door that led into the garden. Rhea saw Jessica; her eyes narrowed. She smiled slowly, smugly.

Jessica stopped in the center of the hall, blocking the woman's passage.

"Were you looking for someone?" Rhea said sweetly, the smile still on her lips.

"As a matter of fact I was, and I have found her."

"Indeed? You were looking for me?" Rhea arched her perfect brows. "Is that not interesting. I wonder why."

"I think you know why." Jessica's eyes flashed in icily controlled anger. "There is no point in mincing words. I am aware of your little games, Mrs. Taylor. I want you out of this house—now, this instant! There is no need to say good night to the other guests, I will advise Mr. Jeffries that you are departing. Go collect your wrap and get out!"

"Who do you think you are to speak to me in this fashion?"

"*I* am the mistress of this house, and I no longer want you darkening my doorstep. You've brought my husband and me enough grief. The exit is in *that* direction, Mrs. Taylor, and if you think you might have the slightest difficulty finding your way to it, I will be delighted to have the butler assist you!"

"Will you now? You are being a trifle hasty, don't you think?"

"I am in the wrong, it's true—I've not been hasty enough!"

"If I were you, I would first find out if my husband agrees with such an assessment."

"And why should he not agree?" Despite herself, Jessica felt her heart constrict. "He acknowledges my equal control over the running of this household. And concerning you, Mrs. Taylor, I know his opinions."

"Do you?" Jessica's rival looked at her steadily. There was no flinching; nothing but self-assurance in Rhea's manner as she languidly perused Jessica.

"You have tried to divide my husband and me since the day I met you," Jessica said through clenched teeth. "Yes, I can understand your anger. You thought yourself engaged to him. You never knew the whole of our love—he never told you. Just as I would not do so now—except to say that our bond together goes far beyond yours to him. I sympathized with you once, three years ago, when you found yourself no longer engaged to the man you wanted. I could understand your pain—but Christopher and I were married before you met him. Yet you haven't given up since in trying to get him back."

Despite the strong words of Jessica's speech, Rhea smiled. "No, I haven't given him up yet. Why should I? When only a few months ago I was in his arms, and you were nothing to him but an obligation."

"That's not so!"

"Ah, but it is. You should have asked him. He sought nothing but a return to the far more congenial relationship he and I had. You see, I understood him. I did not try his nerves. I gave him what he wanted—a woman who was always there at his side; who always smiled, who soothed his worries—who was the perfect companion socially, never having labored as a serving maid."

"He came back to me."

"Did he?"

"He *did!*" Jessica wanted to scream out at the woman, shake her by the shoulders for her cool contempt, her formidable self-possession. But she held on to some shred of sanity. "He has been a good husband to me, before and now."

Suddenly a vindictive, angry spark galvanized her. "He has been with me . . . *night* after *night.* He is here, taking care of my household . . . *our* children. Can you say that, Rhea?"

Rhea threw back her head and laughed. "Ask me five or ten minutes from now—or five or ten hours, at most—when *I* will have him. You see, I have been patient, too; and it has proved its worth. After our very recent discussion"— she glanced, slyly, toward the door to the garden—"I do not think he will agree with you. Why don't you ask him? Then again, if I were you, I would not ask. Why look for more pain? Why look, why ask questions of the husband who is only going to deny you?" Rhea looked at Jessica fully; and as she shrugged her shoulders, the green fabric of her gown slipped farther down her elegant shoulders, making her a more seductive figure than ever.

"If I were you," Rhea continued, having paused long enough to let her prior words sink in, "I might consider my own position. Your husband does not want me out of his life." Again she looked Jessica full in the eyes. "If you will excuse me."

With a smile on her lips, Rhea strolled off toward the drawing room.

For a moment that felt to Jessica like an eternity, she stood frozen to the spot, her face drained of all color. Then, choking with impotent anger and pain, she turned and walked blindly into Christopher's empty study. Halting before the darkened windows at the side of the room, she stared unseeing at her reflection in the glass. After all his promises, all his vows of love and remorse, how could he do this to her? And in their own house! Did he care nothing for her feelings, that he could use her like this? God, how it tore at her! She'd trusted him—believed every word of his remorseful apologies. She didn't want to believe even now that he could be capable of this—not her Christopher, her beloved Christopher!

"Jessica?"

She swung around; Jerome Weitz stood in the doorway. He stepped quickly toward her. "Rhea told me I might find you here—that you were in some distress."

She only stared at him. That Rhea had sent Jerome did not connect with anything else in her jumbled mind.

He had only to see her face to know that her rumored distress was real. "What *is* it?" He came forward, his warm brown eyes filled with concern.

"Christopher . . . Rhea . . . I—you won't believe . . ." It was too much. She couldn't get out the words of explanation, not when her pain was so great. Instead, a sob escaped her; a broken, anguished sound. Jerome reached for her, and he gently, in a fatherly fashion, pulled her head against his chest.

"Good heavens, what has he done to you now! Not the two of them again? My poor dear."

The pain was so intense, she couldn't cry; she only stood

shaking in Jerome's arms. He held her, rubbing his hands along her back, soothing her as he might a small, frightened child.

Suddenly a harsh voice called from the doorway behind them. "Then it *is* so! Rhea spoke the truth! How dare you, Weitz, in my own house!"

In an instant Jerome and Jessica had turned to face the enraged, white-lipped man approaching them.

"Christopher!"

"Yes. Are you surprised to see me, my dear? Did you expect this little meeting to go undiscovered? You might have succeeded had you the presence of mind to close the door!"

"What are you talking about?"

He stared at her in disbelief. "When I see you with my own eyes in the arms of your lover, you have the audacity to ask me what I am talking about? How long has this been going on? Since your stay at the inn, no doubt—or was it before that? You two have always been rather friendly, and fool that I was, I took you at your word, dear wife, that it was only that!"

"Listen, Dunlap," Weitz broke in, as angry now as Christopher. "You are wholly misconstruing reality!"

"Am I? I beg you to tell me how seeing my wife in your arms can be 'construed' as anything but an embrace."

"But not for the reasons you have in mind."

"You have made it no secret that you are an admirer of Jessica."

"Quite true, and I make no secret of it now! She is a fine woman who deserves better than you!"

"I would advise you to watch what you say, Weitz. I once nearly laid you low, and I would not hesitate to try again to do so!"

"Christopher, please!" Jessica's voice was nearly a sob again as she reached for his arm. With her other hand she held back Weitz. "You *are* misconstruing the situation. Jerome was only comforting me—comforting me because I've learned you were just out in the garden betraying me again with your mistress!"

Now it was Christopher's turn to start. "What?" He

frowned in apparent confusion. "You are making no sense. I have been betraying you with *no one!* Nor was I just out in the garden."

"Then where *were* you?" she countered.

"Why, in the drawing room of course . . . and before that I went to the servants' pantry for a few minutes to speak to the butler."

Jessica realized it was time she and her husband spoke alone. She turned to Jerome. Her voice was soft.

"Jerome, can I ask you to please leave us. My husband and I must talk."

Weitz looked back and forth between the two of them. He'd realized several moments before that there were gross misunderstandings on both sides—misunderstandings that, it seemed to him, had been carefully planned by a third party, with whom he himself wished to have a word. Too, he knew that until he'd spoken with Rhea, nothing further he said here would improve matters. "Very well . . . because you ask, Jessica." He gave Christopher a hard stare. "But I will not be far away."

After he was gone, Christopher looked down at his wife. "So tell me what is going on! I find you in another man's embrace, yet you tell me he is only comforting you because you discovered me meeting with my mistress. I presume you are speaking of Rhea, but I have had nothing to do with her. I have not spoken to her— Ah—I take that back. When I was walking on the grounds this afternoon, she came up to me. We did talk. . . . Is *that* what you are so angry about?"

"I saw you, yes, but that alone would not have swayed me. When I woke from my nap this afternoon, I found a note shoved under the door . . . a note of sympathy for my strength in the face of my husband's duplicity and the 'dalliance' he had carried on even the night before with one of the guests in my house. It was unsigned, but in a woman's hand. I would have thrown it into the fire, but then I remembered how late you'd been up the night before, and Rhea *had* been a guest—and then I looked out the window and saw the two of you."

"Why did you not say something to me?" He gripped her

arms. "Not tell me about this malicious note? It is all lies, of course. I was with no one last night before I came up to you, except Bayard and several other men. We could have straightened this out long before now!"

"I don't know. . . . I didn't want to believe it was true. But I was afraid it was, and if I accused you—"

"Jessica, Jessica! How could you doubt me? I had given you my promise. It is over. And this note! I would dearly love to know who wrote it. Do you have it?"

"It's in the bedroom. But, Christopher, I think I know who wrote it . . . to seed doubts in my mind. I guess I always knew it was Rhea; but I just didn't think she would dare do such a brazen thing unless what she wrote was the truth. So I decided to watch you tonight. That was why I was so nervous at dinner, and talked so much with Jerome. I saw her come up behind you when you were playing cards, then stand near you again later, while you were talking to some people. Then you left the room, and a few moments later she followed. I couldn't take any more, and I followed, too. I looked through all the rooms and didn't see either of you. I was just about to head back to the drawing room when she came in through the side door from the garden. She was very sly, very assured. I'd long since lost my temper. I told her she was unwelcome in this house—to leave immediately. She laughed at me, and said it might be wise if I checked with my husband first, because she doubted you'd agree after your very recent discussion. She said you didn't want her out of your life. Then she walked right past me back to the drawing room. I was so sure—she inferred so positively—that she had just met with you out in the garden—what else could I think? I came in here to pull myself together. I wasn't enough in control to face our guests. That's how Jerome found me. I was trembling and upset, and he tried to comfort me—and then you walked in." She stopped as something her mind had ignored before suddenly clicked into place. "Oh—I remember him telling me very clearly that Rhea had sent him . . ."

"Wait here." Christopher released her arms, turned, and strode toward the door.

"Where are you going?"

"To get Rhea. We are going to settle this matter once and for all. She is going to learn that she has interfered in my life for the last time."

It was only several minutes before he returned; yet to Jessica, wondering what the scene ahead would bring, it seemed an eternity. She knew Rhea: the woman would land on her feet, try somehow to twist the truth.

Jessica was watching the door as Christopher walked in, a smiling Rhea on his arm. She saw Jessica, and her eyes narrowed.

"What is this? I thought you sent them both to Hades. You said—"

"Yes, a convenient ploy to get you here, similar to the ones you have used." Christopher smiled.

Rhea's face grew a shade paler. "I do not understand."

"Oh, I think you do. My wife received a very interesting note this afternoon, stuffed under her bedroom door. I will not bore you with the details, since I believe, if we compared your handwriting with it, we would find you were the author."

"What nonsense are you talking?" Rhea frowned. She was not so confident now, but trying to save face.

"No nonsense at all. We have the letter and can prove the point if necessary. A rather foolish thing for you to do, Rhea. But more foolish still was your conversation with my wife this evening. Did you really think you could get away with it? Did you assume that after your insinuations about meeting me in the garden, she would pack her bags and run? Or was that the purpose of your sending Jerome Weitz to my wife's aid—knowing she would break down and take comfort from a man she considered a dear friend? And then to send *me* to walk in on the supposed lovers in hot embrace was, of course, the finishing touch. At that point, husband and wife would be at such odds with each other, there would be no settling it. Your scheming was unique, but far from faultless."

"I *do* not know what you're talking about!" She was flustered now, as flustered as such a coolly composed woman would ever be. "This is total nonsense—lies and exaggerations. I admit to encountering your wife earlier, but when she told me to leave the house, I thought, of course, she was joking. And as for Jerome—"

"Sufficient, Rhea. Remember I know you quite well! Your trying to further deceive us now is pointless. What I am about to tell you is what you should understand." He looked at her levelly, emphasizing his point. "When I said to you we were finished, I meant every word of it—we are; we were. I wish never to see you again. All ties between us are dead. If you decide to go to your father, complain to him, endeavor to sever our business relations—very well. I will stand the loss, although I do not think you will find your father lending you such a sympathetic ear as he has done in the past. You have brought enough unhappiness to my life and Jessica's, and I admit I was partially at fault—I do not try to cast that blame on you—but I will not have you interfering in our lives again. If I find you are, I will make your life as miserable as you are endeavoring to make mine. Am I clear?" He stared hard at her. Jessica felt as though she might as well not have been in the room at that moment.

Rhea's eyes were narrowed, but she didn't avert them from Christopher's face. "You are a bastard." The words were said quietly, but they had the effect of darting knives.

"Perhaps. In fact at many times I probably am. I believe you can find your way to the door. Good-bye, Rhea."

Jessica thought the woman was going to slash him across the face. For an instant she felt sympathy with Rhea in her utter fury at Christopher's cutting and uncompromising words, but then she remembered what Rhea had tried to do to her. After all, Rhea, to reach her ends, would not have given a thought to what Jessica felt and suffered. Why should Jessica give a care to her?

Still, she felt strange as she watched Rhea rush from the room. She stood silent, unnerved by the scene that had just transpired, until she felt her husband's gentle touch on her arm.

"You think I was too hard on her. I can see it in your face."

"In a way."

"Why? Think of what she tried to do to you . . . to us."

"I know, but I think she really loved you—not that I ever want to see her again, but I was just imagining what it would be like to be in her shoes . . . to have tried everything and lost." She had been staring toward the empty doorway; now she looked up at her husband, into his blue, blue eyes. "I know what it is like to love you. I know what it is like to feel I have lost you. Rhea and I are different people, but I know how she feels now. If you and I hadn't found one another again, you and Rhea would have been together."

"Ah, but the two of us would never have loved the way you and I love. That special ingredient was not there—that something that is physical, but also of the mind. That something that kept me thinking of you through those two years we were separated, through all my deceit, so that I always knew that no matter what else I did, you were the woman I loved. That does not excuse my behavior, or make it any easier for me to think of all the lonely days you had, your heartache and suffering, but that was the way I felt underneath, inside. Can you understand that?"

"You may in the end have found happiness with her."

"No. I now see Rhea for what she is. She wants only the prestigious, the secure; a man to maintain her in the social stratum she was born into. If she had ever been faced with the truth of my background, she would have run. Heavens, what is more unstable than a man who jumps through centuries?"

Jessica smiled. "You don't have to persuade me further. I obviously don't want you running back to the woman's arms!"

"I'm delighted to hear that." He, too, smiled, reached out to put his hands on her waist, gazed down at her. His face grew serious again. "Jessica, you are my wife, and I love you to a depth I cannot even describe. We have had some terribly, terribly difficult times, yet I believe, if anything, those times have strengthened the bond between us . . . have strengthened *us*. I will not pretend that there may not still be difficult times ahead, but I promise I will do everything in my power to bring you happiness. You see, I have discovered all too clearly that my own happiness depends on yours. I meant every word I said to you that day a few weeks ago when I found you and the children. Let us continue that new start we began then."

"Yes . . . let us."

Smiling gently, he drew her closer, pressed his lips to her brow. "I love you, dear wife. Even if we should be separated again, God forbid, that love will never die."

Resting his finger beneath her chin, he lifted her face so that his eyes were gazing unwaveringly into hers. "Shall we go upstairs and leave our guests to their own devices?"

"We should tell the servants first that we are leaving."

He chuckled. "Yes, I suppose we should, so we will not be disturbed. Life is never without its small inconveniences."

Yet before they left the room, he drew her against him, and his mouth came down firmly and purposefully on hers.

Epilogue

She stood at the top of the hill overlooking Long Island Sound. In the distance beyond a cluster of bare-branched trees stood her tall, proud home of over fifty years, its stone walls a replica of that great mansion in England, Cavenly, that had stood on its foundations over two hundred years.

The November wind tore at the strands of her silky gray hair escaping the edge of the black-veiled bonnet that was styled, as was the long black cape wrapped about her, in the latest fashion. Lifting her head, she turned toward the sea a face creased with life and time, yet strong boned and still beautiful, full of spirit, the greenish eyes barely dimmed by the haze of old age.

Her gaze dropped to the newly placed gravestone at her feet. An imposing stone—a square granite pedestal with a man on horseback atop; worthy of the man it commemorated—simple and straightforward, so unlike these Victorian fribbles. He had always loved horses, and it had been while out riding that he had met his end—his horse stumbling while jumping a wall, throwing him to break his neck. It was the way he would have wanted to go: quickly, relatively painlessly; no long, lingering illness that brought suffering to his family. Not that she wasn't suffering; not that his death hadn't torn every fiber of her being; not that she didn't wake in the night reaching for the warmth that was no longer there.

He'd been so strong and vital, robust and in good health —a contradiction to his years. His once dark hair had turned a thick silver-gray, there'd been some lines and creases in his face, his muscles and bones had begun to lose a bit of their resilience; yet his joy for life had not diminished one iota, nor had his desire to do the things other men his age would have left to a younger man. She felt

sure he would have lived many years more but for this accident.

She thought of the two men standing silent behind her,
feeling the moment as deeply as she: their son, so the image of his father in appearance and manner that she sometimes had to think twice when he entered a room,
wondering whether she hadn't slipped back thirty years in
time; and Kit's own son, Jeremy, also favoring his father
and grandfather in the tall, well-built frame, the thick
dark curling hair, although his eyes were not his grandfather's vivid blue, but of a greenish-brown cast like his
grandmother's. The other women of the family—her
daughter, Jennifer, and Kit's wife, Anne—were busy at
the great mansion that morning, attending Jeremy's wife
in the birth of their first child. Another generation.

She sighed. How he had anticipated the birth of that
great-grandchild; looked forward to holding the child on
his knee, showing it off to their friends, showering it with
love. She felt so terribly sad that he would not be here to
see the new baby. Yet that new generation gave her a
fresh strength—a reason to carry on now that she was
without him.

She thought of all the years they'd shared together—
good years. There was nothing she regretted except that
those years could not have stretched longer. There had
been those hard times, as in any marriage, but they had
conquered them, and perhaps the hard times had made
them appreciate and cherish the good moments that much
more. . . . It seemed so long ago now, that brief while he'd
strayed from her. That had been a traumatic period, yet in
the long run his infidelity had brought them closer; taught
them that what they had with each other was not something that could be duplicated. There had been the misfortune of her miscarriage a year later, then no more children; but they already had a fine, healthy son and
daughter, and that was more than enough to ask. And Kit
and Jennifer had grown into such admirable adults, making both their parents proud: Kit going on to study at Yale,
and Jennifer, too, wanting and receiving a far better education than most women of the age. She was using that ed-

ucation now, co-editing with her publisher husband a respected newspaper in New York. Kit had married his childhood playmate, then sweetheart, Anne Weldon, which had delighted both families. Mary Weldon had remained one of Jessica's closest friends through all the years and had been anticipating the birth of her first great-grandchild as excitedly as Jessica herself.

At least Mary was alive and well. So many other of their friends had died or drifted away. Robert Bayard still sat on as an advisor in the company he had helped create, but Mawson was gone, as were both the elder Beards. Lucas had died of a heart attack the year before; and after receiving a Christmas greeting several years earlier, they'd lost touch with Jerome Weitz. He'd left New York to set up another banking firm in Boston.

As the children had grown, Christopher's business had grown, too, with his wife as a very active partner; she had wanted something challenging to do with her days. There's been raised eyebrows at first, skepticism in the male business world and in plenty of other provinces, too; but she had proved her worth, and now, with her husband's death, held controlling interest in the firm and the chairmanship of the board of directors. She knew certain of the other gentlemen referred to her behind her back as "the old witch," but that fazed her not in the least. Her mind was as sharp as ever, and she had no trouble thinking circles around any one of them. Christopher had been proud of her; she was proud of herself—and those were the only two opinions she cared about.

The wind was still sweeping up the hill as she turned to her son and grandson, behind her.

"There is something I must say to you both. I will be brief. You know the story of how we met. He told me many times that if we were ever separated again or if he should die before me, it was very important that I remind you of that heritage—"

"Now, Mother." Kit frowned, though the sadness of the occasion and the strong bond of love he felt for his mother softened his tone. "Do you not think it is time you gave up on those fairy tales? We are grown men, and—"

"Are you suggesting your father and I were candidates for a lunatic asylum?" Her pained glance was enough to silence him. "We would never have manufactured a story of that magnitude; every word of it was the truth! You have traveled to England and seen your father's former home—estates that might have been yours. You have also heard me describe the things that will come to be in the future. You are using and have used that knowledge in running the business. Did I not predict to you the coming of the Civil War, its duration and the scars the country would bear at its conclusion? And did you not make a tidy sum for yourself because of that otherwise tragic knowledge? Have you not also used to your advantage other information your father and I gave you over the years? So do not tell me that all of this is the imagining of an old woman and a man who is no longer here to defend himself!" Her voice lost its stridency and reflected the loss she was feeling as she continued. "It is all written down—all the facts, all the details, all I can remember, up to the year 1979—and locked carefully away. On my death it will be yours, Jennifer's, and Jeremy's.

"Your father and I often considered these last years that if we had it to do over, we would have kept the happenings of our past a secret. It is too late now for that. But we have given you a heritage beyond belief. All I can say to you both is to use wisely what you have been given. You really have no choice."

Both men were silent, somber as the full force of her words sank in. The son, at fifty-four, for all he loved his mother and respected what she said, resented her admonishments—he was no longer a child. But the grandson's eyes were gleaming with awe and pride.

She sighed, smiling softly. "That is all I have to say. If you will leave me, I would like a moment alone with him."

"Mother, it is bitter cold. You should come back to the carriage."

"I am well wrapped, and not yet feeble, Kit—no more than your father was when he died."

"Very well. We will wait in the carriage." He touched her arm lightly, gave it a gentle squeeze.

She nodded, then turned to the gravestone, her eyes resting on the letters so clearly inscribed on its surface.

Christopher Robert Julian George Dunlap
Ninth Earl of Westerham
Born Cavenly, Kent, England 26 June 1780
Died Eastport, Connecticut 17 October 1866

A full life, a good one. One I will never
regret and one I feel has no end.

Christopher's own epitaph—one he'd written years before, although he'd had no intention of giving up life for some time to come. Beside his name on the stone was inscribed her own, the dates left blank. She preferred it that way. It would be difficult for her descendants to explain a birth date of 9 November 1950.

She smiled again, although a mist blurred her eyes, and laid her hand on the stone and spoke softly.

"I will miss you so . . . more than you can ever know . . . my love. You have given me such a good life. This world seems so empty without you. But perhaps, as you liked to think, it's not over yet, Christopher. I won't know until my body lies under this stone with yours . . . but I want to believe it. I love you. You will always know that."

With a tear tracing its way down her cheek, she turned, and walked slowly but with straight shoulders toward the carriage where her son and grandson awaited her.

NOVELS BY BESTSELLING AUTHOR

JoAnn Simon

LOVE ONCE AGAIN   83345-X/$3.50
In this eagerly awaited sequel to LOVE ONCE IN
PASSING, beautiful, strong-willed Jessica and
Christopher, her handsome, aristocratic husband,
are suddenly wrenched apart by a strange twist of
time and transported back to the 19th-century. Their
heartbreaking separation is endurable only because
of their unshakable belief that they will someday
be reunited to love once again and for all time.

LOVE ONCE IN PASSING   78154-9/$2.95
While driving to work one morning, Jessica Lund
is startled when Christopher Dunlap, a handsome
and charming 19th-century Earl unexpectedly
materializes on the seat beside her. A deep and
powerful love draws them together but is threatened
by the possibility that Christopher may disappear as
suddenly as he first arrived!

HOLD FAST TO LOVE   80945-1/$3.50
In this sparkling, passionate story, a New York
City career woman is suddenly transported to early
19th-century London. There her unique adventure
turns to romance, and she must decide between a
handsome young Lord and a dashing rogue!

AVON Paperbacks

Available wherever paperbacks are sold or directly from the
publisher. Include 50¢ per copy for postage and handling; allow 6-8
weeks for delivery. Avon Books, Mail Order Dept., 224 W. 57th St.,
N.Y., N.Y. 10019

Simon 6-83

THE CAVE DREAMERS

JEANNE WILLIAMS

THE CAVE DREAMERS is a vivid, passionate
novel of the lives and loves of the women
across centuries who share the secret of
"The Cave of Always Summer." From the dawn
of time to the present, the treasured mystery
of the cave is passed and guarded, joining
generation to generation through
their dreams and desires.
83501-0/$7.95

Dear Reader:

If you enjoyed this book, and would like information about future books by this author and other Avon authors, we would be delighted to put you on the mailing list for our ROMANCE NEWSLETTER.

Simply *print* your name and address and send to Avon Books, Room 419, 959 Eighth Ave., N.Y., N.Y. 10019.

We hope to bring you many hours of pleasurable reading!

Sara Reynolds, Editor
Romance Newsletter